LOVE'S CONQUEST

His mouth found hers and held her captive in
a long, slow kiss. His warm, insistent lips
moved over her throat and up behind her ear.
The rapture of his closeness enveloped her
and she felt loved and cherished.

"How I've ached to hold you in my arms all
night!"

She vibrated to the desire in his voice. Lillyth
turned her face against his shoulder and drew
closer to him. His arms tightened as he felt
her response and a flame ran along his veins.
She felt that her whole body was melting into
his. He picked her up and tenderly placed her
in his bed.

Frozen rain splattered the window shutters
and the wind blew through the chinks, but
they were oblivious to everything except each
other . . .

Other Avon Books by
Virginia Henley

WILD HEARTS

VIRGINIA HENLEY

Bold Conquest

AVON BOOKS ◆ NEW YORK

BOLD CONQUEST is an original publication of Avon Books. This
work is a novel. Any similarity to actual persons or events is purely
coincidental.

AVON BOOKS
A division of
The Hearst Corporation
1350 Avenue of the Americas
New York, New York 10019

First Avon Books Revised Printing: October 1993
First Avon Books Printing: October 1983

AVON TRADEMARK REG. U.S. PAT. OFF. AND IN OTHER COUNTRIES, MARCA
REGISTRADA, HECHO EN U.S.A.

Printed in the U.S.A.

RA   10   9   8   7   6   5   4   3   2   1

For my son Sean (The Pirate)

Chapter 1

Lillyth heard the excited shouts of "Horseman approaches!" and "Rider coming!" that echoed down from the watchtower and were repeated across the courtyard. She lifted her linen kirtle until it was above her ankles and sped from her chamber down to the great hall below, her eyes sparkling with the anticipation of a visitor who might perhaps have news. It would break the dull monotony of endless weeks of waiting for great events that had been rumored for years to take place, but which never seemed to come about. "And like as not ever will," mused Lillyth as she went out of the hall door into the brilliant sunshine of the last day of August in the year of our Lord 1066.

The yard was becoming crowded as word had spread from mouth to mouth, and Aedward, a young Saxon of eighteen summers, rode into their midst. His eyes quickly sought out Lillyth, and they smiled their welcome to each other as he handed his tired mount over to a serf from the stables. "What tidings, Aedward?" she asked breathlessly, her eyes going wide in momentary fear.

"No invaders, if that's your meaning. However, I have news that touches you more closely," he confided, his eyes momentarily clouding. "Come, your mother will be anxious for these letters I carry from your father. You will hear all soon enough."

The Lady Alison, Lillyth's mother, awaited them at the door as they entered the hall together.

"Bring Aedward a horn of ale, my dear," directed Lady Alison to a young serving girl. He handed the packet of letters to the older woman, and as he did so he marveled at the stately appearance she presented. She was small, dark and plump and not nearly so beautiful as her daughter, but she was almost regal in her bearing and always wore an air of serene authority that could set one quaking with a glance if she were displeased. Aedward avoided Lillyth's questioning eyes and watched Lady Alison's hands, adorned with many beautiful rings, open the sealed packet. She scanned the pages quickly, while Aedward drank his ale before he could put the drinking horn down. Fashioned from hollowed bulls' horns, the drinking horns had a crescent shape that made it impossible to set them down before they were empty.

"My Lord Athelstan complains this watch they keep is but another folly of King Harold's," Lady Alison told Lillyth. "No invaders sighted all these long weeks, and their supplies are near run out. Your father says they will keep watch only one more week and then return for the harvest. I think pressing business here at home occupies his thoughts more than rumors of invasions." She was slightly shaken that Athelstan had directed her to make preparations for Lillyth's marriage to Aedward's elder brother, Wulfric, who was patrolling with him on the coast at the moment.

Even though the betrothal had stood for two years now, Lillyth shied from marriage to Wulfric, and her mother knew she would prefer the youth and kindlier manner of Aedward. She looked at the handsome couple before her. Aedward had beautiful blond shoulder-length hair, a fine mustache and a trim golden beard. In her mind's eye Lady Alison contrasted this with Wulfric's sparse red hair and bushy beard, his barrellike chest and his coarser manners. He was strong and brave and would prove a sturdy protector for their daughter; also he was not a poor man, being the lord of the nearest village, Oxstead.

She sighed and laid aside the letters. "Your lady mother will be most anxious to see you, Aedward. My deepest thanks for coming to Godstone first." She arose. "Don't keep him too long at your side, Lillyth—unless you will dine with us before returning home?" she queried.

"Many thanks, Lady Alison, but I must let my mother know of the men's return for the harvest—and the other matters," he finished lamely.

Lillyth arose and walked to the door with him. She wanted to ask a hundred questions, but knew her mother would tell her in her own good time.

"Tomorrow, early," he whispered, "before the others are about. Bring your gyrfalcon and we'll go hunting."

Lillyth nodded quickly, and he left.

"What is it, mother? Something that concerns me, is it not?" Her eyebrows rose in concern.

"After the harvest is in, your father wishes your marriage to take place without any further delays."

"Oh, no!" she whispered. "Mother, must it be?" she pleaded.

"If my Lord Athelstan so directs, daughter, there is no more to be said. However, I will consult the rune stones and see what the future holds."

Lillyth followed her mother up to the solarium, a bright room where beautiful cloth and tapestries were woven, and watched her take the rune stones from a coffer. Lady Alison laid out the oddly shaped stones before her, and sat and gazed at them for a long time. Then finally, "There is much here that I do not understand." She shook her head to dispel the dark images from her mind, but kept her own counsel about these. "However, one thing is quite plain: The marriage will take place. It is preordained, Lillyth—you know the rune stones do not speak untruths, so it is useless to resist further."

Unhappiness and uncertainty filled her daughter's eyes, so she placed a comforting arm about the girl's shoulders. "Come now, when I came from France to wed your father I was terrified, but I managed well enough. You only have to go to the next town. Wulfric's hall is almost the equal to ours, and you will hold the place of honor."

"Forgive me, mother, if I seem ungrateful. What is to be will be. You have told me many times and none has proved you wrong yet."

Resignation quenched hope, and her light step suddenly dragged as she sought solitude in her own chamber. The room was hot, and Lillyth took off her head covering and her linen tunic, which came to her knees, and fingered the delicate embroidery that banded the neckline and hem. In her soft underdress she crossed to a tall coffer and poured cool water into a bowl. She scented it with a few drops of rosewater she had helped her mother distill, and washed her face and hands.

Her red-gold hair fell to her knees and she absently brushed the curling mass back from her brow, sighing all the while.

What if the invaders were to come in the next week and there was a great battle? What if Wulfric were to be killed? She shivered at the wickedness of her own thoughts. There was a soft knock at the door and Edyth, Lillyth's young maid, came in.

"Would you like me to help with your hair before you go down to sup, my lady?"

"Yes please, Edyth. Perhaps if we plait it, it might be cooler." She picked up the brushes. "I'll do one side while you do the other. Edyth," she began tentatively, "you are betrothed to Walter, one of my father's knights—do you love him?"

"Oh yes, my lady. When he returns we are to be wed."

"Does the thought of marriage not frighten you, Edyth?"

The girl giggled. "Of course not. He is only a man, after all, and I cannot hold him off much longer."

"You have always told him nay?"

"I have longed to say otherwise, but if I produced a babe without being wed, you know what your lady mother would do to me," she laughed.

Lillyth blushed at the suggestion. "Suppose you held no affection for the one you had to wed, Edyth? Could you share his bed?"

The girl shrugged. "Aye, and seek a handsome lover as soon as his back was turned!"

Lillyth laughed for the first time in many hours. "Come, we must hurry. Such talk is unseemly." However, she winked at the girl as she handed her the tunic, and she quickly set a gold filigree girdle about her hips and put on a fresh covering. Then she went down to the hall, which held only a handful of women. All the fighting men were patrolling with Lord Athelstan. A few young male pages served the meal, and a few old retainers had been left behind. None of the serfs had gone with their lord, for they were not trained as fighting men. They did not dine in the great hall, but in their own humble dwellings, at their own hearths.

Edgar and May had lived together as man and wife for many years now. Although she had produced a child every year, only one daughter and one male child had survived. Edwina was of an age when she would soon be chosen by one of the young serfs, and they would know the luxury of a hut of their own. Young Edgarson, only ten summers, was still full of mischief that stemmed from the excess energy of the young.

Edgar tended a vast herd of sheep along with the other shepherds, and May had just served her family a succulent stew made from mutton. It was not every day they enjoyed meat, but when an old ewe had died, the shepherds had quickly divided it among themselves. They didn't need to swear an oath of secrecy. All knew the penalty for theft was death. The penalty for murder was not nearly so severe.

Edgarson handed his sister Edwina a pear he had filched from the orchard and bit down into his own pear so hard, the juice ran down his chin.

Edgar knocked his son across the hut in his anger. "Never steal! How often must I tell you?"

Edgarson picked himself up and grinned. Edgar turned on May, "You're too soft with the lad. You don't beat him enough."

May wrung her hands at her son's daring. "I had such hopes for you. I wanted you to become a stableboy and learn to look after the horses, but gathering wood in the devil-infested forests all day has made you afraid of neither man nor beast!" she cried. She carefully touched the small bag of salt she wore at her waist for protection against the evil spirits.

Edgar moved about nervously. He was to take the moon watch tonight to guard the sheep against marauding wolves. He fingered the wolf's tooth he wore around his neck. It was not wolves he feared, but the night, the darkness. In the open, sometimes his nights were filled with terror. Man-eating monsters dwelt in the forests and in wind-swept ridges. All peasants wore charms to protect themselves from everything from elves to swarming bees. May and Edwina did not fear bees, however. They looked after an orchard with a hundred beehives and gathered the honey which was the only form of sweetening. It was also made into mead, a delicious sweet wine, when fermented. The only danger connected with their job was an occasional bear, or "bee-wolf" as they were called, that tried to steal the honey. They were both immune to bee stings.

Edgarson lifted the doorflap of the daub and wattle hut and disappeared outside. May crossed herself, then made a pagan sign. "He isn't even afraid of the dark," she lamented.

Suddenly the boy darted back inside. "Quick, come see. There is fire in the sky!"

For the second time that day a cry went up outside and all ran out in time to see a great comet streak its brilliance across the sky. Men crossed themselves and were sore afraid. The babble of voices was great as each foretold what such a thing could mean, but Lady Alison gazed toward the heavens, and she knew it for an omen.

Lillyth ran swiftly along the mews and lifted her gyrfalcon from its perch and took down the jesses and creance from the wall. Through the high apertures in the wall, the sun slanted down brilliantly though the hour was early and gave a promise of heat for later in the day. At the stables she found Aedward already saddling up her mare, Zephyr. They rode out past the orchards to the meadows beyond, with the worried stableboy gazing after. He knew he should not have let Lady Lillyth ride out alone with the young lord, but what authority did a serf have over his betters?

Aedward unhooded his falcon, and it went soaring after a wood pigeon. Lillyth lifted her arm high and her small hawk flew to the top of a very tall beech.

"Try to lure her back," called Aedward, but the bird flew to a still more distant tree. "She's not well trained." He frowned. His own falcon returned obediently to his wrist and he put the wood pigeon into his saddlebag.

Lillyth watched her little bird fly up into the sunshine and called, "It doesn't matter, let her go. If she wishes to be free, I would not hold her. Would to God I could follow."

He brought his horse close to hers. "Lillyth, I too hate it. Wulfric and your father have become inseparable. They have even begun to share the same tent, no doubt so they can make plans about you."

She dismounted and he followed, fastening his falcon to his saddle, and leaving the horse untethered, to graze in the tall grasses. Although she knew she should not let Aedward see her unbound hair, she removed her head covering and leaned against a tree.

He lifted a tress of hair and pressed it to his lips. "Oh, Lillyth, I've thought about you night and day."

She turned to him with tears welling in her brilliant green eyes, and he took her into his arms and kissed her mouth. She returned his kiss, and his arms tightened and he became more demanding. She had been kissed by Aedward before, but never like this. She had been kissed by Wulfric on a few festive occasions, but she had always managed to escape his advances.

"Oh, Aedward, if only I might wed with you, I wouldn't be so afraid."

"Sweetheart, how can I bear it? To see you together every day will tear me to pieces." His hands slipped to her breasts. "Lillyth, lie with me, lie with me now, please!"

She was deeply shocked and pulled away immediately. High born Saxon maidens were brought up virtuously and their honor guarded well. "I cannot. Aedward, you must not ask it of me."

"But if we love each other—Lillyth, let me be the first," he begged.

"Aedward, nay, I cannot give you what is promised to another." She ran to the horses and, mounting quickly, rode home as if Satan himself were after her.

Lady Alison noted Lillyth's flushed cheeks. "I wonder what mischief that pair has accomplished," she observed shrewdly. "The best thing to occupy your thoughts is work, and believe me, there must be a hundred things to be done in the next sennight. While you've been gadding about, I've set the weavers to finish those two tapestries that are on frames in the solarium. You may have them for your new hall when you wed with Wulfric. His mother has envied my tapestries for years and has nothing so fine, I can tell you. Come up and have a look at them." Lillyth and Lady Alison ascended to the solarium and were met with a dozen women all talking and laughing at the same time.

"Ladies, the Lady Lillyth and Lord Wulfric are to be wed as soon as the harvest is in, and these tapestries must be finished without delay so that she may take them to Oxstead. Lillyth, I want you to choose two or three girls to help you with your new wardrobe. I know you have many beautiful kirtles and tunics, but if you go through them and give some away to the ladies, you may have new ones. Clothes always delight a woman. Get Rose to embroider your borders with pearls. She has no equal, and Edyth has magic in her fingers when she embroiders with gold and silver threads." She left them all busy, Lillyth not the least of them. All the talk had changed to weddings.

Lady Alison called two elderly retainers and bid them follow her to the stillroom. There was so much involved in running this large fiefdom. She was responsible for everyone in the town. I must get on with the real business of life, while the men are off playing their silly games of war. It always falls to the woman to be the practical one in this life, she thought ruefully.

"My lord returns in four or five days' time. Tell the swineherd, the oxherd, the cowherd, the shepherd and the goatherd we will need a couple of animals from each for slaughtering. Tell the barn-men and the stableboys that all must be well cleaned before the men return. We are to have an especially fine feast this harvesttime in celebration of my daughter's marriage. On your way past the buttery send one of the cheesemakers to me here, please."

She would have to send women into the orchards to pick the fruit and then she would have to supervise the preserving and pickling. When would she ever find time to gather herbs and mix her simples and syrups, her decoctions, ointments and electuaries? She had to see to the health of every chick and child on their lands, and she knew there was a time coming when her healing powers would be in demand. When the men returned there would be hunting for game birds, boar and deer, and her husband would oversee the brewing and take stock of the wine and ale.

Meanwhile, Lillyth was deep in the business of selecting materials and colors. "I think perhaps I'd better choose velvet for all my tunics and tabards. The chambers of Oxstead Hall are drafty and it's a long winter."

"I would suggest black velvet, my lady. It would set off your golden hair magnificently."

"But Rose, my head draperies always cover my hair completely," said Lillyth.

"Not in the bedchamber, my lady. Lord Wulfric would be able to see it, and you can wear black velvet over white, or think how striking it would be over red!"

Lillyth considered. "I'll leave black for mother, it reminds me overmuch of mourning. Perhaps purple velvet over a pale lavender underdress?"

"Ah yes, and you must have green, it does wonderful things for your eyes and shows up the red lights in your hair."

"Oh, and could we fashion it with full flowing sleeves in the newest style?" asked Lillyth, feeling genuine pleasure in the new dresses. When Lady Alison returned, she found the women still putting forth arguments for their favorite blue or peach or yellow.

* * *

The ladies who lived in the manor house were the wives and daughters of Lord Athelstan's knights. Lady Adela was relieved that her husband was off on patrol at the moment. She had a delicate nature and much preferred dressmaking to the arts of pleasing a man, especially one as demanding as her husband. Lady Emma, on the other hand, missed her knight sorely, and counted the days until his return to her. She felt incomplete and unprotected without a male close by. She was racked with anxiety for her husband's safety and pushed out of her mind thoughts of invasion and war. Once again, afraid he had left her with child, she decided she must make a visit to Morag's hut. Morag was a crone who lived alone and practiced all the teachings of the "old" religion. She was the daughter of a warlock, and it was whispered that she was a witch. She dealt in horoscopes, spells, dream interpretations and potions. In return, the villagers left her a squirrel or rabbit they had snared.

"Lady Alison, may I be excused? I am feeling unwell," begged Lady Emma.

"Of course, Emma," said Lady Alison graciously. Alison wished Emma would confide in her. She knew everything there was to know about herbal remedies, but no, the woman would visit the old crone and get some vile concoction that would cramp her bowel cruelly. Ah well, she couldn't set the world aright single-handedly, she laughed at herself.

Emma hurried through the village to a familiar hut, set slightly apart from the others. She wanted to be back at the hall before the approach of dusk. A man waited outside.

"Is Morag busy?" Emma asked the peasant.

"Go in, go in, my lady. It's only my lad. He stutters terrible. We've come for the cure."

Emma lifted the doorflap and entered quickly. Morag was giving a peasant woman careful instructions. "Boil this in rainwater. Make him drink it from a bell."

The woman looked blank. "Where will I get a bell, Morag?"

"Brainless!" admonished Morag. "Your man is a cowherd. Use a cowbell."

The woman handed her two small wheaten cakes in payment and hurried off.

Morag's shrewd hooded eyes studied Emma unblinkingly. "Your courses are late again."

It was a statement rather than a question. Emma nodded, amazed at Morag's powers of divination. Morag took down a rush bag from the wall and selected a root from it.

"Bruise this root, then boil it in mead."

"Oh, Morag, thank you. You are so wise." Emma gave her an egg she had saved from breakfast.

Wiser than you, thought Morag. 'Tis only the root of a common fern. You could pick it yourself without coming to me every month.

Emma hesitated. "I have heard that you know about horoscopes, Morag."

The crone nodded.

"It's my husband. I fear greatly for him."

"What month was he born?"

"In November."

"Ha! Under the sign of the Scorpion," said Morag cryptically. "Come tomorrow." She dismissed her. In her wisdom she knew another visit meant another payment. She held up her hand. Her tame magpie, called Greediguts, flew down for a piece of the wheaten cake. "Silly Emma," laughed Morag, "when you come tomorrow I will tell you any man born under that sign is a lone man. He is utterly selfish, will always put himself before you, and when you have ceased to be useful to him, he will put you aside."

Chapter 2

Harold's army had been protecting Winchester and Southampton and all along the southern coast. His ships had been waiting off the Isle of Wight all summer for the Normans when the surprise news came that the Norwegians, led by Hardrada, had invaded the Humber. Harold gathered his army and immediately marched north. He had left behind a small force of knights who owed him military duty, but who were not regular army. This force was to keep a watch and beat off any landing parties.

Athelstan and Wulfric and their knights were among these, but by the seventh day of September their supplies had completely run out. Even fodder for the horses was totally depleted, and they planned on returning home on the morrow.

William of Normandy was obviously not coming. It had just been a false alarm, and the harvest at home was a much more pressing matter. The men, bored with their long vigil, had taken to gambling every night, and there were always plenty of camp followers available.

Wulfric clapped Athelstan on the back in a familiar manner and said, "I've got two plump wenches for us tonight, our freedom will be over all too soon, eh?"

The older man looked surprised. "How did you manage that without money, Wulfric?"

"Easy! I just promised them a place at home. Protection and a regular place at board is very tempting in these times, and we'll be off tomorrow before they awake and find the birds have flown," he laughed.

Athelstan frowned, "I dislike giving my word and then breaking my bond. What harm would there be in acquiring two more serfs?"

"Perhaps our ladies would not take kindly to the idea," Wulfric pointed out.

"Alison would see through them at a glance. I think you have the right of it this time," Athelstan laughed.

Saturday noon saw the two companies of knights arrive at Godstone, and there was a great flurry of activity as all were reunited. Wulfric told his men they would stay the night and go home to Oxstead on the morrow. The horses were stabled, and all the armor and weapons were taken to the armory behind the communal sleeping quarters to be cleaned by the squires. Up on the wall went the chain mail and helmets, along with battle-axes, hatchets, swords, shields and spiked balls, commonly referred to as morning stars. The men were hot, dirty and saddle weary, and they all went down to the river to bathe. Lord Athelstan and Wulfric went to the bathhouse, where large wooden tubs were filled with hot water and the maids from the hall assisted.

As Lady Alison soaped her husband Athelstan's back, Wulfric said, "My bride did not greet me, nor does she help me bathe. I greatly desire her company, my lady. Why does she hide from me?"

"Lillyth is having a new gown fitted. She will sup with us this evening, Wulfric, have no fear. She wishes to appear at her best for you, my lord; you know how it is with young girls these days."

He grunted his disappointment and silently vowed to be alone with her later in the evening.

As soon as the meats were cooked, the feast got under way. Saxon fires were in a pit in the center of the hall and trestle tables were arranged around its perimeter. This evening extra tables were set up to accommodate the knights from Oxstead, and the ale flowed freely because the men had been on short rations for the past few weeks. The sultry weather, combined with the heat from the cooking fires that had been blazing all afternoon, made the hall stifling. This, however, did not seem to detract from the festive air.

Lillyth chose a pale blue silk kirtle and matching tunic, and she deliberately waited for her mother and father and descended to the hall with them.

Wulfric quickly detached himself from a group of his own men and came to the bottom of the steps to greet her with a hearty kiss.

His beard scratches me, thought Lillyth, and was immediately ashamed that she hadn't minded Aedward's beard. She looked into Wulfric's eyes and tried to be sincere. "Welcome, my lord. It is good to know we are safe from our enemies for another year."

She saw his eyes greedily stripping the thin silk robes from her body and almost recoiled from the hot, raw lust she saw in them. Instead of drawing back, she lowered her dark gold-tipped lashes to her cheeks and held out her hand for him to escort her to her rightful place at the head table. She was seated between her father and Wulfric, whose eyes never left her.

God damn the bitch, he thought, so cool, so remote, she always manages to make me feel like a clumsy oaf. Wait, just wait, he vowed silently and licked his lips.

The noise in the room was deafening. There were many attractive serving wenches, and some of Athelstan's wedded knights had their wives with them, but most of the men's eyes fell on Lillyth. One of Wulfric's men said to his fellows, "One night between her thighs, that's all I'd ask, just one night."

His fellows guffawed and winked at one another. One said, "You mean one minute, don't you? One minute with a fancy piece like that and you'd shoot your arrow and your string would hang limp for the rest of the night!" He roared laughing at his own wit, and the others joined in with coarse and ribald comments.

Lillyth nervously spoke the first thing to come into her head, as she wished to avoid the subject that so obviously thrust itself between them.

"The king has taken the army north, I hear?"

Wulfric laughed sardonically. "Two fools!"

"Fools? Two, my lord?" she ventured.

"William, because he has missed the good weather for this year and won't chance the gales of October."

"And the other fool?" she inquired politely.

"Why, Harold of course," he pointed out. "While he looks to Normandy, it is Norway that attacks!"

After searching his mind for something polite to say to Lillyth in the presence of her parents, Wulfric began, "So next Saturday the chains of wedlock are to bind us together, my lady."

"Oh no, my lord, not next week. That is not possible." She was totally taken off guard, although she hid her turmoil well.

Always in complete control, the cool little bitch, he thought.

"Why not?" he demanded.

"The arrangements have been planned for after the harvest is in. There are so many preparations." She tried to smile apologetically.

"I will allow you two weeks from this night," and his brows drew together as he awaited her rebuff and further delaying tactics that he knew would come.

Lillyth turned quickly to her father and deftly drew him into the conversation. "Father, you know we always have a hunt after the harvest is in, and then you give a big feast for all, including the peasants?"

He nodded his agreement.

"Mother and I thought that would be a perfect time for the wedding. It would certainly prove less costly for you, my lord."

Her father looked at her affectionately. "Whatever you wish, child."

Wulfric looked at her and said baldly, "When?"

Her mind raced ahead to the calendar, and she quickly assessed that the most time she could bargain for was three weeks.

"On the thirtieth day of September, my lord, and it please thee?" she said sweetly.

A slow grin crossed his face, now that he had at last pinned her down. "It pleases me," he whispered low, and his hand went down to her thigh under the table. She edged closer to her father, but he arose from the table and joined his men at the far end of the hall to make plans for the gathering of the crops. Her eyes searched desperately, and spotting Wulfric's squire, she bade him refill his lord's drinking horn. Surely this ploy would oc-

cupy his hands. As his squire poured the frothy
ale, Wulfric's other hand came up and lightly patted the boy on the cheek. Lillyth thought in her innocence, He is kind to children, perhaps I blind
myself to his good points deliberately.

He removed his hand from her thigh, and as he
did so they both saw at the same time that he left
a dirty, greasy handprint on the delicate blue silk.
She glanced at the mark with unconcealed distaste, and he was embarrassed that he had not
wiped the grease of the meat from his hands before touching her.

Untouchable—she acts as if I've defiled her, he
thought wildly, and by Christ I will defile her, if
it's the last thing I do.

As soon as opportunity permitted, Lillyth made
her excuses and retired for the night. Wulfric's
men all wanted to toast him, and the entire company became rowdy and drunk before the hour
was too advanced. Wulfric slyly watched for his
opportunity. Lady Alison retired finally, and he relaxed slightly at the thought that the fierce watch-
dog wasn't marking his every move.

He slipped up the stairs and entered Lillyth's
chamber without knocking. She was seated on a
low stool in her thin underdress, and Edyth was
brushing out her beautiful hair, which hung to the
floor. He lowered a cruel glance at Edyth and
jerked his head toward the chamber door. She
dropped the brush immediately and flew, leaving
Lillyth to face him alone.

"My lord, it is not seemly that you visit me
thus!" she breathed.

"Are we allowed no time alone together? Am I
not to woo thee as a lover is wont to do with his
bride?" he demanded.

"My lord, forgive me, I have no experience of
marriage as you have." She was contrite immedi-

ately, "Oh, forgive me, Wulfric, I did not mean to remind you of the pain you must have suffered at the loss of your wife in child-bed."

He waved his arm as he came closer. "Put them out of your mind, girl, I never think of them."

Poor lady, thought Lillyth sadly.

"Perhaps God will bless us with a son for the one snatched away so cruelly," she ventured nervously. She was contemplating whether she should retreat or attack if his advances became suggestive.

He took a handful of her hair and removed it from where it lay across her breast, and his eyes fastened greedily on her nipples protruding through the thin silk. His breath grated hoarsely with desire. "I can get brats aplenty, Lillyth. I want you for fancy."

The chamber door opened without ceremony, and Lady Alison simulated shocked modesty at the sight of him. Edyth had lost no time informing her mistress where Wulfric had ventured.

"My Lord Wulfric, I cannot believe my eyes that you would so dishonor my daughter's reputation," she gasped.

"Nay, madam. Lillyth, tell your mother that we desire only to speak together. It is your desire as well as mine that we should know each other better."

"Speak not to me of desire, sir, for I know where it leads. Nay, not another word. You will leave this chamber immediately and I will forget what I have seen." Lady Alison glared at him until he had no choice but to retreat or make a terrible scene, but silently he added to the score that Lillyth would be made to settle on the last day of September.

* * *

The men, women and children of the fief of Godstone were all in the fields next morning in a majestically interwoven pattern to gather the harvest. It was a strong system, close-knit, based on the land. Each peasant was entitled to eight pounds of corn, a sester of beans and one sheep, so the harvest was a considerable size. The crab apples had been picked from the orchard, and Lady Alison was supervising the making of jelly, which was placed in casks and sealed with beeswax. Men scythed the cornfields and the hayfields and the women and children gathered the crops into bundles and bound and stacked them against one another, until the men collected the bundles on great wagons pulled by oxen. There were many different crops. Rye and wheat for the bread. Oats and barley for the animal fodder and beer making. The washhouse was a busy spot this morning also. The knights had brought back all their chainses, or shirts, and their chausses, or woolen tights. Strings of wash were strung out past the kitchen gardens and into the orchards. Linen kirtles and head scarves and fine linen sheets were all washed while the weather stayed warm and sunny.

Saxon England at this harvesttime was filled with earthly riches and delights. It was a kingdom whose generous earth produced bountiful harvests of grains and fruits. On every side it luxuriated in fruitful fields, verdant meadows, wide plains, fertile pastures, milky herds and strong horses. It was watered by bubbling springs, rising streams and majestic rivers, and its watercourses teemed with fish and fowl. Abundant groves and forests covered the hills and there were chestnut woods abounding in game. England was like a jewel glittering in the sea, and it was a jewel ripe for plucking.

* * *

Lillyth called Edyth into her chamber. "Why don't we go out into the fields today, Edyth. I love this time of the year when everything is most beautiful. All the peasants sing in the fields and the young people have so much fun laughing and teasing. I know they are working, but they enjoy it so much it seems more like playing," she said. "Lend me a plain gown so I may go about without attracting attention, and I'll ask mother what herbs and plants we can gather for her medicines. Hurry!"

She had such a sense of urgency that if she didn't grab the short time that seemed left to her and wring the utmost pleasure from it, it would be gone forever.

The girls set out with large baskets. They had plaited their hair and wore plain white head coverings and serviceable brown linen tunics. The grass glowed with diamond droplets of moisture from the heavy dew as they ran over tussocks of rough grass and wild thyme to the brook where Lillyth gathered dove's-foot for her mother.

"Isn't dove's-foot a quaint name?" she asked Edyth.

"There's oxeyes blooming over there, that's another odd name," answered Edyth.

"Flowers do have funny names, when you think about it. There's goatsbeard and mouse-ear," laughed Lillyth.

"I know one funnier than any of them. The serfs call these dandelions piss-a-beds, I wonder why?"

The girls went off in gales of laughter.

"They are supposed to bring down water from the bladder when it has stopped, that's where it gets its vulgar name," laughed Lillyth.

They came to a cornfield that had still to be harvested. The corn was bowed down before the wind, and the sun-drenched mellow light of autumn made the lines of earth and sky softer, almost melting into each other. Edyth gathered blue cornflowers, and Lillyth started on the poppies. She caught small wafts of perfume as the wind touched their petals, and the disturbed butterflies flitted away. They sat to rest for a moment under the hedge at the side of the field, in the lovely deep grass, and Lillyth thought, The beauty of the earth removes the shadow from my dark spirits.

They heard voices through the hedge, and Lillyth quickly put her finger to her lips to silence Edyth. They listened and heard a youth talking to a maid.

"Faith, we won't need to meet in the fields much longer; our hut is almost built."

"Morgan, I love you so much!" she replied. "But shouldn't you be tending the swine?"

"I traded jobs today because I knew you would be harvesting. Edmund said he was too old to break his back scything corn. He offered to tend the swine in the forest, but I had to promise to relieve him before dusk falls. It's funny how most are afraid of the forest. I'm so used to it, I love it. The floor is rich with pannage from acorns and beech mast."

"You're so brave," Faith sighed.

The compliment encouraged Morgan to take her into his arms. He smoothed her wild golden-brown hair and kissed her full upon her red mouth. Morgan did not even try to conceal his passion. Her touch had aroused him instantly, and he pressed her back under the hedgerow, until she opened to him naturally and willingly.

Lillyth and Edyth both held their breath. Each girl was extremely interested in the goings-on through the hedge. In a remarkably short time the youth lay spent upon the grass. When he made a move to leave, Faith stayed with him. "Nay, Morgan, stop with me a while. I enjoy this time afterward."

It was obvious that they were very much in love. Their coming together was generous and beautiful, and they were so eager to please each other that the mating didn't offend the two young women in any way. In fact, Lillyth felt easier in her mind about this part of marriage now.

"I can't wait until I'm wed, Lillyth," Edyth sighed. "The peasants don't know how lucky they are. They can make love without having to be wed first."

"It's true that we are watched very carefully to make sure our virtue is preserved, but I for one am glad. It's easier to follow rules that are laid down for us," said Lillyth.

"It wasn't so easy for me the night Walter returned. Do you know what it is like to have a man beg you to be with him, and all the while he is kissing you and touching you in ways that make you vulnerable?" whispered Edyth.

Lillyth blushed deeply as she thought of Aedward. She knew the words Edyth spoke were true from her own experience. "My father speaks highly of Walter. He is one of his most trusted knights. Has he asked you to marry him, Edyth?"

"Yes. Your lady mother suggested we exchange vows the same day as you and Wulfric. The church will be nicely decorated and I have been stitching a new gown for your wedding. It is a deep rose-pink with a pale, shell-pink underdress. Walter spoke to the priest, so it is all arranged."

"That's wonderful, Edyth, I'm so happy for you both."

"I was so vexed with you when you chose a day three weeks from now. It will seem an eternity," complained Edyth.

"Nay, Edyth, the time will melt like snow in summer," said Lillyth sadly.

Lady Adela awoke very early in the small chamber she and her husband had behind the solarium. She held her breath for fear of awakening Luke and lay still as death while her mind relived the events of the night just passed. He had demanded his marital rights upon retiring and had awakened her after midnight to slake the hunger that her body always seemed to arouse in him. The trouble was, she received no enjoyment from these overfrequent unions. She almost wished Luke would find diversion elsewhere. She had decided to visit Morag. The thought of revealing these intimacies to another made her go pale, but she had reached the end of her tether. Moving with the lightness of a butterfly, she lifted the cover and slipped from the bed before he could wake and have her beneath him once again. She racked her brain to think what she could spare to pay the old crone, then decided to take her some lamp oil. Morag must do many of her secret rituals after dark. Wasn't the witching hour midnight? She would be glad to receive lamp oil. Adela was relieved that no one was about to see her at this early hour. When she got to Morag's hut, it was empty. She was about to leave in frustration when Morag arrived, her arms filled with herbs and purple fox-glove and prickly thistles.

The magpie Greediguts flew from the old woman's shoulder to a low-hanging branch, scolding Lady Adela with his rasping voice.

"Enter!" Morag commanded as if their stations in life were reversed.

Adela quickly went inside before she could be seen, but once there became suddenly tongue-tied.

"You have come about your man," said Morag wisely.

"No—yes—that is—his needs are so great. I mean, it seems to me that he wants it too frequently." The blood came into her face in her agitation, then drained out leaving her deathly pale.

"Wants what?" demanded Morag, making it as difficult as possible for the gentlewoman.

"My body," answered Adela, low.

"You want a potion that will provoke your lust to match his?" asked Morag. "I will give you aloes, dill and cloves."

Adela was horrified. "Ah no, no! You mistake me. I need a potion that will stop his lust."

"Hemlock," said Morag in ominous tones. "If you give too much it can kill," she warned.

"Ah, there must be another way," begged Adela. "Perhaps a spell?"

"Impotence by use of ligature," proclaimed Morag.

"Yes, yes, tell me how!"

"Take a cord or length of wool. Red is best. Tie knots in the cord and hide it about the bedchamber. A good trick is to stitch it inside the mattress on his side of the bed. He will be impotent until he finds it. Now what is your offering?" asked Morag. She took the lamp oil silently, making sure to offer no thanks.

At Oxstead Wulfric and Aedward were in the brew-house, filling barrels with ale. Aedward was determined to try to dissuade his brother from wedding Lillyth. He knew things about Wulfric that were almost unspeakable, and he trembled at her fate.

"Wulfric, why are you in such a hurry to saddle yourself with another wife? Surely you want to enjoy your freedom a while longer?" he asked.

"That was the shrewdest bargain I ever made, boy. Athelstan gets older, and very soon Godstone will be mine," said Wulfric, hammering another bung into a barrel.

Aedward felt outraged. "You wed Lillyth for her father's wealth?"

"I wed Lillyth because that's the only way I can get her. I would wed her even were she a peasant. I want her—I will have her. It's as simple as that!"

Aedward's hopes died in his breast.

Chapter 3

Saturday, September thirtieth arrived for him too slowly; for her too quickly. The little church was decorated with late-blooming white asters. Even though the church was small, squeezed between the grist mill and the blacksmith's forge, the altar cloth was richly woven in red and gold. In the center of the altar was a large gold cross which had been set with precious stones by a skillful jeweler. Tall candlesticks of silver sat on each side of the cross, and there was a gold chalice, encrusted with exquisite gems, to hold the wine.

There had been a sudden shower which had ended before eight o'clock, and a pale sun crept out but left the morning chilly. By nine o'clock the two families were inside the church. It was a very small group consisting of Lillyth, her mother and father, and Wulfric and his elderly mother, Lady Hilda. Aedward stood up with Wulfric and Lillyth had Edyth, who was a second cousin to her in reality.

Lillyth had on a snow-white kirtle and a white velvet tunic, daintily embroidered with white pearls. A bride's hair was worn loose for the only time in public when she was married, and Lillyth's fell to her knees and was held away from

her face by a circlet of pearls. The couple knelt before the priest and Lillyth's fingers were icy as she
placed them in Wulfric's. By contrast, his palms
were sweating profusely. As a miasma of candle
wax and incense assailed her senses, she was
swept with a wave of nausea.

The priest began, "Dost thou, Lillyth of
Godstone, take Wulfric of Oxstead . . ."

Her response was clear, low, controlled. He
stumbled over his responses, but nevertheless they
were truly wed, as the heavy ring went upon her
finger. He kissed the bride and she managed a
slight smile. Rather than the tears she had half-
expected, a sort of numbness had crept over her as
she seemed to stand aside and observe herself going through the motions. To her husband she
seemed more distant and remote than she had
ever been before.

When the small group emerged from the church
they ran the gauntlet, or passed through a long
line of Wulfric's knights on the right side of the
path and Athelstan's on the left. All the people of
Godstone and some also from Oxstead were
awaiting them. The young girls threw flower petals, and the bride was presented with a sheaf of
wheat, that she be fruitful.

The serfs were having their celebrations out in
the open, and there were huge fires with sheep
roasting over them. Tables had been set up around
the courtyard and barrels of ale were stacked,
ready. The peasants were soon singing and dancing, and the children and dogs were so excited, the
air became deafening. The youths began to acrobat
and one or two were good at juggling. Soon, over
in one corner there was a cockfight and the wagering became heavy.

As Lillyth would have passed the cruel sport by,
Wulfric took an iron grip on her wrist and she was

forced to witness the two black cockerels try to peck each other's eyes out before he allowed her to go inside the hall.

Edgar and May felt more secure than they had in many months. After the harvest they had received their ration of victuals to see them through the winter. Edgar had stacked the sacks of flour he had received from the gristmill at the back of the hut, and he and May had decided not to slaughter their allotted sheep but to tether it to feed on grass until the weather became bleak, when they would have a greater need for the meat. The wedding of Lady Lillyth brought back memories for May. It reminded her that Edgar had not provided her with a hut of her own until she was well along with Edwina. May scanned the merrymakers, anxiously looking for Edwina. She must keep an eye on the girl to make sure that if she went off into the shadows, it was with a youth of her own age and not one of the married men who always had a yen for a young ripe virgin.

Edgarson kept a weather eye open for his parents, and whenever they were not watching he sneaked a cup of ale from one of the casks that had been provided for the serfs. He was full of devilry at ordinary times, but the ale had stimulated him to do something daring. He bet the other boys that he could climb to the roof of the hall of Godstone and steal the wedding banner that flew there so bravely today.

"You wouldn't dare!" laughed his friend, who was two years older than he. Naturally, this was all Edgarson needed. He began a rapid climb of the large oak whose branches spread close to the hall. He had to jump a fair distance from the tree to the roof, but with the confidence of the young he did not hesitate, and landed safely on top of the building. From there it was only a small matter to shinny up the flagpole and make a grab for the banner. By this time he had attracted the attention of many below, who could not believe their eyes at the boy's daring antics. Edwina caught her breath as she recognized her brother. When he grabbed for the flag, a wave of dizzy intoxication swept over him. A gasp of fear rose up from the crowd below as he fell, rolling down the steep roof toward its edge.

Edwina screamed as young Edgarson slipped toward sure death. Suddenly a young man separated himself from the throng and climbed to the roof, unmindful of his amber velvet tunic. Aedward plucked the boy from his dizzy perch, swung effortlessly across to the oak tree and didn't let go until the boy's feet touched the ground. Aedward gave him a short cuff across the ear, then grinned as the young devil scampered off to find more mischief. Edwina was enthralled. She had lost her heart in an instant. The blond curls and golden beard were indelibly etched on her heart forever. She stared after Aedward for long minutes with her emotions clearly visible for all to read. Aedward walked past her without a glance, and disappeared into the hall.

Inside, where confusion reigned, Lady Alison noted Lillyth's waxy pallor and swept the girl up the stairs.

"We will leave the men to enjoy themselves till all is in readiness for the feast. My darling," she whispered to Lillyth, "we must put some of the pink salve I made up from the rose petals to your lips and cheeks. Are you faint?"

"Nay, mother, I will not faint," promised Lillyth. Die mayhap, she added silently. "I'll be all right. Edyth will stay with me for a while. Take Lady Hilda and the other ladies, perhaps they would enjoy seeing the beautiful tapestries you have given me."

When they were alone, Edyth said, "I asked Walter if the priest could say the words over us after your wedding, while the church was so beautiful and I had on my new gown, but he went pale and dashed off, saying Lord Athelstan had need of him. Men are such cowards!" said Edyth acidly. "Why don't you rest for a while and I will finish packing your new gowns?"

"Oh no, I'll help. I must keep busy. I wish you could come to Oxstead with me tomorrow, Edyth," said Lillyth wistfully. "When you and Walter do marry, perhaps Wulfric will be kind enough to let me have you both."

At last all the hall was filled with the wedding guests and the feast began. There were grouse, partridge, wild duck, boar and venison from the great hunt. Sheep and an oxen had also been roasted, and a great black swan had been cooked and then had the feathers carefully stuck back for decoration. Bird and rabbit pies filled the tables interspersed with spiced dishes of pears and pickled crab apples. Whole fishes sat on platters, surrounded by shellfish and dishes of eels. Fruit pies, cobblers and trifles smothered in cream were provided for those who enjoyed sweets. Imported wine and home-brewed ale flowed freely, and the dogs snarled and fought in the rushes for the bones that were dropped.

Lillyth made polite but stilted conversation with her new husband and was vastly relieved that there were no greasy fingerprints left upon the white velvet this day. Musicians gathered, and after a feast that had lasted over four hours, some of the tables were pushed back to make room for dancing. Wulfric was urged from all sides to dance with his new bride, but he laughingly refused. "You know full well I don't dance. A fine spectacle I should make of myself. My skills are better displayed on the battlefield. Aedward? Where is Aedward? Ah, there you are boy. Come, give Lillyth a whirl, she doesn't want to miss out on all the fun."

He was a perfect picture of the indulgent husband.

Aedward flushed and tried to refuse. He knew it would be agony to hold her in his arms in front of this assembly and to know that she would go from his arms to his brother's, but Wulfric's fond looks made him seem ignorant of Aedward's feelings for Lillyth, so finally Aedward gave in and danced rather than create comment with a surly refusal. He and Lillyth didn't speak at first because they felt awkward beneath everyone's gaze, but as the room filled with other dancers and the babble of voices almost drowned out the music, he whispered, "Lillyth, you are so unearthly fair! Promise me that if you ever need me for anything you will let me know? I will come to you immediately. You must know there is nothing on this earth that I would not do for you."

The concern she read in his eyes filled her with apprehension, but she knew how wretched he felt today, so she did not express any of her fears to him.

"I thank you, Aedward. I shall always be your friend," she said softly.

Aedward led her back to Wulfric, and her father claimed her for a dance. Wulfric gave a rich chuckle.

"What's the jest?" asked Aedward.

"The jest is that you are just as hot for Lillyth as I am."

Aedward opened his mouth to protest, but

Wulfric threw back his head and roared with laughter. "Don't bother to deny it, little brother, I'm not blind. The bulge in your groin is almost choking you. Well, Aedward, just to show you what a sport I am, when I've ridden her once, I'll ride her again, just for you!"

Aedward's hand went to the hilt of his dagger, but he kept a rein on his temper. A plan formed quickly. If he could cause Wulfric to become drunk, perhaps Lillyth would find peace and quiet this night. He clapped Wulfric on the shoulder.

"You are boasting again, brother. Like when we were patrolling one night and I heard you brag you could down twelve horns of ale without pause between. Well, I've been practicing, and I wager I can do it in less time than you."

"Done!" shouted Wulfric, who had already consumed a goodly share.

Aedward was having trouble gulping down his sixth when Wulfric banged down his empty horn for the twelfth time. They were surrounded by their knights who were wagering upon the outcome, urging them on to further excesses. Wulfric's knights watched the contest, but none there offered to challenge the winner. Aedward nudged the elbow of Yeowart and said low, "If you beat my brother, I'll let you have that horse back I won from you at dice last night."

"That's a deal, my lad," laughed the knight.

Wulfric was ahead seven to five when he chanced upon Aedward's contemptuous sneer. He knew immediately what his brother was aiming for and, putting down the bull's horn, declared that Yeowart was indeed the winner. Aedward cursed the loss of the horse, but hoped the sacrifice was not in vain. Wulfric was drunk, as was every man in the hall, but he was still on his feet.

He threw Aedward a mocking glance as he and his knight left to relieve themselves.

Lillyth was exhausted from the turmoil of her emotions, but when Wulfric bent his eye upon her from the other end of the hall and jerked his head in the direction of the bedchambers, she pretended not to see him, and suddenly dancing held a great attraction for her. Edyth had been watching for some kind of signal, and she whispered to Lillyth, "I'll go up and make sure the guest chamber is in readiness, and when you come up I'll help you with your hair."

Lillyth was suddenly filled with gay abandon and was prepared to dance the night away. Wulfric made his way to her side and took hold of her wrist. He smiled at the men and women surrounding her.

"My bride has been sending me distress signals this hour past. I believe she desires her bed!"

She opened her mouth to deny him, but his grip tightened like an iron band and all she could gasp was "Oh!"

As he pulled her toward the stairs he glowered at his knights who were preparing to follow, and none mistook his meaning. Reluctantly they backed down the steps, hating to miss out on the fun, but Wulfric in this mood could not be challenged.

"I bid you stay and enjoy yourselves, I need no help, let me assure you."

He was extremely unsteady on the stairs, and Lillyth knew that he was very drunk; nevertheless his grip on her wrist slackened not one whit. Wulfric threw open the chamber door and pulled Lillyth inside. Edyth had lit the candles and turned back the snowy linen sheets and fur coverings on the bed.

"Get out!" he ordered Edyth. She looked inquiringly at Lillyth, who nodded to her imperceptibly.

The moment the chamber door closed, he threw the heavy bar across. He pulled Lillyth roughly to him, and as he put his mouth upon hers, he thrust his tongue in so deeply she almost gagged and pulled away with a shudder. Wulfric chuckled. "So you don't like my kisses, eh? I will find better sport for your mouth, never fear."

Lillyth did not understand his meaning, but she looked at him contemptuously and rubbed her wrist, which was covered with blue bruise marks. "Wulfric, you hurt me. That is not the way to win a new bride's love," she said.

"I don't want you to *love* me, I want you to *obey* me," he shouted.

"When I say strip, you strip. When I say kneel, you kneel!"

The contempt she felt was quickly replaced with a blazing anger. Although a woman was expected to obey her husband without question, Lillyth had been treated with deference all her life.

"How dare you, sir, speak to me thus? Your drunkenness does not excuse you!" she hissed. "I think they have wed me to a madman!"

He grabbed her hair, wrapped it around his fist and gave it such a vicious jerk that it brought her to her knees.

"You have many lessons to learn, Lillyth. Obedience is only the first lesson. You she-bitch, I will master you and you will be glad to do my bidding!"

He was swaying on his feet because of the drink, but it didn't diminish the strength of his cruel hands. He took hold of the neck of her beautiful gown, so lovingly embroidered with seed pearls, and tore it from top to bottom. The pieces fell to the floor, and she was helplessly naked before him. Her anger rapidly dissolved into blind fear, and her limbs began to tremble.

"Help me off with my clothes," he ordered, and he took her breast and squeezed it cruelly. Lillyth screamed and reluctantly helped him to remove the last of his clothing.

"If you scream again, I will make you take this into your mouth." There was no mistaking his meaning this time, as he held his hard member close to her face.

Loathing mingled with mute terror. Her mind formed plans of escape, and she could see herself running naked into the crowded hall. She eluded his fumbling grasp and lunged toward the bar on the door. He tripped going after her but managed in spite of his drunkenness to lay hands on her again—hands that bit into her flesh, not caring what damage they did.

Lillyth was sobbing in her throat as he threw her facedown onto the bed. He separated her buttocks and mounted her from behind as he had mounted his young squire for years.

Lillyth screamed with pain and with one tremendous surge of energy drove her elbows upwards into his gut. He gave a large groan, followed by a thunderous belch, and as he rolled off her he vomited all over the bed and quietly passed out.

She didn't know how long she lay there. When she came to her senses, her pain was almost unbearable and she was sticky with blood. Dimly she became aware of a terrible clamor. Men were shouting, women screaming, and a great din of panic and pandemonium arose. Someone was hammering on the door, so she arose from the bed and wrapped herself in a velvet robe, then went to the door and lifted the heavy bar to find her mother.

"I am sorry to disturb you, my dear, but your father needs Wulfric immediately."

Lillyth waved her arm toward the naked man lying in blood and vomit. "My father is welcome to him. The next time I lay eyes on my husband, I shall kill him," said Lillyth quietly.

"My God, what has happened here? The Normans have landed at Pevensey. A great horde of invaders, seven or eight hundred ships, and our men all left their posts. Harold will go mad when he learns."

Lillyth swept past her mother as if she didn't hear. She heard all right, it was just that she simply didn't care. She walked purposefully down the stairway, ignoring the people who would speak to her, and made straight for the armory. It was filled with drunken men who had suddenly been sobered and were frantically sorting out chain mail and weapons. She searched until she found a sharp dagger in its jeweled sheath, and then she went back the way she had come. She climbed to her own chamber, slammed the door, pulled down the bar, and dragged her large coffer, packed with her belongings, in front of the heavy wooden door. She lay down on her own bed, and the tears pricked her eyelids and slid softly down her cheeks.

Before dawn arrived on the first day of October the lord of Oxstead had been revived and the knights held a meeting. Something had to be done immediately, but the first suggestion of returning to the coast to meet the invaders seemed too foolhardy and was rejected. A vast army was needed to stem the flow of Normans. They discussed riding north by the shortest route and meeting the army on its rapid descent south, but finally the majority agreed to ride out into Suffolk to recruit all the soldiers they could and march to London, where Harold was certain to pass through on his way to confront William of Normandy.

Wagons were loaded with provender and sent to Sevenoaks where the knights could pick them up on the march south. The armory walls were stripped of weapons as the knights scrambled to equip themselves with arms and chain mail. Everything was done with such haste that there was not time for any formal good-byes. Lillyth stayed barricaded in her chamber for twenty-four hours, and when she at last withdrew her bolt and ventured forth to break her fast, the men had long been gone.

Chapter 4

An anxious week of waiting for some kind of news was endured at Godstone, and then they got some good news and some bad. Aedward came riding in, bursting to tell all he knew of the momentous events taking place around them.

"I've been sent for horses, my lady," he addressed Lady Alison. "I've taken all Oxstead can provide us with and Lord Athelstan said you would be able to send another six or eight mounts. Harold is unbelievable! There was a huge battle at Stamford Bridge in Yorkshire on the twenty-fifth of September, and Harold wiped out the Norwegians that invaded up the Humber. As soon as a rider gave him the news of the Norman invasion, he started south immediately. He's already in London and it's only the eighth day of October. An impossible feat, you would think! He's traveled so swiftly, the main body of the army has been left behind. That is why they are in need of fresh mounts. The horses have been pushed too hard. As soon as the foot soldiers arrive, perhaps tomorrow, we go straight to the coast to teach William a lesson." He was flushed with pride for Harold's energy and invincibility.

Lady Alison said, "We have had many rumors

this past week of Norman doings, and if only half of it is true, God help us! William brought at least eight hundred ships, not counting boats and skiffs carrying arms and harness. He has hundreds of knights on armored war-horses. Hundreds of archers, all shaven and shorn and clad in short garments. He even brought his own carpenters to build forts and his own cooks and provender to feed his army of men and horses. But the worst part is they have burned every hamlet and town along the coast that they have spotted. Pillage, murder, rape, mutilations and burnings, and it is too close for comfort, Aedward."

He glanced hastily toward Lillyth and wished her mother would not use these frightening words in her presence.

"Have no fear, Lillyth. No doubt these things are greatly exaggerated, and our army should arrive at the coast in less than a week's time. We will set them fleeing across the Channel, whence they came. You will have no cause to use that dagger you are wearing, my dearest sister."

"You are right, Aedward, guessing at my cowardice, but it is one Saxon I fear more than the whole bloody Norman army!"

Lady Alison spoke up quickly. "Take whatever horses you think necessary, just leave Lillyth's Zephyr and one of the mares for me if you think you can spare them to us, and Godspeed, Aedward. May you bring us good tidings next time we meet. I've told your mother to come and stay with us until all this is over. She was quite ill after we got news of the Norman landing. We will do our best for her until you return."

Lillyth kissed him and smiled sadly as he prepared to take the horses to Sevenoaks to await the army.

"Aedward, you have never fought in a battle.

Do not let your bravery be your undoing, I beg you. Good-bye, and go with God." She didn't allow the tears to show until he had departed.

"Lillyth, go to the stillroom and get some bayberry oil," said Lady Alison. "It will take away those bruises. If your arms are a sample of what the rest of your body looks like, something must be done immediately. I'm sorry I didn't think of it earlier, my dearest." She looked at her daughter sadly. "I'm sorry I didn't think of a lot of things earlier."

When Lady Hilda arrived at Godstone with her serving woman Norah, Lady Alison was appalled at her appearance. She took Norah aside quietly and said, "She looks most unwell. Do you think you could persuade her to go straight to bed? She will need her strength in the days to come. We all will, for that matter."

"I think she will be glad of a bed, Lady Alison. She was ill all the way over," replied Norah.

In a bracing voice Alison said, "Come, Hilda, your chamber is prepared, and I've just had a warm fire lighted for you. I want you to rest. I will stay with you a while and we can have a talk. You can tell me what is worrying you so badly."

"It's war, Alison! It took my husband from me while I was but a girl and now it will take my sons. It is a voracious monster that cannot be satisfied. I will never see my sons alive again!" she cried.

"What nonsense!" laughed Alison, showing a confidence she did not feel. "Invaders have been trying to take your beloved England for hundreds of years and they haven't succeeded yet. Our Saxon army is incomparable, invincible! They turned back the Norwegians, vanquished them completely, and now they go to turn back the Normans. Enough of men, they are well able to take care of themselves." She changed the subject. "Tell me about you. Have you been poorly of late, Hilda?"

They helped her into the bed. Norah pulled the bedcovers over the older woman and brought her a cup of mead.

"Well, I've had a strange dream," she said wearily. "It's a recurring dream that I have a splinter in my breast. It was so real that I began to believe it. I've examined myself carefully, and though I have found no evidence of a splinter, I can feel a lump, I'm afraid."

A cold feeling gripped Lady Alison, but she said quickly, "If you would let me take a look, Hilda, I am sure it's one of those things called a slippery mouse. We all get them from time to time. Just a little piece of gristle that moves about, and they disappear on their own quite mysteriously."

When Alison's fingers made contact with the tumor, her worst fears were realized, but she said lightly, "Yes, just as I suspected, a slippery mouse!"

"That is a great relief, Alison," the older woman said, closing her eyes.

"Norah, come to my stillroom and I will give you a soothing syrup that will let Hilda sleep."

On the way to the stillroom Lady Alison warned Norah, "I'm afraid what Lady Hilda has is most unpleasant. She is feeling pain, but trying to deny it. Very soon that will be impossible. Fortunately, I grow the white poppy in my garden. When the flower falls off as they do at this season, it leaves a seed vessel as large as an orange. These are filled with a bitter milk, but mixed into a syrup with honey and water it takes away the pain like magic and brings blessed sleep. I must warn you that half an ounce is enough for a grown person.

Never give her a larger dose, no matter how she begs."

"Will it cure her?" asked Norah hopefully.

"I'm afraid not."

"I understand," said Norah with sad resignation.

The Norman invaders, totaling between five and seven thousand, had landed on the coast of England. William, duke of Normandy, had had the forethought to bring horses so that his army could be mounted. William was inspecting the temporary buildings his carpenters had erected for their shelter when two of his scouts rode up at breakneck speed.

"My lord, we have spotted the English army. At first the numbers seemed small, but they are growing rapidly."

William stood a tall five feet ten inches. "Where are they?" he demanded eagerly. So convinced was he of his sovereign rights that no shadow of a doubt of his success crossed his mind.

"About seven miles hence, my lord, on the northern slopes beyond the town of Hastings."

"Good work! It is a sign of bad luck for the English that we spotted them on Friday the thirteenth," he said shrewdly. He knew how superstitious the men were, looking for signs and omens everywhere. "Summon all knights and lieutenants to my tent," he ordered, "there isn't a moment to be lost!"

When William entered the tent he found his two older half-brothers in deep conversation. Robert, count of Mortain, was the handsomest one of the family, while Odo, bishop of Bayeux, had the bearlike girth of a warrior, which belied his religious title.

"The enemy has been sighted. We do battle tomorrow!" announced William shortly.

"Is there a need for such haste? Will the men be ready?" asked Robert. "Better to be sure than sorry."

"If they are not ready now, they never will be," said William firmly. "Our men are rested. Harold's men have just fought a battle with the Norwegians. They have had to travel half the length of the country to meet us. I don't think I need spell out in what condition his fighting men will be."

Odo cut in, "Are you so sure of our own men? The only warfare they have known is besieging castles. They have never fought in open battle."

William said, "The choice is a simple one, brother—fight and survive, or fight and die!"

When his captains were assembled, he began, "The English have arrived." The babble of voices ceased the moment William spoke. "Tomorrow at dawn we go forth to meet them. We are smaller in number but we have a higher proportion of select men. We are fresh, we are eager for conquest." He paused dramatically to let this sink in, then announced, "I am open to suggestions for battle plans."

A great chorus of voices arose. Each Norman was eager to stand out in the eyes of his leader. William was a man who could make sound choices swiftly. In a little over an hour it was decided to divide the men into three divisions. William, duke of Normandy, along with his brothers Robert and Odo, would fight in the central one among the highest-ranking Normans. The division to the right would contain all the lesser-ranking Normans, and the one to the left would be made up of men from Brittany.

"My spies tell me the Saxons employ few archers for warfare. When they see what damage my multitude of archers can inflict, they will rue the day," laughed William shortly. He was a hard man, hated and feared by many, but as a leader he was respected by all.

Saturday, October fourteenth dawned early, but before first light the Norman army was assembled, ready and awaiting the address they knew would come from William. As he rode front and center on his great destrier, he felt nervous excitement in the pit of his stomach. He knew he must convey the excitement without revealing the nervousness. He must somehow infuse his strength into them. His words must somehow convey that they had no alternative! He removed his helmet with a flourish and paused dramatically while the cheering rose up and died away.

"For God's sake, spare not," he shouted. "Strike hard at the beginning!"

He lifted his voice again. "Do not stop to take spoil. All booty will be taken in common—there will be plenty for all."

His throat felt hoarse now.

"There will be no safety in asking quarter or taking flight. The English will never spare a Norman!"

He took a great gulp of air.

"Show no weakness, for they will have no pity on you."

He shouted contemptuously. "If you fly to the sea, the English will overtake you and slay you in your shame!"

He stopped, allowing a full minute to elapse before he resumed.

"Fight and you will conquer!"

His voice rose. "I have no doubt of the victory!"

His voice rose again. "We are come for glory!"

As the sun came up, the autumn morning was

revealed in all its brilliance. The woods were a blaze of orange and russet and red—blood red. The Norman army was no less colorful. They advanced with their painted shields slung around their necks. Every emblem and device was a different, gaudy work of art. William's minstrel had chosen to ride ahead of the army. He swung his sword like a baton and he began to sing the Song of Roland. Each man joined in until the entire horde rode forward to the accompaniment of song.

The Saxon army, hardly able to believe their ears, began to shout taunts and curses, and some blew horns to show their contempt. The two armies closed in battle, each sure of victory. They were so well matched, each soon realized it would be a long and bloody fight.

By noon the Normans were not winning the day as they had thought they would. The Englishmen returned blow for blow with their axes, fighting with a stubbornness that was alarming.

In the early afternoon, Harold's men, tasting victory, took it upon themselves to launch an unauthorized attack. They could not be held in check. The moment they broke rank, William's lieutenants wheeled their chargers and began to annihilate the Saxons. This allowed William the time he needed to regroup. He bade his archers aim their arrows high to fall upon the enemy like a deadly shower of rain.

The Saxons raised their shields to protect themselves from this heavenly onslaught and William's knights and foot soldiers hacked their way through. By nightfall, the sheer weight of the horses and the blows of the knights won the battle. Total exhaustion forced them to make camp alongside the battlefield, knee-deep in death.

Inside his tent, William grinned at Robert de Mortain through his exhaustion. "In hundreds of years no other invader of this isle has achieved victory!"

Robert drank his health, then said, "Before I seek my couch I must see how many of my knights were lost."

William gazed at him with hard, unblinking eyes. "Get your sleep, brother. Today we won the Battle of Hastings, tomorrow we must conquer the country!"

Althelstan lay dead on the field, surrounded by most of his knights. Aedward saw them while keeping his eyes skinned for Wulfric, and when he finally tried to flee it was too late and he was captured. The Normans dealt swiftly and surely with their prisoners, thinking themselves merciful in sparing their lives. Aedward managed to escape again, but not before his hand had been chopped off for "daring to raise it against William."

On Sunday, the fifteenth of October, while Aedward was desperately making his way home, William called his top-ranking knights together to plan their strategy. "There is a great fortified castle at the port of Dover. This will be our first target. We will take it by siege, then move on to Canterbury, and thence to London. I will take half the men with me. My brother Robert de Mortain will take one-fourth of the men with him and go westward and come to London the other way around. The remainder will separate and go north toward London, securing all towns in my name. Each commander is to take his own knights, and any towns that you can hold in my name, I will give you lordship over. If you meet resistance, burn the towns, but try not to slaughter the people wholesale. These are now my people. Rebuilding huts before the cold of winter arrives will keep them occupied and give them pause before they rise up again. If they still resist, chop off a limb. Kill only when necessary—I would not make enemies of these Saxons, but loyal subjects. If we secure all roads into London, the country will fall to us. As in our other campaigns, all valuables or treasure will be gathered and your share distributed when all has been tallied. Be sure to keep a true tally. Theft from me will not be tolerated, petty or otherwise."

Chapter 5

Guy de Montgomery had a force of forty knights,
including his two younger brothers, Nicholas and
André. He was thirty years old and had been father and brother to these two for the last ten years
of his life. Nicholas was only nineteen and André
twenty. The young men were very close, went everywhere together, did everything together. They
were always laughing and would hazard any bold
adventure life offered, their arms slung about each
others' shoulders, their handsome dark faces filled
with mirth.

Guy often sighed and shook his head at them,
realizing he took life too seriously, but circumstances had demanded he take responsibility for the
whole family at an early age. He was a natural
leader of men. They respected him, gave him their
complete loyalty, and some, like his second-in-
command, Rolf, loved him. Guy called his brothers and Rolf. "We are not to go with William, nor
with my good friend Robert de Mortain. It has
fallen on us to go north from here and claim the
towns close to London for William as his sovereign right. Many others go north also, but we will
travel with only our own forty knights. When we
get closer to London we will pick out a few

wealthy towns and hold them in lordship. As we go through the villages and towns we will strip them of any treasure or valuables and take it with us. Nicholas and André can be in charge of transporting this and bringing up the rear. It may be quite dangerous as there will be a constant threat of looting. If you two do your jobs well, perhaps there will be a town for each one of you to hold. Rolf and I will take the lead and decide the route. I will give you command over twelve knights," he told Nicholas and André. "Try to keep them in check," and he winked at Rolf, knowing the difficulties this would encompass. Men faced with riches and women laid out like a feast for their taking would tend to be greedy and gorge themselves to excess. William's soldiers had often gone hungry, and they were restless and had torn France into small pieces in their greed. They had been a danger to their ruler until he found land for them across the seas.

The pale golden Saxon maidens were very desirable to these young conquerors from France. They were such a contrast to the black-haired women of their own country, who often had a tendency to sallow skins.

The knights presented a terrifying sight to the Saxon countryside. They were extremely tall and large in their hauberks and chain mail; shields slung at their necks and their helmets laced each with a nose guard. Each knight sat astride a huge war-horse with its own armor, their lances raised and their pennons flying in the breeze. They were determined, turbulent and strong men, not given to compromise or half-measures. When they came to a very small hamlet the villagers quaked and trembled at the very sight of these Normans. In the smaller places they only had to announce, "William, duke of Normandy, claims England his by sovereign right," and if the people swore fealty, they took only the valuables and of course ravished any women who took their fancy. When they came to a larger town that showed a force of resistance, they sacked it, burned the houses, killed or maimed their attackers and afterward raped if they felt so inclined.

The horse found its own way into the stables at Godstone, and Aedward fell from the saddle unconscious. The man on night duty in the stables did not recognize him at first, so filthy was his appearance. It was long past midnight, but the stableman saw his condition was poorly and carried him up to the hall. A young squire was urgently dispatched for Lady Alison.

"Carry him upstairs for me," she directed, "we'll put him in the very last chamber at the back, I think. Thank you, I can manage now. Go back to the stable and say naught of his return," she warned. She went swiftly along to Lillyth's door and tapped quietly.

"Lillyth, I will need your assistance with something." She hated to do this to Lillyth. If she could have spared her the shock, she would have done so, but a woman had to face so many terrible things in this life, and she knew Lillyth was woman enough for anything, as she herself was.

"Put on a warm robe. Awaken some of the servants, send down to the kitchen for boiling water. I'll get my medicine box. Be prepared for a shock, Lillyth. Aedward is in the back bedchamber— they've cut his hand off!"

Lady Alison watched her daughter covertly for any recoil as they looked down at the young man. His appearance was one of filth, his beautiful hair and beard matted with dirt and blood. The stump of his arm was red and raw in parts, festering in others where the cauterizing had not done its job. Lillyth gently felt his brow, and as she touched him he roused slightly. "He's fevered, mother."

"Yes, I'll give him camomile, and reach me that green balsam made from adder's-tongue, it is very effective in taking the inflamation from wounds. Help me strip him."

They took off his chain mail and his leather tunic and he sat up with wild, fevered eyes and tried to prevent them, but his strength soon ebbed and he fell back into a faint. Edyth came in with hot water and they stripped off his chainse and chausses. His body was very pale and he looked so thin.

"I'll wash him, mother," said Lillyth quietly. "Did he come alone? Did he speak to anyone?"

"He was alone, perhaps others follow. He has told us nothing so far. I put him in this back chamber so we wouldn't arouse Lady Hilda. Do not tell his mother of this for a while, the shock would be too much in her poor condition."

Lady Alison bound up his stump and they put him in the clean bed and piled up the furs. Aedward began to mutter and then to ramble, "All dead . . . all dead . . . battlefield terrible . . . slaughtered, dead . . ." He quieted after a while.

"I'll stay with him until morning, mother."

"No, daughter, go to your chamber and get what rest you can. Tomorrow, when he wakes up he will benefit from your company, and we will have much to decide on, I fear."

When the dawn streaked the sky with pink, Lady Alison came quietly to Lillyth. "Aedward is awake and much improved, God be praised, but he brings terrible tidings. My Lord Athelstan is dead, Lillyth. Aedward saw him with his own eyes."

The girl put her hands over her mouth to prevent the anguish from rushing out.

"He saw all our knights slain. Wulfric is dead also—we are both widows this day."

Lillyth felt giddy with relief and bereft with sorrow all in the same moment. She had such a mixed welter of feelings within her breast, she shook her head in bewilderment. How can I feel sad and happy at the same time? she wondered. It's like I'm two different people.

"We can't even bring them home for burial. All the English are dead or fled north, and Aedward says there is such a Norman horde, none can stop them, and believe me, Lillyth, they are almost upon us. Wake everyone, all the girls and women, and all the squires and servants. I will come down and speak to them after they are gathered in the hall."

"Mother, are you all right?" she asked anxiously.

"I will grieve later—now there is no time for such luxuries."

Lady Alison stood before the household and held up her hands for silence. "Listen to me, ladies. Harold was killed at Hastings and the Normans are come to conquer us. The lord of this hall is dead and all our men with him. Your fathers and husbands are slain. As far as I know, Aedward is the only survivor. The Normans are almost upon us. They are killing, burning and pillaging everywhere. We stand only one chance, and it is a slight one. I intend to surrender this fiefdom when they come and beg for mercy."

"But we will be raped!" cried one of the girls.

"Rape is the least that can happen to you," emphasized Lady Alison.

"Saxons can rape as well as Normans," sneered Lillyth, clenching the dagger at her waist.

"Get rid of that dagger, Lillyth," her mother ordered. "Listen to me, all of you. They are men, and they are conquerors. The only thing that ever conquered a man is a woman. If we are fortunate enough to escape with our lives, we will have nothing but our lives, but that will be enough! We will own nothing, have no status whatsoever—we will be their slaves, but clever women have made slaves of men before this, and I am counting on each one of you to play her part. I want no treachery. You catch more flies with honey than with vinegar. I will do all I can for you. The rest will be up to yourselves. I will go out to the serfs and talk to the men and women myself. We will take up no arms against them whatsoever. No weapons must be found, and the long and short of it is, what will it matter to the serfs if they have new masters, so long as they are not harmed?"

Edyth was crying beside Lillyth and young Rose looked wildly about as if she were ready to take flight.

Emma clutched her breast and whispered, "Dead? All our men dead? That cannot be! Oh please, dear God, no. Mark, Mark, please don't be dead, please don't leave me alone." She was growing quite hysterical.

Lady Adela came up to Lillyth and said quietly, "Let us get the ladies away from the household servants or they are going to start a wholesale panic."

Lillyth gathered the ladies and said gently, "Come up to the solarium where we can be private." She felt a calmness she knew was irrational under the circumstances. Lillyth was relieved that Lady Adela seemed to have a firm grasp on herself even though she was in the same position as Emma, and her husband Luke was lost to her.

"They will torture us. They will nail us to crosses and crucify us! They cut open your stomachs and set fire to your entrails!" screamed Emma.

Lillyth slapped her face sharply. "Stop that, Emma. We must think, we must plan. Pull yourselves together," she admonished Edyth and Rose. "That is absolutely enough weeping, wailing and gnashing of teeth! They are men without women. Their needs will be the same as other men. They will need feeding, they will need their clothes washed and mended," said Lillyth, trying desperately to point out what use they might be.

Emma stopped wailing. "Do you think they may spare us because we are women?" she asked desperately.

"We must hope so. To think otherwise would be unbearable and self-defeating."

Emma was looking somewhat relieved, but now Adela, who had been so calm, started to tremble uncontrollably. "Dear God, they will ravish us. You know what soldiers are like when they have been deprived of women!"

"Adela, I don't believe Rose has any knowledge of men. I see no point in frightening her witless."

"If only I'd let Walter have his way," sobbed Edyth. "I feel so guilty because I denied him and now he's . . . dead!"

Lillyth knew she must use strengthening, not softening words. "Yes, Edyth, they are all dead, my father among them, but I beg of you to dry your tears. Your life may depend upon your face being pretty. Mar it not with tears; men cannot abide them," said Lillyth softly.

Edyth looked so webegone, Lillyth said, "Remember when you chided me for being afraid? I will give you back your own words—they are only men after all. Come, let's have a drink of mead."

Lady Alison stood before all the serfs. They had gathered nervously in tight family groups. The swineherd with his wife and children, the oxherd with his family, Edgar the shepherd with May and their two children. Similarly the men who tilled the fields and grew the crops bunched together silently, their fear of the unknown overwhelming them.

"I know you have all heard rumors and have been wondering just what is the truth. Lord Athelstan and our knights have been killed in battle. I will not lie to you. We are all in grave danger, so we must help each other. The Norman conquerors are almost upon us. If we make no resistance, we may be safe. I plan to surrender this fief, the hall and all its buildings and animals. No weapons must be found in your huts. I am certain if you raised up against them, the punishment would be death! However, if you obey them and work hard, I see no reason why your lives should be very much altered." She felt a panic rising within her but crushed it instantly before the peasants sensed her fear. She said a silent prayer under her breath that the words she spoke so confidently would not be too far from the truth.

News had traveled quickly. The peasants already knew what Lady Alison was telling them. Her calmness in the face of danger lessened their fears only slightly. Most of them would have run off into the forests, if fear of the consequences had not held them immobile. Anyone found in the forest was officially deemed an outlaw and could be killed by anyone with complete legal impunity. They feared these Normans greatly, and did the only thing they could. They resorted to prayer as a means of insurance, and to be doubly sure of divine protection, bribed Morag for a spell, an amulet or a talisman. Morag's business had never been so good. She was working night and day to keep up with the demand. She was almost being wooed as she was plied with food and firewood to keep her all winter. The problem was, this was one situation where she derived no pleasure from duping her neighbors, for her salvation hung with theirs. She wished for the hundredth time that there really was a spell that would keep the sinister gods at bay.

In all that fiefdom only one young man decided to take his chances with the elements. To live in the open air, in the forbidden forests, but to remain free of the Norman yoke, Morgan would brave it out. He quickly sought out Faith, hoping he could persuade her to join him, but if not, he would chance the winds of fortune alone.

"Faith, I'm leaving today. I'll take only the bow and arrows I made ... and you, if you will trust yourself to me." He slipped a strong protective arm about her and drew her to him.

"I'm afraid, Morgan," she whispered, wide-eyed, clinging to him.

"I know, love. You are afraid to stay and afraid to go. But consider if you stay they may kill you or rape and torture you. At the very least they will enslave you. Come with me and we will take our chances together. Is not just a short time of freedom better than a lifetime of slavery?" he demanded.

She could not disagree with him.

"If you will not come with me, I will go alone," he vowed.

Faith could not contemplate life without him. If he would stay with her at Godstone, she could put up with serfdom if they could spend the nights in each other's arms, but take that away from her and existence was like ashes in her mouth.

"I'll come," she whispered, as his courage flowed into her.

He sensed the moment was upon them. "We'll

go now," he said, pulling her after him into a stand of oak trees. He led her to a lightning-blasted tree where he extracted the homemade bow and arrows.

"We have no food," she realized aloud.

He grinned. "Don't worry, I will snare us a cony and we can spit it over a fire. I've done it many a time rather than go hungry," he confessed.

As they made their way deeper into the forest, Faith clung to Morgan's hand desperately because the forest seemed so dark and sinister, but as the hours passed and their eyes grew accustomed to the gloom, a calming quiet slipped over them. He caught the rabbit, just as he said he would, and they licked their fingers over the strong dark meat. They gathered bracken for their bed and piled it under a low-sheltering evergreen. Morgan built up the fire and pulled Faith close in his arms. He caressed her for hours until finally her body relaxed against him and she began to respond. It was the closest they had ever been to paradise.

Lady Alison knew that Aedward would be killed if the Normans discovered him, so she decided to move him into a hut with one of the peasant women, and fastened a long-sleeved work shirt over his stump so that the newness of the wound would not be noticed.

"Aedward, are you feeling well enough to get up, my dear?" Lady Alison asked urgently.

He grimaced. "I think the fever is gone, my lady. I don't want to endanger you with my presence, nor endanger your people in the huts. I'll go home to Oxstead and take my chances."

"Aedward, we are all endangered. The people at Oxstead are no exception. I'm sorry you must live with a peasant family, but I think that is the safest place."

"If you are willing to have me at Godstone, I shall stay, but please do not apologize, Lady Alison. I see no hardship whatsoever," he assured her.

Her eyebrows rose in mild amusement. "Oh, Aedward, you will find it vastly different from life in the hall as a young lord. These one-room huts are used for everything—cooking, eating, sleeping. There is no privacy whatsoever. They have an open fire, very little furniture, not even light except from the doorway."

He silenced her gently. "It is enough."

She took him down the long row of huts to where Edgar and May lived. "May, I want Lord Aedward to live in your hut for the time being. I will come each day to dress his wound. I will see that you get extra food so that your children won't go without, that is, if I can find it humanly possible to do so. I want the Normans to think he is a peasant. If they learn he is a soldier there is every reason to think he will be slain. Do not treat him as a young lord, I beg of you. That will draw attention to him instantly. Try to treat him as you do your son and daughter. I know I am asking a lot of you, but nevertheless, I am asking it."

May dipped her knee. "I will do my best for him, my lady."

"God bless you for your kindness," said Alison.

As Aedward made himself known to Edgar and thanked him for his willing hospitality, Edwina sat in a trance. This was like a miracle! Here was that beautiful godlike creature who had rescued her brother from certain death. He was to stay here in their hut. She had dreamed about him so often that her dreams were beginning to come true! She tried to swallow, but her mouth had gone dry. She could hear her heart pounding in her ears so loudly, she was afraid the others would hear.

Then they would know! For the first time in her life she blushed.

Edgarson had also recognized Aedward. He thought this entitled him to familiarity.

"Let me have a look," he said, wide-eyed, pointing to the arm with breathless anticipation.

"Forgive him, my lord!" begged May, horrified.

Edgar cuffed his son with the back of his hand.

"No, it is all right," said Aedward, "we all have to get used to it, myself included."

"Please sit by the fire," said May, offering a rough stool. "I'll get food. Edwina, look after his lordship's needs."

Shaken out of her trance, she came shyly forward and went down on her knees before him.

"Please, don't do that," he begged, raising her up.

"My lord," she whispered, "what are your needs?"

He searched desperately for something the girl could do. Perhaps it would put her at ease if she had a task to perform.

"Water," he asked, "could you bring me water, so I may wash before we eat?"

She stared at him as if he had asked for the moon. Finally she brought him a cup of water. It was then it dawned upon Aedward that they did not wash. He realized that accounted for their darker skins and unkept appearance, to say nothing of the miasma in the hut.

May handed everyone a wooden bowl containing a deliciously fragrant soup. She served a coarsely baked barley bread with it. Aedward realized there was no table. They ate on stools drawn up to the fire.

Edgarson had eyes for only the food, but Edwina had discovered food for her soul as she watched Aedward eat with rapt attention. They retired early once the fire grew low as there was hardly any light.

May laid out rush mats on the floor. She shared her sheepskin with her husband so that Aedward could have one for himself. He lay hour after hour wondering what the morrow would bring, not daring to sleep for fear of the nightmares. Edwina drowsed instantly, her dreams filled with never-before-wished-for delights. Outside there was a new moon and the comet streaked across the skies.

Chapter 6

Guy de Montgomery rode at the head of his knights. He liked what he saw about him. The villages and countryside grew richer as they rode in the direction of London. As soon as he approached the lands surrounding Godstone, he knew this was his chosen place. He felt almost a welcoming, a homecoming. He regretted nothing he had left behind in Normandy, least of all his shrew of a wife. When the landowner who lived next to him had joined with him to defeat a common enemy and had lost his life in the cause, the young knight had felt a responsibility to the daughter who had suddenly been made fatherless, and he had married her. They soon discovered they were not suited. She was of a grasping nature, never satisfied with the living he provided and jealous that he made himself responsible for his young brothers, Nicholas and André. She had a sharp-featured face and a sharper tongue, and he found his soldiering took him farther abroad for longer and longer periods of time, which seemed to suit them both. She is even a bad-tempered bitch to our two little girls, he thought coldly.

* * *

Lady Alison had sent lookouts to watch for soldiers approaching and when they brought back the word, she filled the courtyard with the household of ladies. All the young squires she positioned with white flags, and standing before the entrance to the hall with Lillyth beside her, she awaited the invaders.

Guy rode with the main body of knights while Nicholas and André and their dozen knights were a few minutes behind with the wagon containing the spoils of their pillaging. As these giant apparitions rode into Godstone on their huge armored war-horses, the nose guards of their helms covering their faces, the assembled Saxons trembled like leaves in a storm.

Guy rode straight up to Lady Alison, who stood out clearly as the head of this household. He reined in his mount, fixed her with a fierce, proud stare and in a loud ringing voice commanded, "I claim these lands for William, duke of Normandy, by sovereign right." He looked at Lillyth and saw the exquisitely beautiful face and upthrusting breasts, and one word went through his mind— Mine!

Lady Alison spoke up clearly and calmly in French. "My lord, I willingly surrender this town to you." She had the temerity to smile at him, and shrugging slightly she said, "I am a practical Frenchwoman, my lord. Will you *parlez* with me?"

He bowed his head slightly. "I will, madame."

He dismounted and turned to Rolf. "Hold your hand unless you find treachery afoot," and he followed Lady Alison into the empty hall. His tread was so firm, his spurs rang as they struck the flagstones.

They sat down facing each other across a table.

Lady Alison placed her chatelaine's ring of keys and her jewel case before him.

"I hereby turn this fiefdom and all its people over to you, my lord. Likewise this hall and all I possess of any value. My daughter and I find that we are both widows since the Battle of Hastings, so since we have no protectors we shall have to bend the knee. I can only pray that you will be merciful." Her mouth was dry with fear. Her heart thumped so loudly, it almost deafened her.

Montgomery removed his helm and set it upon the table and placed his huge gauntlets next to it. He ran his hand automatically through the short black curls, and Lady Alison was surprised to discover his eyes were as green as Lillyth's, with shrewd, slightly hooded lids. With his sun-bronzed skin he was a most attractive man, yet his expression was so fierce and his jaw so strong, the set of his head so proud and his eyes so piercing, that it took all the courage Lady Alison possessed to confront him in this manner.

"Guy de Montgomery, madame," he said shortly, and waited for her to speak again.

"I am Lady—I beg your pardon, my lord—I am Alison, and this is Godstone."

He nodded his head. He did not like women and had had scant dealings with them the past few years, except in bed. Women were only of use to assuage lust, yet here was one that he could not help but respect for her courage. She held herself like a queen before him instead of the defeated Saxon she was in reality.

"What do you mean by merciful?" he demanded.

"You could slay us all and set a torch to the town, but I think you are too clever for such wanton destruction and waste. The harvest has just been gathered and we are a rich town. You could

turn us all out to fend for ourselves, but I believe
you would be wise to let us work for you. This is
a large undertaking and I am used to running the
household smoothly, no small feat, you will understand. Also I am wise in the ways of healing and
medicine and am willing to look after the health of
your knights. The women of this hall are expert
weavers of beautiful cloth as you will perceive
from our rich clothes. Other of the women are accomplished cooks—in short, my lord, a household
with women in it can be made more comfortable
for its men in many ways."

"And in return for these—feminine ministrations?" He raised a questioning eyebrow, black
and arched as a raven's wing.

"A roof over our heads and a place at board—
also protection against any further marauders,"
she bargained desperately.

Nicholas and André rode into the courtyard,
pleasantly surprised at the number of young
women standing about. Their eyes fell on Lillyth
at the same moment and they were immediately
spoiled for all other women. In a flash, Nicholas
dismounted and picked her up in his arms. She
struggled frantically and suddenly found herself
flung to the ground as André's fist smashed into
his brother's face.

"This one's mine, little brother, choose elsewhere," he roared.

She prepared to flee, but André reached out a
long arm and pulled her to him, ripping off her
headdress in his rough handling of her. Her hair
swirled about her like a glorious cloak. She raked
her nails down his cheek, and with an oath and an
ironlike grip, he bound her wrists with a rough
rope and pulled her with him into the watchtower.
Nicholas found his feet in a hurry and, drawing

his dagger, followed in hot pursuit. André dragged her up the steps and pushed her into the room at the top, which contained only a bed. He quickly slammed the door on his brother and bound the rope holding Lillyth about the bedpost.

Guy de Montgomery looked at Lady Alison and said shrewdly, "With your knowledge of medicine you could poison us all in our beds, madame, if I gave you the freedom of the place."

"I could," she acknowledged, "and you could have us killed any day or night of your choosing," she countered.

"I could, and will with provocation!" he acknowledged. "Therefore, if we do not underestimate each other, I think we should manage admirably," and picking up his helm and gauntlets he went outside. Lady Alison followed, her legs threatening to give way in relief.

"My daughter Lillyth . . ." cried Lady Alison. Guy looked at Rolf, who jerked his thumb in the direction of the watchtower.

Guy took the steps three at a time.

"You whoreson bastard, I'll gut you," snarled Nicholas.

"She warms my bed, if I have to kill you for her," spat André, lunging at his brother's throat.

"Splendor of God!" roared Guy, "you are supposed to be controlling your men, not whoring!"

His anger at the two brothers who had never exchanged an unkind word before this day was something to behold.

He saw Lillyth trembling before him, her breast bare, her golden-red hair tumbling to her knees. She was so exquisitely fragile; he saw before him the classic *damoiselle en distrait*, and the chivalry of his knighthood rose up in him. He quickly crushed the softening thoughts and took out his dagger to cut the rope from Lillyth's wrists.

He took her hands, and upon contact green eyes looked deeply into green eyes, and suddenly they went tumbling down the eons and centuries in mutual recognition. He drew back sharply to deny the images of déjà vu being thrust upon him.

"She is mine," he stated flatly. "Get below."

He picked her up and carried her down the stairs and across the yard to the hall. Her head pressed against his chest, she could feel the thud of his heart beneath her cheek while her own beat wildly in her ears. Without pausing, he took her up the stairs to the bedchambers. He chose the largest chamber and dropped her onto the bed.

"Stay put," he commanded, and left, slamming the door behind him. He went below to Lady Alison.

"The first obstacle to be overcome will be the language barrier. Until such time as my men learn the Saxon tongue and your people learn French, I will have to ask you to interpret for me. We will see to the horses first."

He looked toward Nicholas. "I want the horses rubbed down well, fed and watered and their armor cleaned. You will see that the stableboys do their work properly and there will be no mistreatment. These people are mine now. Do you suppose I can entrust you to execute this duty?" he asked dryly.

"André!" he bellowed. "I want the hall and all those outbuildings searched for weapons, also the mill and the church. The wench you covet is in my chamber, where she will remain—unmolested! See to it, sir."

He turned to Rolf and Lady Alison, who seemed to be exchanging pleasantries. In her practical way

she was almost relieved that the commander of
these men had marked her daughter for his own.

"Come, we will round up the peasants and
search their homes for weapons. I must speak to
them all and you will interpret for me. I will make
plain what I expect from them and what they can
expect from me."

Lady Alison was impressed with Guy de Montgomery and his knights. They must have been
tired, and she knew their full chain mail and armor were extremely heavy, but they moved about
easily, completely used to the weight. Their bodies
must be in excellent physical condition, she mused.
No wonder our men were no match for them. She
was also pleasantly surprised to see them drink water to quench their thirst rather than the ale that the
Saxon men had swilled so freely.

Methodically and thoroughly the buildings were
searched for weapons, then the peasants themselves were searched. When they had been
brought together in a group, Guy asked Lady Alison to tell them they were now his people and
would be treated fairly if they obeyed him completely. He was well pleased with what he saw.
They were handsome people, not scrawny or sul-
len as the peasants seemed in Normandy. They
were well fleshed and well clothed.

"Tell them there are many differences between
us, but in time I will try to minimize these. They
must make an effort to learn our language and our
ways and we will do the same. If they have any
grievances they must come to me. Treachery will
be dealt with swiftly and surely." His expression
was so stark, none doubted it.

Lillyth sat motionless for a long time after Guy
left. Her emotions were tangled like the silk
threads on the back side of a tapestry. Her nerves

tingled along her body with an excitement she had never felt before. A man had picked her up and carried her a short distance, and this brief encounter had changed her whole life. He was frightening, yet thrillingly so. He was strong enough to kill her with his bare hands, yet his hands were gentle on her body. His face was fierce and stark, yet he was so handsome that her heart turned over in her breast. He was all male, and he made her acutely aware that she was female. His nearness had been most pleasurable and arousing. She slowly became aware of her surroundings and her disheveled attire. Her clothes were in her own chamber next door to the one he had put her in, and she was almost afraid to disobey and leave, but her breast was bare and she must change her clothing. She listened at the door and, when all was quiet, slipped into her own chamber.

She deliberately picked the plainest thing she could find, which was the brown linen kirtle and plain white headdress she had worn in the fields with Edyth that day that seemed a lifetime ago. She hated these overbold Normans who were come to put their heels on her neck. She would make herself plain and ugly so as not to invite their lustful eyes.

All the other women will be in their finery in the hall tonight when we dine, he can look elsewhere.

Why did this thought displease her so much? Quickly she took off the plain garments and instead picked a soft green, sheer silk underdress with a green velvet tunic and fastened her gold girdle about her hips. She replaced the plain white head covering with a matching pale green sheer silk which was most daring in the way you could see her hair right through the material. She even put on a touch of red lip salve and perfume, then, feeling more satisfied with her appearance, she prepared to slip back into the next chamber where he had bade her stay.

She gasped as the tall figure of André loomed before her in the passageway. She opened her mouth . . . "Please, mademoiselle, do not scream, I beg of you. I will not harm you, my word on it!"

His face had taken on a grayish tinge; the scratches she had made stood out sharply and he looked unwell. Her eyes caught sight of the red oozing through his chain mail.

"You are bleeding—come sit down," and she took him into her chamber.

Lillyth looked into sherry-brown eyes and realized he was only a youth of approximately her own age. Some of her fear of him subsided and he smiled. "It is a wound I took for you, *chérie*."

"Two grown men fighting over a woman, 'tis ridiculous!" she scolded.

"Three grown men, mademoiselle," he said with a wicked glint in his eye.

She tried to help him lift off the chain mail. "How do you walk about in such heavy garb all day long?" she marveled.

He shrugged his shoulders and winced at the discomfort. She helped him take off the short tunic underneath and blushed as he sat before her naked but for his woolen chausses. She washed the shallow wound in his shoulder and spread on some of the green balsam from her mother's medicine box. She shook her head as she knelt before him. "Two brothers using daggers on each other. You should be ashamed!"

"Three brother, *ma petite*," and he threw back his head and laughed at his own folly.

"By the Christ, what goes on here?" demanded Guy from the doorway. He strode into the chamber, his anger mounting with every step, until he saw

the wound Lillyth was tending. Slowly the anger
ebbed away and with a glint in his eyes he said,
"By God's bones, André, you are going to have to
give me lessons. Not five minutes with a woman
and you have found an excuse to strip off and display your well-muscled chest for her. Out of here
before I take my whip to you, you young dog!"

André picked up his clothes, but before he
closed the chamber door on them, he kissed his
fingers at Lillyth.

She lowered her eyes but could feel Guy's intent
scrutiny of her. She felt her cheeks flush and
busied herself, putting the ointment back into the
medicine box and tidying all the little pots. Finally
he broke the silence that stretched between them.

"Why do you cover up your hair, Lillyth?"

" 'Tis the custom, my lord, all decent Saxon
women do so," she explained.

"Take it off," he said quietly.

"My lord, I cannot! It would be an unseemly
display," she protested.

"We will start a new custom," he said softly,
reaching up and taking the scarf from her hair.

"Why?" she asked wildly.

"Why?" he repeated, raising an eyebrow. "Because it pleases me," he said simply, and made the
color deepen in her cheeks.

"Am I a slave to do your bidding?" she demanded hotly.

"You have put your finger on it exactly, mademoiselle."

Lillyth moved away from him to the other side
of the room. "I believe I chose the larger chamber
for us," he said, emphasizing the last word. She bit
her lip to prevent herself from answering his deliberate provocation.

He looked about. "If these things are yours, remove them to my chamber." He took off his heavy chain mail and washed his hands.

"Shall we go down to dine now?" He gave her a mocking bow.

She took her usual place at table. All was the same, yet all was different. Could it only have been three weeks before that she sat here at her wedding with all eyes upon her?

Guy sat beside her and shared his plate with her, cutting all the choicest pieces of meat for her with his knife. Lillyth had a scant appetite with his eyes never leaving her.

"How do you like my seating arrangement? Man, woman, man, woman, throughout the hall. I believe the fastest way for my men to learn Saxon is from the women. The women will no longer serve the food, the esquires can do that. The woman can dine with my men and exchange conversation. Before long you won't be able to tell this place from William's court." He grinned.

She felt very daring with her hair uncovered, but before the meal was over, Lillyth was amazed when Edyth, who was sitting with André, took off her head covering to display her long, wheat-colored tresses.

Nicholas was sitting with Rose, who did such beautiful embroidery, but she was only fifteen, and Lillyth could see she was white and frightened. Lillyth was determined not to talk to Guy de Montgomery. She gazed about the hall and was surprised to see her mother sitting with Rolf and not even holding herself aloof as Lillyth was determined to do. One or two of the knights had chosen peasant women to dine with them, and it was the first time the women had ever eaten in the hall. The men drank wine as they were used to back in Normandy, but some tried the home-brewed ale and seemed to like it. In spite of their differences, the men and women were communicating on many levels.

"Ah, *chérie*, you draw every male eye in the hall. They all envy me—little do they realize you will neither look at me nor speak with me," he sighed heavily. His thigh brushed hers beneath the table and it was like a shock wave going through her. Lillyth pulled sharply away, and her cheeks burned hotly. She glanced across at Rose and saw Nicholas whispering in her ear. Rose began to cry softly. Lillyth turned to Guy and broke her resolve not to speak.

"My lord, the young girl your brother Nicholas is forcing his attentions upon is little more than a child!"

He regarded them through lazy, half-lidded eyes. "Neither is he, mademoiselle, they should suit each other very well."

"I hate you!" she spat at him.

"If that is true, Lillyth, you are free to choose another," he challenged her.

She tossed her head in disdain and a wide grin crept over his mouth. "Since you have made your choice, shall we go upstairs?"

His hand closed over hers before she could make her escape, and he arose and took her with him to his chamber. She could feel his hand at the small of her back, gently urging her forward. As she went through the doorway ahead of him, his hand went lower and he caressed her bottom. She whirled instantly and slapped his face. She gasped at her own temerity and fear sprang into her eyes as she realized what she had done.

He dragged her against his body and his mouth possessed hers. His kiss was scalding, searing. She squirmed and wriggled in his embrace in a futile effort to free herself. His thighs pressed tightly to hers and she felt his manhood harden and rise up against her. She stopped moving immediately when she realized her movements excited him. He took his mouth from hers, and she fought for breath.

He whispered, "You have something I want, Lillyth. I shall want it from you every night." He paused and looked deeply into her eyes.

She lowered her lashes and her cheeks flamed scarlet.

"Ho, I know where your thoughts are leading, *chérie!* For shame! I merely want you to teach me your Saxon tongue." He grinned and set her free.

She fled across the chamber. "You are playing a game with me! 'Tis just sport you are enjoying!" she accused angrily.

His eyes followed her, lingering on her hair and her mouth in the candlelight. She is so unearthly fair, I'll never get my fill, he thought.

"I wish to retire to my own bedchamber, my lord," she demanded, her chin held high.

"Lillyth we both know you are sleeping in my chamber this night," he said quietly.

She began to tremble. "I will not share this bed with you, Norman." She had a prickling fear of what he would do as he bent his ruthless gaze upon her and she had nowhere to flee to safety. Then the humor came back into his green eyes.

"There you go again, mademoiselle. I know the sorry plight a young widow must be in, but I must decline your tempting invitation. I promise we will have many nights before us to quench the fires in our blood. At least four men will be on guard duty every night patrolling this land. None will take it from me, for once I mark something as mine, it remains so. Rolf, my brothers and I will take the first night's watch." He reached for his hauberk.

"But André is wounded," she said, feeling relief and pique at the same time.

"A scratch merely. If you treat him as a baby, how am I to make a man of him?" His face softened as he looked at her. "Lillyth, I am not playing games when I tell you to bar the door after me. I cannot answer for your safety tonight unless you remain here with the door securely barred."

Chapter 7

The four men rode the perimeter of the land every two hours and met back at the hall at midnight, two and four o'clock. At four André looked haggard. Nicholas said, "Stay here and rest; I'll ride double patrol."

"Nay," protested André, glancing at Guy. "I'll manage."

Guy handed André some hot mulled wine. "Your brother is trying to make amends for stabbing you. Let him do your patrol and ease his conscience at the same time. André, get up to bed, and mind which chamber you pick," he warned.

Nicholas grinned, and André was bold enough to ask, "There's no chance of you tiring of her, is there?"

"Splendor of God, you can't straddle your horse, but you are thinking of straddling a wench! Do you think of naught else, boy?" Guy demanded.

"Very little," admitted André. "I don't know what's wrong lately, but it's on my mind constantly," he laughed.

"It's all this blond hair and creamy flesh these Saxon maidens possess. I've heard it is dangerous to your health to remain stiff for a day and a night. Better ask the widow for some medicine," laughed Nicholas.

"The only medicine he needs is a bed wench three times a day until he can think clearly again," advised Rolf.

"Speaking of the widow, how goes it with you in that direction, Rolf? You've a great deal of courage to tackle that one, I'm thinking," laughed Guy.

"Nay, I've not tried her yet, man, I've only been here one day. How goes it with your young widow, if it comes to that, Guy?"

"I'm in like case, Rolf. Let's go!"

The morning dawned cold and gray. At six o'clock the three men eased out of their saddles and went to the bathhouse. The young squires ran to do their bidding and by the time they had stripped, the wooden tubs were in readiness for them. Guy sank into a tub of hot water and let it soothe the knots from his aching muscles. His eyes met Rolf's in amusement as they observed that Nicholas had fallen asleep in the water.

"This young generation is a trifle soft, I'm afraid," said Guy.

"Give him his due. Sometimes the standard you set is too hard," said Rolf.

"Better waken the young devil before he drowns," said Guy, his face softening.

The hammering on the chamber door awakened Lillyth. She wrapped a fur pelt from the bed close about her body and went to the door.

"Who is it?" she called.

"Your lord and master. Why do you keep me waiting? Open up immediately before I break it down," he laughed. He sounded in good humor and she wondered if she could take the time to dress, but the loud hammering started up again, so timidly she took down the bar and opened the door.

He looked at her and thought, She is even more desirable with the sleep still in her eyes and her mouth all soft and warm.

She looked at him and thought, He doesn't even look tired after riding patrol all night. He is fresh and clear-eyed as if he'd just slept the night through.

"I have men coming up here to build a hearth so we can have a fire on cold winter nights, so if I were you I wouldn't stand about naked." He pointed to her bare legs and feet.

She whirled about angrily. Damn him, she thought, he is always putting me in an awkward position and then making a fool of me. She tossed her head and went next door to her own chamber to get dressed.

Her mother caught sight of her and followed her into her room. She raised an eyebrow at Lillyth's attire. "I've seen the way he looks at you and I can tell you now he is lost. But do not yield too easily, Lillyth; he would not treasure anything that came too easily, that one. He will enjoy the chase as much as the victory. Let it be as lengthy as you can make it."

Lillyth gasped open-mouthed at her mother. "Whatever you are thinking, you are wrong. I wouldn't let the Norman dog even touch me!"

"Lillyth, he will force you, and I don't want you to be hurt, child. I don't suggest for one minute you defy him."

"I am not afraid of him!" she shouted boldly, then clapped her hand over her mouth in case he should hear her boast.

Rolf ran up the stairs. "Guy, trouble with the villiens. A fight has broken out between Norman and Saxon."

Both men ran swiftly, swords to hand.

"Aedward!" breathed Lillyth to Lady Alison.

Fear rose up in her throat as she hurried her dressing. She grabbed the first thing that came to hand, a rose-pink underdress and tunic. She brushed her hair quickly and flung it back, not bothering to cover it, then she ran as fast as she could.

They had not discovered Aedward as Lillyth had feared, but Rolf held one of the villiens in an iron grip, and one of the Norman knights was laid out on the ground. His head had been bashed with a wooden club and he was bleeding profusely.

Guy knelt to examine his young knight. "It's Giles. Take him up to the hall and ask Lady Alison to tend his hurts."

Lillyth was surprised to hear him call her mother Lady Alison.

"Now what happened here, what started this?" he demanded.

"The Saxon swine was laughing at our short hair and clean-shaven faces, so Giles hit him across the face with his gauntlet. The Saxon picked up a club and nearly killed him," answered Gilbert.

"Strip him," ordered Guy. He took a whip from one of his men.

"Know this, Saxon. If you had used your fist, I would not have punished you thus. Never use a weapon on a Norman again. If it happens a second time your life will be forfeit. Twenty lashes!"

They strung him between two trees, and Guy drew back his arm and let the first stripe fall.

Lillyth screamed, but he didn't even glance in her direction. Coldly and methodically he laid lash after lash across the Saxon's back until the blood dripped. On the nineteenth stroke Lillyth fainted, and Aedward, who had been standing close, picked her up and carried her into his hut. She came to almost immediately.

"Oh, Aedward, thank God you are all right. He is a monster! I thought he was kind. I didn't know he was so cruel and inhuman." Her face was white and she was trembling slightly.

"He did what he had to do, Lillyth, but you should not be exposed to these things."

"I came because I was afraid for you, Aedward. How is your arm? Let me see."

He stripped off his chainse and displayed the stump. "It is healing well."

A huge shadow fell across the doorway. Lillyth jumped guiltily and sobbed, "Oh my God!"

Guy came into the hut, eyes glittering dangerously. He said very quietly, "I'm always finding you with naked young men, *chérie*."

Fear choked her, making her breathing so difficult her breast heaved. She saw the blood on his hands. "Stay away from me!" she cried.

"I don't have to explain my actions to you, Lillyth, but I will. My judgment was harsh because it had to be. He used a weapon that almost killed my man in front of all the fiefdom. His punishment had to be swift and sure or every last one of them will try it. By William's justice I should have chopped off the arm he raised against a Norman."

"He's right, Lillyth," said Aedward quietly.

"Like all women you are full of deceit. You told me all your men were dead, yet this is obviously a knight who fought against us at Hastings. How many more are you hiding?" He advanced upon Aedward and Lillyth threw her arms wide to protect him and cried, "He is my brother!"

Guy looked at the young man, and indeed his blond beauty reminded him of Lillyth's. He was puzzled. "Surely you could trust me not to take your brother's life. Do you think so ill of me, Lillyth?" He turned to Aedward. "If you will swear your fealty to me, you may come to the hall. I have need of an interpreter. There is more than enough work for all. Do we have a bargain?"

"My thanks, sir. We have a bargain," said Aedward, wishing that Lillyth had not lied for him. As they entered the hall, Lillyth made a sign to her mother to be quiet. She rushed on to say, "My brother Aedward has permission to dwell in the hall with us again."

"Thank you, my lord," Lady Alison said to Guy. "Come upstairs, Aedward, and I will see to your arm. Lady Hilda will be pleased to see you are re-covered somewhat."

Guy followed them upstairs. "I want to check on the progress of the fireplace. They should be finished by tonight. A fire in our chamber should be welcome this cool night, don't you agree, *chérie?*"

Aedward clenched his teeth at these words, and Lillyth pressed her lips together and ignored the taunt.

Lady Alison turned to Guy. "I tended the man you had whipped, but he had better remain here tonight along with the Norman with the broken head. Let us hope there is no more trouble, all my beds are filled to capacity. I am sharing with Lady Hilda down there."

Guy caught Lillyth's eyes and said, "My bed will hold two."

Rolf came into the hall for further instructions and Guy directed him to cut the Saxons' hair to-morrow and order them all to shave their faces. "The differences are too marked. The sooner we all look alike, the sooner we will all think alike. I want a man to ride across country to see how Wil-liam's forces are doing, and to let him know we hold towns secure close to London. If I know William, he will have taken Dover by now and be on his relentless way up the coast. You pick a man for me, Rolf. We had better ride over to this place Oxstead and another town close by called Sevenoaks, I think. Once we have secured these, I had in mind to establish Nick and André. A little responsibility wouldn't hurt them right now. By the way, remember the wolves we heard last night? I want to talk to the flock herders and find out how many they lose to these wolves. I have an idea to cut down the numbers. We'll take young Aedward with us, it will make explaining somewhat simpler."

"Can't you save some of your improvements for tomorrow? My bones are crying out for sleep," said Rolf.

"Must be getting old," laughed Guy, clapping him heartily on the back.

When Guy returned it was almost supper hour. From where Lillyth sat in her own chamber she could hear the workmen next door and knew the moment Guy returned. She had braided her hair with some rose-pink ribbons and was admiring the effect in a hand mirror of polished silver when Guy tried her door and finding it barred, banged on it heavily. Her heartbeat quickened against her will as she lifted the bar and opened the door.

"Do you bar the door against me, *chérie?*" he inquired with a lazy lift of the brow.

"I bar it against all, my lord," she said quietly.

He looked at her admiringly. "You have many lovely clothes, Lillyth. I feel quite shabby beside you."

"You could have some new ones made without difficulty. We have lovely velvets and linens, and I could make you some fine new shirts."

"If you would do that for me, it would indeed give me pleasure." He smiled. "It will also give me pleasure to escort you to dinner. I'll be back as soon as I speak to the workmen for a moment."

He went back into the larger chamber where the men had finished building the fireplace.

"Excellent work!" he praised them. "I have another task for you before you go to sup. Cut an archway in the wall here to make these two bedchambers into one. The wood is thick, but you have done such a skilled job with the fireplace, I'm sure you can accomplish miracles. Be sure to get help in cleaning up the mess and get one of the servants to build me a fire. Many thanks, men!"

Guy was hungry; he had a large man's healthy appetite. Beside him Lillyth seemed to eat very small portions and occasionally dallied and played with her food.

"You should try to eat more, Lillyth. You are too delicate, too slim," he urged.

"Do you like your women fat, my lord?" She smiled.

"No, I most certainly do not, *chérie*, it is just that you do not seem strong. If you took sick, you would not be able to recover quickly." He picked up her slim hand and toyed with her fingers.

She quickly averted her eyes from his and looked about the hall. She counted a dozen women who had left off their head coverings.

"I told you we would set a new custom. Tomorrow they will all have ribbons in their plaits, now they have seen how lovely you look." He smiled.

She was amazed that he was able to read her thoughts. Her thigh brushed his under the table, and he was immediately aroused. He was thankful that the table concealed his condition from his knights.

"My lord, I have a problem," said Lillyth, turning the full impact of her green eyes upon him. "I cannot use the bathhouse, there are always too many of your men about. Could you assure me privacy tomorrow and keep them all away?"

"I will have a bathtub taken up to your chamber and then you may bathe anytime you desire."

The images that danced through his mind did nothing to lessen his physical discomfort. "May we go up soon?" he urged.

She noticed that Aedward dined with Nicholas and André, and they showed great interest in his mustaches and rich mode of dress. All about the same age, they were deep in conversation. Rose, the young girl with Nicholas who had been crying the previous evening, was chattering happily with Aedward, but instead of being jealous, Nicholas seemed to be studying the Saxon's manner with the girl in the hopes of learning something. Aedward's eyes rested on Lillyth every few moments, and she wondered if he had some desperate plan in mind. She fervently hoped not; he had suffered enough at the hands of the Normans.

Guy led her upstairs, and she was surprised when they stopped outside her own chamber door. He lifted her hand to his lips, and her heart softened as she saw the lines of fatigue etched around his eyes. He had had no sleep for at least thirty-six hours.

"Good night, mademoiselle, pleasant dreams. Be sure to bar your door," and he was gone.

She entered her chamber and there he stood, leaning negligently against the archway cut into the wall. Tears of anger and frustration welled up and she cried, "My God, what have you done? How could you, how could you?" He threw back his head and laughed. "Come, *chérie*, none will be any the wiser. Come and warm yourself at my fire."

She was outraged. He was determined to tear down all barriers between them. If walls would not stop him, what defense did she have? His amusement only made it worse.

"It is just a game to you, but this is my life you are playing with, Norman! You kill my father, take my home, and now you do not even permit me my privacy," she cried.

"Come, you make more a fuss than needs by half. I admit I cannot give you back your father's life, but you have a place of honor here beside me. Your mother and your brother Aedward have free rein. I think you have been much indulged and spoiled, Lillyth. You know well how to receive, but you haven't learned how to give yet."

"You want me to be your whore to make life softer for myself, but I will not—you cannot make me!"

He swiftly advanced upon her and dragged her into his arms. "I could make you, wench, never doubt it."

"Yes, get your whip, my lord! Bloody another Saxon back. We are no better than the dirt beneath your feet. Well, what are you waiting for?" she taunted.

"I have other weapons," he said slowly, and he bent his head and took her lips softly. She was filled with the taste of him, and her senses reeled with his masculine scent. A tiny spark of desire to be his was kindled, and it grew and swept along her veins in warm pulsing waves. Her thighs were pressed to his and she could feel his desire for her raging against her body. With a tremendous effort she pulled her mouth from his and sobbed.

He was greatly disappointed that she was not the complacent widow he had thought. He took his arms from her abruptly.

"Women—every one a bitch!" he snarled.

She went and sat upon her own bed through the archway and cried softly. By the time she had dried her eyes, she could hear his even breathing from the other room and knew he was already asleep.

Chapter 8

At first light Guy was out among the Saxon villiens. By his presence alone an air of law and order prevailed.

"Hugh and Roger," he directed, "get water and razors and shave every last one of them. D'Arcy and Gilbert will be in charge of haircuts. I want them cropped close. If shears won't do the trick, shave them bald. You other men, line up these fellows in an orderly fashion."

Rolf approved. "It is a damned good idea. Their hair and beards must harbor vermin. Shaving them is easier than delousing them," he laughed. "We'll light fires here outside. Hugh, get pots from the women to boil water."

"Aedward, tell them each man must be barbered before he leaves for his work this morning," instructed Guy. "Where are all the villiens? I know there are more people than this in the fiefdom."

"My lord, they are hiding in their huts. They are afraid," said Aedward.

"Then we will have to go in after them," decided Guy. He entered the first hut and herded the occupants outside, then he cleared five more huts in succession.

"Line up six huts at a time. That should be enough to be going on with."

The peasants were muttering loudly, grabbing and shaking the magic charms they wore around their necks. Out of curiosity, Rolf pulled a small leather bag from around a peasant's neck and inspected its contents.

"Fah! Whatever it is, it stinks to high heaven!" said Rolf, holding it at arm's length.

"Let me see," ordered Guy. He emptied the contents and poked at them curiously.

"It looks like a dead bat!" he said incredulously. "Get me another," he directed Rolf.

The serf wildly tried to prevent the removal of his charm bag, but Rolf prevailed. They examined the contents.

"It looks like chicken or pigeon bones," offered Rolf.

"It looks like witchcraft!" Guy exploded. He turned to Aedward and demanded, "The source of this abomination?"

Aedward pleaded ignorance, but Edgarson, who was at his elbow to relish the spectacle of men being shorn like sheep, spoke up eagerly, "Morag, the witch!" and he pointed out her hut. With the agile mind only children possess, he had already picked up a few Norman words. Coupled with Guy's small knowledge of Saxon, they communicated adequately. Guy ruffled Edgarson's hair as a sign of his approval, then, grim-faced, strode back to the hall at such a pace that Aedward and Rolf could not keep up with him.

"Alison!" he bellowed at the top of his lungs.

She came quickly, dreading what had caused him to raise his voice to such a pitch.

"My lord, whatever is amiss?"

"Madame, are you aware that these people are

practicing witchcraft under your very nose?" he demanded.

"Witchcraft?" she protested.

"The villiens are so weighted down with talismans and magic charms they can scarce hobble about," he accused.

"Oh, you mean the things they get from Morag, my lord," she said, relieved. "They are harmless enough."

"Do these people not attend church as God-fearing Christians?" he asked incredulously.

"Well, no one prevents them attending church. We of the hall go, of course, but I can't say the peasants are regular attendants."

"From now on they will be. All of them! Even if we have to enlarge the church," he thundered.

She lowered her head to him. "Whatever you say, my lord."

"Lady Alison, I am shocked. I can scarce credit your attitude!" he exclaimed.

She smiled ruefully. "The English are not as pious as we French."

"Pious?" he exploded. "Rolf, find that Morag and hang her!" he ordered.

Alison went pale. "Nay, my lord, I beg you, what harm can her love potions and horoscopes do?"

"Horoscopes? Love potions?" He laughed. "You can't be serious!"

She quickly pressed her advantage while he laughed. "When they learned the Normans were almost upon us, they flocked to Morag for lucky charms that would protect them. And you see they worked—fate sent us a man with compassion!"

"You suppose if you flatter me, I won't hang the old hag," he accused.

"Do I suppose wrongly, my lord?" she asked with great daring.

He paused, then met her halfway. "I will see her for myself before I pass judgment."

Guy entered Morag's hut without ceremony. Aedward stood at the entrance, realizing he was going to be caught between two very strong forces. While Greediguts screeched from his perch near the roof, Morag met the Norman's stare of scrutiny without blinking.

Guy said, "Aedward, you will interpret for us. Word for word," he warned, "I don't want your watered-down version."

He narrowed his eyes and said to Morag, "If you have the Power, you must know I have come to hang you."

"No," she said slowly, "you have come to intimidate me."

His eyebrows rose at her temerity. "Bones of Christ!" he swore. "And do I intimidate you?" he demanded.

"You are born in April under the sign of Aries. You would intimidate anyone," she said, maintaining eye contact.

"I was born in April. How did you know?" he demanded.

"It is written all over you for anyone to plainly see. By nature you are aggressive, self-willed and determined. You enjoy power and are fond of being looked up to by others. You are restless and courageous to the point of daring. You have a quick temper and will make or break your own destiny. You are intolerant, impatient, overconfident and overbearing."

Guy grinned a wolf's grin. "These are just my better qualities; what of my faults?"

"An Aries has no faults," Morag said dryly.

Aedward hesitated to translate. Guy gave him a look so commanding he translated—"An Aries has no faults."

Guy gave a sharp bark of laughter.

"By God's bones, she must have some powerful magic to deliberately goad me. Madame," he warned, "you are on probation. Your activities will be closely watched. You will attend church twice a week and if you dispense anything stronger than a lovecharm I will lock you up permanently."

When he had left, Morag sagged to the floor as relief swept over her. In her wisdom, she knew he would flourish here and remain long after she was dead and buried. His will was even stronger than her own; she had no choice but to obey him.

Outside Guy told Rolf, "I am going over to inspect Oxstead. God knows what I'll find over there if this is any indication. I'll take my brothers, but I want you to stay and see that things progress here in an orderly fashion."

Aedward went back to where the peasants were being shorn, glad that the encounter with Morag was behind him. He heard the Norman called D'Arcy laugh, "My God, this one's fainted from fright. These Saxon youths are gutless."

Aedward looked down to see Edwina lying on the ground with her head shorn. He elbowed the knight away and went down on one knee to her.

"This is a maid," he said angrily. "Your orders didn't include the women!"

"They all look alike to me with their long blond tresses. She hasn't even got tits, how was I to know?"

Aedward helped Edwina to her feet. She was

terrified and clung to him desperately. Tears streaked her face and her short, chopped hair stood up hideously. He put a comforting arm about her, but her whole body was trembling. He gently led her back to her hut.

"Hush, Edwina, everything will be all right. They didn't really hurt you." Once inside the privacy of the hut, she really gave vent to her emotions. She sobbed and rocked back and forth until Aedward was beside himself to console her.

"Listen Edwina, I have an idea. If we wash it, I bet it will look quite nice."

"Wash my hair?" she said, the fear coming back in her eyes. She drew away from him before another indignity was forced upon her.

"Yes, yes. The ladies up at the hall wash their hair every other week. Come to the bathhouse with me. We'll get some soap and I'll help you to wash it."

"I will do it if you desire it, my lord," she offered, trying her best to swallow the tears.

At the bathhouse Aedward filled a deep wooden tub with hot water.

"It would be much simpler if you got into the tub, Edwina."

"But I would wet my clothes," she protested.

"No, no, you take your clothes off first," he explained patiently.

"I cannot swim. I'm afraid of water," she said miserably.

"It's not deep enough to drown you. Come, be brave," he encouraged. "I'll turn my back. Do it quickly while there is no one about!"

When she slipped into the water she let out a sharp gasp. This made Aedward glance over his shoulder in time to see that Edwina did indeed have breasts. They were young, delicate, budding and quite tempting. Aedward took a linen towel from a bathhouse shelf and a cake of soap scented with lemon verbena.

"When you have lathered your hair, rinse out the soap and dry yourself on this towel. Then quickly put your clothes back on before you take a chill. I'll come back to the hut with you and build a fire to dry your hair."

Aedward knelt to the dry kindling. He held the flintstone steady with his bad arm and struck the sparks with a small concealed dagger. He fed the fire until it blazed warmly.

"Come, sit closer. When your hair is dry it is going to be quite beautiful, Edwina. Now that it's clean, I can see its true color is a lovely flaxen shade, and it's curling softly around your face. Actually it is much prettier than it was before."

Edwina sat shyly, basking in his admiration, saying nothing.

"Tell me about yourself," urged Aedward.

"There is nothing to tell," she said simply.

"Of course there is! What work do you do?"

"I look after the bees and gather the honey."

"Bees must be fascinating; tell me about them," he coaxed.

She smiled. "Did you know the ones that do all the work and gather the honey are female?"

He laughed. "No, I didn't know that. Tell me more."

"When a bee finds a lot of flowers she flies back to the hive and does a little sort of buzzing dance. She touches the others with her body and tells them where the flowers are. If the flowers are a long way away, the bee does her buzzing dance, then walks in a straight line, then buzzes again, then makes a right turn, buzzes again, then walks another little line and turns again and buzzes again, and when the others leave the hive, they know exactly where to go to find the flowers."

He laughed delightedly.

"Don't you believe me?" she asked.

"Well, I don't think you would make it up, so I must believe you. Tell me, how do they survive the winter?" he puzzled.

She said with a wisdom far beyond her years, "They survive only because they have learned to cooperate with each other. They all cling together in a mass and keep moving very, very slowly. As the ones on the outside become cold they move to the inside and the warm bees from the middle of the mass move to the outside."

"Edwina, that is exactly the way it will be here. We will all survive and, yes, even prosper, if Saxon and Norman learn to live together and cooperate." He took a small ivory comb from his tunic. He reached out carefully and ran it gently through her blond curls.

"I want you to have this. I probably won't have any use for it after today if they make me cut my long hair and shave off my beard."

She cupped it in her hands wonderingly. No one had ever given her a gift before. It pleased her. She reached out a finger to touch his curling mustache and as she did so, Aedward's arm swept about her, and he pulled her against him and kissed her. She was enthralled by his touch. Her fragrance filled his senses, as his hand sought her delicate breasts that had tempted him earlier. He knew she would allow him to have his way with her, but something in her vulnerability stayed him. She had so few choices in life, he could not bear to impose his will upon her. He drew back and said gently, "I dare not stay longer."

That evening May shook her head as she tried to get used to the appearance of her husband and her daughter. Edgarson ran in, mad as fire. He wanted his hair cut so badly he could taste it, but the Normans had paid no attention to the boy.

"I want to look like him!" he insisted.

"Who?" asked May.

"Him! The new lord," shouted Edgarson.

"When I was at Oxstead yesterday, I discovered the people are suffering with what you call St. Anthony's Fire or dysentery of the bowels. We don't want it to spread, so I spoke with your mother and she has something she calls alkanet, I believe. Would you ride out there with me this morning, Lillyth?"

"Oh, I would enjoy a ride. I can bring some of Lady Hilda's things back for her." She ran upstairs to change her slippers for soft leather boots.

In the stables Guy had Zephyr saddled for her. All three Montgomerys were going to Oxstead, while Rolf was left behind in charge of Godstone. Lillyth admired Guy's magnificent horse.

"He is called Tempest. Is it not strange that both our horses are named for the wind?" he laughed. "When she is ready, perhaps we could breed them?"

Lillyth blushed and said stiffly, "He is too big—he would hurt her."

Guy looked amused. "Nonsense!"

The sun was shining, but the air was cold and Lillyth wore a warm woolen cloak.

Guy thought, I would like to give her a cloak

lined with fur before the winter sets in, and his mind went over the various animals that he might hunt which would provide this luxury for her.

Lillyth enjoyed the ride tremendously. Her cheeks were scarlet from the wind and her hair whipped about wildly. The autumn leaves were thick upon the ground and the horses' hooves made a rustling, swishing sound as they progressed. She laughed at the squirrels scampering about with nuts and acorns, preparing for the winter. All at once her horse screamed and reared in fright. A wild boar rushed from the underbrush, and almost immediately Guy had him spitted with a short lance he carried. Lillyth quieted her horse and Guy asked, concerned, "Are you all right, *chérie?*"

"Of course," laughed Lillyth, "what need to fear with such a brave escort?"

"Truss up the boar and we will collect the carcass on our way back, André," he called. He decided that Lillyth was quite brave and not easily frightened. "Perhaps you would enjoy the hunt. Will you ride with me the next time we have one?"

"I think not, my lord. It grieves me to see animals die, unless of course they threaten our lives."

Upon arrival at Oxstead, the men went to give out doses of medicine, and Lillyth went into the hall to collect Lady Hilda's clothes and also some for Aedward if she could do so undetected. She called one of the hall servants to her and explained to the woman quickly that Aedward had been discovered by the Normans, but she had claimed him as her brother to protect him. The woman promised to spread the word quietly and

Lillyth ran up the stairs toward the bedchambers.

She gazed about her, thinking how strange fate was that she wasn't living here now with Wulfric. She suddenly shuddered at the thought. The place was quiet and had a queer, deserted air about it. She went into Lady Hilda's chamber and lifted the lid of a coffer and began sorting the contents. A bang from one of the other chambers made her jump, and she listened intently for further sounds. As she looked around her at the dust, she had an eerie feeling that she was not alone. But hearing no further sounds, Lillyth quickly gathered together the things she thought would be most useful and placed them in a small trunk. She went quietly to Aedward's chamber, which was next door to the one Wulfric always slept in. There she shook out three long velvet tunics, heavily embroidered at the hem with gold thread. She felt nervous, as if unseen eyes were watching her. When she was about to rise from her kneeling position, she heard stealthy shuffling footsteps in the next chamber. Fear closed her throat and her heart started to pound uncontrollably. She sensed an evil presence, and all she could think of was Wulfric. She began to shake, and a scream rose in her throat as a shadow fell across the doorway.

"You look as if you have seen a ghost!" laughed Guy.

"Oh, my lord, thank God it is you." She ran to him as if seeking his protection, and the look of relief on her face was so marked he put his arms about her and held her gently.

"You are trembling, *chérie*, what is it?" he asked softly. "Strange that you can face a wild boar without a tremor, yet you jump at shadows."

She shook her head and managed a tremulous smile.

He did not press her for an explanation, but there was a perplexed crease in his brow as he regarded her. He would find out more of the mystery if he could, he promised himself.

"That small trunk has to be carried home. Could you get someone to carry it for me, my lord?"

"*Certes*, lady, but we will be a while yet. Won't you stay here and rest until we return?"

"Nay," she said quickly. "I will come outside and look about, I think. Don't worry about me, I will find occupation until you are ready to return." She ventured no farther than Lady Hilda's herb garden, where she picked some rosemary and thyme for the kitchens of Godstone.

On the ride back, late in the afternoon, the rain started, and it came down in unrelenting torrents. Guy gave Lillyth his mantle to put over her own, but it was of little avail against the downpour. They left the horses in the stable and ran across the courtyard into the hall. Guy said, "By God, they told me this England was a dark, wet hole, but until today I didn't believe it."

Lillyth threw over her shoulder, "You can always go home if you don't like it, Norman," and they ran upstairs laughing at the puddles of water they left on every step.

Once inside their chamber, Guy began to strip off his soggy clothing and Lillyth quickly retreated through the archway into her own chamber. Guy stripped off his chausses and put on dry ones, then, bare-chested, he sought out Lillyth. She was huddled on the edge of her bed with only her cloak removed.

"Get those clothes off, lady, you will catch your death," he commanded.

"I have no privacy. I shall not remove one stitch until you quit this chamber," she flared.

"Splendor of God, are you back to defying me again? Undress this instant or by the Christ I will do it for you," he threatened.

She tossed her dripping hair and threw him a challenging glance of disobedience. In one stride he jerked her up from the bed and pulled her soaked tunic over her head. Lillyth struggled in vain as he pulled her this way and that. Her wet kirtle clung to her body and revealed its outline completely. He set his hands upon it and managed to pull it up to her thighs, and she struggled against him and begged, "Please, please, my lord, I will remove it if you would get me a towel for my hair. Please?" Her eyes implored him.

Reluctantly he left in search of a towel and returned with it. He also brought wine. She had stripped off her last garment and put on a velvet robe. She wrapped her head in the towel, turban fashion, and Guy held out some wine to her.

"Drink this, it will keep out the chill. I've set the fire to blaze. Come and be warm, *chérie*."

"I do not drink wine, my lord, it is intoxicating," she said prudishly.

"This is Chablis—a rich white wine, and you will drink it now, Lillyth, or do I pour it down your throat?" he challenged.

She took the wine and sipped it slowly, looking pointedly at his bare chest. "Aren't you cold, my lord?"

"If you would but warm me once with your eyes, I would never be cold again," he said quietly.

He refilled her glass over her protests and lifted

it to her mouth, insisting that she drink. He then lifted the glass to his mouth and pressed his lips to the spot where she had drunk. The wine warmed her considerably, and she felt it running along her veins and making her legs weak. She felt his eyes upon her and pretended to study the flames in the fireplace. It was safe and warm and very intimate here drinking wine with him before the fire, utterly alone, with the wind and rain lashing against the roof.

"We have an hour before supper. Fetch yonder great book and teach me to read this heathen Saxon of yours," he directed.

Glad of the diversion, she carried the large book to the fire and sat down beside him. She opened it and showed him the beautiful illustrated pages. "This is the legend of Beowulf," she began.

He interrupted her. "Come down here on the rug before the fire, so I can see it better."

She slowly sat on the furs beside him and began to read. He looked at the words and protested that he could make no sense of them. His interest soon strayed from the book. He studied her profile intently while she read, and though she pretended otherwise, she was completely aware of him. His nearness did strange things to her, or was it the wine?

Swiftly he closed the book in her lap, and pulled her across his chest. His mouth took hers in a demanding kiss. She put her hands up to push against him and felt his naked chest. The muscles rippled under her hands and she thought, How magnificent he is.

She pulled violently away from him, afraid of her own reaction to his maleness. He did not pursue her further but contemplated her intently while he finished his wine. The silence stretched between them, so, womanlike, she said the first thing that came into her head.

"You will never learn Saxon if you allow your attention to keep wandering to other things," she rebuked him lightly, and to her dismay she heard herself giggle. It must be the wine, she told herself hastily.

"I can learn Saxon in one hour if I put my mind to it," he boasted. She threw back her head and laughed. "Ridiculous, impossible for a thick-headed Norman to learn a civilized language in a year, let alone an hour," she ridiculed him.

"A wager! Tonight I will study your Beowulf for one hour. If I read it back to you perfectly, you will have to pay a forfeit."

"Done!" cried Lillyth boldly, then instantly knew what he meant by "forfeit."

His teeth showed in a grin. "Who wagers against me loses."

She arose hastily, wondering at what she had done. He had a power over her that set her shivering. She retreated through the archway to dress for dinner and hoped fervently that he would not follow her, then when he didn't, she wondered why he had not.

At the evening meal Nicholas had again chosen Rose as his dinner partner, while André sat next to Edyth. Lady Adela had attracted Hugh Montrose for the past two nights from across the great hall. Tonight he was bold enough to take the seat next to hers.

"My orders are to dine with one of the ladies so that I may learn some Saxon. I have chosen you," he said very deliberately, glancing boldly at her neat figure and light, ash-brown hair.

Her lashes swept down over her cornflower-blue eyes. "My lord, I do not seek company."

"Then why did you uncover your hair?" he asked pointedly.

She glanced at him swiftly, fearing he would be more demanding than Luke, her husband, had ever been. She must go slowly, just keep his thoughts on impersonal matters. Her mind raced quickly for a subject that would fit the moment. "I will try to teach you Saxon, my lord. It is indeed fortunate that I have a little French."

In Saxon she told him her name was Adela.

"You need a protector, Adela," he said plainly.

She blushed. "I have just lost my husband, sir."

"Call me Hugh. A young widow needs a protector," he repeated.

"I'd rather not speak of it, sir, I mean Hugh," she said politely.

"We will speak of it, Adela. Lord Montgomery has over forty men. Any one of them could take you any time he felt the need. The only way to avoid being continually molested is to chose a protector. Lady Lillyth understands that very well, if you do not." He indicated Guy at the head of the table. "If we pair off, the other men will not dare bother you." Her mouth had gone dry and her lips went white. Hugh lifted his goblet of wine, but before he held it out to her, he took out his dagger and plunged it into the blood-red liquid to the hilt. It was a sexual symbol which she understood completely. She hesitated for long minutes, then slowly accepted the wine and drank it.

Lady Emma had come to dinner determined to acquire whichever knight was the tallest and strongest. She felt lost without a man. She felt betrayed by her husband, as if he had abandoned her, and the sooner she replaced him, the safer she would feel. She eyed the company of knights who were still available after eliminating Guy, his brothers and Rolf. By the look of things, Hugh Montrose was also out of the running.

Three men sat together. They had discovered a fondness for English ale as well as the good plain food which was always served so generously in this newfound country. Emma had a plan. She would flirt with all three. They would argue over her, perhaps even fight, then the strongest would emerge the victor. Such a knight would make her feel safe and protected again. She soon caught the eye of Fitzroy, the youngest of the trio. She smiled at him. He looked owlishly back at her and said to his companions, "God's feet, I just received an open invitation from across the hall."

Gervais, a muscular, powerfully built man with a dark brooding quality, glanced over at Emma. She immediately smiled at him before lowering her eyes. "You are wrong, my young cockerel, 'tis me she fancies."

Esmé, the only tall blond Norman in the group, asked, "Do you mean the one with the lovely big ta-ta's? I've had my eye on her since the beginning."

"Well, we had better decide this thing fast, or while we are arguing over her some other son of a bitch will have bedded her," laughed Fitzroy.

"I make first claim," drawled Esmé lazily, as if all had been decided.

Gervais lifted a dark brow, looked like thunder at his companions and announced shortly, "There is only one way to decide." As he reached into his doublet for a pair of dice, the clouds cleared from his brow and a sunny smile broke through.

Fitzroy set aside the pewter tankard of ale with the leather handle to make room for the cast and said to Gervais with resignation, "We don't stand a chance, *mon frère*. Esmé always gambles with the devil at his shoulder. He never loses."

Each man cast the die and, as predicted, Esmé's negligent cast proved to be lucky.

He stood up from the table, stretched his long legs and sauntered over to Emma. Naturally, she had witnessed what had transpired, and humiliation stained her cheeks. He cocked an eyebrow and drawled, "Dearest lady, to the victor goes the spoils."

She wanted to turn from him in disdain, but his beauty held her in thrall.

Guy cracked walnuts with the hilt of his dagger. Most of the knights got out the dice, and the room was filled with such boasts as, "I'll nick three throws out of three."

Rolf looked across at Guy. "Will you hazard with me?"

Guy put up his hands. "Nay, I've a deal of studying to do. While you waste your evening, I'm learning to read Saxon."

He bowed low to Lillyth. "Come, little tutor."

She blushed vividly and with lagging steps followed Guy upstairs.

Without a word he took up the book and began to read intently. She tried to distract his attention by poking at the fire, and then by brushing out her hair in front of him, but he never looked up. She walked about nervously and finally took her courage in both hands and said, "My lord, what will my forfeit be?"

He met her glance evenly. "My bed has been cold to me for many nights, Lillyth. This night you will warm it for me, *chérie*," and he bent his attention upon the book again. The room was filled with silence.

Lillyth retired to her part of the room and took up a shirt she was making for him. Slowly and thoughtfully she plied her needle. It had such a calming effect that her confidence returned and she knew he could never do what he had boasted.

She went to him before the hour could be up and said, "You have had the time we agreed upon, my lord, let us hear what you have learned."

He flashed her a wicked grin and began to read the first page in perfect Saxon. As he neared the bottom of the page, he glanced up triumphantly and saw such dismay in her face, such distaste for what lay ahead, such marked fear in her eyes, that he faltered and, clearing his throat, asked, "I cannot understand this last bit here. Will you translate it for me, lady?"

Her lashes were beaded with tears. "Thank you," she said softly.

"Lust is a hard horse for a man to ride and control, Lillyth. Good night."

After a short time she began to relax and finally drifted into sleep, but Guy found that he was unusually restless. He tossed and turned in the great bed and longed for Lillyth to be beside him. Finally, he slipped quietly from the bed and sought her out. He gazed down upon her sleeping form, then knelt beside the bed and took her hair between his fingers. Its satiny texture aroused him further and he ached to know the feel of her skin. He had never wanted a woman like this before. His desire almost overpowered him. He longed to slip in beside her and caress every curve of her body. He wanted to put his mouth to hers and to go inside of her. He wanted to give full rein to the passion he had dammed up too long, and know the luxury of her response to him. He fought his raging desires and let her sleep on peacefully, but it was the greatest agony he had ever endured. The captor was completely captivated.

Chapter 9

With the rain still coming down, the next day brought the return of the rider Guy had sent to William. Guy watched with approval as the knight saw to the needs of his horse, rather than turn it over to a stableboy. The knight grinned. "William took Dover Fort after besieging it for only eight days. He was most pleased to get your messages and sent this." He handed Guy a sealed packet.

Guy said, "Come to the hall and take refreshment. Tell me the temper of the people at Dover."

"Well, they hate us Normans, but they have grudgingly accepted William." He laughed. "What choice did they have? He's already nicknamed William the Conqueror. I don't think he'll have any trouble taking London and once he is crowned king, perhaps a lot of this hatred and resentment against us will die down."

"You could easily hate William, but you could never despise him. I think these Saxons will never become Normans, my friend. We shall all have to change and become English. We may not accomplish that until the next generation. Saxons are obstinate as the devil and everything goes by custom or superstition," said Guy.

"In my travels I have discovered that England is

full of odd people, but that is one of its charms."
They both laughed.

Guy poured them both wine, then opened the
sealed packet and studied the contents. He
smiled to himself that William had writ plainly
his plans to go immediately to Canterbury and
take hostages, with no care if this message was
discovered and made common knowledge. None
could stop William—he was that sure of his own
destiny. He had written that once he was
crowned king, he would grant Guy deed to the
manorial demesne of his choice, but he would
need his help in London. He intended to completely surround it with a show of force in such
overwhelming numbers that none would dare
say him nay. He commanded Guy to be in London in full force by the end of November. This
was only the end of October and therefore Guy
had another month before he need take up arms
again. William had signed the letter in Latin:
"Ego Willelmus cognomine Bastardus."

That night at the main meal, Guy told his men
of William's request and outlined how much there
was to do before their departure. He smiled at
Lillyth. "I'm afraid I am turning into a farmer.
You'd be surprised at all the things I have had to
learn since coming here. For instance, half a beef
herd must be killed for winter salting at Martin-
mas, but with sheep you can get enough cheese
and wool to pay for their winter keep. However, if
you let sheep feed on grass that has hoarfrost
upon it, then they suffer from aphtha about the
mouth, which prevents them from feeding. I could
go on and on through foot rot to scab, but it
would bore you to death."

"I think you are the one to be bored, my lord,
and will be glad to go back into battle, slaughter-

ing my poor people. You are all cruel barbarians!"
she said hotly.

"Nay, lady," spoke up Rolf, "when we have
fought the infidel we saw such cruelty you
wouldn't believe. Blinding, castrating, or using human heads for footballs were common. We are
Christians."

She looked at Rolf and scoffed. "You fight the
infidel so he won't swarm over your country,
burning your towns and raping your women, but
as dutiful *Christians* you swarm over my country,
burning our towns and raping our women!"

Guy gave her a warning glance. "Gently, *chérie*,
in all fairness, no woman of Godstone has been
badly used. War is no pleasure. It is simply chaos
and it's every man for himself. Some blossom and
rise above themselves in the horror of battle, others just go rotten. Look about you, Lillyth. My
knights are all eating and drinking themselves into
a convivial stodge, to use a Saxon phrase. Think
you they would rather be on Senlac Field holding
a blade plastered with thick blood to the elbow,
catching some poor bastard under the armpit as he
lifts his shield?" he asked.

"You enjoy conquest, do not dare to deny it to
me!" she challenged.

He shook his head slowly and his green eyes
glittered. "I cannot deny it. I have mastered
Godstone and Oxstead, and I shall master you,
Lillyth, so have a care how you speak to me in future, wench!" he warned.

She looked boldly into his eyes and vowed silently, I will bring him low!

Her mother passed her and bent low to whisper,
"He looks at you as if he would devour you, like
a hound at the throat of a doe. The pliant bough
bends to the wind, Lillyth, do not unleash the
beast in him," warned her mother.

But Lillyth's appetite was whetted and she licked her lips over him.

Aedward approached Guy as soon as Lillyth moved away.

"My lord, may I have speech with you?"

"*Certes*, Aedward, is there a problem?"

"As a matter of fact, there is. The Saxons have approached me with a couple of complaints against your Normans. Since you instructed me to inform you when things were not going smoothly, I promised them I would speak to you about them."

"I see." He frowned slightly for a minute, then said, "Tell them we will hold a court tomorrow morning if this infernal rain ceases. I will give them a hearing if you will tell them to assemble, and I will get my knights together and we will thrash out any problems."

"Thank you, my lord," said Aedward, turning to leave.

"Aedward," Guy recalled him, "what is your sister Lillyth's connection with Oxstead?"

Aedward started slightly at the mention of his home, and he searched Guy's face to see if there was hidden meaning behind the question.

"Why, that was Wulfric's hall," he answered carefully.

"Wulfric?" questioned Guy.

Aedward hesitated, then answered, "Wulfric was Lillyth's husband."

"I see," answered Guy. "Thank you."

Jealous anger flared in him for a few moments, and as Guy watched Lillyth ascend the stairs, his imagination was tortured by visions of her lithe form in the arms of his predecessor. He could see her trembling at Oxstead and his brain suddenly cleared as he realized there had been trouble be-

tween them. She seemed to be afraid of a man's
touch. She probably refused him his rights and he
forced her a few times, thought Guy. I'd better
leave her alone for a while before I do the same
thing. I've almost forced her a hundred times, and
will one of these nights, yet I want her willing, he
thought quietly.

"Who rides patrol this foul night? I vow he will
gladly trade with me, eh?" Guy ran upstairs to
fetch a heavy cloak and as he opened the chamber
door Lillyth was seated, brushing out her hair. It
fell in gold-red waves to the floor and presented a
very seductive picture, as she had fully intended
to do. The wistfulness of her beauty took his
breath away. He thought, There is no greater torment than hope eternally deferred. He picked up
his cloak and said, "You may rest easy tonight, I
ride patrol."

A look of disappointment crossed her face and
she tempted him with a sideways glance. "I hoped
you would join me in some wine, my lord."

"Stay me with flagons," he quoted from the
Song of Solomon, and realized that he had fallen
into a trap of his own making. He could not possibly tell young Gilbert he had changed his mind
about riding patrol. "Golden bitch!" he cursed,
and left the chamber, slamming the door after
him.

The only invaders he encountered were a wolf
pack in the sheep pens and he killed three, thinking they would line a cloak for Lillyth before the
bitter winter set in. He chuckled to himself,
thinking, Now I will woo her with gifts, I've tried
everything else. At six o'clock when the men finished their night patrol, the rain stopped falling.
Guy was soaked to the skin as he went up to his
chamber. He thought he would have the pleasure

of awakening Lillyth, but she was already up and dressed, waiting for him. She worried about him when he went thirty-six hours without rest and knew he drove himself by willpower alone.

"I have a hot bath ready for you, my lord, and dry clothes laid out." She smiled.

His eyes widened in surprised pleasure. "Playing the wife, *chérie?*" he laughed.

She blushed at the remark and retreated quickly, as he was already stripping his clothes off. She thought, I'd like to see him naked, why do I run away? and then she was immediately ashamed of her brazen thoughts.

"I want you to be beside me this morning. I'm hearing complaints from your Saxons against my Normans. I don't want them to be afraid to speak up, so I think your presence will help."

She heard him splashing about, and finally he got out of the water. "What chance do my people stand against your Normans?" she shouted through to him. "You will punish any who dare to speak up."

"Lillyth, are you daring to suggest I won't be impartial?" he demanded.

She rushed to the archway, crying, "Don't forget your whip!" and found him standing naked before her. She gasped, but found her feet rooted to the floor. Her eyes took in the splendor of him. His skin was dark and tanned above the waist and white below. The corded muscles of his thighs and sinewy torso gave the impression of powerful strength. A thatch of black hair covered his chest and another his groin.

"I—I'm sorry," she stammered.

"I'm not." He grinned slowly.

"Has the rain stopped?" She quickly sought for something to say, and clung to the subject of the weather. "I'd better get a warm cloak," and she retreated quickly.

Guy and Lillyth were seated on wooden stools with the knights to one side and the assembled peasants in front. As Guy looked over the people in front of him he realized that he could put a name to many of the faces in the crowd. He could see young Edgarson had pushed his way to the front in case he missed something, and yes, there Morag stood listening at the back, hoping she wouldn't be recognized. Guy asked Aedward to bring the first complainant forward.

A man approached hesitantly and said, "My lord, one of your Normans stole my wife."

Guy raised his eyebrows and asked Aedward to explain. Aedward cleared his throat and said, "This man's wife, Elfrida, has taken up with Giles St. Aubyn, I believe he is called. She has moved out of her husband's hut."

Guy sighed inwardly as he remembered this was the second time Giles had antagonized a Saxon. He looked toward his knights and called out to Giles. "Is this allegation true?"

Giles hesitated for a moment, then spoke quietly. "Yes, my lord, it is true."

Guy looked at the aggrieved husband. "Did he take her against her will, or did she go freely?"

Aedward interpreted, and turning to Guy said, "It was of her own free will."

Guy swiftly looked at Lillyth, then said to the peasant, "You can have no cause for complaint. A man who cannot hold his own woman does not deserve her!"

A great murmur went up among the villagers. They had known they would never get fair treatment from a Norman. Lillyth almost scathingly asked if this was an example of his impartiality, but bit back the words for when they would be more private.

"There was another man with a complaint, was there not?" asked Guy.

"Yes, my lord," said Aedward, and beckoned to the Saxon in question. For a few moments no one moved, and then resolutely a man stepped forward. He spoke to Aedward who explained to Guy, "This man traps furs and cures them. Two knights rode over his furs stretched out on racks he had constructed himself and ruined both the furs and the racks."

"Who were the two knights?" Guy asked.

The Saxon hesitated again, then pointed out two men. They were two of Guy's youngest knights who were always in one scrape or other.

"Fitzroy, Gilbert, is this true?" Guy's countenance was dreadful to behold.

"Aye, my lord, but we meant no harm. It was a race, that's all!" protested Gilbert.

"Splendor of God, you are Norman knights, not children playing destructive games. This day you will reconstruct this man's racks for him to his satisfaction. I myself will help him replace the furs."

He looked at Aedward, who was now smiling. "No, my lord, that's all for the present."

As the assembly dispersed Guy left Lillyth and spoke to the Saxon who had lodged the complaint.

"What is your name?" he asked in fairly good Saxon.

"Alfred, my lord."

"I killed three wolves last night. Could you cure and soften the skins for me so that they could be fashioned into a cloak, think you?"

"Aye, I could make them as soft as doeskin, my lord."

"Good. Do you always trap your furs or do you hunt them with a weapon?"

"Nay, I am allowed no weapon, but I could increase the number of furs greatly if I were taught to hunt," said Alfred.

"Have you never shot a bow?" asked Guy.

"When I was a boy I fashioned a crude bow and arrows, but that was many years ago."

"We will have a hunt soon, and you will join us, Alfred. I will soon teach you to shoot." Guy held out his hand and smiled.

The Saxon took it wonderingly, asking himself what manner of man this new master was.

After the first two days and nights in the forest, Morgan and Faith did not fare too well. They thought they would be able to supplement their diet with nuts and berries, but it was so late in the autumn that the squirrels had stripped the trees of anything edible and then stayed safely in the high treetops.

Rabbits were scarce this deep in the forest. They liked to stay at the edge where they could hop into the sunny green meadows.

Morgan had had a close miss with a wild boar. They had startled it while it was rooting for pannage and it had charged without hesitation, its little red eyes wild with rage. Faith knew if Morgan were wounded she could not survive alone. The days were turning quite chilly, but the nights were extremely cold. They were not adequately clothed to spend the winter outdoors. After three days, Faith was considerably weakened from lack of food and shelter. They could not travel many miles with her in this state, so they decided to go back toward Godstone, if they could find their way. On the fourth day, while they were resting, close to exhaustion, they were quietly surrounded.

Morgan could tell they were Saxons, though by their weapons he knew they were not serfs.

He asked, "Are you hiding out from the Normans?"

"We are outlaws, who have banded together to survive in the forest. As you must have learned by now, it is impossible to survive alone," one of the men said.

"We need food," said Morgan, "can we join you?"

"That is up to our leader, Red Wolf. We chose different names now to mask our identity. If he will take you in, we share everything," he said, looking at Faith.

Inside, Morgan railed against the fate that thrust such a decision as this upon him. He knew Faith wouldn't last another day without warm sustenance, therefore he knew he had no choice.

"Take me to Red Wolf. We will work in return for food."

The tall man helped Morgan get Faith on her feet, and they supported her through a pathway that had been worn in the woods. They soon emerged into a clearing that had been made into a camp. There was a welcome fire with a black iron kettle of food cooking over it, and three rough-hewn huts had been built from cut logs and thick tree branches. Morgan heard a gurgling brook nearby and saw two horses tethered to trees. Tall John presented them to Red Wolf.

"There was no point in killing them, they had naught to steal. Besides, they were Saxon peasants, runaways. If you have use for them, they want to join us."

The leader looked over the woman first, then said to Morgan, "Can you obey orders?"

"Yes, sir," he answered promptly. He was almost certain he recognized Red Wolf's true identity, and he was not about to anger him.

"Do not be too quick, boy. Consider before you answer. Can you kill?"

"If I have to," answered Morgan slowly, "I could certainly kill a Norman."

"We rob and kill anyone who ventures into this forest, except someone who looks wealthy. Those we hold for ransom. Also, we share the woman," he stated flatly.

Morgan hesitated.

"Quickly boy! Food or starvation, the choice is yours."

"Food!" Morgan replied, and a great wave of relief swept over him.

They were free to go close to the fire to warm themselves and were given a wooden bowl of stew. Morgan knew he had made the right decision when Faith began to revive with the hot food inside her. They provided her with a fur pelt covering and she sank into an exhausted sleep beside the camp fire.

Red Wolf said to Morgan, "Tomorrow I will map out where we are in relation to Godstone, Sevenoaks, Oxstead and other towns not too distant. Learn the locations well. We need many things. Weapons, food, winter clothing, horses. We have a plan to make concerted raids for the supplies we need to survive. The one law that must never be broken is never, under any circumstances, lead anyone back here. It means certain death for all."

"You have knives and long bows," said Morgan.

"You must steal yourself a knife, but we will help you fashion a bow and arrows. However, if you are smart enough to steal a horse, I will make you a gift of a knife, gladly. When the woman is recovered she will gather fuel and do the cooking, to free one of my men for other activities," ordered Red Wolf.

Chapter 10

Simon Fitzroy and Gilbert de Clare came crashing into the communal sleeping quarters in the middle of the night. They awoke Nicholas and André de Montgomery for extra support before they faced their lord with their bad news. Already fallen from grace because of the business with the Saxon Alfred, they quaked at the thought of Guy de Montgomery's reaction to the report they must give him. André, believing Guy and Lillyth shared a bed, offered to go to their chamber and break the news to his brother. For this the two knights were duly thankful.

André entered his brother's chamber softly, but before he could close the door, Guy was on his feet with his broadsword in his hands. André raised his brows at not finding Lillyth with him, but made no mention of her.

"What is wrong?" snapped Guy.

"Fitzroy and Gilbert are below. We have been raided and they fear what you will do when you learn they did not catch the bastards."

"Splendor of Christ, I govern a motley crew!" he spat as he reached for his chausses. "Did they say what happened?"

"Yes, they saw one of the peasant's houses on

fire and all those on patrol rode over and helped put it out. In the meantime two horses were stolen and food supplies taken from the storehouse. They never even saw a sign of them." He shrugged.

Guy ran his fingers through his hair, thinking rapidly. "It's got to be someone who knows this place well. Was anyone hurt?"

"No, the peasants got out safely, but the hut was destroyed before they could save it," said André.

Guy put his head through the archway to see if their voices had aroused Lillyth, and to his utter amazement, he found she was not there. He swore under his breath, then an idea sprang into his mind.

"Aedward! Find him. If he is not in bed, it is possible he has got a band of men together and is provisioning them from our stores. Who would know this place better than Aedward?"

Aedward was not in the communal sleeping quarters behind the armory where most of the knights slept. He was not in the servants' sleeping quarters where the men spent many of their nights with the serving wenches. Guy sent André to search the stables and he himself went back upstairs to look through the many bed chambers. He opened the door to the last one on the right and found Lillyth standing beside the bed in a dark velvet robe and Aedward rubbing the sleep from his eyes, still abed. Guy was relieved that he had found Aedward safely in bed, and thus he could remove the suspicions he had had from his mind. He wanted to ask Lillyth why she was with her brother in the middle of the night, but he was in a hurry to question Fitzroy and de Clare further. He did this privately, saving them from humiliation. His scathing words reduced them to errant boys, only playacting at being knights.

At breakfast Guy outlined a new plan for patrolling. Some knights were to set up permanent sleeping quarters in the stables and in the storerooms where food and provender were kept. There was to be a permanent guard on the hall door, lest those who had slipped in and out so easily should do so again and kill them all in their beds. The peasant family who had been burned out were brought to the hall until their home was rebuilt, and their children ran about laughing among the dogs. A wolfhound bitch that had taken to following Guy about lay at his feet, and he had another notion.

"These bloody dogs should be trained better too. We want watchdogs that will set up such a howl they will awaken the dead! At night some must be fastened in the stables and storehouses. Find out how many supplies are missing; that should give us an idea of how many there are to feed. Young Gilbert is supposed to know a deal about dogs," he told Rolf. "Get him to whip this lot into shape and train them to be fit for more than eating and shitting!" he said bluntly. "All except this one here," he added indulgently.

He thumped his fist into his palm and swore, "By the bones of Christ, I will know who has dared raid my demesne and lift my horses." He went outside and crashed the door of the hall so violently the pigeons rose in a flock from the watchtower. The day was taken up with plans and counterplans for the capture of the raiders and in the evening Guy took the wolf skins he had killed over to Alfred's hut. His purpose was twofold. He wanted him to cure and soften the skins, and he also wanted to find out if Alfred had seen anything, or if not, at least what his ideas on the subject were.

Guy looked at him directly. "You are absolutely sure you saw no one? I am almost sure it must be a Saxon and I know I am asking you to betray your own kind."

Alfred spat on the floor. "Saxon peasants are afraid of the dark. I am almost certain none here at Godstone is involved. As lords go, you suit us all well enough. A great deal better than our last one, or that Wulfric our Lady Lillyth married. We all feared him greatly, my lord."

"I must confess my first suspicions fell on Lillyth's brother," admitted Guy.

"Lady Lillyth's brother?" questioned Alfred.

"Aedward," said Guy absently.

"Aedward is not my lady's brother, my lord. He is Wulfric's brother." Alfred chuckled, "Brother indeed! They were more like sweethearts until along comes Wulfric and marries her from under Aedward's nose!"

Guy went rigid and his eyes turned to green ice.

Alfred immediately knew he had said too much.

An unbidden picture arose in Guy's mind of Lillyth and Aedward as he had surprised them in Aedward's bedchamber. Guy walked so swiftly back to the hall that small startled things scurried out of his path in the darkness. His step was loud and firm as he entered the hall, and all heads were turned in his direction.

He pointed a finger at Aedward, who was playing dice with Nicholas. "Seize him!" he commanded. "Chain him in a stall in the stables until I have time to deal with him." His voice carried such cold authority they did not dare disobey him, or question him while this mood was upon him.

Guy strode up the stairs so purposefully, the torches spluttered in their cressets. As soon as he entered their chamber he threw down the bar and fastened his eyes upon her. Lillyth was dressed in yellow and had never looked more beautiful, with her hair swirling about her thighs. She smiled at

him, but found no answering smile in Guy's countenance. His eyes never left her as he pulled off his
heavy cloak and leather tunic and stood before her
in only his chausses and chainse. He poured wine
and sipped it thoughtfully, rolling the horn between his palms. She began to feel uneasy with his
steady gaze upon her and was about to retreat to
her own side when he said very crisply and
clearly, "Come here!"

She turned, puzzled and apprehensive at his
tone.

"What were you doing in Aedward's room in
the middle of the night?" he asked quietly.

Basically, she told the truth, but the coldness of
his eyes disconcerted her so much she stumbled
over her explanations. "His mother—that is, our
mother was ill in the night and I went to fetch
him," she said.

"Aedward is not your brother," stated Guy so
quietly that she did not know if she had heard
him right. Fear sprang into her eyes.

"Ha! You fear for your lover, and by the bones
of Christ you have good reason to fear!"

She took a step toward him to plead her case. "I
did not lie overmuch, my lord. He is my brother,
in the law, since I married his brother Wulfric, and
indeed I think of him in terms of a brother."

Guy's lips pulled back to show his teeth. "You
mock me, lady! The whole fief knows you for
sweethearts. I am the last to know—a fine figure
of fun I must be to everyone."

"We were never really sweethearts, and besides,
that was a long time ago," she pleaded lamely.

"You deny me night after night, but dispense
your favors elsewhere with such frequency it
makes my senses swim. How many men have you
known, Lillyth? I admit you had me fooled with
that 'touch-me-not' business. But you are very

good at the game, Lillyth, luring me, then re-
buffing me, daring my manhood."

He went toward her and she turned and ran
from him, but he simply reached out and took her.
She knew all her time had run out and he could be
denied no longer, yet in a totally futile effort she
struggled and hit out at him instinctively. He
picked her up and threw her down onto his bed.
He held her down into the furs with one hand and
pulled off her tunic with the other. She went wild
and scratched his face, but he didn't even seem to
notice. He simply took both her wrists in one hand
and pulled her underdress from her, leaving her
naked.

Her bare thighs and breasts excited him more
than he had dreamed possible as she thrashed
about the bed, entangling them both in her long
golden tresses. A white searing jealousy consumed
him as his mind's eye pictured her with Aedward.
Aedward was such a handsome, blond youth of
Lillyth's own age, compared to his thirty. What
made it harder to bear was the fact that he knew
he was jealous. Inside, he laughed bitterly at himself for the fool she had made of him. He had been
falling in love with Lillyth and had been determined to wait until she yielded to him, but now
he was wild to have his way with her.

Lillyth knew she loved him. It was no use deny-
ing it to herself any longer, but she hated him for
what he was thinking about her, and she did not
want to be taken by force. She cursed herself for
not yielding sooner, when he had been in a gentler
mood.

He slipped out of his clothes so easily she
hardly blinked before she found him naked and
almost on top of her. His thighs were like iron as
he knelt above her body. Lowering his mouth to
hers, he kissed her savagely. His mouth moved to

her throat and down to her breast as she fought for breath. As she fully realized the extent of the towering passion she aroused in him, she was stunned at its intensity. His combined lust and anger formed a tidal wave that swept her begging denials aside ruthlessly. Her nipples stood erect and she realized hopelessly that he was arousing her even as she fought him. He forced her legs apart with his knee and tried to impale her, but something prevented him from entering all the way, and she cried out in pain.

"You are still a maid!" he said thickly, as realization dawned upon him. He withdrew immediately and looked down upon her in great wonder.

"Does that matter, Norman?" she cried.

"I am no ravisher of virgins, lady." Gently, he wiped a smear of blood from her thigh with the soft linen sheet and tried to take her in his arms. She curled over onto her side in a tight little ball and was racked with sobs. His heart soared heavenward as the thought that none other had had his way with her. He bent over her and asked gently, "How long were you wed, love?"

"One day only, before he rode away to his death," she said simply.

"It would have been long enough had you been my bride," he whispered, and took up the soft fur covers and placed them over her to keep out the cold.

She offered him no explanation and he got off the bed and dressed himself again. He stroked her hair gently and whispered, "Forgive me, Lillyth," before he took himself downstairs to spend the night with his men and give her the privacy she had begged him for. He deeply regretted the black-tempered mood he had gone to her in. He felt savage toward those who had dared to raid his property. His nerve endings felt raw when he thought Lillyth had lied to him. The trait he most disliked in a woman was deceit. He had never met one before now who was not deceitful. Suddenly, his spirits soared as he thought of the treasure that no other man had touched. Nay and never would, he swore. As he descended, all eyes looked up apprehensively and he remembered his entrance earlier. He bethought himself of Aedward and started for the stables, then changed his mind. Let the young devil sweat it out until morning.

Edgarson ran into the hut agog with news. His mother grabbed his arm. "Where have you been at this hour? You should be abed."

"The new lord has chained Aedward in the stables," he told Edwina.

She went white and gasped, "Why? What happened?"

"They would not tell me. Probably kill him, come morning," he babbled.

"Ah no, please God. I must go to him," Edwina cried, throwing back her bedcover and slipping into her tunic.

"You cannot go out at this hour. Do not go looking for trouble, Edwina," her mother begged.

Edwina took May's hands in her own. "I must, mother. I love him."

"I know, child," said her mother sadly, shaking her head and letting her go.

Edwina gave no thought to the darkness, even though she had never ventured out alone in it before. She ran to the stables and found Aedward chained to a stall. He sat dejectedly upon a pile of straw. She knelt down before him and he looked up startled.

"Edwina! What are you doing here? You should not have come," he warned.

"I had to know. What happened, Aedward?" she pleaded.

He shook his head. "I don't know, but I think it has something to do with last night's raid. He must think I am connected with it in some way because I am a Saxon."

"He must know you could never have anything to do with setting fire to our people's huts," Edwina protested.

"Men would really have to be driven to go to such lengths to steal supplies, but, Edwina, if I were on the run, I might be driven to such an act."

"Never," she asserted. "You are a man of honor."

"I only hope it has no connection with Lillyth," he thought aloud.

"Lillyth?" she whispered, really afraid now.

"She came to my chamber last night to tell me my mother was very ill. He found us together."

"Do you love Lillyth?" she asked fearfully.

"Who could know Lillyth and not love her?" he mused.

"God, I fear more for Lillyth at his hands than I do for myself."

"You should not waste pity on her; he will be blinded to her faults as are all men."

"Edwina, that was unkind," he rebuked her.

"I cannot help it. I am so worried for you. What will he do to you? My brother said they will kill you at dawn!"

"Edwina, I have done nothing. If I receive justice, I certainly shall not be killed. I want you to leave now. I do not want you to be in trouble on my behalf. It is best not to fraternize with a prisoner."

"Fraternize?" she asked.

"It is a French word. It means treat me as a brother."

"I do not think of you as a brother, Aedward." She blushed.

"Go now," he insisted. "It is not safe to be about after dark. If one of the knights sees you, you could be molested."

Edwina left the stable, but instead of going to her family's hut, she made her way to Morag's.

"Morag, you must help me, please! The Lord Aedward has been chained in the stables and I fear for his life," she begged.

"The Norman will not take his life," said Morag with conviction.

"How do you know?" sobbed Edwina.

"Power shared is power halved," said Morag cryptically.

"Is the trouble connected with Lillyth?" asked Edwina.

"Where Aedward is concerned, you would do well to fear Lillyth, and not Montgomery," warned Morag.

"He loves her!" cried Edwina.

"Aye, and you love Aedward," said Morag.

Edwina stared at her wonderingly, then she lowered her eyes and admitted, "I do love him and I want him to love me. Will you help me?"

"You are the little girl who looks after the bees?" asked Morag.

Edwina nodded.

"Bring me beeswax and I will fashion you and Aedward out of wax. It will work better if you can get me some of his hair for the doll. Then we will bind them together with a red thread or ribbon. The material you use does not matter but it must be red. Soon he will love you as you love him."

"What will I give you for payment, Morag? I do not have much to give, I'm afraid."

"I need wax. Bring me wax to make many images, and do not forget to whisper your wishes to the bees, for they take messages to the gods. Be silent," she admonished, "or the Montgomery will have me put to death for casting spells."

Guy de Montgomery found Aedward chained to the stall as he had ordered the next morning and immediately unshackled him.

"I discovered the lie you are living, Aedward," he said sternly.

"My lord, I hated the lie Lillyth gave you, but she only did it to protect me. I am Wulfric's brother. Lady Hilda is my mother and Oxstead our home, not Godstone."

"You swore fealty to me," stated Guy.

"I did, my lord, and I kept my vows."

"Do you swear you know nothing of last night's plunder?" Guy demanded.

"I do so swear, and I will help track them down with a vengeance. I have been wondering what will be left at Oxstead as it is virtually undefended."

"We will ride over there as soon as we have eaten. I will give you another chance to prove yourself, but it will be your last chance, Aedward."

The hall was agog as the two men walked in, seemingly on good terms.

Morgan's head swam with his own daring. The raid had gone off as simply as one, two, three. Of course, that was because Red Wolf was as familiar with Godstone as he himself was. Morgan had simply walked into the stables where he had always worked and led out two horses. Because he was such a familiar face around there, none questioned him. He had been shocked when he found out one of the peasant's huts had been fired, but when he realized no one had been injured, he reasoned that was probably the only way his companions could have drawn attention away from the storehouses while they helped themselves to the food supplies. Later, back at camp, Red Wolf praised him generously for his accomplishment. "Not one horse, but two! I am proud to count you among my men. Here is that dagger I promised you."

Red Wolf drew the large knife from his belt and held it out to Morgan. His pride swelled within him as he went forward to claim the prize the leader had promised him. Red Wolf grabbed him by the arm and plunged the knife into Morgan's gut as deeply as it would go. Morgan's eyes opened wide in horror as he realized he was finished, and he had not only provided this pig with horses but had provided him Faith as well. Red Wolf called two of his followers. "Bury him," he ordered, as he went to his knees to wipe the blood from the dagger on Morgan's tunic.

Faith awaited Morgan's return from the raid with mounting apprehension. She fingered the talisman around her neck and sat with her fingers crossed tightly. She willed her eyes to see that dear, familiar blond head appear through the door of the homemade hut, then finally she heard a step and rose with a glad cry. It froze in her throat as the head that appeared was not blond, but red!

"I have bad news for you, little one," he said low.

"Morgan?" she whispered.

He nodded. "He was caught in the raid and killed."

She sat motionless, numbed by the blow fate had dealt. It had been an ill-omened day when they had decided to run away together. Morgan had escaped the Normans, but at what a price!

"Fear not, I will take care of you," said Red Wolf.

Faith knew if she showed her distaste for this leader her life would be misery from this moment until she went to her grave, so she sat passively as he told her of his plans for her. Something inside her died that night along with Morgan. She did not notice him begin to remove his clothing. She hardly felt his thick avid fingers as they tore her garments off to reveal her nakedness. She made no protest as his rough beard scraped her tender breasts. However, she screamed in pain as he bit down on her nipple. "Bitch! Respond to me!" he growled. She moaned and reached for him in a frenzy of pretense.

Chapter 11

Lillyth saw Guy ride out with a sizable number of his men early in the morning. She recognized Rolf and André and was glad to see Aedward ride out with them, apparently none the worse for wear in spite of Guy's threats. She knew it would be a good time to take a bath, so she called a couple of young esquires and sent them off to the kitchen for hot water, while she dragged out the wooden bathtub. As the young lad was struggling up the stairs with the hot water, Nicholas, who had not gone to Oxstead with the others, spotted him and asked his destination.

"This is for the Lady Lillyth's bath, my lord," he said importantly. This was all Nicholas needed for a morning of sport to dispel any boredom he felt. He waited until Lillyth had time to get into the tub and walked in on her.

She gasped and slid down as far as she could under the water.

"Get out, immediately!" she demanded angrily.

"Sweetheart, you shouldn't have left the door unbarred. I'll do it for you," he grinned, and deftly dropped the bar into place.

Lillyth was so dismayed at her predicament that the tears sprang to her eyes and she hopelessly pleaded with him to leave.

"Don't take life so seriously, Lillyth. You should laugh and play more; have a little fun. I know my brother is a dull dog, but he is getting old and that excuses him. But you, *chérie*, are just a little girl and you should smile more often."

He picked up a flacon of perfumed oil she had used and sniffed it appreciatively. He spread his arms wide and said, "I promise to leave if you give me just one glimpse."

"No!" she shouted, and desperately sought to keep her breasts beneath the water.

He laughed, "They keep bobbing up like apples in a wassail bowl—delicious!" He took a step closer. "Come out of the water and let me see you. One glimpse of heaven and I'll leave."

"I have no intentions of getting out of this water until you depart, sir," she stated flatly.

He perched on the edge of the tub and said, "I'll wait. Sooner or later you will have to come out, or freeze to death."

"Oh please, what can I do to make you leave me alone?" she wailed.

He considered for a moment and said, "Well, you realize I cannot give in without you paying a forfeit of some kind? My honor is at stake!"

"You have no honor! Besides, I've learned to my sorrow about Montgomery forfeits. What do you want?" she asked suspiciously.

"I have a great desire to see Sevenoaks. If you will ride out with me today, I will consider leaving you to your ablutions in privacy."

"All right, I will come with you, if you promise that I will be completely safe."

"I won't ravish you, *chérie*, but I shall woo you

every step of the way." He winked and left, and she found herself laughing at his audacity.

They rode alone without escort, and to her surprise Lillyth found that she was enjoying herself. Nicholas was very gallant when he chose to be so. He was witty and she laughed a great deal. The smooth French compliments fell from his lips with such ease she did not believe a word, but his undivided attention was very flattering.

"You must learn to speak the Saxon tongue. From now on I shall only answer when you speak English," she threatened.

He tried a few phrases out and then said, "Lillyth, my beautiful flower, you are absolutely worthless!"

She was engulfed with giggles. "I think you mean 'priceless,' " she corrected.

"Worthless—priceless—what is the difference?" he puzzled.

"I cannot really explain. Your brother begins to speak Saxon very well, though. Tell me about his childhood."

"Well, Guy learned knighthood in the discipline of servitude. I imagine by the time he was eight he was exhausted from bringing, fetching, errands, slaps and scoldings as both a page and an esquire. He believes if you must know how to govern men, you must first learn how to govern yourself. It was much easier for André and myself, as we grew up in his household. Enough of Guy," he grinned, "he must plead his own case."

It was getting colder and soon the snow began to fall lightly.

"Nicholas, I am very cold. I think we should return."

"It's only another mile. We will get warm and have something to eat before we return," he promised.

Sevenoaks was the crossroads to London and the coast. It boasted no hall, but it did have a small inn for weary travelers. They dismounted, and Nicholas asked for a private room with a fire. The innkeeper hurried to do as the Norman bid him. He was thankful to still be in possession since the Normans had taken over.

Lillyth was almost blue from the cold, and Nicholas drew her into the private room. "Come and be warm, love," he said.

She sank into a chair before the cheerful blaze and Nicholas knelt to remove her boots and rubbed her feet between his hands. He bent and placed his lips to her instep. "I kiss your feet, Lillyth. I've given it a lot of thought, *chérie*, and I have decided that I would like to have you for my wife."

She looked at his serious face and thought, A while back I would have been in heaven if I had had to take a husband such as he—young, handsome, always laughing, instead of the beast that was forced upon me, but now he seems like a boy, and I need a man.

Her silence encouraged him. He rushed on, "We could build a fine hall here at Sevenoaks. I don't think you fancy Oxstead overmuch, and I know you hate being thought a loose woman. That is why I am offering to wed with you, Lillyth. I would have to get permission from William first, but apart from that you know I'm mad in love with you."

The landlord brought them wine and bowls of hot stew and freshly baked bread.

"Nicholas, I don't want to hurt you, but I am in

love with your brother." She blushed as she put her feelings into words for the first time.

He sighed. "Ah, I was afraid so. But you must understand it makes no difference to me, and I am still offering you marriage, something that Guy will never do!" he said passionately.

"Why not?" she asked simply.

"Because he is already . . . ," he hesitated and could not betray Guy, "because he is too old for such games, too set in his ways. He often says how much he hates women. Oh, I know he wants you for himself, and has warned us to keep hands off, but he will soon tire of you, and believe me I do know what I am saying when I tell you that he won't offer you marriage."

"I'm very honored by your proposal, Nicholas, but he has spoiled me for all other men," she said softly.

He puzzled over this statement that could be taken in two different ways. "Eat now, I won't press you further. Perhaps if I give you time, you will change your mind." He smiled into her eyes and held his hands over hers for a moment.

They wrapped their cloaks about them tightly and started the ride back to Godstone. The bitter wind had dropped, but the day had closed in and it seemed much later than it actually was. The snow was falling thickly and the visibility was poor. All at once a group of riders came out of the trees at them. There were too many for Nicholas to contend with, and when Lillyth realized they were only after the horses she begged Nicholas to let them go and put up his sword before he was slain. The outlaws joined their leader, who was waiting in the woods, and Nicholas and Lillyth were left with no choice but to carry on, on foot, to Godstone.

"Lillyth, forgive me. I have covered myself in shame. I gave you my word you would be safe with me!"

"Nick, I am safe. We should never have started out alone." She knew the men to be Saxons, but recognized none of them. They had only gone part of a mile when Guy and Rolf came upon them at full gallop.

"Bones of Christ, boy, what are you about?" Guy shouted angrily.

"We were set upon and the horses stolen," Nicholas explained lamely.

"We will overtake the bastards, fear not. Wait here, both of you," he commanded, and sent Lillyth such a baleful glare she shivered involuntarily, and not just from the cold.

Within half a hour they were back, but they only led one extra horse, Zephyr.

"Here, you mount Lillyth's horse and Lillyth, come up with me, although you deserve to walk." He bent and lifted her before him.

"What happened?" she asked Guy.

"We killed some of them, but their horses bolted and the leader got away with Nicholas's mount. But I shan't forget him! He was a burly bastard with a bright red beard."

Lillyth started violently at his words and he looked at her intently. "You know someone like that?" he demanded.

"Nay, no one in this world, my lord," she said thankfully.

He pulled her against him and wrapped his mantle about them both. The warmth seeped from his body and thawed her a little. She couldn't stop shivering, so he opened his knees wider and pressed her body with his own, almost completely protecting her from the elements. The cavalcade soon reached Godstone, and before he dismounted he whispered into her ear, "I want you to get into bed immediately. I'll be up for an explanation shortly."

Guy saw to the horses personally and totally ignored Nicholas as he tried to explain his actions. Guy strode from the stables without a backward glance and ascended the stairs without a pause.

Lillyth was in bed with the furs pulled up to her chin. He strode to the fire and put a couple of logs on it, then came to the bed.

"Are you warm now?" he inquired kindly.

She nodded and waited.

Patiently, as if dealing with a five-year-old, he asked, "Now, what were you doing with Nicholas?"

"He wanted me to ride with him to Sevenoaks. I refused at first, but I then agreed to go with him," she faltered.

"You did not wish to go, but he changed your mind for you? Did he threaten you?"

"Nay," she replied softly.

"Did he force you in any way?"

"No, not really," she evaded.

"What does that mean?" he asked evenly. "Answer me, Lillyth!" he shouted.

"When I was taking my bath—he . . ."

"Splendor of God!" roared Guy.

"Please, he acted honorably and asked me to wed with him."

Guy left the chamber and sought out Nicholas.

"Get you to Oxstead and stay there!" he thundered. "In a few days we ride to London; perhaps into battle. Until that time, stay out of my sight and take that blasted Saxon, Aedward, with you. I'm up to my eyes in lovesick boys!"

Lady Adela had just finished tidying her small chamber off the solarium when she heard a polite tap on the door. Hugh Montrose stood upon her threshhold, holding his hand tightly bound with a cloth.

"You've injured yourself!" she said, alarmed.

"I gashed my hand while cleaning a weapon. I know it will not stop bleeding until it is stitched. I was wondering if you would be kind enough, Adela?"

"Of course. Come in and sit down. I'll just get needle and thread."

He looked downcast. "I thought perhaps you wouldn't want to see me again, after last night."

"Hugh, you must not be so sensitive. That can happen to anyone," she said gently.

"It's never happened to me before!" he swore.

"Then perhaps it was my fault. I'm not desirable enough," she confessed.

"The desire was there, Adela, I swear to you. I just couldn't perform. I shamed my manhood!"

"Hush now, while I see to your hand." First she unbound it, then bathed it. It was a nasty gash, but he didn't wince when she touched it with fox-glove juice to keep out the infection. She carefully held the edges together and sewed steadily, first through one side of the flesh, then the other. Her needle made small neat stitches. He never flinched.

"What was that nonsense about shaming your manhood? You are a most brave knight in my eyes."

He reached for her and drew her onto his knees. He kissed her until she struggled to get up.

"Hugh, it is the middle of the day," she protested.

"Let me prove myself," he urged.

She needed much persuading; all the while his desire raged ever keener. At last she gave in and took him into her bed. The moment he reached for her, his member became limp and once again he was shamed before the lady.

"Hugh, it doesn't matter to me. I have never much enjoyed that sort of thing. I swear to you, my lord, it means naught to me!"

"It means all to me!" he said bitterly. "Swear to me you will reveal this to none," he demanded.

"Hugh, how could you even think such a thought?" she asked, hurt.

"I'm sorry, Adela. Thank you for tending my wound."

With as much dignity as he could summon, he dressed and left the room. Adela decided she had no option but to visit Morag.

She was surprised to see the inside of the old woman's hut. The clutter was gone and everything was considerably cleaner. A few herbs hung drying from the thatched roof, and Greediguts sat up there cackling to himself. If it hadn't been for the magpie, Adela would have thought she was in the wrong hut.

"I need a spell, Morag."

"I am forbidden to cast spells. You must know what the Norman has decreed, it is no secret for those who dwell in the hall."

"Oh, Morag, I brought you a lovely ripe cheese. Perhaps a spell is not necessary. Perhaps you can recommend some herb that will work just as well?"

"Are you still seeking something that will subdue lust in a man."

"No!" Adela said quickly. "I need something that will provoke lust."

The old woman rocked back and forth on her stool, laughing.

"Morag, it is not amusing," wailed Adela, embarrassed beyond measure.

"It is, it is! Do you remember the cord you tied the knots in, and hid in the bedchamber? Find the cord, untie the ligatures and your troubles will be over."

"You have stripped the church and the hall!" Lillyth said accusingly.

"William needs money. You can't be a king with empty coffers," Guy answered shortly.

"Here, take my girdle," she said angrily, stripping it off, " 'tis gold, and I've nothing else left to offer."

He came to her and gently replaced the girdle about her hips. "You have much left to offer," he said softly. "I've tried everything, even rape. Lillyth, why will you not yield to me?"

Her lashes brushed her cheeks and she whispered, "You spoke . . . no words . . . of love . . ."

A great surge of excitement raced through him and he swept her up into his arms and sat cradling her before the fire.

"Oh, my lovely one, I adore you." His green eyes laughed into hers. He picked up a tress of hair and curled it around his fingers possessively.

"You have the most wondrous hair I have ever seen, and all men who lay eyes upon it must ache to caress it and play with it like this. Oh love, you enthrall me. Your image is before me day and night. Your loveliness haunts me, how am I ever to leave you?" He kissed her eyelids. "I have an unquenchable thirst for you. When I see you across the room, I have to come close to you, and then when I'm close to you, I have an uncontrollable desire to touch you. I want to touch you all over. Here, and here." He cupped his hand around her breast, caressed and stroked it gently. "When I hear your voice and your laughter, it arouses me immediately, no matter who is there to see, and when I am close to you, your fragrance fills my senses until I can taste you almost."

His mouth found hers and held her captive in a long, slow kiss. His warm, insistent lips moved over her throat and up behind her ear. "Always, until you, a voice whispered to me 'This is not she.' "

The rapture of his closeness enveloped her and she felt loved and cherished.

"How I've ached to hold you in my arms all night!"

She vibrated to the desire in his voice. Lillyth turned her face against his shoulder and drew closer to him. His arms tightened as he felt her response and a flame ran along his veins. She felt that her whole body was melting into his.

He had seen her naked only briefly when he had forced her; now his blood beat thickly with the knowledge that she would allow his hands to unclothe her and caress her naked beauty at his leisure. His hands lifted off her gown and he quoted from the Song of Solomon, "And the smell of thy garments is like the smell of Lebanon."

Frozen rain splattered the window shutters and the wind blew through the chinks, but they were oblivious to everything except each other. His powerful hands stripped off her undergarments and his breath caught in his throat as she stood before him, her glorious red-gold hair her only adornment. He lifted handfuls of it to his face to feel, smell and taste, then draped it back from her shoulders to fall down her back, leaving her breasts exposed to his smoldering green gaze.

"Do not move," he commanded huskily as his fingers unfastened his own garments and impatiently removed them. She reached out a tentative finger to touch the dark fur pelt on his chest, then she ran her hands along the hard muscles of his arms and shoulders, and her fingers burned to explore him further. His hands reached out to encircle her exquisitely small waist and he lifted her high against his heart, allowing his throbbing erection to brush down across her belly and slide between her thighs.

"You are the most beautiful, breathstopping creature I have ever seen." Her arms slid up about his neck and he held her velvety breasts against his chest. Her excitement made her gasp for breath, her breasts rising and falling against him, her thick-lashed eyes closing with heavy desire. He wanted her to cling to him like this every night for the rest of his life.

His mouth covered hers softly, warmly; seeking, rousing her blood to catch fire, to flame and blaze. "Come to bed, love. I want to show you how much I love you, not just tell you." He carried her to the bed and lowered her, still clinging to his body, until she lay upon the furs, then he backed off the bed to stand at the foot with her full beauty open to him. She trustingly allowed him to place her knees on either side of his thighs with her feet dangling.

His fingers could no longer resist the lure of the red-gold triangle of curls. He touched the luxuriant tendrils then dropped worshipfully to his knees, the better to enjoy the pink bud between the tiny folds which would blossom for him once she was fully aroused. His fingers traced the folds, then gently opened her to tenderly probe and tease. When he heard her moan, his mouth wanted to follow where his fingers played, but he knew she was not quite ready. He would build her desire until she was longing for his tongue, then with his tongue he would build her desire until she was ready for his shaft. The tension at the base of his groin became almost unbearable at the thought.

He began his kisses at her feet and moved slowly, lingeringly up her legs. His lips moved from her white thighs, across her belly, up to her breasts. As he towered over her, she thought him magnificent. His wide shoulders and hair covered chest tapered to a flat belly. The powerful symmetry of his hard muscles hinted at dangerous strength. Her eyes widened, drinking him in as he was her.

Her hair spilled across the silver fur in shimmering splendor. He dipped his head and took her erect nipples between his lips and toyed with them until she cried out in ecstacy. All the while his hands moved upon her, caressing her, seeking love's secret places. She touched his hair, loving its thick softness. He lifted her hand from his face. Each finger received his kiss. His tongue moved across her palm, up her wrist and along her arm to her shoulder. Then his mouth was against her throat, exploring its fragile hollows with his lips. He lifted her hair and ran his lips across the fragrant curve of her neck, and finally he found her mouth and kissed her with such a demanding passion that she responded with her whole body, arching up from the bed.

She moaned and moved against him in such an inviting manner that he cautioned her, "Not yet, sweetheart. You think you are ready, but I don't want to hurt you." He placed his hand on her mound of Venus. His hard, erect organ brushed her thigh and she quivered with anticipation. "Little wanton," he teased, "do I excite you? Tell me what you feel," he whispered.

"You know you do! I feel I shall die if you don't come into me quickly," she breathed.

"How long have you loved me?" he demanded, softly.

"Since first I set eyes upon you."

"Say my name, I've longed to hear it upon your lips."

"Oh Guy, please, love?" she begged. "Guy ... Guy ..."

He moved lower and allowed the tip of his tongue to trace the tiny folds between her legs, then opened her to seek the pink bud which was ready to burst into bloom. She screamed with excitement as he thrust his tongue deeply, then she sprawled involuntarily, spread-eagled upon the furs, surrendering completely to his wicked mouth.

When he felt her shudders begin, desire pulsed up the long length of his shaft with a sweet, tortuous ache. Quickly he moved up until his body covered hers and she gasped as he penetrated deeply. She was so tight and hot that she burned and scorched his flesh as he moved inside her. In a short time their ecstacy built to an unbearable peak and they dissolved into each other with simultaneous shouts.

She cried softly in her fulfillment. Without withdrawing, he held her in his arms until they both slept. Hours later when she awoke, his body enveloped her in a warm cocoon. In his strong arms her body curved into his; she had never felt so safe in her life. It was as if their bodies had been made for each other. So attuned were they that they had awakened together. His arms closed about her fiercely as he turned her to face him.

His mouth sought hers with its full underlip as beautiful as sin, and again the head of his shaft sought the satin-slippery sheath which tightened upon him as he thrust deeply like some mythic beast. Their mouths crushed together hungrily, fiercely, savagely until they climaxed together in a flooding warmth.

Lillyth awoke at the first light of dawn and felt the weight of his arm curved possessively around her. She was so warm against him, she lay very still so she wouldn't disturb his slumber. His mouth, which was always so hard and firm, was softened in sleep, and his hair curled darkly on his neck. She was glad that she had awakened before him. She felt very vulnerable and was half-afraid of what he might do or say when he awoke. He could destroy her with a word after their intimacy of last night. She held her breath as he stirred. Guy opened his eyes sleepily and looked at her for a long time.

"Will you always love me, Lillyth?" he asked hungrily.

"Forever," she promised.

"I cannot bear to leave you for a while yet," he

said, reaching for her. "Try to go back to sleep, love."

"Your men will be awaiting you," she said.

"Let them wait," he said comfortably, and stroked her back until she relaxed against him.

Chapter 12

After only one night, the Lady Emma knew herself
to be in love. She had never before had an experience in life like Esmé. The tall blond knight
thrilled her with every glance. The smooth French
phrases that rolled from his tongue enchanted her.
She could listen to him all night. Esmé knew that
words brought a woman to her final rapture more
quickly than the most passionate physical exertions. When he arose to dress before dawn, she felt
desolated. She wanted to beg him to return to her
at nightfall, then thanked all the saints in heaven
that she had not blurted out her need when he
murmured, *"Je suis desolé* that I must leave you
now, *ma petite*. As soon as the light fades from the
day, I shall return to your arms."

Emma wanted him forever. She wanted no other
for her husband. How to get him to marry her
filled all her thoughts. She wrapped up an old
warm shawl that she could manage without, and
took it along to Morag.

Morag sighed, "So the cycle begins again. Wherever men are present, there is always the fear of
pregnancy."

"Morag, I want a child desperately, now. Give
me something that will make me fruitful."

"You have drunk so much boiled fern that you fear you are barren?" chuckled Morag.

"Is that what you gave me?" asked Emma, surprised.

Morag ignored the question. "Orache is the cure for barrenness. Make a syrup of the orache herb with honey."

"Where will I find this herb?"

"It is plentiful enough. It grows on dungheaps," laughed Morag at the fastidious Emma.

To Guy, the day seemed to have a hundred hours. There were many preparations to be made before they left to rejoin William's army. He knew that he could not leave many behind to guard all he held dear, because William had ordered him to be in London in full force. So although he knew Rolf would prefer to be at his side, he had asked him to remain at Godstone because he was the only one in whom Guy could put complete trust. He worried not one whit about the dangers that lay in wait for him, but only those that might befall his beloved, once he could not protect her with his own presence. There had been no more attacks or thieving in the night, and he hoped feverently that it had been an isolated incident. When he returned, he was determined to build and fortify his holdings so this fear would never be with him again. The Saxons were great fools when it came to defending their land. Normans were better builders, stronger leaders, greater at fighting and defense. Guy thought it a great waste that the thanes who were shepherds, swineherds and sowers were not trained to defend their own land. This was another thing he intended changing. He believed a lord need not fear a revolt because his peasants bore arms if they had a fair master who offered their families protection inside a strong motte and bailey when attackers threatened. He was leaving Aedward in charge at Oxstead because he was so familiar with its workings, and he could hardly take him to London. Each knight was responsible for his own armor and weapons and those of his horse. Guy had refused many a fighting man in his mesnalty because he could not furnish himself with a horse. He didn't want foot soldiers for obvious reasons. The forge was going day and night, repairing, cleaning and sharpening. Lances were fashioned from newly trimmed larchwood, and everywhere could be seen men-at-arms lolling on spears or resting on the quillons of their swords, blades pointing downward. Victuals for the men and fodder for the horses had to be loaded on wagons and the loot, carefully packed and guarded, had to be taken to William. It was November and he had promised William he would set out then. He could delay his going no longer. It must be on the morrow. He was impatient to be with Lillyth, and when he told the men it must be approaching time for the evening meal, they smiled behind their hands since the day hadn't even started to fade yet.

In the hall he looked about for Lillyth, but could only see Lady Alison busy about her household duties.

"Where is Lillyth?" he asked.

"She has not shown her face belowstairs all day. Is everything all right between you two?" she asked doubtfully.

"Everything is perfect!" He smiled at her, and took the stairs three at a time.

Lillyth lifted her head from the fine sendal silk shirt she was stitching for him and blushed as his eyes rested upon her boldly.

"Wear something beautiful for me tonight,

chérie, I want to make every male at Godstone mad with jealousy."

"I thought perhaps I wouldn't come down to-night," she said hesitantly. "Perhaps I will have something sent up here. I'm not really hungry."

"Splendor of God!" he stormed. "You are ashamed men will call you my leman. I shall not make you wear a sign that says whore, Lillyth," he sneered.

The hurt sprang into her eyes, and he had her in his embrace in an instant. "Forgive me, love, I didn't mean it. You wounded my pride, and in all truth I did want to display you like some prize I'd captured. We will both eat up here away from everyone, if it makes you happier to do so," he promised.

"Oh Guy, it is only that I could not bear anyone to spoil this beautiful thing between us with sniggers or ribald jests. You know what the men are like."

He mock-sighed, "Ah well, tomorrow you will be rid of my burdensome presence and will be able to show your face without embarrassment."

"I am so afraid for you," she said hollowly.

He threw back his head and laughed. "Foolish one, 'tis I who am afraid for you. I fear you will be snatched from me when it has taken me a lifetime to find you."

She reached up her arms behind his neck and stood on tiptoe to lift her mouth to his. He picked her up from the floor and swung her about. "I thought the day would never end," he whispered.

"You are early, it's still an hour before supper. I'll ask Edyth to bring our food up here."

"I'm not hungry for food," he teased, taking her earlobe between his teeth. He unclasped her girdle from her hips, and just as quickly she fastened it again and whirled away from him.

"I want you to get measured for some new clothes so that while you are away, I can work on them and have them ready for you when you return. Come to the solarium now and we can pick out material. See the shirt I have just finished for you?"

He took the soft silk between his fingers. "It is almost too fine for me. I'll tell you what, sweetheart, I'll come with you now if you will put this on later and let me see what it looks like."

"Your suggestions are all scandalous!" She pretended to be shocked, and he grinned at the mental picture he conjured of her.

They went into the solarium and in just a few minutes the room was filled with attractive young women who circled about Guy, giving him every attention. Lillyth was amazed to see them openly flirting with him and sending him the most inviting glances. She knew for the first time what the pangs of jealousy felt like, but as she watched Guy closely, he seemed unaware of the female lures being cast his way. The materials were spread in gorgeous array and each girl gave him her advice on what would suit him. Saxons loved sharp, bright colors, but Normans had more sober tastes, their clothes being dark and colorless for the most part. He touched the black velvet, but Lillyth shook her head quickly. He lifted a brown dun-colored cloth and she pulled a little moue with her mouth.

"When you do that sweetheart, I don't know if you are going to spit on me or kiss me," he laughed, and the women sent her envious glances. He finally chose a rich wine-colored velvet, some fine dark green cloth and velvet in a deep russet shade. Measurements were taken and style of sleeve discussed. When they had finished, Lillyth asked Edyth to send a page with their supper.

"Will you need me to help you with your hair?" Edyth asked.

Guy whispered in Edyth's ear and she blushed and ran quickly from the room.

"What did you say to her?" asked Lillyth.

"I told her we wanted to be alone and that I would put you to bed tonight."

"You didn't!" said Lillyth, scandalized.

"No, no of course not, sweetheart. I can't resist teasing you! I only sent her to fetch a surprise I had made for you."

Edyth came back with the fur-lined cloak over her arm. Lillyth was delighted with it. The wolf skins were soft and the workmanship was exquisite. Envious eyes followed the couple as they left, Guy with his arm held lovingly about Lillyth.

They sat across from each other at a small table, and Guy carved a succulent stubble-goose, and tender slices of venison. They ate most things boiled in Saxon England, and there were many dishes of boiled vegetables and freshly baked, coarse bread spread with thick, creamy butter. The food was different in Normandy. Everything was very heavily spiced or dressed with frumenty. Guy found that the plainer English fare suited his taste better. He poured wine for Lillyth and urged her to drink. Guy always seemed to have a healthy appetite. He ate quickly as a man who was used to taking meals on the march, while Lillyth dawdled and nibbled delicately on this and that. He was finished before Lillyth and, unable to stay away from her any longer, came around to her chair and slid her into his lap.

"I think I have had enough, Guy," she said.

"No, no, you must eat everything I gave you. Here, let me help you," and he lifted a choice piece of meat to her lips and made her eat it.

"Now some wine, it will warm your blood when we lie naked by the fire," he said into her neck.

He took it completely for granted that she would lie with him whenever he wanted. He acted as if she were his property, as if he owned her body and soul. Lillyth thought she should be angry at this, but deep inside she wasn't really. It was her turn to tease him. She slipped from his knee and crossed the room to wash her hands and face. Then, ignoring him completely, she unbound her hair and began to brush it. Guy took the fur coverlet from the bed and some pillows and spread them before the fire.

"Come and be warm, love," he invited, removing his doublet and chainse.

"You assume too much, my lord," she said haughtily.

His eyebrows shot up in surprise. "What? Would you deny me on my last night?" he demanded.

He was beside her in an instant and tried to take her in his arms.

Lillyth hit him with her brush. He crushed her in his arms and carried her to the fire.

"Whether you will or no, I do not intend to forego the joy of you, my darling."

He lay beside her on the furs and despite her struggles, managed to disrobe her.

"I know you are stronger than I, but I intend to fight you," she promised.

"That will just add a fillip to our lovemaking," he laughed.

She raked her nails down his back and bit him sharply on the shoulder.

"Little bitch," he gritted, then caught the flicker of a smile at the corner of her mouth.

"You are just playing with me," he accused. "All

right, my little golden witch, I will make you beg for mercy before this night is over," and he found the softness of her mouth.

He knelt above her to watch the firelight play over her lustrous skin. She was like a gift from the gods as she lay naked before him. Her glorious golden hair was highlighted by tiny red tendrils where the fireshine touched it and he reached out to spread it across the dark furs so that it framed her lovely shoulders and breasts. Her body was all delicious light and shadow as his eyes traveled from the curve of her throat to the rosy globes of her breasts with their tiny wine-dark crests.

She drew in her breath as he reached out with his powerful hands to possess them. Guy was an experienced lover who knew better than to immediately touch a woman's nipple before the rest of her breast had received his full attention. His strong fingers stroked and caressed. Then he took them into his hands to weigh and fondle them with his palms.

She turned her face from the fire and lifted her lashes to watch him. Guy felt the warmth of her radiant look as her breasts began to harden. Only then did he allow his thumbs to gently brush the tips and a flame of desire ran along his shaft as they swelled in arousal. She glimpsed his look of intensity before his head dipped to kiss, taste, lick then finally suck the hard little fruits which thrust up at him so temptingly. She moaned softly and he raised his head once more to gaze down upon her loveliness.

In the firelight his tanned body turned a deep mahogany and his eyes smoldered with green fire. He was like a dark predator who mesmerized her so that she wanted only to lie beneath him forever while he worshipped her beauty with his eyes, hands and mouth.

As his sex branded her thigh, she knew an over-whelming curiosity to explore him. She reached down and as her fingers touched his shaft, he arched above her with a ragged cry. He raised from his haunches, full upon his knees, and thrust his pelvis toward her. Then he took her fingers and drew back the velvet foreskin so that its bold head sprang up hot and taut in its natural state.

As her fingers caressed him, her thighs opened of their own volition and he was astride her instantly. As his lips sought hers to take her soft sighs into his mouth, the tip of his phallus slid against her tiny slit nestled beneath her golden triangle. She almost scalded him and as he rubbed himself against her, all the time kissing her, she became moist and slippery.

His mouth and his manhood worked in unison. As her lips parted to take the tip of his tongue into her mouth, so the pulsing head of his manroot thrust inside her tight sheath. It was not long before this was not enough for her and she opened her mouth to encourage his tongue to delve deeply. At the same time his fingers reached between her legs to open her so that he could bury his entire length inside her sugared walls. He stilled to allow her to grow accustomed to his bursting fullness, then amazingly her tight sheath gripped and squeezed and sucked him deeper, as with a half-sob she experienced the first pulsation.

Lillyth surrendered completely to his seeking mouth and pressing shaft as his fierce hunger devoured her. He swept her away with him to a place she had never known existed. Their hearts beat, and their breaths came and went, in unison until they moved as one. His domination was so complete she wanted to yield to him forever. Then, as they began to peak, they both cried out in fulfillment and regret, wishing they could go on and on without end.

Guy arched his neck as his head fell back and Lillyth came up from the furs with him inseparably, her lips clinging to his throat. His ejaculation was like a volcanic eruption and she went limp and almost swooned.

Much later as she slumbered in the firelight, he gently lifted her to his bed and she half-roused and murmured against his shoulder, "Would William let a Norman marry a Saxon?"

His heart constricted, but with his lips against her hair he said, "If it were possible for me to wed you, Lillyth, I would have done so long ago."

She missed his meaning and said, "Be sure to ask William when you see him," and she was asleep.

Chapter 13

When Lillyth awoke, she knew immediately that he was gone. He must have slipped away before dawn, taking pains not to disturb her. She felt desolated. Would he ever return? If he did, would he still feel the same way about her? Would he be faithful? Would he be killed? Oh God, do not let me think such things! she prayed fervently. I will go to the church every day and burn candles, and I will keep so busy that the days will fly past swiftly, she promised herself. I will start with this chamber. I will put up my tapestries and if there are any more wolf pelts, I will get them for before the fire. She blushed at last night's lovemaking and smiled a secret smile to herself. She would make some pine-scented candles, and perhaps the smithy could make a little incense burner for beside their bed. If only it were spring she would fill this chamber with flowers. She decided to strip the room and give it a thorough cleaning. She would get a couple of the girls to help her and beeswax the wooden floor.

Guy's men traveled eastward to meet William's army. He knew that after Canterbury the goal was

London, and Guy hoped to meet the army somewhere between. The men rode in full chain mail,
but Guy carried his helmet on the pommel of his
saddle and the upper catches of his coif were un-
done, and it was pushed back from his head and
lay across his shoulders. This wasn't war, it was a
matter of subduing small villages. There was only
token resistance, and Guy found himself more in
sympathy with these Saxons, no doubt due to the
weeks he had spent at Godstone.

Whenever Guy met fierce resistance he quickly
discerned that instead of wholesale killing, only an
example of one man need be demonstrated or a
single dwelling burned, and they were ready to
lay down their arms and swear fealty to William,
who was claiming England as his by divine right.
The Saxons had no other strong leader to follow
and could easily be persuaded. Guy met William's
troops near Rochester. Many of them were suffering from dysentery, which they had been fighting
for over a month. Guy told his men to ride
through the camp and go upstream. He forbade
them to touch the filthy water that had been pol-
luted by thousands of soldiers, but bade them fill
their casks upstream before contamination had set
in. He quickly sought out William and the leaders,
among whom was William's half-brother, Odo. Guy
wanted to unload his treasure wagons and get an
official tally, as looting would be rife in an army of
this size.

He found William suffering from the same complaint of dysentery, and Guy told William's physician, Nigel, about the plant alkanet. How, when
boiled in wine, it would help to bind up the bowels. Scouting parties were sent to pick great quan-
tities of this miracle plant, which grew wild along
the streams, and although many a soldier drank

boiled weeds from the wrong plant that night, many others got the correct dose, and within a couple of days the army was back on its feet and ready to move again.

William was always in the midst of a crowd and it was a difficult task to gain a word with him, but finally Guy managed to see him.

"Congratulations, Montgomery, you have done well by me. You brought in more silver and gold than many another. When it has been counted and our due taken out, the rest will come back to you."

"My lord king, I would rather have my share in land. The towns I hold in lordship for you I could continue to hold if you will grant me legal deed of lordship so that none other can claim them. My own men I can pay myself."

"I am not crowned yet, Montgomery, but it is only a short time away. I will have the treasurer draw up deeds of ownership, not lordship, then it will be up to you to keep what is your own."

"I deeply appreciate your generosity, sire," said Guy honestly.

William laughed. "Don't thank me too soon, Montgomery. When you learn the taxes I will levy on your holdings, you may begin to curse me. So many are eager for territory, you would not believe the hunger for land that is about these days. It is basic animal instinct coming out in us, to stake out a territory and defend it to the death." William laughed. "How can you afford to pay your men? Keeping a coffer of silver deniers from my tally?" he jested.

"This is a rich land. Among my people at Godstone there are many artisans. The cloth alone that the young women weave is so beautiful it will bring in a fortune if exported to France," answered Guy.

"Soon all the ladies and the whole court will be at London. You would be wise to give us first choice, before exporting it to France. What other artisans have you discovered?"

"When you have examined the treasures more closely you will see what exquisite jewelry is produced. I have also noticed the quality of the wool is much thicker, probably something to do with the climate. All you need do is look at the sheep and you can see they are superior to ours."

"Splendor of God, watch out or they will turn you into a farmer, Montgomery," he laughed.

"Any word from Robert, my lord?" asked Guy, referring to his friend Mortain, another of William's half-brothers.

"Ah, splendid news indeed. A rider arrived yesterday to tell me he is far west of London in the Chiltern Hills. He hopes to take a castle called Berkhamstead. With Robert I have thrust a spearhead between my enemies before they could join forces. You will be seeing him before this campaign is over, once London capitulates."

Guy smiled to himself. William spoke as if it were a foregone conclusion, but of course that was William's way.

"All your men are mounted, are they not, Montgomery? Join up with St. Cloud, I believe his unit is mounted also. Go out as a scouting party. Sweep the country before the main body of the army and clear out any hot spots."

As they sat around their camp fires that night, a company of traveling players came among them to entertain. They sang, danced, and bedded with the men; in fact anything to get their silver coins from them. Guy sat with his men, silently contemplating the girl who was dancing at his camp fire. She was young, slim, exciting, inviting, and her voluptuous beauty and flaming red hair were a vivid contrast to the Saxon women.

He gazed into the flames and ached for Lillyth. The dance was purposely taunting and suggestive, and sex was uppermost in the mind of every man who watched her. They kept one eye on their leader because if he wanted her they would concede, but if not they were ready to fight one another to see who would be first.

Guy's loins throbbed, and a dull ache started deep in his belly and spread uncomfortably to his groin. The wineskin he had been drinking from was half-empty, and more than just keeping out the chill, the wine had heated his blood to a fiery degree. He beckoned the girl to his tent. With a flash of white teeth and a contemptuous sidelong glance at the other men, she followed him quickly. She slid against him boldly and her hand went immediately to the enormous bulge in his chausses. She stuck her other hand out and waggled the fingers in front of his face. "First you must show me the color of your money," she said, darting her tongue quickly around her lips.

Guy looked down at the girl and he noticed she was none too clean. An odor of sweat, acrid and pungent, assailed his nostrils, and he was filled with revulsion as he thought about the disease he might pick up and pass along to Lillyth. He quickly slipped a coin into her hand and whispered, "Not tonight, sweetheart, I've changed my mind."

She spat on the coin, as she would have liked to spit on the Norman pig, but she wanted to keep her skin whole, so she settled for a volley of derisive laughter as she ran out of the tent and back toward the other men. Nicholas came in and said,

"By the face, that was fast. She must have satisfied you standing up!"

Guy laughed. "I told her to go. Upon closer inspection I discovered she wasn't my type."

Nicholas shook his head. "Lillyth has you bewitched, she's spoiled all other women for you."

"Splendor of God, what bullshit you spout!"

Guy exercised control over his men, but was disgusted to find that St. Cloud did not. They killed and raped at will, and the unnecessary violence sickened Guy. The first day they rode out, they brought to heel the men of a large village. Guy caught sight of a young woman with her little son come running forward to beg mercy. He pictured Lillyth in her place being a supplicant for his son's life, but St. Cloud was before him. He hacked the boy almost in half and carried the woman off to rape her.

Guy mustered his men and quit the vicinity. He kept a distance between his men and St. Cloud's the rest of the day. That night he sought out William to tell him that he would ride no more with St. Cloud, but William was not available until later, and after he had time to cool and reconsider his position, Guy realized that William would not appreciate dissension in the ranks and might consider it petty squabbling. The next day he bade his knights not to mix indiscriminately with St. Cloud's men, but to follow his lead. However, in the late afternoon the two groups again came together, and Guy was outraged to see St. Cloud run down a female child of about nine or ten and rape her. Guy called Hugh Montrose, who was closest to him, and asked, "Is your bow hornbacked?"

"Of course, and I carry only candle arrows.

They will reach five hundred paces," he assured Guy.

"Good. Lend it to me," he ordered.

He waited tensely until St. Cloud came out of the trees, and after taking very deliberate aim, he loosed an arrow which went straight to St. Cloud's heart.

"My God, you've killed him," said André at his shoulder.

"Vermin!" spat Guy.

"If any saw, you will be in serious trouble! Let's bury him before any find him," urged André.

"Hold. Let his own men find him. They are such dishonorable bastards, they will concoct some lie of an accident to keep blame from their door. Let us quit this place."

The army was on the move at last. They arrived at London and camped on the south bank of the River Thames. The English came out of the gates at Southwark and attacked the Normans, but they were soon driven back. William gave the order that all the houses on the south bank of the Thames were to be burned. Norman troops rode down the narrow streets, killing any in their path. They were followed by torchbearers who in a systematic manner fired the houses. Men threw down their weapons and cried for quarter. They received none. The wooden houses burned quickly, and the place soon became an inferno, with acrid black smoke burning the eyes of soldiers and citizens alike. Flaming shells of buildings crashed inward upon themselves. Great towers crumbled and churches blazed. A few children were seen with their clothes afire, and some women's hair caught flame, but most citizens of London had the good sense to flee before the holocaust. The men began looting and plundering what the fire did not destroy.

William had many important hostages from Dover and Canterbury. Because Guy de Montgomery had a fair knowledge of the Saxon tongue, he was relieved that he had been chosen to guard them, rather than sent out to kill and burn. William moved the army west of London and crossed the River Thames at Wallingford. Here he was met with messengers sent from his brother, Robert de Mortain, who was now in possession of Berkhamstead. William passed by Icknield Way to the gap in the Chiltern Hills at Tring, and thus on to Berkhamstead. He had given the decision makers in London a taste of his ruthlessness, now he would give them pause to think on it. After a hurried discussion among London's important men, they decided to capitulate. William received the crown of England for the first time in the grounds of Berkhamstead.

Space was at a minimum at the castle of Berkhamstead, but Robert was delighted to find room for his old friend Montgomery, although his men had to be camped on the grounds.

Guy found himself in exalted company. William's other brother, Odo, the bishop of Bayeux, was very much in evidence, and a more ungodly bishop one was never likely to meet. William's cousin, William Fitzosbern, was a great personal friend to the king, as well as being a relative, and was seen much in the "Conqueror's" company. Richard de Rules, William's chamberlain, and Eudo Dapifer, his steward, rubbed shoulders with Hugh de Grandmesnil, a baron who supplied a vast number of knights and soldiers for the Battle of Hastings.

In the vast dining hall at Berkhamstead, Guy de Montgomery sat down to sup with Robert de Mortain and other important lords and barons. They were served sumptuous meals at which Guy's palate rebelled slightly. There were whole boars, their heads stuffed with spices and cloved apples in their mouths. Porpoises dressed with frumenty lay in sickening poses on huge platters. Cranes and peacocks were resplendent on silver dishes, but when carved gave off such highly spiced flavors that only stomachs accustomed to such rich fare could digest them. Everything was surrounded by dyed jellies or candied rose leaves. The rich fare, mixed with the wines that flowed from Normandy, caused many a lord, suddenly discovering he had overindulged, to excuse himself.

The talk turned to the castle of Berkhamstead where Robert was in sole charge, and he decried the poorly built Saxon fortification. "These Saxons have no idea how to build a stronghold," he told the other men at table. Guy listened intently, as he was very interested in improving his own hall.

"All this place is, really, is a timber fort with an artificial motte around it," said Robert, waving his arm.

"I agree. The Saxons seem more inclined to be artistic than practical. Look at the beautiful tapestries that cover every wall and the intricate patterns on the silver plate, yet all these riches are housed so poorly, we have no trouble taking their castles and cities," answered Guy.

"Come upstairs and let me show you the plans I've drawn up for this place," Robert invited Guy, warming to his favorite subject of building. The two friends left the crowded dining hall. Robert laid out the plans on a long narrow table and pointed with his finger. "I'm going to build a stone wall at least sixty feet in diameter and about eight feet thick around a shell keep. There will be a rampart wall on top of this for lookouts. Steps up the earthworks will be protected at the top by a tower and a ditch filled with water at the base of the earthworks."

Guy studied the plans intently. "You will have an inner and an outer ward?" he queried.

Robert nodded. "Surrounded by flint rubble walls at least seven feet thick with bastions and gates, plus two ditches and bank between."

"Splendor of God," commented Guy, "you don't intend to give this place up easily."

"Do you blame me?" Robert winked as two serving wenches came in to repair the fire and put a bedwarmer between the sheets.

"That's not the kind of bedwarmer I need," he teased the girls, who giggled and seemed inclined to linger over their duties.

"Are you forgetting that you are a married man?" laughed Guy.

"Bones of Christ, with William about I'm not likely to. Do you know, I don't believe he has ever once been unfaithful to Matilda. You don't suppose he's afraid of her, do you?" Robert asked Guy.

Guy laughed out loud at such a suggestion, that William could be afraid of anything. "More likely, William being bastard, he is determined never to father one. Matilda is only four and a half feet tall, how could he be afraid? Although I know some women can be the very devil," he added grimly.

Robert knew he referred to his own wife back in Normandy, and he cleared his throat and said, "Let me give you a little advice. Every castle both in Normandy and England is full of wenches who will do a man's bidding, and wives expect it and shrug it off, but let a man take a mistress from the nobility or one that is highborn, and the wife will make such a damned jealous scandal, life isn't worth living."

In that moment a beautiful, clear picture of Lillyth flashed before Guy. He had to clench his fists and dig his nails into his palms to still the desire that flamed through him.

Robert glanced at the two girls and spoke in a low voice to Guy. "I will share whatever I have with you, friend."

"Done," grinned Guy, "but be warned now, I intend to steal some of your carpenters and masons when I leave. I want to build new fortifications at Godstone. In fact, I was thinking of moving the great hall up one floor, instead of using the ground floor, for a greater sense of security."

"Enough, Montgomery, or by the face I shall begin to suspect your manhood," he laughed.

Guy kept his men busy by organizing half of them to hunt and half to help with the new building fortifications that were already under way. Each day they would switch about. This way there was less likelihood of them becoming bored, or coveting the next man's job. Guy felt the need to contribute in this way to their keep. Also, leaders who left their men idle soon found they had an unruly bunch of drunken, whoring gamblers on their hands. However, none of this showed up in William's presence. He was a stark man and in the hall or at board he would tolerate no disorder. He was also a man who believed in setting an example for his men. He never drank to excess, he was always in the front ranks on the battlefield, he was a good, faithful husband and a strict father to his growing brood of sons and daughters.

Guy noticed that when William left Berkhamstead and went to London for two days, the hall took on a bacchanalian air in the evenings, with drinking, cursing, gambling, lewd entertainment and womanizing.

"By the face, Robert, you allow things William would never countenance."

"Let them enjoy themselves while they may; William returns tomorrow. He has gone to make arrangements for the coronation and Odo has gone with him. I think Odo will remain in London, but I'll keep possession here, thank you. You can keep London."

"When is the coronation to be?" asked Guy, feeling a longing for it all to be over and done so he could return home.

"Well, we all thought New Year's Day would be a good choice. You know, the symbolism of a new year, a new reign, that sort of thing. We reckoned without William! He insists he conquered England in 1066 and he will be crowned in 1066. It will look better in the history books," winked Robert, "so he has decided it is to be Christmas Day!" Guy raised his eyebrows, but held his tongue from a sarcastic jest that could be repeated.

At night, Guy lay awake long hours going over and over his last night with Lillyth and the shame he had brought upon her, when he only wanted to give her love and happiness. Splendor of God, how he wished he could marry her. A thought stirred, then took shape. Why couldn't he wed with her. Why not have the priest say the words over them? It wouldn't be legal, but if

Lillyth truly believed they were wed, she would hold her proud head high and not be ashamed before the others. It was hard enough for her now, but if she bore him a bastard, it would be intolerable for her. His mind followed that path for a moment. A son! It was what he had longed for but never achieved. He was past thirty; he had better make haste. Sons! He wanted his seed to spring from his loins into Lillyth's body and give him sons. He would legitimize any child she bore him. He dismissed the idea of marriage as an empty dream, but it came again and again, and he found himself practicing the phrases he would use to his brothers and Rolf, to ensure their lips would be sealed over the matter of his previous marriage. He thought of it in those terms because, by all the saints, they would be married in God's eyes. He already thought of Lillyth as his wife, and this surely was the only way to keep her for himself forever. He wanted to ask her to marry him, to see her eyes light up with the love she felt for him. When he had settled it all in his mind, he relaxed and fell asleep. When the cold, clear light of morning arrived, he dismissed his thoughts as impossible, but again at night as he lay abed, they came creeping back, intruding up through layers of subconscious thought to the surface of consciousness, and he knew that he would never be whole until the other half of his soul, Lillyth, was joined with him, mated for life.

Guy was impatient to be home again, even though he had only been away for the month of November. When he thought of Godstone he was filled with unease that it wasn't well guarded and chafed at the bit when he thought of all the month of December that had to be gotten through before he could return. He began to keep his ears and eyes open for an excuse to return home. He could take his men back up to London in time for the coronation.

Chapter 14

As December dawned, Lillyth longed for Guy's return. The people at Godstone prepared for the Yule season as they had done in the past. All the girls were busy making Christmas gifts and Lady Alison asked Rolf to find them a big yule log to bring into the hall to be decorated. A merry party of ladies went into the woods and, with the men's help, cut garlands of holly from the great oak trees and also mistletoe, and they spent hours trimming the walls and tables and even the sleeping chambers.

May said to her husband Edgar, "I am glad the Lord Aedward was sent over to Oxstead."

He said, "You mean you are glad to have him away from Edwina?" May nodded. "She has formed an impossible attachment for him. I have tried to tell her that nothing can come of it."

"She will soon forget him," said Edgar. "She will take up with Alfred's grandson or young Lucan."

May shook her head. "She will not look at another man. She asked me not to make any arrangements for her, at least until Aedward returns to Godstone."

He said, "She has set her sights too high, I am afraid. He no longer owns land, but he is still of noble blood. I am afraid if she persists she will receive a broken heart for her foolishness."

May sighed. "Why are all maids foolish when they are in love?"

"Men too," he chuckled as he slipped his arms about her.

"Hurry then if that is what's on your mind. The children will be in for supper any minute."

Edwina had walked about in a melancholy state since Aedward left for Oxstead. She had received the wax images from Morag and faithfully bound them together with a piece of red wool, but her wishes looked as if they would never be fulfilled. That night she took the little dolls into bed with her and prayed with all her heart that Aedward would return soon. The next day she took them out to the bees and whispered her longings to them as Morag had advised her to do. It was too bad that Samain had slipped by without her noticing, on November first—the pagan festival when the barriers were down between mortal and immortal, between the visible and the invisible.

At last she received her wish. Aedward had walked all the way from Oxstead. She spied him through the trees going toward the hall. Breathlessly, she ran to him, then was at a loss for words when he stopped politely to see what she wanted.

"I . . . I missed you," she blurted out, unable to conceal her feelings.

He smiled sadly. "I came to see my mother. I fear she is gravely ill."

"Oh, Aedward, I am so sorry. Is there anything I can do?" she begged, longing to take his hurt onto herself.

"Only pray," he said simply.

Lillyth and her mother took turns looking after Lady Hilda, who seemed a little worse each day. Lillyth sat beside the bed and did her sewing. She had decided that Guy should have a new mantle and she was determined that it wouldn't be of a somber hue, so she picked scarlet wool and chose an amber jewel to fasten it at one shoulder. How brave he would look in the bright color with his dark hair for contrast. She looked up at a low knock on the door, and setting aside the material, she rose to answer. Aedward came into the chamber, took her hands and said quickly, "I came to see how my mother fares, and to see you too, Lillyth."

She smiled at him sadly. "She is sleeping now thanks to the potion my mother brews for her, but I am afraid she gets no better, Aedward."

"I appreciate everything you are doing for her, Lillyth, thank you." He hesitated. "Lillyth, you know I still love you. Why don't we steal this opportunity to get married while they are away. Who knows, perhaps we will be lucky and they will never return." He went on his knees to her. "Oh, love, it would be a *fait accompli* and there would be nothing he could do about it."

"He would simply kill you," she said softly.

"Perhaps not, perhaps he would not want you after I'd had you," he begged. "I am willing to risk all for you."

She looked at the boy before her, and thought, That's exactly what he is, a boy, and not nearly man enough for me.

She took his face between her hands and said, "Aedward, if you had only said to me those words 'I am willing to risk all for you' before I was wed to Wulfric, I would have gone away with you and wed you. You should have taken me that day we went hawking and never allowed me to go to him. Now I do not love you—I love another." She thought silently, You were not man enough then, and for me, you are not man enough now.

Her denial cut him deeply. He held up his stump and cried, "Is it because of this?"

"That is unworthy of you, Aedward," she said quietly.

He looked at her and knew the truth of her words.

The Lady Hilda lingered a few more days, and during the night when it was Lillyth's turn to sit with her, Aedward's mother drew her last labored breath. Lillyth went to the next chamber where her mother was resting, pondering whether she should first awaken Rolf to send a man over to Oxstead to bring Aedward. She went into her mother's chamber without knocking and checked on the threshold. Alison and Rolf, naked, were in the most passionate embrace Lillyth had ever witnessed. Her mouth fell open and she went pale, then finally murmured, "Lady Hilda . . ."

Alison reached smoothly for her robe and said, "I'll come at once."

Rolf said quietly, "I'll send word to Oxstead."

They laid her out and washed her, and put fresh linen on the bed, all without a word to each other. When the incense had been burned to freshen the room, Lady Alison motioned for Lillyth to follow her. They went into Lillyth's chamber and Alison closed the door.

"I'm a passionate woman, Lillyth, and Rolf is all man. What did you expect? Do you think you and Guy are the only ones permitted to sport naked in your chamber? Don't be a hypocrite, Lillyth!"

"I'm sorry, mother," she said humbly.

Aedward took his mother home to Oxstead for burial after the service in the church at Godstone. As the priest said the words over the small coffin and the dirt fell into the grave, Lillyth looked at Aedward's haggard face and felt a terrible remorse over the cruel words she had said to him. As she watched him, she realized he was a boy no longer, as she had accused in her heart. He had indeed become a man. Her attention was inexplicably drawn to one of the windows in the hall. What had she seen? A figure or watcher of some sort, someone out of place who was odd and unnatural. A shiver went over her and she was covered with gooseflesh. She had exactly the same feeling that had crept over her the last time she had visited Oxstead, and suddenly she couldn't bear the place a moment longer. Ghosts, it was filled with ghosts, and they haunted her peace of mind. She turned sharply away and slowly the others followed her, away from the grave, away from Oxstead and its dead, toward Godstone, home, life!

Edwina had watched them place Lady Hilda's coffin on a wagon, and the mourning party set out for Oxstead. She followed the riders on foot, at a distance. She did not know why she did this, she only knew she must. Aedward needed comfort. If no other would provide it, she would. She arrived in time to see them offering a prayer for the lady's soul. She watched Aedward invite the party from Godstone into the hall. She watched Lillyth shake her head and turn sharply away. She watched them all leave for Godstone, but this time she did not follow. Aedward kept vigil beside the grave until dusk began to fall. Edwina knew he would stay all night if she did not intervene. Quietly she approached him and said his name softly.

"Edwina, what are you doing here?"

"I did not want you to be alone this night," she said simply.

He looked deeply into her eyes and saw that she shared his pain. They shone with so much love for him he could neither deny it nor refuse it.

"Let me be with you tonight?" she pleaded.

"I would like you to stay with me a while. Then I must take you home."

She smiled up at him, indicating that whatever he decided for her would please her.

Aedward said, "Come, I will take you to my old chamber." He took her hand and she followed him, excited now.

"I have never been inside a great hall before," she told him.

"Then I am sure you will be favorably impressed. Of course, it is not the equal of Godstone, but we managed to live quite graciously."

Edwina's gaze swept about the entrance hall, admiring the fine tapestries. She jumped guiltily. "Someone is coming!"

"It's only one of my mother's ladies. It's all right, sweetheart. Norah, I thought you went back to Godstone."

"No, my lord. It seemed so peaceful now that

the Normans have gone, I thought I would stay a few days and enjoy the way it used to be."

"You must not call me 'my lord,' Norah. Remember, they will return."

She curtsied to him. "Can I fetch you come supper, Aedward?"

"No thank you, Norah." Then he realized that Edwina would be hungry. "I have changed my mind. I would appreciate it if you could choose food enough for two and bring it to my chamber. Fetch me some ale and some mead for my lady. I think she would enjoy that." He smiled.

Edwina was enthralled to be called his lady and followed him up the staircase to his bedchamber.

"You must be cold, Edwina. Forgive me, I never thought," he apologized. He bent to the fire and in a few moments had a small starter fire blazing in the open hearth. Edwina fingered the fur coverlet on the bed.

"This is where you sleep?" she asked because she had only ever seen bedmats on the floor. "I've never slept in a bed," she said.

He stood up from the fire and came toward her. "You will tonight," he promised.

She shook her head. "I would fall off."

"I will hold you too tightly to fall off." He laughed for the first time that day. There was no need for candles. The fire lit up the small chamber, making it a warm haven for the young lovers.

Norah knocked softly. She brought a platter of cold meats and cheeses. The fine white bread with butter to spread upon it took Edwina's fancy. She had never before tasted butter. Shyly, she waited until Norah left.

"Can I have some of this?"

"Of course. Put some meat on it," he urged.

"What is it?" she asked curiously.

"I think this is cold venison. Have you never had it before?"

She shook her head, and he watched eagerly for her reaction when she tasted it.

"It is very good," she laughed.

"Now try this. I think these are slices of wild boar. The taste is much stronger."

"Mmm, that's good too," she praised.

Aedward was delighted with her. How thrilling it was to give a maiden her first taste of life's pleasures. He felt himself harden at the taste of the pleasures still to come. He knew she was virgin, so did not want to frighten her with his haste. He plied her with partridge, insisting that she take the leg while he picked at the wing. Then he poured her a horn of honey-sweet mead and held it to her lips until she almost drained it. He saved the last drop for himself, putting his mouth to the spot her lips had touched, then he took her into his embrace and touched their lips together, while they were still sweet from the mead. "We have shared the loving cup," he whispered. He lifted her to the bed, and she raised her face to receive his kiss. He paused to gaze down at her as the firelight flickered across her delicate features. Her short blond hair curled about her face, making her look like an angel.

"Oh, my lord Aedward, I love you so much!" she cried.

"Edwina, you are so pretty; so sweet."

He gently removed her woolen tunic and traced the delicate, budding breasts with his forefinger. When he removed his clothes and lay beside her, she knelt up on the bed to gaze down at him. Her lips fell upon his chest with hundreds of little, hot kisses. She moved so quickly, down his chest, across his belly, down to his groin and back up again, he could only lie groaning in his need. With a swift movement he had her beneath him. She was extremely small, but by persistently pushing an inch at a time, he penetrated as deeply as he dare go this first time, then slowly he began to make her his. He was so inflamed he reached his climax after only a dozen thrusts and was greatly relieved that he had not hurt her.

"Are you sure you are all right, Edwina?"

For answer she curled against him, rubbing her cheek against his chest.

He said wonderingly, "You are so selfless, you receive pleasure from giving it to me."

"Must we go?" she dared to ask him.

"Not tonight. Neither of us wants to leave this bed. Early tomorrow I must take you back and explain to your mother. She will be ill with worry for you."

Edwina smiled up at him and snuggled down against him under the soft fur pelt.

When Aedward awoke he found himself alone. He rose up from the bed quickly, about to search for her, when she came in carrying hot water. He laughed in his relief. "You remembered that I like to wash."

"Let me wash you, my lord Aedward."

"Not unless you allow me the same pleasure," he teased.

"We must hurry. Lady Norah is bringing food."

"Ah Norah, you are just the one to solve my problem," said Aedward as she entered the chamber with a tray. "I wish to see my lady in a fine gown. I would like it to be blue to match her beautiful eyes. See what you can do, my dear," he directed Norah, as he had often done in the past.

Summoning all her courage, Edwina asked softly, "Can I be your woman?"

"My lady," he corrected her. "After I see your mother and father I will bring you back with me."

Guy gambled seldomly; however, when he saw the stakes were two sets of golden bracelets, one small delicate pair for a lady, the other larger, thicker to fit a man's arms, he decided he wanted them as a gift for Lillyth.

Probably the man didn't realize they were real gold, and for just the hazard of a few silver denier, he soon had the bracelets safely stowed in his doublet. Guy burned to be home before Christmas so he could give Lillyth the present, but of course he didn't need this spur, he just wanted to be with her again. He sought out Robert immediately and came directly to the point. "I must return to Sussex for a few days. I'll be back in London in time for the coronation."

Robert smiled at him. "There is such a crush around here, I don't even think you will be missed, but I'll say you have gone on a mission to the coast for me to hurry along building supplies that are long overdue, if there is any question. Godspeed!"

Robert made a silent promise to himself to visit this Godstone and find out for himself what drew Guy so irresistibly.

Guy startled his brothers by telling them they were leaving for home in the morning.

"See that the men are ready before dawn," he ordered impatiently.

"We are not missing the coronation, are we?" Nicholas asked incredulously.

"You're not worried about any coronation—it's London you can't wait to get your hands on," laughed Guy.

"And it's Lillyth you can't wait to get your hands on," Nick taunted.

"We are to be back in London by the twentieth, so we had best break camp and head out without any delay. See to it."

Faith sat huddled in a corner of the hut while Red Wolf dressed and checked his weapons carefully. She knew they were going out on another raid. Her plan was made; her decision reached. She would carry it out the moment the band of men quit the forest camp. She could bear this life no longer. The depth of degradation she had suffered at Red Wolf's hands could not continue.

It was her job to prepare the men's food, and she went about her work calmly. She cut large chunks off the roe buck they had hunted and killed and placed them in the iron pot over the fire, with water she had carried from the stream. She put in the last of the wild turnips, along with some mustard greens, then walked upstream to where she remembered seeing a laburnum tree growing.

She gathered the deadly poisonous pods from the tree, returned to her cooking and threw them into the iron pot. As the mixture bubbled, it gave off such a savory fragrance her mouth began to water. She took a wooden bowl, filled it with the stew, then ate every mouthful with relish. She lay down beneath a gnarled oak and gripped her arms about her middle, tightly, knowing what was to come.

Soon she would be with her beloved Morgan; soon she would escape the cruel torture of the Red Wolf.

Lillyth awoke with a sore throat, and she felt flushed all over. She was considering going back to bed for the day when Aedward rode in like a madman.

"Fire! Fire!" he shouted. He ran into the hall to find Rolf.

Aedward was blackened from smoke and sweat, and he had a wild look in his eyes. "Half the peasants' huts are on fire at Oxstead. Some people are badly burned. I don't know how it started; it must have been set, I think. We'll need help. How many men did Guy leave behind—only five?"

Rolf considered for a moment. "I'll get more men. Our peasants will come gladly. Giles, take the men and go immediately. I'll get Alfred and he can pick the men he will need. Aedward, you can take them to Oxstead. I'll stay here in case it is some kind of diversion to get everyone away from Godstone."

Alison organized her ladies. Some tore strips off sheets and others rolled them into bandages. She went to the stillroom and began to mix ointment to soothe burns. She sent Adela to ask at every hut for any clothing, especially for the children, that they could spare. She sent word to the kitchens to prepare extra food, and Rolf went to the stables to prepare some wagons to take the necessary supplies to Oxstead. He had just returned to the hall when the sound of horses coming at a full gallop filled the yard. About a dozen men thrust their way into the hall, and Lillyth raised her head and looked straight into the eyes of Wulfric. She felt the walls coming together and the floor rose up and almost smacked her in the face, and she realized she was fainting. She grasped the air in front of her and hung onto consciousness, though oblivion was to be desired in the face of this evil.

Rolf reached for his sword, but a knife was thrust into his back and he fell in a pool of his own blood. Alison screamed and sprang forward, but Wulfric struck her across the face and she fell to her knees beside Rolf.

"Tie her," he ordered.

The girls were screaming and the men grabbed them and began their atrocities. Wulfric had his whip in his hand and he bared his teeth in anticipation as he motioned Lillyth up the stairs. She picked up her skirts and ran wildly up the steps toward the back chamber where they had spent their wedding night. All the while a voice screamed in her head, I knew! I knew! She repeated it over and over with her heartbeats. One moment she was freezing and her teeth were chattering, the next moment she felt overheated as though she would suffocate. A part of her mind told her it was the influenza, so she dismissed it to secondary importance. Another voice in her head said quite clearly and calmly, You are no longer a child, you are now a *woman!* If you can control a real man like Guy, you can control this scum, this nothing! He has a whip, but your weapons are more deadly, and then very clearly she heard herself say, "I almost feel sorry for him, the poor bastard doesn't have a chance!"

As he came through the chamber door she was waiting, facing him. Her mouth caressed his name as she whispered, "Wulfric, thank God you are alive!"

He narrowed his eyes suspiciously and raised his whip arm, but as smoothly and easily as an otter slips through water, she slipped under the whip arm and cast herself into his arms.

"No, love, please don't use the whip on me. That is what the Norman dogs use. They are not man enough to handle a woman without a whip, as you are, Wulfric," she purred. She lifted her mouth to his, but not quite all the way. Holding her lips very close to his, and every few seconds darting out her pink inviting tongue to moisten them, she told him, "I did not know what a man was until I married you. You are so masterful it sends shivers down my spine."

He was concentrating on her mouth and was compelled to kiss her as he had longed to do for months. She quivered with a simulated ecstasy and he growled, "Let us see what fancy tricks these Normans have taught you, slut!"

"They only use us as slaves to fetch food and water and carry wood. They do not find Saxon women attractive." She breathed her warm words at him and managed to sensuously touch every part of his anatomy with hers. He was breathing heavily now. Her sore throat gave her voice a seductive, voluptuous huskiness he had never heard before, and his fantasies began to build in spite of himself and the determination he had of revenging himself on her. Her eyes were filled with undreamed-of promises, and with a sensuous movement she reached behind him and put the bar down across the door so they would be alone without interruption. Her hands began to lift off his leather tunic, and then her fingers were inside his chainse doing tantalizing, indecent things to him. He allowed an involuntary groan to escape his lips, and she whispered, brushing burning lips against his ear, "You have made me wait too long, Wulfric. Let's see what you have for me," and she slipped her hand between his legs and cupped his testes.

He gasped, "I never thought I'd see Lillyth of Godstone play the whore!"

"For no other man, but I'll be your whore, Wulfric," and she took the tip of his penis and stroked it with tender featherlike fingers. He squirmed with unquenched lust and moved toward the bed. She clung to him and between kisses said, "I know which way you like it best, but I want to feel you between my thighs the first time, then afterward I will turn over and you can have it your way."

The whip slipped nervelessly from his fingers as he fell onto the bed and pulled her down on top of him. His hands slipped up her dress to her hidden thighs, and her hands slipped under the mattress to her hidden knife.

It fit so well into her palm and felt so right that it became an extension of her hand. She raised her arm and swiftly plunged it into the middle of his chest. His eyes flew open and his mouth gaped foolishly as it plunged in. He screamed and raised his arm to smash her, but quick as lightning she stabbed it into his arm and tore it down the length of his muscle. The arm dropped uselessly. Oblivious to the spurting blood, she plunged it into his chest again, over and over. He thrashed about wildly, and her other hand closed on his whip and she lashed out at him with all her force. He screamed again and tore up from the bed, propelled by the stinging lash of the whip. The knife stayed in her hand and she stabbed and stabbed, and when he fell to the floor mortally wounded, making only animal sounds now, she plunged it in again and again, not knowing or caring where the thrusts struck.

He was a mass of wounds from his throat to his belly and groin, and when she knew that he was quite, quite dead, she splashed in his blood until it splattered the ceiling. She sank down upon the bed and felt very ill. Her body burned with fever and she stared fixedly into space.

Chapter 15

Guy and his men could see the pall of smoke in the air while they were still some miles away, and it impelled them to double their speed. However, as they drew closer to Godstone they could see the smoke coming from the east and surmised that it was from Oxstead. Guy divided the convoy in half and bade Nicholas take his men to Oxstead immediately. Guy could not dispel the fear that was clutching at his heart, and he urged his men make every possible speed with him to Godstone. He saw the strange horses tethered in the yard immediately, yet not so strange, noted his quick eye. Some of those horses had been stolen from them. Their approach had been heard from within, and eight or nine armed men rushed them as they dismounted. Wulfric's men were outnumbered two to one, but they fought like wild animals in their desperation to get away from the Normans.

When the melee was over and all the Saxons lay dead, Guy's men had suffered more wounds than they had received at Senlac. André had been wounded in the thigh. Guy could see how severe it was, with the muscle and tendons hanging from the cut the huge sword had carved open. He picked André up in his arms and carried him into the hall. Rolf lay unconscious in a dried pool of blood. The knife still stood between his shoulder blades. Most of the women were tethered with ropes, their garments were torn and their faces were bruised, eyes blackened and lips burst open from trying to resist their attackers. Guy took the gag from Lady Alison's mouth and cut the ropes at her wrists.

"Thank God you have returned. Pray he isn't dead yet," she sobbed as she knelt beside Rolf. Edyth and the other ladies immediately took charge of André and the other wounded men, and Alison ministered to Rolf.

Guy eased the knife out and felt for his heartbeat. "I don't know how, but he is still alive," he told Alison.

"God be praised, I'll swear an oath to keep him that way." She hesitated a moment. "Guy—it was Lillyth's husband, Wulfric. He's got her upstairs—I am afraid they have been there for hours."

He mounted the stairs steadily, not three at a time, but with the grim determination of death on his stark face. Two of his men followed at his back, determined not to leave him unprotected. All the chamber doors were ajar, so it was easy to discern that they were in the back room. The door was barred and he turned toward his men for an axe. He called, "Lillyth!" but was met with an unearthly silence. He swung the battle-ax with mighty strokes, rhythmically, one stroke after another without pause, and the door soon splintered from its frame and fell in shards about him. He stepped inside and saw a wild-eyed, bloody thing, staring at him, unseeing.

"Bones of Christ, what has happened here?" he said almost to himself. Lillyth was soaked with blood. He saw the sticky knife and whip upon the bed beside her and whispered hoarsely, "Where are you hurt, love?"

She tried to speak, but no sounds came from her throat. He saw the high, bright spots of fever on her cheeks and her glazed eyes, and placed a hand to her forehead.

"She is burning with fever," he said over his shoulder. "Get the women to prepare a bath for her," and he picked her up very carefully. He glanced at the thing on the floor.

"Bury that—what's left of it, but not at Godstone!"

By the time he carried her to their own chamber, young esquires were building him a fire. He shielded her from their curious glances with his mantle and impatiently ordered, "That's enough, send one of the women to me," but Alison was moving Rolf to her chamber and Edyth was giving instructions as to which chamber the men should bring André. Suddenly the chamber was filled with women ready to do his bidding. Very gently he began to peel the blood-soaked garments from Lillyth. Miraculously, there were no stab wounds. He stripped off her underdress and turned her bare body over carefully. There were no whip marks on her back; in fact nowhere could he find even a small bruise upon her white limbs.

"Thank God!" he kept muttering as he lowered her into the hot water and gently washed away the streaks of blood.

Lady Alison came into the room. "What did he do to her?" she asked anxiously.

"He is dead, she's alive. That's all I know—that's all that matters," he said. "She is burning

with fever, what do you suppose it is?" he asked
distractedly.

"I remember she had a sore throat this morning
before all this happened. She has probably just got
a bad dose of influenza. Adela, get her some hot
bricks for the bed. Keep her warm and I will mix
some camomile which you must make her drink.
By tomorrow Rolf will be fevered. I am afraid his
wound was left too long without being tended.
André should be all right as far as fever is concerned. His wound was cleansed immediately, but
I can tell you now, his leg will never be the same
again. I do not think he will lose it, but it will heal
stiff and he will be lame," said Alison, and hurried
back to Rolf.

Guy felt her scalp for cuts or lumps. He sighed
with relief when he was sure she was uninjured.
He wrapped a cover from the bed about her, to
warm her blood, then laid her before the fire and
gently wiped away the streaks of blood. He sat in
his big chair, spread his knees wide and pulled
her between them. He vigorously rubbed her
from head to foot. He wrapped her in a soft
woolen blanket and laid her before the fire. He
looked up as Alison came in with a potion for the
fever.

"Stay with her a moment, I want to see how
Rolf and André are," said Guy quickly.

Rolf was still unconscious. Guy inspected the
dressings and knew Alison was doing everything
she could for him. He could leave his friend in her
capable hands and know that none could do more
for him than she would. He then went in to
André, who received him with a grin slightly
pulled down at the corner because of the pain
from his thigh.

"Is Lillyth all right?" he asked Guy.

"She has a wild look in her eye which I do not

like, but apart from that, she doesn't seem to have been harmed. I cannot understand what drove her to such bloody vengeance. She is so gentle—fragile, almost."

André hesitated, then said low, "Aedward told me that his brother sometimes practiced sodomy."

Guy stiffened. His questions were answered.

Nicholas came in with Edyth, who carried food on a tray for André. Nick joked, "I've been doing all the work, and he's the one to get fed."

Guy turned to Nick, "Come away, let André rest. I must get back to Lillyth, so that Alison can attend to Rolf. What happened at Oxstead?"

"The bastards set the peasants' huts afire to draw what few men we left here at Godstone, but Rolf stayed behind to guard the women."

They entered Guy's chamber and he knelt to have a close look at Lillyth, who had fallen into a doze that was obviously filled with delirium. Alison hurried back to Rolf.

Guy looked up at Nicholas and said, "Go below and find a woman to stay with Lillyth. I must get help to those poor devils at Oxstead."

"Stay where you are," Nick ordered him. "What do you think I've been doing? The wagons are already loaded to take food, burn dressings and clothes to Oxstead. We will house the peasants in the hall, the armory and the mill until their homes are built again. Aedward is working like a demon also. There's another wagon loaded for Oxstead—full of corpses. I gathered you didn't want them buried at Godstone!"

"Thanks, Nick, you're a good man," offered Guy, and Nick smiled inwardly at the praise that Guy gave only sparingly and not at all unless it was so deserved.

"Ah well, it has its compensations," said Nick, making light of the day's happenings. "Little Rose who used to run and hide when I approached has flown to my arms for protection."

Guy hovered above Lillyth, tucking the blanket more closely and soothing her brow, and Nick said, "I asked Lillyth to marry me, you know, but she would have none of me. Said she was mad in love with you. I can see you love her too—Guy, what will you do?" he asked.

"I am going to take her for my wife just as if that bitch in Normandy didn't exist, and if anyone ever breathes a word of it to Lillyth, I'll slit his throat."

Nick raised his eyebrows, but kept his own counsel and went in search of food before making the journey back to Oxstead.

Edyth brought Guy a tray of food and some steaming broth for Lillyth.

"How is my brother?" asked Guy.

"Lady Alison mixed him a sleeping draft and it has finally taken effect. How is Lillyth?" she asked, concerned.

"She has been asleep for a while. I'm sure she will be all right," he assured the worried girl.

After he had eaten he roused Lillyth, and she took a few sips of broth and drifted off to sleep again. He settled himself in the chair before the fire and put his head back. He aroused sometime later to hear her murmur, "Guy?"

"Yes, love. What is it?"

"I'm cold," she whispered.

The fire had gone down and he bent and placed two logs onto the low embers, then he picked her up and put her into his bed. Her teeth chattered and he piled the furs up around her. She still shivered, so he quickly stripped off his clothes and slipped into bed beside her. He took her into his arms and held her against his warm body. After a long time she stopped shivering and lay still against him, and then, very softly at first, she began to cry. He held her tightly as her crying turned into heavy sobs. Her body was racked, and when no more tears came she shuddered with dry heaves. He dreaded the question, but finally asked, "Lillyth, did he violate you?"

She shook her head. "If he had, I would have used the knife on myself as well as on him."

He relaxed as if a great weight had been lifted from his shoulders.

"I am a murderer, my immortal soul is in danger," she whispered in a dread voice.

He searched his mind for words of comfort. "Love, I have killed many men. If your soul was pure, how could we hope to meet in the hereafter?" He laughed softly. "One little blot won't matter. After all it was in self-defense."

"I keep telling myself it was in self-defense, but maybe the real reason was that he stood between us. Perhaps the real reason I killed him was so that I could have you."

His arms tightened about her. "Hush, love. Put these ideas out of your head, you are only torturing yourself. Promise me you will never think of him again! He couldn't come between us while he lived, and by Christ he won't now that he is dead!"

"I—I promise," she whispered.

He quickly changed the subject. "Are you warmer now?"

She snuggled against him. "Hmm," she replied drowsily.

He tucked her head underneath his chin, and knowing that his strength would be there to comfort her whenever she awakened, she slept in the protection of his arms.

At dawn she was wet with perspiration, so he arose and bathed her in bed. He left her naked, but put fresh linen sheets on the bed. He took her hand. "Are you feeling any better?"

"My throat is still very sore, you should not have slept with me, you will catch it."

"I am too healthy, but I warned you, didn't I, about eating more? You are so frail." He lifted her slim wrist to make his point, then slid his hands beneath the covers to encircle her waist. "You are so small I can span you with my hands." He took them from her body before they explored her further, and he moved from the bed quickly. "I'll get one of the ladies to bring you some breakfast, and you must try to eat it. I don't want to leave you, but I must go to Oxstead to see to the things over there."

She shivered at the mention of Oxstead and said, "I knew the day we went there that he was watching me."

His thoughts went quickly back to the time she had run to his arms so eagerly for protection, and his eyes narrowed dangerously.

"Bones of Christ, I will have Aedward's head if he has been harboring my enemies!"

"No, oh no, Guy, he knew nothing of Wulfric's whereabouts. Please do not harm him, and remember he only buried his mother last week," she pleaded.

"You know nothing of the matter," he said sharply.

"I have proof that Aedward did not know," she cried.

"What proof?" he demanded.

She faltered. "Aedward begged me to wed him while you were gone. He couldn't have done that if he had known Wulfric was still alive."

"Splendor of God," he said, jealousy flaring

in his face, "is there no end to your conquests, lady?"

Guy was out all day. He was pleasantly surprised to discover that his people were more than generous and welcomed those who had been burned out into their homes. Rebuilding had already begun, and he directed and advised them on building sturdier, larger huts. Fortunately there had been few injuries, save for burned hands when people had desperately tried to salvage their belongings. The people had become almost friendly when they saw the lord roll up his sleeves and pitch in beside them, clearing away debris, felling new timber and sharing their humble meal at dinnertime. Before the day was done, he called most of them by their names, and this was a novelty indeed. Their Saxon lord had known them all their lives, yet had never bothered to learn their names.

It was after dark when Guy and Nicholas directed their men back to Godstone. They were begrimed and decided to make use of the bathhouse before dining. Guy sat soaking his tired muscles.

"I'm worried about Rolf. I don't think he is going to make it."

Nick hesitated. "I know how badly you feel, Guy. He's been like a father to you, hasn't he?"

"Ah, well, let's not bury him before the corpse is cold," Guy said bleakly. He stepped from the tub and viciously rubbed himself dry.

"Do you think André will lose that leg?" Nick ventured.

"Splendor of God, now who's being morbid? Alison can do wonderful things with her potions and medicines. Give her a chance!"

"Yes, she reminds me of a witch."

"As a matter of fact, boy, I think she is a witch."

They both laughed and went to join their men for the evening meal. Guy ate with all possible speed and went immediately to see Lillyth. She was asleep, but she had moved into her own bed, so he quietly withdrew and went along to see Rolf. There was no change. He was still unconscious and extremely fevered.

"I am coming along shortly to change your brother's dressings," said Alison. "If I do it in your presence his pride will forbid him to shout the roof in." She smiled at him with kindly eyes.

Guy found Nicholas visiting André, who was cursing because he'd had to spend the day abed. "I'm bored to death! Find me a willing wench, Nick."

Guy fixed him with a steely eye and said bluntly, "Stay off that leg, or you will lose it."

André paled for a moment and licked his lips nervously as he tried to assess the truth of Guy's words.

Alison came in carrying her box of healing tricks. Behind her, Edyth carried a bowl of steaming water and Emma carried fresh cloths and bandages. Alison put a sprinkling of herbs into the water, and it turned purple and gave off a pungent aroma. Without ceremony she stripped back the sheet, tucked one corner between his legs to preserve modesty in front of the young women and gently but firmly stripped the old dressings from André's leg. The bone and muscle were visible, and as the wound was disturbed, it started to bleed brightly.

Emma slumped over in a faint and Alison, blinking rapidly said, "Whatever is the matter with the girl, there's been enough blood let hereabouts lately, she shouldn't be that squeamish."

Nicholas picked the girl up and sat her in the nearest chair, and Edyth put her hand up to Alison's ear and whispered to her.

"So!" Alison stormed at the three brothers, "this is just the first of a whole crop of Norman bastards we will be harvesting by summer." Her eyes blazed her indignation as she washed the wound carefully, and André ground his teeth to keep from crying out. She was secure in the knowledge that her nursing skills were indispensable for the moment, so she turned her wrath upon Guy. "After you left, Lillyth was in a frenzy of fear counting the days until she got the sign that she was not with child, and when you leave again in a few days, the worrying and counting will start over."

Guy stiffened. "That will not be necessary, madame. Lillyth is ill, I won't take advantage of her."

Alison took the dark green balsam ointment made from adder's-tongue boiled in oil and spread it thickly onto the wound to keep out the inflammation.

"Edyth, hand me those clean dressings and take Emma and make her lie down."

After the two girls departed, Alison began to bind up the leg, making sure the bandages were not too tight.

"Do you think if we had a wedding it would set the fashion, madame, and others would follow?" Guy asked carefully.

"A marriage between a Saxon and a Norman is exactly what we need. It would set a precedent and things would be as they should," she agreed.

"I intend to wed Lillyth when I return from William's coronation."

Her eyes kindled as her fondest wish was about to be realized.

"There is only one problem—I am already married," he stated bluntly. André and Nicholas caught each other's eye and quickly looked away.

Alison sat with her hopes shattered, and Guy continued, "She is no wife to me—none know of her existence outside this room, save Rolf, of course. I am telling you this, Alison, but I don't want Lillyth to ever find out. I do not want to hurt her, not ever. I want her to have a wife's place of honor here, and if there are children, they will be my heirs. I don't hold this land for William; he has deeded it to me outright. André is to have Oxstead, and Nicholas, Sevenoaks. I hope they will follow my lead and marry, as will my other knights." He looked at her keenly, trying to gauge her reaction. "If you do not agree to my plan, we will say nothing more of the matter."

She gathered her things together quickly and said, "I will think on it, my lord."

It was past midnight, and Guy sat with his head back and his eyes closed before the fire. He was trying to summon the effort to arise and go to bed when Alison knocked lightly and came in.

"I need your help, my lord. It is Rolf; he is much worse!"

His lethargy disappeared immediately as he followed Alison to her chamber. Rolf's face was dark red, his whole body had a dull flush over it. He was still unconscious but he thrashed about the bed like one demented, and the bandage covering his wound had become displaced.

"We have to break his fever and make him sweat. I have made a clyster from camomile flowers beaten up with oil. We have to spread it on his body from head to foot and pray that the fever breaks. If it does not he won't last the night."

They spread the mixture all over his body and piled the blankets and furs on him, then sat down to their vigil. Alison knew that any claims Lillyth and she had to Godstone could only come through Guy. Her practical mind could weigh sentiment against advantages, and the advantages won.

"My lord, I have been thinking about the matter we were discussing, and I have decided that any marriage would be better than no marriage at all."

"So think I," said Guy. He held her eyes for a moment and said, "Do not worry, I shall be good to her."

"I have no doubts about you, my Lord Montgomery."

Within two hours the concoction had worked its magic, and Rolf started to sweat profusely. They worked together, washing and changing him throughout the night, and finally he succumbed to an exhausted sleep. At three o'clock all seemed to be well, and Guy left Alison dozing in a chair. He felt that a great weight had been lifted from his chest as he quietly entered his own chamber.

Lillyth was coughing because the cold had settled in her chest. He quickly poured a drink and took it to her. She took it gratefully and drank it down. "Is it morning yet?" she asked.

"No, I have been helping your mother with Rolf. We thought he would never last the night, but your mother came up with another miracle and he should be all right now."

"Thank God," she breathed. "You must be exhausted! You came home only to work yourself to a standstill. I'm sorry about everything that has happened. I must get up today and make myself useful."

"Your chest sounds terrible. You will stay in bed until you are better. This room looks lovely, you have worked hard too." He smiled. "In a few short days, Lillyth, we have to leave for London. I gave my word we would return for William's coronation, or I would never leave you right now."

"I have a gift for you, my lord. Since you will not be here for Christmas, I want you to have it now, to wear in London. It's in my coffer by the wall."

"I wish you would use my name, Lillyth," he said wistfully. "When I return and we are married, it will be ridiculous to keep 'lording' me, don't you think?"

Her eyes opened wide with delight, and he watched her reaction with deep pleasure. He opened the coffer and took out the scarlet cloak. "Why it's magnificent," he said, twirling it in a wide arc and settling it on his shoulders.

"It looks wonderful," she said proudly.

"I have something for you too," he said. He took a small parcel from his saddlebags and, unwrapping it on the bed, gave her the gold bracelets. She put them on immediately and held up her arms for his admiration.

"I'll have these others made smaller for you."

"Oh no, they are for you, Guy," she said.

"Me in bracelets?" He laughed incredulously.

"Oh yes, put them on! They will make you look like a pagan god." She smiled seductively.

He clasped them onto his thick arms and his muscles bulged above them. "They make me feel pagan. How will you fare if they make me act pagan?" He laughed and clasped her tightly to him and began kissing her neck and breasts, and laughing together they tumbled back and forth across the bed. Suddenly she was racked with coughing, and he was all tender concern for her, his passion dissolved.

"I'd better get a couple of hours' sleep. Cover up warm, love, and try to rest. I'll see to the fire."

She felt such a stab of disappointment that he was going to his own bed. She wanted to feel the long, hard length of him against her. Then, remembering his promise of marriage, she contented herself with the thought of all the nights to come and snuggled down, closing her eyes.

During the next couple of days it became evident that Rolf would recover and that André's leg was doing as well as could be expected. Guy decided to take only twenty-five men with him to London and leave the rest behind at Godstone. He left the choice up to them, and as he had supposed, it worked out well, because some really wanted to see London and others preferred for one reason or another to remain at home.

Lillyth insisted on dressing and coming down for their leavetaking, and Guy drew her aside and said, "If you had been well enough I would have taken you to London with me. I feel such a great need of you when we are parted for a long time."

She looked at him archly and said, "I do not intend to share your bed again until we are wed, my lord."

He gave a mock sigh and said, "Ah well, I had better keep my eye open for a likely wench then."

She slapped him playfully and in front of the assembled men he pulled her to him and kissed her deeply. He looked full into her eyes and said,

"And by God, madame, if you receive any more proposals while I am gone, tell them you are pledged to me."

"Godspeed, my love," she whispered.

Chapter 16

As Guy's small cavalcade drew close to London, the travelers upon the road increased in number with each mile, and then the roads became clogged completely. London was every man's destination, it seemed, from Norman knights to Saxon peasants. There were many parties on horseback, including soldiers, rich merchants and highborn Saxon ladies. Every denomination of holy man was traveling to London. Some, poor priests and friars on lowly donkeys, and some, rich corpulent bishops in ostentatious litters. Wagons and carts hauled and heaved their way slowly on the badly rutted roads that had started out frozen and passable, but were now so mired with mud and befouled with animal dung that a journey that should have taken hours now took days. Farm carts carrying provision into the city dropped everything from autumn apples to winter cabbages, but these were soon picked up and devoured by the travelers in the wake of the oxcarts.

Flocks of sheep and geese were herded between the crowds of people. Even whole herds of cattle and goats were driven forward in one large concerted attempt to reach the capital and turn a profit.

It took a great deal of patience on Guy's part not to ride roughshod over the people on foot, but when he saw others on horseback doing this he determined to push through at a slower pace that left none behind killed or maimed in the throng. He amused himself, with Nicholas beside him, watching the different kinds of people that made up the humanity about them. There was a gaily painted wagon whose inhabitants tumbled and did acrobatics all about the cart and then passed a hat around for coins. Fashionably dressed minstrels with their viols or harps were present, and when the crowds came to a full stop for more than ten minutes, these troubadours strolled about, playing and singing the Song of William and other popular chansons.

The air was thick with insults. The Norman insulted the Saxon; the Norman insults were pale compared to the curses that fell from the lips of the English. Merchants cursed farmers, men swore at women, the young railed at the old and the poor directed their hatred toward the rich. When the travelers passed by huts, the inhabitants tempted them with warm food or drink, or other commodities depending upon the tastes or morals of the passers-by. When they reached the gates of London they surged through with the mass only to discover every street and thoroughfare plugged solid. Their horses became very agitated, and to keep in the saddle required all the expertise their long experience in warfare had taught them.

Every inn seemed overflowing, and the people in the city presented a motley mixture greater than they had ever encountered upon the road. There were black men, men in turbans and Jews everywhere. It seemed that people from every corner of the world were assembled in this one place at this one time. It was almost an impossible task to keep his men together as they sought accommodation, and their quest seemed hopeless until Guy espied Richard de Rules in the throng, and he hailed him as a drowning man would claw at straws. Richard de Rules was very young, only eighteen years old, but he had covered himself with glory at Senlac and ably ruled over a mesnalty of about a hundred knights.

"Montgomery! Well met!" he shouted joyfully.

"We promised to come, but now that we are here, where the hell are we to go?" asked Guy bluntly.

"Follow me, we've taken over some houses along the Strand. We will make room for you somewhere, never fear."

They made very slow progress, and it took an hour before they clattered up to a large mansion with vast stabling facilities in the rear. Despite the cold, they were covered in sweat and needed to bathe and change clothes before they were fit to sit down in the dining hall. Excitement permeated the air because of Christmas and because of the coronation. There were serving wenches aplenty, and Guy noted indulgently that Nick and other of his young knights were already making their selections for their evening's entertainment.

"Enjoy yourselves tonight," he told them sternly, "because tomorrow you will spend the whole day polishing your armor and tack. I want a smart turnout for the coronation."

After supper he left them to their carousing, and Richard de Rules went to seek out Robert de Mortain at William's court.

Christmas Day, 1066, dawned cold and clear. Guy's instructions were to place his men outside Westminster Abbey, along with many more companies of Normans, to guard against any interference with the ceremony taking place within its sanctified walls. They held back the surging crowds and allowed William and his nobles unimpeded access to Westminster.

The highest nobles of Saxony were also present. Inside, they were seated on one side and the French on the other. William's half-brother, Odo, was there, resplendent in his bishop's robes, but it was Archbishop Eldred of York who officiated. The ceremony seemed endless, but finally it came to a climax when the archbishop asked, "Do you consent that he be crowned as your lord?" once to the English and once to the French. There arose such a thundering tumult inside Westminster that the Norman soldiers outside thought William had been set upon. They immediately set fire to the buildings opposite. The soldiers closest to the doors knew that everything went well inside and began shouting to the knights who were creating havoc outside, and in a few minutes the pandemonium without was louder than within. Everyone rushed out to see what was happening, and William received the crown of England alone in Westminster.

It took hours to bring everything back to order, and by the time Guy got back to the palace, the banqueting was well under way. There were so many to be fed and they had to wait so long between courses that an elderly knight remarked, "These benches are so hard, my arse is as sore as a virgin's crotch on her wedding night."

William, who lived austerely for a ruler, usually allowed no drunkenness at his court, but tonight he relaxed his guard and turned a blind eye to the merrymaking festivities. Guy was surprised that so many ladies of the court had come from Normandy and remarked on this to Robert.

"Aye, they can't get over the narrow sea fast enough. Some of them swam over, I think! My own lady will be mad as fire that she missed the celebrations. I received a message only this morning that she has brought my son William and awaits me on the coast. I think I will travel down with you, Montgomery. May I bring them to Godstone to break the journey?"

"It will be my pleasure, my lord," he answered gracefully.

"I wish it were my pleasure," said Robert, wrinkling his nose slightly at the thought of being reunited with his wife so quickly. "We had better make hay while the sun shines. By the rood, Montgomery, you are getting a lot of inviting glances. It must be that scarlet mantle you are wearing." He winked.

Guy awoke very early. He had the clear mind of a soldier whenever he opened his eyes, and he found it almost impossible to go back to sleep. An unbidden picture of Lillyth arose before him, and he could not dispel it. He feared greatly when he was away from her. It was funny that he had only experienced the feeling of fear in connection with her. Never, even before battle, had apprehension filled him as it could nowadays. His mind drifted to a more intimate fantasy, and the desire was upon him. It became so great that his loins ached with longing. He threw back the covers and stepped out upon the cold stone floor. Something must quell this ache that reached clear up to his guts. He fervently hoped that Lord Robert would not keep him waiting too long. He knew that Robert wanted to get his wife and son with the least possible delay and return to Berkhamstead and the enormous building task he had set himself. What kept him in London at his brother's side was obvious. Land was being given out wholesale and all wanted a fair share.

William planned to return to Normandy by March, set everything to rights at home and return to England with his family and full court before the end of the year. Before he left for Normandy he wanted the land distributed to the strongest advantage, and it was a massive undertaking. Guy entered the vast council chambers and eighteen-year-old Richard de Rules made room for him on a crowded bench. Eudo Dapifer, the king's steward, read from a parchment:

"The king has declared that all English lands are forfeit wherever the said English opposed William's coming. The king has appointed the bishop of London and Ralf, master of the horse, as the dual legates responsible for organizing land settlements. Ralf is made earl of East Anglia and receives the manors at Tring. Bishop Odo of Bayeux is to receive the earldom of Kent, and Hugh de Montfort is henceforth sheriff of Kent, and receives as his divisio the castle of Saltwood above Romney Marsh."

Guy was watching Robert's face, for Robert was seated on the main dais with his other brothers. Guy had asked him yesterday what he wanted, and he had replied, "Cornwall."

Guy had lifted an eyebrow. "All of it?"

"All of it!" answered Robert. "William gives generously with both hands, but many have their eyes on Cornwall. What William gives me will tell me immediately where I stand in his favor."

The steward cleared his throat and drank water before he continued. "Count Robert of Mortain to receive Cornwall and to stay in residence at Berkhamstead during the king's absence."

Robert did not betray his pleasure on his square features, but Guy knew he would be well satisfied indeed.

Eudo Dapifer continued, "For his generous

pledge of men, horses and supplies for the English venture, Count Eustace was promised one hundred Essex manors." A gasp went round the room at William's generosity. "William Fitzosbern is to receive the earldom of Hereford. Richard de Rules"—he stiffened beside Guy as he heard his name—"is to be created lord of Deeping and receive Lincolnshire." Eudo lifted his head and commented, "Lincolnshire lies sixty or seventy miles to the north and has not been brought to heel as yet, but we have no doubt young de Rules will have no difficulty in that direction."

Richard's mouth split into a grin and he was well pleased that he would see action again so soon.

"Likewise Richard de Bieufaite is to have Suffolk, sixty or seventy miles to the east, territory not yet secured. The castellaria of Hastings to go to Count Robert of Eu."

William held up his hand at this point. "I should like to make it clear that land can be bought from the crown. I do not want this to degenerate into a scramble for land. Saxons as well as Normans are free to bring me their gold in exchange for land or for the redemption of their own land. I have promised land to many privately and as you can well imagine there will be mix-ups and two or more men claiming the same castle or manor. Let this not bring bad blood between us. In Normandy there was too much of that. I do not want this England to be torn apart with strife and petty wars. I command you all to keep the peace and should difficulties arise, the bishop of London or Earl Ralf have my authority to settle them as they see fit."

It took Guy two days more to make certain that his lands were registered to himself and none other, and he also discovered that other land in his area was up for sale. The going price for a town seemed to be eight or nine ounces of gold.

It was a large party indeed that left London. Guy and Robert de Mortain traveled with Robert of Eu, who was going directly to Hastings, which he had just acquired.

Chapter 17

Rolf grew in strength daily, for which everyone at Godstone heaved a collective sigh of relief. Lady Alison examined André's thigh and pursed her lips.

"I am afraid as the leg heals the muscle will shorten considerably and you will only walk again with the aid of a crutch."

André's eyes burned brightly, and he turned his face to the wall while the horror of her words swirled around and around in his brain. She tried to get him to talk about it, but he would not respond, and later she learned from Rose that he would not eat. Lady Alison sought out Lillyth and confided her fears for André.

"Your words were cruel, mother. Could you not have softened the blow?" she asked.

"It will have to be faced sooner or later; I thought it best sooner," said Alison in her practical way.

"Is there absolutely nothing we can do?" Lillyth asked anxiously.

Alison pondered for a moment, then said without much conviction, "Perhaps if the leg was massaged it would keep the muscle more supple, but it's only a gamble." She shrugged. "Ah, Lillyth, my hands are filled with too many patients, and tomorrow is Christmas. I want our people to enjoy it a little, as in the old days, but I have so much to do."

Quickly Lillyth cut in, "I will take over André's nursing. He will be my patient from now on." She ran quickly up to her chamber and took a small chess set from a low table. She entered André's chamber in time to hear him yell savagely, "Get out!" to Edyth. Lillyth motioned for her to leave the room and went up to the bed.

"I have come to entertain you, my lord."

He turned upon her with cutting words. "It is my brothers who are being entertained at the coronation. I'm being pitied!"

She bit back the quick retort about self-pity that sprang to her lips and smiled at him prettily.

"Come, André, it's Christmas, and I am here to relieve your monotony." His eyes narrowed and his lips set stubbornly in a tight, hard line.

"We will play a game of chess . . ."

"Chess!" he spat contemptuously.

"We will play a game of chess, and if you win, I will tell you a secret I have learned about your leg." The corners of her lips crept upwards, and his eyes opened wide at the mention of his leg.

"What about my leg?" he demanded quickly.

She shook her head and her hair cascaded about her. "First the chess!"

The first fifteen minutes André played without interest until Lillyth said, "I will not tell you about your leg unless you beat me, André." His interest quickened and in just over half an hour and five moves he had maneuvered his queen and shouted triumphantly, "Checkmate!"

"How impatient you are. A Montgomery trait, I think," she laughed. "It will help your leg muscle if we rub it with oil every day. Perhaps we can prevent it from shortening too much."

"Go and fetch the oil now, Lillyth, and I will rub it not once, but ten times a day."

"No, you cannot do it yourself. You must relax the leg and I will rub it for you. I will do it every morning and every evening. I will bring the oil now." She smiled.

She returned with a small stone bottle and a large clean linen cloth. She blushed as she told him, "Drape yourself with this and put the rest under your leg so we don't get oil all over the bed."

Under cover of the sheet, André draped one end between his legs and pulled the other end under his leg and threw back the sheet. The wound had closed, but the edges were red and puckered where flesh and muscle had been cut away. Lillyth took out the stopper and a pungent odor filled their nostrils, not unpleasantly, as she poured out a handful and applied it to the leg. His leg was very sore to touch, but the oil soothed it, and Lillyth's hands were so gentle as she massaged the skin that he lay back and relaxed to the even, sensual strokes of her hands. He became quickly aroused and knew that it was obvious to Lillyth, but she tried to ignore it and kept on rubbing with long, smooth movements. When she had finished she said, "I will bring you some supper now. Would you like me to eat up here with you?"

"There will be merrymaking in the hall tonight; go and enjoy yourself."

"I care nothing for that, André, I will spend the evening with you. Tomorrow we will play another

game of chess, and I will not let you win so easily,
I can promise you."

"Ha! Don't pretend you let me win, for I don't
believe you."

"We shall see," she laughed.

The next day she took out an old game of
snakes and ladders she had had as a child and
they laughed their way up the ladders and down
the snakes.

She rubbed his leg morning and evening, and at
her touch he became aroused every time, but as
Lillyth always ignored this, it soon subsided and
he half-closed his eyes and studied her lovely profile and the golden-red tresses that fell so prettily
about her. It was decided that André could get up
and walk about with the aid of a crutch during the
afternoon, if he were back in bed by six each evening. On the fifth night Lillyth massaged his leg
and he pretended to drift off to sleep, then with a
movement so swift she could not prevent him, he
had her in bed with him, cuddled against his side,
and he was showering her with fiery kisses. She
did not immediately struggle against him, but relaxed and allowed him a few kisses.

"Let me up, André, or I will tell Guy when he
returns."

He laughed in his throat and said thickly, "I
have been thinking about that, sweetheart, and I
know that I can take you here and now and you
will never breathe a word of this to Guy."

She stiffened and tried to pull away from him.
She was a little frightened now.

"He will kill you!" she cried.

"Yes, he would kill me, and that is why you will
not tell him, *chérie*. You would never be the cause
of his having his brother's blood on his hands, because you are clever enough to realize he would
come to hate you for it."

She was fast losing her argument at the logic of his statements.

"Do not be afraid, my darling," he whispered, and she saw her opportunity plainly and laughed until tears came to her eyes.

"Why should I be afraid of such a little thing?" she asked pointedly, stressing the double entendre.

He was immediately offended.

"You are a poor substitute for your brother. He is a magnificent lover." She removed herself quickly from the bed and said lightly over her shoulder, "I will be back tomorrow, and do try to be a good boy!" She spoke to him as she would to a child.

The next morning she went out to the huts of the peasants and sought a young, unmarried wench who would be able to help with André's nursing. Her notice fell on one of the girls who was quite pretty in a cheeky way. She had a head full of saucy red curls and a pert, turned-up nose. Lillyth asked one of the older women her name.

"Ah, lady, you would not want that one up at the hall. She is not a good girl," and she looked at Lillyth knowingly to make sure she got the message.

Lillyth beckoned the girl and said, "I think she is just who I am looking for."

She took her up to her own room and made her bathe and wash her hair. Then she picked out a pretty turquoise blue underdress and tunic for her. "Do you know any games, Bertha?"

"Oh yes, my lady, I know plenty." She grinned suggestively.

"I mean games such as chess," said Lillyth lamely.

"Let me see. I know hide-the-thimble and blind-man's buff, and such as that."

"Well, they might serve. Our patient is the lord's brother and he gets bored very easily. He is getting to be too big a handful for me to manage, so I want you to help me amuse him."

When Lillyth walked into André's chamber with Bertha in tow, their eyes met in amused understanding, and when Lillyth had administered the massage to the leg, she left Bertha and André to their own devices.

Emma counted the days until Esmé's return. She was positive now that she was with child. She felt such security in the knowledge that the moment she told him of his baby he would do the honorable thing and marry her.

Rose discovered that she missed Nicholas with all her heart. The days he spent away in London filled her with apprehension, lest another maid catch his eye, perhaps one who was less shy, and more willing to do his bidding. She had almost decided that if he came back to her, begging for the same favors and liberties, she would give in to him. A picture of his dark, laughing face came into her mind, and she sighed with longing. Then she saw Emma across the room, jabbing at her needlework impatiently, and remembered her fainting and the things that were being whispered about her. She sighed again. Perhaps she would not let Nicholas have his way completely, after all.

Since Hugh Montrose had been gone, Adela had received constant attention from one of the knights Guy had left behind. Adela did not welcome these attentions. In fact, she did everything in her power to discourage the man. In truth, men frightened her. All except Hugh Montrose. Somehow, he did not pose a threat to her. She found herself wishing for his return, for when she shared the evening meal with Hugh, she was safe from unwanted attention.

Edyth was completely miserable. While Guy had been gone, Lillyth had taken over the care of André and had almost excluded her from nursing him. Edyth was sick with worry over his wound. She did not mind if he had a crippled leg, but she knew it would be such a blow to his pride that he would never be the same carefree young man again unless something could be done for it. Lady Alison and Lillyth had wonderful healing skills, and she prayed that their ministrations would be successful, but must they monopolize his every waking moment? When she found out about Bertha, she was so angry with Lillyth she vowed not to speak to her and avoided her at every turn.

Guy and his men, along with Robert de Mortain and six of his knights, rode south with Robert of Eu and his eighty men. Guy offered Eu the hospitality of Godstone, knowing full well what eighty men and their horses would cost to feed, but Eu declined the invitation, saying he wished to reach Hastings with all possible speed.

When they neared Sevenoaks, Guy drew him a map of the fastest route to the coast. At the crossroads they stopped for ale at the inn and Guy took this opportunity to send Nicholas with all speed to Godstone to warn Alison and Lillyth of the exalted visitor who would soon be upon them.

Lillyth looked out from upstairs and saw the huge horse approaching with the tall, dark rider.

Her heart gave a leap and she ran down the stairs and outside without stopping for a cloak. When she saw that it was Nicholas she was only slightly disappointed, as she knew Guy could not be far behind.

"Lillyth, the men are at Sevenoaks and Guy has the king's brother with him. I came on ahead to give you notice," he said.

"Splendor of God," she breathed, "it is not much notice! How many are there?" she asked.

"He's only brought six of his own knights with him and they can be bedded in the armory, so it's just Robert you will have to worry about, at least for the present."

"What do you mean?" she asked breathlessly.

"Mortain is traveling to the coast to bring his lady and his son, William. He is bringing them to Godstone to break their journey, and they will have their whole household with them."

Lillyth turned and fled without listening to more. She found her mother and told her the news as quickly as she could.

"I'll go to the kitchens, you go up and prepare the large chamber, Lillyth."

Lillyth moved all her belongings over to her mother's room, then she took Rolf's clothes from her mother's room and put them in the small chamber next door. She went back to the large chamber and debated about Guy's belongings. Should she leave them here so that he could share with the king's brother? Then she thought about his wife's arrival, and thinking they would wish to be together, she took Guy's things and put them in the small chamber with Rolf's. It took a considerable amount of time before the large chamber was vacant, and she found herself wondering why Edyth never seemed to be about these days. She went to fetch fresh linen sheets for the big bed. She could hear the riders arrive at the stables and hoped Nicholas had had enough forethought to send for plenty of men to tend and feed the horses, as the travelers would be weary and always appreciated help in this direction.

Rolf met Guy and Robert at the doorway to the hall, and Guy swept his arm about Rolf and laughed with great relief to see him on his feet again. Robert shook hands with Rolf, whom he knew from many campaigns. Guy looked about for his women, and seeing none in evidence, he urged Robert to go upstairs and pick out a bed-chamber while he fetched wine to clear the dust of the road from their throats.

Robert looked about the hall with great interest. It wasn't as large as a castle, but by the face, it was well appointed and rich tapestries hung every-where. He idly walked up the stairs and spied Lillyth bending over the huge bed, spreading a fine linen sheet. He went swiftly up to her, picked her up and held her in the air for a moment, as large men are often wont to do when they see a small-boned woman who attracts them. Her mouth formed an *oh*, but no sound came out, so startled was she. "By the face, you are a beautiful little wench, and these damned Montgomerys have you working as a menial. I will take you back to Berkhamstead with me, where I promise you will only have to look beautiful and do the things that amuse you."

Guy coughed behind them and said, "My Lord, this is the Lady Lillyth of Godstone—Lillyth, this is my good friend, Robert de Mortain."

Robert's countenance changed visibly. "My humble apologies, my lady. Montgomery, we should offer every courtesy to our highborn Saxon countrymen. Why is she doing menial work?" His plain, square face showed his annoyance.

Lillyth quickly said, "My lord, it is my pleasure and honor to prepare your chamber for you. Indeed I do not usually do this work, and my mother and I have received every courtesy from our new lord."

"Very prettily done too! My heartfelt thanks, my dear lady. Will you do me the great honor of dining at my side this evening?" he asked formally.

"Why, I humbly thank you, my lord, I would love to. I will have a bath prepared for you immediately. Have you had any refreshment, sire?"

"There is ale and wine below. Will you join us, Lillyth?" asked Guy in a formal tone.

"It would be my pleasure." She smiled at the two men.

When they went downstairs, they found Alison and Rolf serving wine to Robert's men.

"May I present Lady Alison—Robert de Mortain," introduced Guy.

"Ah, it is indeed an honor for me to entertain my countryman," said Alison with great warmth.

Robert replied, "The honor is mine, madame."

Guy smiled. "She is a wonderful chatelaine and indeed none of us could manage without her. Her nursing skills are unsurpassed—witness Rolf here who was done near to death. How is my brother André mending?"

"He is Lillyth's patient, my lord, but you will find she has him completely in hand."

Guy's eyebrow raised at Lillyth, and she hid a smile behind her wine. "He cannot manage the stairs without aid yet, so I think it would be better if you went up to him," she suggested.

Robert quickly spoke up, "I'll come too, lead the way, then I'm for that bath I was promised."

Lillyth could not forestall them and they burst in upon André and discovered him in bed with

Bertha. Raucous laughter assailed Lillyth's ears, and she went quickly into her mother's chamber and closed the door. Only when Robert was safely in his chamber did Guy seek out Lillyth. He enfolded her in his arms and said her name over and over. She felt the prod of his manhood against her thighs, and demurred and tried to pull away from him.

"Sweetheart, don't you know it is the greatest compliment a man can pay a woman?"

"You pay me too many compliments, my lord," she smiled.

He threw back his head in laughter, "Ah, you lay me low, wench. Sweeting, as soon as we are rid of our exalted company, we will be wed, but word of this must not reach William's ears, lest he try to stop it, so we will have to be careful." He bent his head and took her lips, his hands caressing her lovingly.

"I can behave myself. The question is, can you?" she teased.

"I don't know, it has been so long and I have missed you damnably, Lillyth!"

"Is that a present for me?" she asked.

He handed her the parcel. "It is a gown from London, made all in one piece, not an underdress and tunic. As soon as I saw it, I wanted to see you in it. It will cling to your body and show off all your lovely curves." He slid his hand down her body and drew her to him again. "But by all that's holy, if you wear it in front of Robert I will take my whip to you."

He looked so ferocious that for a moment she feared him. She told herself it was ridiculous to fear a man who would soon be her husband, so on impulse she kissed him and whispered, "Or one of your other weapons, my love?"

"You saucy baggage!" he said, but the ferocity had left him.

"I must go and help mother. At this moment she probably needs me more than you do."

"That cannot possibly be." He shook his head.

"Thank you for the present, my lord."

"I will enjoy it as much as you, I have no doubt," he grinned.

Robert de Mortain was a square-built, large man. He looked like a plain soldier except for his rich garments. He had nothing of the polished courtier in his looks; however, his manner toward Lillyth was all gentle courtesy. When she joined him for dinner, Guy was pleased to note that she dressed with extreme modesty, in flowing apricot velvet, and her hair was covered with a matching head scarf. She did not even glance in Guy's direction once during the meal, but he could not accuse her of flirting with Robert, because she kept her eyes lowered and answered him only when he ventured some remark or question to her. She listened to the men's conversation and gathered that they were leaving for the coast on the morrow and that Robert had requested Guy to accompany him. The party that would descend upon them within a couple of days threatened to be a large one, as most of the Mortain household was expected, along with furniture, baggage, servants, horses and priests.

Lillyth glanced down the table and caught Guy watching her. Alison looked at them both. The way they looked, they were mentally caressing each other while separated by the broad expanse of the table. She reflected that she would be glad when their guests had gone and they could get on with the wedding. When Lillyth no longer shared her chamber, Rolf would be able to return to her.

Lillyth retired early and left the men to their wine and conversation, which seemed to be all about land grants and building fortifications.

Emma wore her prettiest gown to welcome Esmé back from London. He was extremely attentive to her every need and sent her promises with his eyes. She was encouraged to the point where she shared her secret with him. He looked at her blankly, almost as if he had not heard her correctly. As the silence stretched out, Emma was at a loss and ventured, "Did you understand me, Esmé? I am enceinte."

"My dearest lady, how could you have allowed such a thing to happen?" Esmé inquired, almost politely.

Emma wanted to tell him it was her dearest desire to have his child. She wanted to cry *"je t'aime,"* but the words stuck in her throat.

He bent his blond head close and murmured, "You must do something about it immediately, before it becomes too late. If you will excuse me, my dear, I have to see the king's brother while he is a captive audience here at Godstone. It is not often such opportunities drop into our lap."

She was devastated but schooled her face so that it gave no hint. How could he have been so cool, so remote? This could not be happening!

Adela sat at a table lower down the hall. When Hugh had looked her way, she had encouraged him with a warm smile, but he certainly had not responded to it in any way. She felt conspicuous sitting without a partner. The room, filled to capacity, was overheated and noisy. When she heard men laughing, she imagined they laughed

at her. With hot, flushing cheeks, she left the hall
and went outside for a much-needed breath of
fresh air. She walked across the courtyard toward
the watchtower. The air was still, but extremely
cold and frosty. Adela's cheeks soon cooled and
she decided to go back inside. When she heard a
noise behind her, she turned, startled that someone was there in the dark with her. She was
grabbed from behind by strong hands, and she
fought wildly to escape his grip. She fell to her
knees, gashing one upon impact with a cobble-
stone. Then she heard someone scream and realized she was making the terrified shrieks.
Suddenly the cruel hands fell away as Hugh
rushed upon the scene.

"Adela! By God, I feared this would happen one
night. Who was he?" he demanded angrily.

"Oh Hugh, thank God! I did not see his face. I
have no idea who it might have been." She was lying. She felt sure it was the man who had been
pressing his attentions upon her while Hugh had
been away.

"I'll find him," swore Hugh, unsheathing a very
nasty weapon.

"Hugh, I cannot walk. I have gashed my knee.
Will you help me to my room?"

"Of course, sweetheart. Here, lean on me. Oh to
hell with it, I'll carry you," he decided. They went
up a back staircase which led to the solarium and
the rooms beyond. Hugh placed her on the bed.
"Let me see your knee," and without waiting for
her to show him, he lifted her skirts back and exposed her limbs. "The blood has come through
your hose." He reached up her thigh to the garter
that held up the hose.

Adela blushed, but made no protest.

"The damned lout!" he swore as he gently
pulled off the hose and looked at the gash. "I

think when it is washed, it won't look so badly, sweetheart. Hold still while I pour some water." He bathed her knee and wiped away the blood that had trickled down her leg. "There now, that's not too bad, is it?"

"You should not be nursing me, Hugh," she protested.

"You looked after my hurt when I needed stitching up. I am just returning the favor." He looked at her differently now. "You look so damned tempting on that bed with your skirts around your thighs," he grinned.

She smiled up at him prettily. "Well, aren't you going to finish the job? Surely you are not going to leave me with one stocking on?" she teased.

As his hand reached up her thigh for her other garter, he bent forward to claim her lips. "Shall we try again?" he whispered.

She responded by fusing her mouth to his in a most inviting manner.

Determined to perform well tonight, he proceeded slowly. He would not rush into bed, only to disgrace himself. He lifted off her head covering and let the soft brown tresses ripple through his fingers. He kissed her eyes and her throat, encouraged when she lifted her face to his for more of his kisses. He lifted her into his lap to finish undressing her. Her fingers, wrists and palms each received his kiss before he moved on to more intimate places. He made love to her with his hands before he trusted himself to make love to her with his body.

Adela lay in blissful abandon. That she was at last receiving joy from a physical encounter filled her with wonderment.

Hugh was also overjoyed that every inch of him responded to her loveliness. His body stayed hard and demanding until he had received all her sweetness, then he allowed himself his final release. It was the first time in her life Adela had ever reached climax, and she silently thanked Morag.

Chapter 18

Three days later, the Mortain household descended upon them. Alison and Lillyth made their curtsies to Lady de Mortain and her serving women. She was a plain woman to look at, but very gracious and friendly, and Lillyth liked her immediately. Lillyth showed her upstairs to the large bedchamber and said, "This is where you and your lord will be sleeping, madame."

The older woman started to laugh and Lillyth was momentarily disconcerted.

"I see you are puzzled. I laugh because we always have separate rooms."

"Oh, madame, I am sorry, please forgive me."

"No, no, my dear. I like the arrangements as they are. I do not get to see my husband often enough to suit me, and if Robert objects to the arrangements, we will tell him your accommodations are not as large as he is used to, and see if we can pull the wool over his eyes, no?"

Lillyth's eyes sparkled as they shared the joke, but the joy left her face a moment later when Lady Mortain said confidentially, "I hope you can put all my ladies together, and preferably away from those Montgomerys. They are the very devil with women, you know. In fact Simonette cannot keep her hands off the eldest one. They had a little affair a few years back, and I can see she will have to be watched closely or it will happen again."

"I will put them in the solarium," Lillyth stammered, and ran lightly down the stairs to see what was keeping the ladies. At the far end of the hall, Guy stood in conversation with a tall, dark-haired girl whose figure could only be described as voluptuous. Her generous curves bent toward Guy as she placed a possessive hand on his sleeve.

Lillyth was oblivious to the crush of people and baggage in the hall as her heart constricted painfully. She was seized with a violent attack of jealousy, a feeling she had never experienced before. This was rapidly replaced by anger, a blinding, red fury that filled her brain and left her panting for breath. She pushed her way through servants and tutors and musicians and priests, caring nothing for the problem of where to stow them all, but only rapidly assessing where she could possibly go to be alone with her thoughts.

She took down a warm cloak from a peg by the door and swept outside, not knowing if the cloak was hers and caring less. She ran out past the watchtower and outbuildings until she came to the mews. She ran swiftly past the surprised falconer and climbed into the loft and dropped down into a pile of hay in one corner. The birds set up a deafening screech, but Lillyth's thoughts were so loud they blocked out the cacophony. Never before had black hair become so ugly, nor full red mouth so utterly repulsive, nor large dark eyes so hateful, and yet, withal, Lillyth had to admit the woman was attractive. She berated herself for a fool and asked herself, Where do you think he learned to make love so expertly? How many beds had it taken before he became so sure and accomplished? Her face was hot with shame as she recalled how easily she had gone into his arms because of a few words of love. He had promised to marry her, but what had he promised the others? What did she really know of him? Her mind whirled, tears came to her eyes, but she dashed them away with angry fists. She was cold and wrapped the cloak about her twice and scrunched down into the hay, trying to bury her misery.

Nicholas had a hasty word with the falconer and climbed into the loft. "My God, what are you doing here? Guy sent me to look for you and it has taken the best part of two hours. Come along quickly, he will be furious."

"Tell him no," said Lillyth firmly.

"I cannot tell him no. He won't take no for an answer," he said flatly.

"From now on that is the only answer he will get from me!" she said passionately.

"Lillyth, what is this all about?"

"If he prefers Simonette's company to mine, I shall be free of his attentions, thank heavens!"

Nicholas left abruptly, and within ten minutes Guy's huge shadow loomed above her. She glared at him defiantly.

"You are being ridiculous," he said shortly.

She raised her chin, and even in the dim light he could see the cold green of her eyes.

"As if I don't have enough on my hands," he said. "Half these people have had to be put up at

Oxstead. I've had to organize a hunt for tomorrow to get meat to fill all these extra bellies. You'd think the least you could do would be to arrange to entertain our guests for the evening."

"*Your* guests," she stressed, "and I am sure you will not have to look far for entertainment."

His eyes narrowed warningly. "Our guests, wife," he asserted.

In icy tones she said, "I think not, Monsieur Montgomery!"

He picked her up and she struggled furiously, but his arms were like bands of iron and her struggles were useless.

"Would you make a spectacle in front of Robert?" she asked incredulously.

"I am master here, not Mortain," he said sharply, and started off for the hall, as straw dropped from the folds of her cloak all the way. Ten yards from the hall he set her on her feet. She brushed herself off furiously and ran toward the kitchen entrance. She shot him a look of pure venom and was shocked to see him laughing at her.

"I'll show him!" she swore angrily.

She bathed quickly and spent a full hour brushing her glorious hair until it fell in shining waves to her knees. She took out the new gown Guy had brought her from London but had forbidden her to wear. It was the finest white wool with a silver thread running through it, and it fitted her body to perfection, accentuating the curves suggestively. She colored her lips and cheeks and stroked perfumed oil between her breasts where they rose from a revealing neckline. She deliberately waited until Robert de Mortain and his wife were descending to dine, and joined them. Robert graciously seated his wife on his right hand and sat Lillyth on his left.

Guy came up immediately and sat beside Lillyth. Points of fire glittered in his eyes as she looked at him.

"Go up and remove that gown immediately," he said quietly.

She looked at him triumphantly and said, half under her breath, "Tear it off me here, or better still pick me up again and carry me from the hall kicking and screaming!"

He lifted a sardonic brow and said, "Ah, *chérie*, there is a much simpler way." He picked up his wine, and she immediately discerned his intention to spill the contents upon her. She quickly raised her hand and as if by accident the wine splashed across Guy's new tunic. Momentary fear took hold of her, but she saw his lips twitch and a look of admiration came into his eyes. He excused himself to change, and as he left the hall Simonette stood in his path. He brushed past her as if he did not even see her. Simonette immediately sought out Nicholas and laughed up into his dark face at every opportunity.

Lillyth felt a moment's satisfaction, then immediately fell to brooding in case Guy ever walked past her in such an insulting manner. She looked past Robert and addressed his wife, "Do you go on the hunt tomorrow, madame?"

"Heavens no, traveling is far too exhausting for me. I shall just rest up for the journey still to come."

Robert turned to Lillyth. "Will I have the pleasure of your company, mademoiselle?"

"I am afraid I find hunting not to my taste, my lord, but I should love to ride with you sometime when you have only pleasure in mind."

He looked at her quizzically and said, "Will you ride with me early tomorrow morning, before the hunt?"

She smiled up at him prettily, and Guy was just in time to hear her say seductively, "It will be my pleasure, my lord."

Guy sat beside her and the more she tried to ignore him, the more aware of him she became. He silently overwhelmed her with his nearness and the charm of his green eyes and magnetic smile.

Ah, God, if only I had the ability to affect him as he does me! she mused, smiling at something Robert said.

If only she had known in what torment Guy sat there, looking calm. He wanted to plunge a dagger into the heart of his friend Robert every time Robert smiled at her. He wanted to take hold of Lillyth and master her and bend her to his will once and for all, so that hereafter she would cleave only to him.

Emma sat down beside Adela so she would have someone to converse with, should Esmé not join her again. As soon as Hugh Montrose entered the hall, his eyes quickly scanned the assembled company for one pretty face. He spotted Adela and slipped in beside her. When Emma saw them smile intimately into each other's eyes, a sharp pain stabbed her in the heart. Ah, God, where were Esmé's adoring glances being bestowed this night?

Eagerly, she watched the entrance for his arrival, but toward the end of the meal it became apparent to Emma that he was not going to put in an appearance. Adela was not unaware of her friend's plight. Although Emma had not confided in her, she had guessed that Emma was with child, and Esmé was conspicuous by his absence!

Adela wondered if she should discuss it with

Lady Alison, but she was almost sure Lady Alison was aware of Emma's condition and had done nothing. Adela decided to tell Lillyth, who had such influence with Monsieur Montgomery. Perhaps pressure could be brought upon Esmé to make him accept responsibility. She looked across at Lillyth, who had her back toward Guy in a most insulting manner and was giving all smiling, gracious attention to her guest. Oh dear, what is going wrong there? wondered Adela. I had better wait until all these people have departed. At the moment it looks like Lillyth is biting off more than she can chew.

The Mortain musicians played throughout the meal and afterward French troubadours with viols and harps entertained. They heard the Song of William and then a young man with poetic dark eyes bowed before Lillyth and asked if she would like to hear her favorite. She hesitated a moment before all these Normans and then deliberately asked if he knew Beowulf. He sang it so beautifully that none was offended at the heroic exploits of the Anglo-Saxon.

Robert smiled at her and said low, "I find much to admire in your England, Lillyth."

"I admire some things that are French, though not all," she said, glancing at Guy.

The dancing began and Robert first danced with his wife and then with Lillyth. Guy watched them, his face marblelike in its set expression. Lillyth slipped away to bed, as she knew she would not be able to bear it if Guy danced with Simonette, or any other woman for that matter. She withdrew before she was humiliated. Guy was in a dangerous mood and she knew he was capable of anything.

* * *

It had only just become light when Lillyth made her way to the stables, therefore she was most surprised to find Robert there before her, personally seeing to the saddling of their horses. They rode out a while until finally Robert said, "'Let us walk a little."

They dismounted, and taking the reins in their hands, they walked slowly over the snow-covered ground. He stopped and took her hand in his. "Lillyth, you could very easily steal my heart. Is that what you are trying to do?" he asked.

She blushed lightly and stammered, "No, my lord."

"Would you consider coming to Berkhamstead? I cannot offer you marriage, but I can offer you my protection, and anything you desire that is within my power to give shall be yours."

"My lord, you both flatter and honor me, but indeed, I cannot accept," she said quietly.

He took a ring from his little finger and placed it on her hand. She shook her head. "It is too costly."

"It is not a gift. I shall merely lend it to you, but should he ever hurt you, Lillyth, bring it back to me." He raised her hand to his lips, and his shrewd, kindly eyes told her that he understood all.

It was still quite early when they returned, and Lillyth hoped she could get back without being observed. Guy was in the stables, however, ostensibly readying for the hunt, but Lillyth knew he had been waiting for her. Like a queen she swept past him without a glance, and went on up to the hall. Guy and Robert looked at each other silently, but their eyes told each other everything that needed to be said about the woman who had just left their presence. Guy's penetrating look conveyed the message that if Robert pursued things further, there would be a showdown, and Robert's cool glance told Guy that he would leave be, for now, but if opportunity arose in the future, he would not hesitate to take advantage. They decided on a truce for the nonce, and all the men at Godstone hunted that day. They came back with such an abundance of deer and game that they wondered how it would ever be eaten.

After breakfast the ladies of Godstone showed their visitors their beautiful cloth and tapestries.

"Ah, these tapestries are a sheer delight. Matilda, William's wife, does wonderful work on tapestries, her ladies are trained specially. At the moment she is planning one all about William's conquest of England," said Lady Mortain thoughtlessly.

Lady Alison asked, "When will the queen be coming to England?"

"Oh, Matilda will not come dashing across the channel as I did. Too much pride! She will make William go and fetch her. Funny is it not, everyone quakes before William, but Matilda, who can't be much over four and a half feet tall, rules him with an iron hand. They are the queerest couple!"

Lillyth hid her smile as she sensed a great deal of rivalry between these two.

"Really, I must sound repetitious, but this is truly the most beautiful cloth I have ever seen. Do you really make such lovely things right here at Godstone? The colors are so bright! How do you obtain this vibrant shade of red?" asked Lady Mortain.

"From the madder root," answered Alison.

"Why of course!" said Lady Mortain. "Why did I never think of that?"

"All our colors come from plants and wild flowers and roots. I have a stillroom full of lovely dyes," answered Alison.

Lillyth spoke up quickly, "Guy de Montgomery has an order for some of our embroidered cloth from King William. He no doubt wants it for when the queen comes to London," she said ingenuously.

Lady Mortain picked up on this immediately, as Lillyth had hoped.

"Oh, but Matilda may not be here for months yet, while I and my ladies are in desperate case for fine material such as this for our court clothes, and of course the climate is slightly different here, and we cannot make do with what we have."

"Why, madame, we would be honored to make cloth for you, and deliver it long before we fill the King's order. After all, yours is the greater need. You may buy whatever you fancy from what we already have made here and take it with you. Mother will be best to advise you on the materials. Just have my Lord Robert pay Monsieur Montgomery for whatever you choose." She swept a low curtsey and was well pleased with the bit of business she had just transacted. They would need gold to buy more lands. Lands that her sons would own someday. She reminded herself for a moment that she was not even speaking to Guy, and the corners of her lips tilted merrily. She would goad him to the end of his endurance. She shivered rapturously over what would happen then.

Lillyth went up to André to massage his leg. Bertha had returned to her home until after the visitors had departed, and André was avid for company. "When the hell is everyone leaving, Lillyth? I am dying to try the stairs, and I am sure

I can get about really well without a crutch, but I'm damned if I am going to do it in front of this lot. I will not be a laughingstock or the butt of their jokes."

"With any luck they will leave tomorrow, but it will take all day to get them on their way, and probably Guy will give them escort for the first few miles."

"Well, I will be glad to see the back of them, how about you?"

"Some of them. André, is it true that Simonette was Guy's mistress?"

"Good God, you do not expect me to keep track of his women, do you? They are legion." Then he saw the hurt in her eyes and became serious. "Lillyth, do not be foolish. I don't think Guy ever looked twice at a woman until he laid eyes on you. And now he is like a dog with a bone!"

Lillyth bared his leg and André lay back against his pillows and let her hands soothe the tensions from him.

Guy swung open the chamber door and checked on the threshold, a look of utter disbelief upon his face. "How long has this been going on?" he demanded.

Lillyth ignored him completely and continued massaging André's limb as if they were completely alone.

"It's not what it seems, Guy. Lillyth is massaging my leg to keep the muscle from shortening. I am determined not to hobble about on crutches for the rest of my life, and Lillyth has been generous enough to help me."

"After these exertions, it is a wonder you do not end up in bed together!" Guy thundered.

Lillyth and André dissolved into gales of laughter. They laughed so long and so hard it brought tears to their eyes, and Guy grew livid that they did not share the joke with him. Finally to try to mollify him, André said, "Do you know what we have been doing here every day while you were enjoying London? Playing chess!"

Guy's scowl did not lessen, and Lillyth tossed her head and threw at him, "If you are jealous, go and rub Simonette's leg!"

She thought he would slam from the room, but he looked at her coolly and said, "Hmm, very pretty legs as I recall. Perhaps I will ask her to stay." Then he left, shutting the door quietly behind him.

André looked at her and said, "You goad him too far, Lillyth."

"If he had seen how bitter and hopeless you were with your face turned to the wall, and compared that with the laughing, optimistic man you are now, he would be thankful for what I have done for his brother; or he ought to be."

"I have been a sore trial to you, Lillyth, but I am determined to walk well again, and then you will know it has been worth all the trouble."

Lillyth put the rubbing oil away, washed her hands and put the ring Robert had given her back onto her finger. Her thoughts went over Guy's words and she believed them to be idle threats. It was all part of a taunting game they played with each other, but at the same time she knew there was a point beyond which she was afraid to go with him. Guy's real anger and Guy's feigned anger were two very different things indeed. She smiled to herself; she was almost to the point of forgiving him.

A soft knock on the door drew Lillyth's attention. She was pleased to see that it was Edyth, but when Edyth saw that André was not alone, she quickly withdrew.

"Edyth, don't run off. I have not seen you in days, where have you been hiding?" called Lillyth.

Edyth came back unsmiling and said stiffly, "I thought perhaps André might need some company for dinner, since he will be missing all the festivities below."

"That is a lovely gesture, Edyth. I am sure André would love some company." André's eyes had kindled at the sight of Edyth. She had taken pains to wear a very pretty pale pink tunic and underdress. He looked at her and said, "Edyth, your hair is like silver moonlight. Would you really prefer my company to the fun of the hall?"

Lillyth smiled to herself as she left. They hadn't even noticed her going.

Lillyth dressed very carefully for dinner, painstakingly fixing her hair in a more elaborate style with ribbon threaded through the curls. She put on a lime-green silk gown that was not really suitable for a winter's evening, but the great press of people below in the hall, coupled with the huge fires, would make the hall stifling. She hurried as she realized she was later than usual. She passed her mother in the hall with a heavily laden tray.

"Lady Mortain has a migraine, so I thought she would be better off to sup in her room."

"Is there anything I can do to help you, Mother?" asked Lillyth.

"No, child, she has more than enough ladies ready to run and do her bidding, it's just that I was damned if I was going to let them take over my kitchens."

"You had better hurry down, Mother, or everything will have been devoured," Lillyth laughed.

She walked into the hall to find everyone already seated. Her eyes went straight to Guy and she stiffened in horror as she saw Simonette sitting next to him in her own place. *In her place!* How could he offer her this insult? Her head went up proudly and she walked slowly and deliberately to Robert's right-hand side and smiled brilliantly at him as he arose to assist her into his wife's place. The ale and wine flowed freely, and Lillyth watched in disgust as Guy kept refilling his horn.

Robert said to her, "I have some goblets which I would like you to have. I don't much care for drinking from these horns. The only problem will be locating them among all the baggage, but never fear, I shall set one of the servants to searching until they are found."

"Thank you, sire," she smiled.

"No, no formalities please, Lillyth. This is wine from my own vineyards we are drinking."

"In that case, I will have some more," and she drank until she was a little giddy. The inhabitants of the hall were in a boisterous mood. The voices and music grew louder and one or two quarrels broke out, mainly because too much alcohol was being consumed. The men and woman were conducting themselves with an abandon unusual in Guy de Montgomery's hall. Dancing began, and the tables were pushed back to make more room. As soon as Guy took Simonette's hand and led her out into the dance, Lillyth seized upon the moment to take Robert by the hand and coax him from the hall. She had made good her escape, and Guy would not notice they were gone for a few moments. She would stay away long enough to make him suffer damnably!

She smiled up at Robert. "The hall was so unbearably hot and stuffy, I thought I was going to faint. You do not mind, do you, if we go for a walk?"

"I always allow a beautiful woman to have her way," he assured her. "Where shall we go?"

"I don't care! Let's get cloaks and go and see the horses, and then we can have a look at the falcons in the mews, and then we can go up in the tower and I can show you the view."

"But it's dark," he laughed.

"Exactly!" she said, closing one eye in an exaggerated wink.

They purloined cloaks from behind the door and went out into the night like two conspirators. The snow was falling thickly, and Lillyth lifted her face to let the snowflakes fall on her. She ran across to the stables. "You can show me your horse," Lillyth suggested.

"You saw him this morning," he laughed.

They stopped before the magnificent black beast and she ran her hand along its glossy flank. "What do you call him?" she asked.

"Satan," he answered, "because he's a devil. I think there is a devil in you tonight, Lillyth."

"Come up into the loft and I'll show you some newborn kittens," she invited.

He looked round at the gaping stablemen and put a restraining hand on her arm. He whispered low, "We cannot. Your reputation would be in shreds if we went up into the hay. Behave yourself."

They went outside again, where she playfully made a snowball and threw it at him. He chased her and caught up with her down by the stream.

"Let's see if the ice is thick enough to hold us," she said excitedly.

"Be careful!" he called.

Lillyth was standing on the frozen surface and she shouted, "Don't be a coward, come on." He took a tentative step and she cried quickly, "No, no, Robert, I was only teasing, it will never hold your great weight. I'm freezing! Come, let us go up in the old tower." She led the way up the spiral staircase, pulling him along behind her.

"Oh, someone has been using it as a trysting place. There are wine and cushions and some wood. Light a fire before we perish. Oh look, here's some chestnuts, let's roast them."

"I would offer you some wine, but perhaps you have had enough?" He eyed her, amused.

"Of course I shall have some wine," she said, rubbing her hands before the welcome blaze he had created.

They settled by the fire to roast the chestnuts, and she leaned against him contentedly.

"I know you are not being serious, Lillyth. I think you are only playing with me."

She looked him full in the eyes and asked, "Well, aren't you playing with me?"

He took her into his arms and kissed her very gently. "You are a widow, are you not, Lillyth?"

"Oh, the marriage was never consummated, let's not talk of it," she pleaded.

"Then you are still a virgin?" he asked.

She blushed and said, "That is not a question a gentleman asks a lady, my lord."

"I'm sorry, forgive me," he said contritely.

A silence fell over them and she gazed into the flames, and gradually her eyelids became heavy and then closed. He did not move to disturb her. Instead he studied her face, which was so close he could see the fine grain of her skin, the flare of her delicate nostrils and the curve of her lovely mouth. After she had slept for about an hour and the fire had died down, he roused her. She opened sleepy eyes and looked at him. He kissed her softly and murmured, "Come, sweetheart, we must be getting back."

She obeyed without question and thought him quite the nicest, most comfortable gentleman she had ever met. They slipped in the back way and crept quietly up the stairs. They paused before his chamber door, and putting her fingers to her lips in a gesture to indicate quiet, she watched him gently open it and disappear within.

She tiptoed along the hallway to her own sleeping quarters, and as she passed Guy's door a strong arm shot out and jerked her from her feet. Before she could cry out, a rough hand clamped across her mouth and she found herself inside Guy's chamber with the door closed firmly behind her.

"You hurt me," she flared, rubbing her lips.

"I am not gentle by nature. In fact I have a reputation for being harsh and cruel."

She turned to flee and Guy swung her around. "Never turn your back on me again," he commanded.

"I am going to bed," she said coldly.

"You will not leave this room," he ordered.

A smoldering defiance took hold of her and she struck out with her nails at his dark, haughty face. He snatched her wrists.

"Very pretty behavior!" His eyes caught sight of Robert's ring and his anger exploded. "You whore! Damn you to hell, you little whore!" A pulse throbbed savagely in his jaw and he raised his hand and struck her full across the face. Bright red blood ran across her cheek and down her neck, where he had opened up a gash in her delicate skin. She swayed toward him and the red madness receded from his eyes.

"My darling, forgive me! Oh, my little love; *mon petit chou*, what have I done?" He cradled her in his arms and was distracted at the damage he had caused her face.

She thought oddly, Well, I asked for it. Her manner toward him did not soften, however.

"Let me go! My mother will attend to me," she said coldly.

Helplessly he let her go, as he knew she needed immediate attention. He had probably scarred her for life.

The cavalcade got under way just before noon the next day, and before they left Guy sought out Lillyth, who had stayed in her room all morning. When she saw him she said, "We have nothing to say to each other," and turned her face away. He saw with relief that the cut on her cheek was not as bad as he had feared, but she was bruised.

"You are mistaken! We have a great deal to say to each other, but it can wait until my return. We have a wedding to arrange," he said, and turned on his heel and left.

Guy held himself stiff and aloof from Mortain and his knights, and made himself useful to the ladies and the baggage train, urging them to keep up with the rest of the party. After they had ridden for three hours, Guy told his men they were to start back to Godstone. He rode forward to take his leave of Robert, who looked at him with kindly eyes.

"She loves you very much, you know, and would have none of me. However, I was at a distinct disadvantage with a wife hovering about, while yours is off safely in Normandy." He smiled. "For friendship's sake I did not tell her you were married."

Guy smiled back. "Good-bye, old friend, and I thank you."

They saluted each other, and Guy's heart was happy that they were not parting as enemies and that he was turning "home," as he fondly thought of Godstone.

Chapter 19

The first thing Guy did upon his return was to put all his things back into the large chamber. When he was finished he looked around with satisfaction and vowed before long to have his Lillyth sharing it with him. During the next couple of days Lillyth avoided him, and try as he might, he could not seem to get her alone. When he realized it was by her design, he finally got a grip on the situation and strode into her chamber briskly.

"Get the fur cloak I gave you, we are going riding," he said.

"I think not, my lord," she answered.

He ignored her words, found her cloak and wrapped her in it. Then he took her arm and pulled her after him, ignoring all protests. In the stable he ordered that Zephyr be saddled, while he saddled his own horse. They rode out side by side into the crisp morning air.

"Lillyth, I am sorry I hurt you. I will never strike you again."

"Ha!" she retorted.

"Why did you deliberately provoke me with Robert?" he asked.

"Ha!" she said again.

He began once more, holding his patience. "This business of Simonette—she means absolutely nothing to me."

"Ha!" she said, louder than ever.

They rode on in silence for a while, then Guy said reasonably, "I am offering to share the present and the future with you, Lillyth. I cannot give you my past."

"Ha!" she repeated.

"Stop making that annoying noise!" he shouted.

"Ha!" she provoked, then added, "You are a lecherous monster, an insufferably arrogant, cruel and whoremongering Norman!"

"You are never again to speak to me in such a manner. I will not tolerate your insolence," he ordered.

They rode on a few more miles, until Guy said, "This is ridiculous. Dismount so we can converse properly."

They got down and stood face to face.

"Our marriage is to set an example to the others at Godstone. I am sure that once our marriage takes place, others will follow."

"I would not marry you if you were the last man on earth!" she taunted.

"Be silent!" he thundered. Lillyth's horse was immediately startled into action, and she galloped off in the direction they had come before either of them could grab her. Guy mounted and picked Lillyth up before him. Her nearness affected him immediately, and he said coaxingly, "I've not had another woman since the first day I saw you, Lillyth, even though there were dozens who would have been willing. I have been completely faithful to you."

"Ha!" she said once again.

"If you make that bloody noise once more, I will put you down and you can walk home."

She felt the statement to be ridiculous since they were many miles from home, so she immediately tossed her head and said, "Ha!"

He stopped his horse and put her to the ground. Then he rode off and left her alone. At first she couldn't believe that he would do such a thing and she stood and waited for him to return. He did not return. Reluctantly, she began to walk. With every step her resentment against Guy melted, and anger built against herself. What a fool she was to deny him, for he was her heart's desire. She loved him, and when his face was dark and arrogant, that was when she almost worshiped him. She had goaded him in the hope that he would take her in his arms and crush her resistance. After the horror of the fate that was her first husband, she was mad to anger and cruelly deny this beautiful man who was her love, her life!

She trudged on, weary and cold, fearful lest he had finally turned from her in disgust. She walked what seemed forty miles, which in reality was closer to four miles, and when she almost sank down with numbed limbs, she saw him coming for her. She gave a glad cry and ran forward with her arms upheld appealingly. In an instant he was beside her, holding her, lifting her before him.

"My love, honey sweet. Let me warm you. Come inside my mantle. There, sweeting—I have been so cruel to you."

She slid her arms around his strong body and buried her face in his shoulder. "I'm sorry for everything I said, my lord. Please forgive me?" she begged.

"Only promise we'll be wed soon, for in truth, my heart, I cannot wait longer."

"Whenever you will," she promised, all submission.

His arms tightened about her and he bent his head for a swift, fiery kiss.

"You will lie with me tonight? You won't deny me?" he asked ardently.

She was silent for a moment, then said very low, "It is my desire to come to you on my wedding night, not before. Indulge me in this, my lord, if you love me?" she begged sweetly.

How could he deny her? He groaned, "Oh, Lillyth, you know not how cruel your request is, but so be it. I have waited this long. We will be wed in two days' time, and if that is not long enough for you, I am sorry, but my mind is set and I will not be swayed."

She smiled her secret smile and thought, It will seem an eternity for me also, does he but know it.

Guy de Montgomery decided to exploit this wedding to the best possible advantage. The actual ceremony itself, which would be totally invalid, would be as private as possible. They would take only Rolf and Alison to the church with them, but afterward he wanted all the knights and ladies to make a large wedding procession and ride slowly past every hut in the village with Lillyth and him. He wanted everyone down to the peasants' children to see the bride and rejoice in the wedding celebrations. The Saxons would see that their lady had accepted the Norman as her lord, and they could do the same without any guilt or resentment. They would invite everyone to come to the hall and feed themselves from tables heavily laden with food. Stag, deer, rabbits and boar from the recent hunt were plentiful and would be supplemented with sheep and perhaps an ox. He wanted the wedding party to ride over to Oxstead and Sevenoaks so the people there would not feel left out of things. All would wear their best clothes, and the celebration would help to make up for a dull Christmas and New Year's. He did not want the feasting to deteriorate into a drunken brawl but genuinely wanted everyone to be happy and share the joy which he felt.

The household was busy from dawn to dusk with preparations, and everyone seemed in an especially good humor. If Guy happened upon Lillyth, he would caress her cheek with a loving gesture and whisper words of love to her. "I will give you slow, shuddering kisses," he would say, or "Do you smile so dreamily, so seductively, because you are filled with love for me?"

She awoke slowly and remembered this was her wedding day, January 20, 1067. She knew she was wanton to marry again so quickly, but she was filled with happiness. Only three months since that other wedding. She put the cloudy thought away from her before it spoiled one moment of this perfect day. She moved slowly, as if in a dream, and, with the help of Rose and Edyth, she dressed in her wedding finery.

She did not wear white, but had chosen a cream-colored velvet trimmed with marten, and her hair was done in elaborate twirls with ribbon and sequin-covered flowers threaded through the loops. They draped her fur cloak about her shoulders and handed her the matching fur muff; she stepped from the hall with her mother, into the pale January sunshine.

This is the end of my winter, she thought, as they made their way to the church. Inside, the priest stood waiting with Guy and Rolf at the altar. Guy wore wine-colored velvet, and her breath caught at the sight of him, so handsome was he.

The air was filled with the spicy scent of incense, mixed with the smell of melted candle wax. Guy's warm hand encompassed hers, and when she made her responses, her breath left traces of misty, white vapor upon the cold air. She was surprised when he put a golden wedding ring upon her finger and murmured, "I have had it for weeks." He bent and took her mouth tenderly, released her, then hugged her to him again. Hands clasped, Lillyth and Guy slipped from the church and ran back to the courtyard. With every step she took, she thought over and over, Lillyth de Montgomery.

A throng of laughing men and women, all mounted, awaited them. Even André had decided that the pain in his leg would not prevent him from riding out with the party. They had decorated her horse's bridle and stirrups with tiny bells, and as Guy lifted her into the saddle and tucked her fur about her, they tinkled merrily.

She was so radiantly happy, it infectiously spread to the whole party and then to the people of Godstone, who came out of their homes to watch the procession go by. Every child that Guy passed was given a coin from his pocket, and all were given their invitation to go up to the hall for the banquet.

"We are on our way to Oxstead, so do not wait for us," he bade them.

When the cavalcade reached Oxstead they did

the same thing, and they all went into the hall to break their fast. The cooks had been extremely busy and most of the guests did justice to the food. However, Lillyth took only a small portion of omelet and followed it with freshly baked bread and honey.

"Don't you think she is sweet enough?" asked Nick.

"I do indeed," laughed Guy.

"Maybe you should have some, it will sweeten your disposition," laughed Nick.

"Me? Why, I have been an angel for the past three days," said Guy, amused.

"Well, one of you is angelic, but I do not think it is you, brother," laughed Nick.

Aedward sat at the end of the hall and Lillyth turned to Guy impulsively. "You don't mind if Aedward comes to the dinner tonight at Godstone, do you?"

He searched her face for a moment, then answered, "I don't mind, but do you think you are being kind? If he is still in love with you, it would be like licking your lips over the poor bastard."

"I have heard a rumor that he has found consolation. Do you not see the pretty little blond by his side?"

"Mmm, how did I miss such a delectable armful?" teased Guy.

"That was an unhusbandly remark, my lord, but I will forgive you for it," she smiled, "if you give Aedward your personal invitation."

Rolf looked at Alison and said, "Shall we follow their lead and be married next week?"

"I thought you would never ask," she answered gaily. "Lillyth, come and kiss your new father."

"Oh, Mother, that is wonderful!" exclaimed Lillyth.

"Congratulations, Rolf," said Guy. "I hope yours will be the first of many."

The wedding party made its way back to Godstone by way of Sevenoaks, and when they arrived the hall was overflowing with the villagers. They were so merry from the food and ale and the happy atmosphere of the celebrations that they began to dance. Guy danced with nearly every village woman, no matter what her age or size, and he encouraged Lillyth to dance with the men. It was nearly three in the afternoon before the last stragglers departed and the ladies of the wedding party made their way upstairs to rest and refurbish their appearance before the formal wedding banquet.

There were many hands willing to ready the large bedchamber. The new linen sheets and pillows had been embroidered with Guy and Lillyth's initials, intertwined. Two of the precious goblets Robert had given her were set out with a flagon of fine French wine, and scented candles were placed about the room. All Lillyth's clothes were brought to Guy's chamber and placed in large coffers with lavender sachets. Her toilet articles and silver hairbrushes, which Guy had never confiscated, were polished and laid out for her. A white silk nightrail and a voluminous white woolen robe were laid across the bed. Logs were laid ready to be lighted before they retired. Lillyth bathed her hands and face with rosewater before she went down, and her hair was rebrushed.

As she descended the stairs, he was awaiting her at the bottom. She took a deep breath. How handsome he is, she thought, seeing his eyes crinkled with good humor. He took both her hands in his and brought them one at a time to his lips. "You look radiant. I'm the luckiest man alive."

"Will you always love me?" she asked.

"More, I will cherish you," he vowed.

The dishes had been prepared lovingly and lavishly. Steaming breast of partridge with sweet almond sauce, roast venison surrounded by spiced crab apples, pickled ox tongues and huge cauldrons of ale with roasted apples floating in raw sugar and ginger filled the tables. One large platter contained a boar's head stuffed with roasted chestnuts. There were no dogs underfoot since Guy had given orders long ago that they be kept at the kennel with a fewterer to see to them.

While they ate, a minstrel sang a song newly composed for Lillyth and Guy, and afterward they played games and danced. Guy couldn't get near Lillyth because all the young knights, with his brothers as ringleaders, claimed their privilege of a kiss and a dance with the bride. When she was returned to his side, he bent close and asked, "Are you weary, love?"

"Oh no, I am enjoying myself, but we can leave whenever you wish." She blushed.

"Nay, love, it is for you to say. This is your day." He touched her cheek with the familiar loving gesture. "When you have had enough, just say some common phrase such as 'No more wine for me, thank you,' and I will take you upstairs."

In a few moments an esquire came by with his wine flagon and Lillyth said quickly, "No more wine for me, thank you," then immediately looked up into Guy's laughing eyes and said, "You tricked me. You saw him approaching."

He hugged her to him, and the assembly banged their dagger hilts on the tables and shouted for him to kiss the bride. He did so, lightly, but a flame shot up between them and Guy's eyes kindled with desire. They needed no words, but rose together in mutual agreement and made their way through the guests. Many followed, and they did not have the heart to forbid them. Guy was borne aloft on the shoulders of two knights, and the girls ran ahead giggling and laughing. The men dropped Guy onto the bed and the girls ushered Lillyth to the opposite side, and from then on the jests became a trifle lewd and most suggestive. Laughing heartily, Guy appealed to Rolf, and within a few minutes he and Alison had herded them all from the bridal chamber.

The fire had been lighted and the candles flickered shadowed patterns on the walls. Lillyth found snowdrops on her pillow, and she looked a question at him.

"I saw them growing in a sheltered spot beside the church this morning. Winter is almost past."

She was suddenly shy, and Guy went to busy himself with the fire and to pour them wine. Lillyth undressed in the shadows, and as she stood hesitant in her silk nightrail, he turned toward her and said, "Come and be warm, love."

He pulled her into his lap tenderly, the wine now forgotten. His mouth was close against her neck, and when he lifted his head and looked at her, she traced his lips with her fingers. She smiled. "Your mouth is blunt at the corners."

"Whenever I lift your hair just so, there is a little tendril that curls upon your neck." He kissed the spot. He wanted to prolong the sweetness and magic of the moment and make it last. The act of domination and submission was coming, but he wanted to temper his mastery with the subtle art of courtship.

Her body was soft and warm beneath the thin material as he caressed her with loving hands, murmuring words of endearment against her hair, and his lips touched her temples and eyelids and finally her mouth. She kissed him back with a tender longing, her hands slipping behind his neck. He carried her to bed and undressed quickly, then quenched the candles. Naked now, he rolled against her. His arms went about her and pulled off her nightrail, and her skin felt like satin beneath his hands as he caressed her back and stroked her legs. Pleasure built and receded as he kissed her breasts and nipples and felt them respond and bud. Every nerve was kindled by his arousing hands and lips. She felt his hard-muscled legs against hers, and her hands caressed the great slabs of muscle in his back. When he moved over her, she arched pleasurably against his hardened manhood. Her body opened to him, and at the shock of his entrance closed on him tightly. Kissing her mouth the whole time, he made agonizingly slow love to her and did not allow himself the final joy of fulfillment until she had reached her peak, and her last shudder of ecstasy had stilled.

Once more he was beside her, holding her tenderly.

"The act of love," he mused. "It is rarely that—an act of love, but it was tonight between us two. I love you so very much, my beautiful one. Always remember that, promise me?"

"How could I ever doubt it?" she asked softly, tracing her finger over his heavy eyebrows and along the strong line of his jaw.

Her mind was like quicksilver, reliving the events since the day she had first met this man to whom she was now bound forever. Part of her felt guilty that she had fallen in love with a man who

should be her enemy. These Norman conquerors
had invaded her country and were sweeping away
the old order and establishing a new one. She did
not know if it was good or bad, right or wrong for
England; she only knew that for her it had been
very right. She offered up a prayer of thanks that
the Norman who had come to conquer Godstone
had been Guy de Montgomery. He was indeed a
chivalrous and honorable knight who had rescued
her from the dragon as surely as any prince in a
fairytale. Here in his bed, in his arms, it all felt so
right. Was it because they were under love's magic
spell or was it preordained, written in the stars,
their Fate inevitable?

Guy's thoughts ran a different course. In this life
you made your own Fate. When you wanted
something, you set about getting it. His mind and
his heart were in agreement that he had made the
right decision to follow William from Normandy
to claim this country for its rightful king. He saw
with clear vision just how great this England could
become under its new rulers. For the most part the
Norman influence was a positive one. They were
clever builders, just lawmakers, strong warriors
who would defend this new land they had
claimed so it would never be conquered again.
They would take the best from the Saxon's way of
life, blend it with the best from Normandy and
produce a new race of Englishmen. He knew a
fierce desire to breed sons upon this lovely creature who had come to him like a prize from
heaven. His arms tightened around her possessively. "Lillyth, my little love."

Her cheek, pressed against him, felt his heartbeat accelerate. She raised up to fill her eyes once
more with his dark beauty, just to be sure she was
not dreaming. With a groan he lifted her hair and
let its silken torrent bathe his chest. He lifted her

onto his body with fierce impatience to be one flesh again. His kiss was so demanding, it stunned her in its intensity. In the last hour he had loved her with a gentleness that had been poignant; now his desire for her raged almost out of control, as if he were making love to her for the first time, or the last.

His savage strength frightened her a little, but she was determined to meet his need. If he wanted everything from her, she would give it; more, she would welcome it. She opened her thighs and slipped over him like a glove.

His hands captured and cupped her bottom frantically in his need to bury himself in her loveliness. Earlier, she had seemed so fragile, so helpless, but now she seemed the mate he had always sought. He was consumed by a virile desire to overpower her, to brand her as his woman and his alone. His mouth possessed hers in his desperate urgency.

Desire coiled in her loins and struck with the piercing force of a serpent. The last barriers between them crumbled and they went over the edge of the precipice together, tumbling into love everlasting. Mated for life. As his hot seed flooded into her, each of them longed to give the other a child.

"Sleep now," he murmured.

"I cannot sleep, it is all so new and strange, and wonderful."

He smiled in the darkness and knew she would be asleep in minutes. He drew her closer in a more comfortable position and offered a silent prayer of thanks that his life finally was set on a course that was satisfying to his soul.

She awoke slowly and stretched luxuriously in the great bed. Turning toward her husband, she found him propped on one elbow, looking down on her. "You have been watching me!" she accused. "I must look terrible."

"The most beautiful sight I have ever seen," he assured her.

She snuggled down under the furs. "The room is cold."

"I'll see if I can rekindle the fire, but be warned, I am coming back to bed."

She giggled as he threw off the covers and swung his legs from the bed. She watched him shyly at first, and then became fascinated at the lithe movements of his naked body. Surely it was the most beautiful body in the whole world. Wide shoulders sloped to the well-muscled back and then on to narrow hips. His belly was flat, his strong legs were long, and between them . . . !

When the fire blazed warmly, he came back and jumped in beside her. He dived for her beneath the covers. "I saw you watching me," he teased her. "Now it is my turn. I want to see you all over."

"No, no," she cried, clinging to the sheets.

"Come on, walk about for me, so I can see you in all your loveliness," he coaxed.

"Oh, Guy, please do not ask me to, not yet. I feel too shy," she pleaded.

"When then?"

"Tomorrow! Tomorrow I promise, but not now, please, love?"

"You should not be shy with me. I can see I shall have to take you in hand." He chuckled deep in his throat, and she turned from him and tried to escape. His arms went around her from behind, and he cupped her breasts with his hands. He nuzzled her neck, sending delicious tremors down her spine. It tickled her; she squirmed as she laughingly tried to evade him. But he pulled her closer until her buttocks came in contact with his swollen phallus and she pretended outrage. "Are you always in that dreadful condition?"

"How unfair! You are the cause of it, and only you have the cure," he laughed. He playfully turned her to him and showered her with kisses, but the playfulness vanished as his passion mounted. He took her mouth almost brutally in a searing kiss that had no end. He was hot with desire and soon lit a matching fire within her that threatened to consume them both. "Lillyth, you drive me mad," he gasped hoarsely. He thrust deeply and she cried out with pleasure-pain. It was soon over, and she went limp in his arms as his tenderness returned. He cradled her and whispered all the things she longed to hear.

Guy was in the armory with maps, drawings and sketches strewn about when she finally tracked down his whereabouts. Plans to enlarge the hall and make it a fortified stronghold were foremost in his mind. The work had to be started while winter gave the men many idle hours, for once spring was upon them the daylight hours would be taken up by planting, along with all that the sowing of crops entailed.

"I want to add two more wings to the hall. One for my own family, the other for you men. When you marry we cannot have you sleeping in the armory, can we?" Everyone laughed, and there were several rude rejoinders.

"Before we start on the hall, we will erect a stone wall all the way around. We will redirect the stream and have a moat and a drawbridge. We will have a bailey, see, like this"—he sketched quickly—"with an inner and an outer ward. These will be large enough to house everyone in Godstone in the event of an attack."

He spoke to Rolf, "Will you go to the smithy

and see that the shovels I ordered to be made are ready? Mortain promised to lend me one of his master builders. One of the monks from Mont St. Michel, I believe, so we are getting the best. He will be directing the masonry when he arrives, but in the meantime the stone can be gathered and the channel for the moat can be dug. Work on the building will not be compulsory for the peasants, but any villagers who work get extra food for their families. I strongly believe that when given a free choice, a man does a better job. Nick, I want you to work with the miller. See to it that more grain is ground. You will be in charge of distribution—so much grain for so much work—you can work it out fairly."

His eyes lit up as he saw Lillyth. "Come in, love, come in."

She blushed as she came among the throng of men.

He beamed. "Come and see the plans we are making. The whole wing here is a nursery." He winked over her head at his men. Her cheeks flamed and her eyes were cast down. Every man's heart went out to her in that moment. Rolf's gruff "For shame to tease the child in front of these rough men," made Guy cease his nonsense, and he drew her to his side with a protective arm. He said low, "Some of the ewes are dropping their lambs already. Would you like to come to the south fold with me to see the lambing?"

She nodded happily, and, hands clasped, they slipped from the armory, the plans momentarily forgotten. Rolf shook his head. "Cooing like doves in a dovecote."

André nudged Nick and laughed. "Listen who's talking! Next week this time, he'll be sighing and carrying on in like case."

Rolf cuffed him over the ear, albeit lightly.

* * *

The little lambs that had been born a couple of days ago were adorable to watch. They frisked innocently around their mothers, jumping over imaginary obstacles.

Guy asked one of the shepherds, "Have we lost many?"

"Hardly any, my lord. It worked out evenly—we lost two ewes and two lambs, so we took the orphans, put the skins of the dead lambs on 'um, and the other ewes took to 'um right away."

"Oh look, Guy, that one has just delivered twins," Lillyth said excitedly.

"They look pretty small. I don't think they stand much chance," he said.

The shepherd said, "If they are left out in the fold all night they won't, but I'll take 'um to my wife. If they stay beside the fire all night they'll be just fine come morning."

"Oh, let me have them?" she asked. "I'll wrap them up and keep them by the fire."

Guy shot a quick frown at the shepherd, who said, "Beggin' yer pardon, my lady, but I think they stand a better chance if yer leave 'um here to us. There's a knack to it, you see."

"Of course. I'm sorry, I didn't think." She smiled.

Guy hugged her to him and said low, "You would be too upset if something happened to them. It's better to leave them here."

Elfrida, a peasant woman, approached Lillyth. "May I speak with you, my lady?"

"Of course. Is there some kind of trouble? You look very upset."

The woman eyed Guy and decided there was nothing for it but to state her mission. "My daughter, she married a man over the next fief to ours."

She pointed off to the west. "They don't want to stay there no more."

"They are quite welcome to come here. We can use willing hands on our land anytime," said Lillyth.

"Ah, my lady, if only it were so simple." She hesitated, and kept sending quick furtive glances in Guy's direction. "The Norman lord over there is so cruel, my lady, they are treated like animals— worse, like slaves. They are kept in chains and whipped and given no decent food. My daughter escaped, but they caught her husband and took him back. I have hidden her in my hut." She looked defiantly toward Guy.

Lillyth turned to Guy, ready to plead the woman's cause, but he cut in quickly. "I think it is time I made the acquaintance of my neighbor. How far is the next fief, love?"

"At least ten miles, perhaps as much as fifteen," answered Lillyth.

"Have no fear, Mother, I will get your daughter's husband released from this man, and gain her lawful release also."

"Oh thank you, my lord, thank you." Elfrida knelt before Guy and the tears of relief fell down her face.

"Come, Lillyth, I must tell a few of the others to saddle up and come visiting with me."

She looked at him fearfully. "Oh, Guy, I don't want any trouble."

He laughed. "Neither does William, by God. The last thing he wants here in England is petty wars and fighting between the landowners. In Normandy there was so much of it he was sickened."

"But how will you get what you want without trouble?" she asked.

He looked at her worried face. "There are many

ways, dearest, stop worrying. If necessary, I will trade for the people we want, or if all else fails, I will have to buy them."

Lillyth felt uneasy all afternoon but tried to keep telling herself that Guy knew how to take care of himself. The afternoon drew in fast, and the light went from the sky early. She kept listening for his return and thought she heard horses approaching many times, but whenever she looked out she was disappointed. When he had not returned in time for the evening meal, Lillyth found that she was too worried to eat. She took some food for Guy up to their chamber and placed a clean cloth over it, then sat down by the fire to await his return. She found herself praying for his safety, Just when I found him, do not let anything happen to him. Do not let him be taken away from me, she pleaded. Another hour passed. It was completely dark outside when she heard the unmistakable sound of galloping hooves. She fled from the room, down the stairs, and ran out to meet him.

"Oh, Guy, thank God you are safe!"

He picked her up and swung her around. "What's all this? Tears? Whatever is the matter with you, you silly child?" he chided her.

Each man with him wished he had someone to give him such a welcome as this.

They went up the stairs with their arms entwined about each other.

"Why are you so late? Was there any trouble? What happened?" she asked.

"Nothing happened, love." He shut the door.

"What do you mean, nothing happened?"

"I simply made the acquaintance of our neighbor."

"But what about the poor woman's husband, wasn't there any trouble?"

"I never mentioned him," he said.

"Do you mean to tell me that I have been here worrying myself to death about you and you did nothing you set out to do?" she flared.

"Lillyth, you must not fall into the habit of worrying about me whenever we are apart for a few hours. It is foolishness! You are a nervous wreck, filled with anxiety for me, and all for nothing. As for the other matter, it is not so simple that I can walk in and take a man away just because I want him. It is a deeper game than that. As a matter of fact, I have invited our neighbor and his wife to your mother's wedding."

"In God's name, why?" she asked.

"For one thing, to let them see there are other ways for Normans and Saxons to live together than the way they are going about it."

"Was it very bad?" she asked anxiously.

"Yes, but I refuse to depress you by discussing it further." His voice held a note of finality. "Come and give me a kiss."

In the circle of his arms, she said, "I have saved you some food, are you hungry?"

"Yes, very, but not for food," he laughed, and his hold tightened. "Besides, I have already dined."

She pulled away from him. "I would not break bread with people I did not approve of; that is being a hypocrite."

He cocked an eyebrow at her but held his tongue. "I saw some lovely land on my travels today." He grinned at her. "If we are to have sons, I will have to get busy acquiring more land."

"Does this land belong to the Norman?" she asked.

He shrugged. "Some of it. Here, let me show you." He quickly drew a map for her, showing their land, and then the river along the western boundary, and then the land the Norman held in the next fief.

"The fields on the other side of the river are very good land; they must yield bountiful crops. I have my eye on those, but there is more land just north of the fief that certainly doesn't belong to St. Denys—that is his name, by the way. The sooner I can get my hands on the land around here that is not claimed, the better it will be for all of us. You know I have half-promised Oxstead and Seven-oaks to my brothers when they wed. Does that bother you, Lillyth?"

"Of course not. They are my brothers now."

He poured himself some wine. "I thought perhaps you might wish to keep that land for our children."

"If you are so generous to your brothers, what will you not do for your sons?" she said smilingly as she undressed and got into bed.

"Most women would be jealous of my generosity to my brothers. Thank God you are not one of them." He studied the map. "Ah, Lillyth, I have great plans for the future, you will see."

"I also have plans. I want André to marry Edyth and of course Nicholas is to have Rose."

"Save me from your matchmaking. Men like to do their own hunting, love."

"I am content to let things take their natural course. For the most part," she amended quickly. "Darling, there is one man whom I wish you would give a good talking to. I believe his name is Esmé. You remember when Emma fainted in the solarium a while back and we suspected she was with child? Well, it is Esmé's child, and since she told him of it, he has been avoiding her like the plague."

"What do you want me to do about it?" he asked.

"Order him to marry her!" she replied.

"And what chance would she have for happiness if he was forced reluctantly to wed? Do not ask it of me, Lillyth."

She decided she would handle the matter herself. "Drink your wine and come to bed, or we will never have those sons you keep talking about."

"Can't wait to get your hands on me, can you?" he grinned.

He undressed quickly and came to her. He took her hair in great handfuls and buried his face in its exquisite perfume. "Oh, Lil, I love you so much."

When daylight filtered into the room, Lillyth slipped quietly from the bed and dressed quickly, one eye on Guy's sleeping form. He was not asleep, however, and smiled to himself as he guessed what she was up to. She tiptoed from the room and closed the door behind her very quietly. As soon as she was through the door, he sprang from bed and pulled on his woolen chausses and was out the door after her. He listened for a moment and heard her voice, along with the other women's, coming from the solarium.

He went in and without a word picked her up in his arms, and on his way out said, "Sorry, ladies, Lillyth has a little matter of a promise to fulfill."

"Guy, whatever are you doing? What will they think?" she asked, outraged.

"They will simply think that we are newlyweds playing love games, *chérie*." He set her down inside their chamber and said, "Your promise, my lady."

"I don't know what you are talking about." She blushed.

"You know exactly what I'm talking about."

He took off her tunic and dropped it on the bed, then he took off her underdress and placed it with the tunic. He took off her slippers and stockings and unbound her hair. She shielded her nakedness with her arms. "Don't be shy, my beloved," he pleaded.

She stood before him proudly now, and saw the light come into his face as he looked at her worshipfully.

"Do I please you?"

For answer he went down on his knees before her. He drew her to him tenderly, and his lips explored all her private beauty he had been longing to know. She had to bite his shoulder to prevent herself from screaming in excitement.

She was secretly delighted that he could receive such deep pleasure from kissing her there. Her cheeks were pink with pleasure. Surely if she allowed him this intimacy in the full light of day, she would never be shy with him again.

His thumbs spread her woman's center so he could fit his mouth more closely and enter her with his tongue. Now she could not contain her cries of excitement. The tip of his tongue licked the hard rosebud hidden within, then circled it slowly over and over until she was swollen with need. She sighed and panted and begged him to move faster to give her release, but Guy knew that the slower she built to her peak, the more profound would be her orgasmic climax.

When she began to writhe and cry, "Guy, please . . . sweet god!" he knew she was reaching the limits of her newborn sensuality. He sucked her hard, then thrust his tongue within her honeyed sheath to experience her every tremor.

Later, when she recovered from his loveplay, she

walked about the room for him, enjoying his eyes upon her newly awakened body. She had the tawny look of a lioness. She was ripe, she was ready, she was woman.

Chapter 20

Edgarson was thrilled about the building and was trying to fire his father with enthusiasm.

"I could watch them all day! Please say you will work on the building and then I can help you. I want to learn all about it!" he pleaded.

"I thought you wanted to work in the stables?" asked May.

"No. This is what I want to do. I heard the master telling his plans to some of the men. It's going to be like a big castle. When I have learned all about building, I will be able to build us a big house with two rooms, one for cooking and the other for sleeping."

He was so enthused, his mother smiled to herself. Well, it was nice to have dreams. Edwina was deliriously happy with Aedward, and he had taken her to live in the big hall at Oxstead. So sometimes miracles did happen.

Edgar looked at his son and shook his head in disbelief at the youngster's passion for this building.

"All right, I'll do it, and I will speak to the master about letting you help."

"Tomorrow!" insisted Edgarson.

* * *

This time the church was filled to overflowing.
The smells of incense, candle wax and sweat inter-
mingled as the priest said the holy words over the
middle-aged couple. Lillyth held Guy's hand
tightly, and they stole glances at each other every
few moments. Guy wished with all his heart that
his own wedding could be as true and binding as
this one, but with a sigh he vowed over again to
cherish his "wife" who was in truth more of a wife
to him than the real one had ever been.

The St. Denys party did not arrive until later in
the day. Guy was the jovial host while Lillyth was
looking to a dozen things at once, making sure
that her mother's day went as smoothly as her
own had. The St. Denys party brought along two
knights for escort, and Guy ushered them into the
hall with a hearty welcome. They were outraged
to find Saxon peasants strolling about, laughing
and helping themselves to food.

"Montgomery, if you let these people have free
rein of the fief, I warn you that they will murder
you in your beds!"

"These are my people, St. Denys, and I assure
you I have had no problems whatsoever with
them," Guy said.

"They are just biding their time. This system of
yours cannot work. They hate Normans worse
than poison! They are a conquered people and we
are their masters, therefore there is no way possible for friendship to flourish."

"Relax and enjoy yourselves. I am sure nothing
will happen today at any rate." Guy went to bring
them wine. Across the room André walked with
his arm across Aedward's shoulder. The two
shared a joke and the blond head of the Saxon was
close beside the black one of the Norman. St.
Denys glared his disapproval. Marie St. Denys

was staring at Lillyth, who had just come downstairs.

"By the face, look at this one all decked out like a queen. Obviously someone's whore! I never saw such a brazen bitch in my life." She dug St. Denys in the ribs. "Look at her hair all uncovered, and the way she walks. She is plying her trade right here in the hall."

St. Denys stood slack-mouthed at the vision his wife referred to. St. Denys was darker of countenance than the Montgomerys, with a thin, almost evil face, but at the moment it was filled with unconcealed lust. The Saxon women were very much to his taste, and his wife hated all Saxon women because of it. He took them on his own fief whenever and wherever he felt like it.

Guy took Lillyth's hand and brought her over to be introduced. Marie St. Denys almost turned away, as she was loathe to meet Montgomery's leman, but she did not quite have the audacity.

"Madame and Monsieur St. Denys, this is my lovely lady, we were only wed last week." Guy looked into Lillyth's eyes and brought both her hands to his lips, then, putting a protective arm about her, he looked at his guests so that he could gauge and enjoy their reactions. Envy stood out all over St. Denys, while his wife gave birth to a hatred that needed a vent.

"Darling, please see what is keeping Rolf. I think Mother is ready to come down now," said Lillyth.

As soon as Guy left, Marie St. Denys said to her, "Surely the ceremony that took place last week was not a legal one. Did you never suspect that Montgomery might have left a wife behind in Normandy?"

For one moment Lillyth felt as if a knife had been plunged into her, but she instantly dis-

missed the hateful words and smiled her own secret, seductive smile. "Ah, what a delightful
sense of humor you French ladies have. I discovered that when we entertained my lord Robert de
Mortain and his lady two weeks ago." Lillyth
swept away from them with this parting shot
and determined not to hold further conversation
with them.

"The king's brother stayed here?" bristled Marie
St. Denys to her husband.

Later, when much wine and ale had been im-
bibed, Guy put forth a suggestion to St. Denys. "I
am so sure that my theories will work that I
would be willing to make you a proposition.
Give me your worst man. Someone who runs
away habitually and needs the whip to make him
work, and I'll keep him for two months. If at the
end of that time he has attempted to run, or
needs the whip just once, you can have all my
fields for planting on this side of the river," Guy
said.

"What would you gain from that, Montgomery?"

"Nothing! However, if he turns out to be a willing worker without the lash, then I will plant the
fields on your side of the river."

St. Denys laughed shortly. "I have a man who
has tried running three times in spite of whippings
upon his capture that have nearly killed him. You
are welcome to him for two months—in fact,
you are welcome to him permanently, but it is a
sure thing that I will be planting your fields when
spring comes."

"It's a bargain. Send him over tomorrow. Now,
can we offer you hospitality for the night?" Guy
asked.

"No, no, we must get back. I'll have one more

cup, then I fear we shall have to depart. It has been a pleasure, Montgomery. I will be over in a couple of weeks to see how that Saxon is doing."

After the nuptials had been thoroughly celebrated and the couple was bedded, Guy and Lillyth were the last ones to seek their chamber. "My little scheme seemed to work sweetheart! We should have our man back here tomorrow."

"What terrible people they are, Guy. She was so unpleasant to me, and for no reason whatsoever."

"Sweetheart, she had a hundred good reasons. Your beauty was enough to put her in a jealous frenzy. I am afraid she hates you very much. Do you mind?"

"The whole world may hate me, save you," she smiled.

He bent his lips to hers, and mouth fused to mouth, he caressed her tenderly. He drew her closer until their bodies touched at every point, then without taking his mouth from hers he lifted her into bed. His loveplay went on and on until she lay beneath him in a wanton sprawl. His iron grip told her that he could wait no longer, as in truth, neither could she. She arched her body to meet his, and he was pleasantly surprised at the passionate responses he had unleashed in her. Afterward, as they lay in the haze of love, she whispered, "Was I very wicked?"

"Deliciously so," he whispered back.

She cried out once in the night from a dream of dark shadows, but he was there instantly, drawing her down into strong arms.

The monk from Mont St. Michel, who was called Sebastian, arrived, and the building and fortifications went ahead with great speed.

Edgarson was always to be found at the center

of things, so much so that his father was afraid he was under everyone's feet. One day he spoke to Montgomery. "Forgive him, my lord, but I cannot keep him away."

Sebastian the monk spoke up. "The boy has a love for building equal to my own."

Guy asked, "Do you think he could learn from you?"

"The best time to learn anything is at his age. I will apprentice him, and by the time he is a grown young man, he will be the master builder of Godstone."

Guy agreed readily. He was all for teaching his people new skills.

Once more Emma found herself compelled to visit Morag. It was obvious to Morag that Emma was at the end of her rope, not knowing which path to take. She had wanted to conceive badly enough, but now that the child was beginning to show, she wanted to be rid of it.

"Morag, you must help me," she pleaded.

"No. The master has forbidden me. This is no simple matter of bringing your courses down because they are a few days late. This is to deliberately destroy a child!"

Greediguts spotted a sparkling brooch at Emma's neck and flew down to peck at the shiny object.

Emma screamed. "It tried to kill me!" she sobbed.

"Nonsense, woman. Magpies are collectors." The intelligence of the average woman is abysmal, Morag muttered to herself.

"Then if you will not give me a potion to drink, make me a spell," begged Emma.

"Foolish, foolish! Think you if you walk backward, or spit in the fire or bow to the raven it will keep the sinister gods at bay?"

"Are you trying to tell me the old beliefs are all nonsense?" asked Emma.

"Some believe one thing, others another. Do you really think a deformed child is one the fairies have replaced? And do you believe if you whip it enough they will come and take it away?"

"I could not whip a child," said Emma, sinking onto a low stool.

"You will make a good mother. Go now and believe with all your heart that the father will decide, for one reason or another, to support you in your great need," declared Morag with total conviction.

The ladies spent their days weaving and embroidering the beautiful cloth which had been ordered by the king and by his brother Robert. After the evening meal, Guy usually went over building plans with his men, but if he went upstairs to get drawings or maps, they knew he would not return that night, for as soon as he saw Lillyth all thought of buildings and plans vanished from his mind.

On days when there was such a downpour it was impossible to work outdoors, Lillyth knew that Guy would begin to tease her and then to steal kisses and sooner or later find an excuse to lure her to their chamber, where they would lose themselves in each other's arms in the huge bed.

Guy decided to have the sheep-shearing as early as possible so that he could take some of the winter fleeces to London along with the cloth. When he got back, it would be time to start thinking about planting.

"I am so excited about going to London, Guy. I

have never seen it, you know," Lillyth said as she mended one of his chainses before packing it for the journey.

He looked at her in astonishment. "Sweetheart, you aren't coming with me to London. What gave you such an idea?"

"Oh please, Guy, you wouldn't leave me behind, would you?" she pleaded.

He shook his head. "Nay, love, we sleep on the road the first night. It wouldn't be fitting."

She could not believe he was saying no, as he had been able to refuse her nothing since they were wed. She went up to him, stood on tiptoe and slipped her arms about his neck. "I have been so looking forward to it, Guy. We can spend time alone together away from the hall for the first time. Please?"

Green eyes looked down into hers and he could not hide his amusement. "Playing the temptress will not work, Lillyth. It would be unsafe for you, so the answer is no."

She was disappointed and angry, so she left him. He treats me like a child, she thought. Then she conceived of a plan to go without Guy knowing. If she could get part of the way without his discovering her, she did not think he would make her return home. She packed her things along with his and put them in the baggage cart, along with the bolts of cloth and the bales of wool. Guy was taking his campaign tent for the night on the road, as it was still quite cold. Provisions for the journey for both the men and the horses were also packed in the baggage cart.

Lillyth waited to see which men Guy would take with him. He chose his three most seasoned knights, skipped Rolf because of his recent marriage, and as an afterthought told Nicholas he could come along. Lillyth was delighted. She explained to Nick that she wanted to go in his place; she would need his horse and his armor.

"And what do I get in exchange for giving up my trip to London?" He winked at her suggestively.

"Oh, Nicky, do not tease me. I am deadly serious! It is a surprise for Guy."

"It will be a surprise, all right," he chuckled. "By God, it's worth it! It's a fine joke to play on him. Mind you, do not involve me in this when he discovers you. He has eyes like a hawk, you know; likely you will not get away with it."

"I'll get away with it," she vowed.

The night before they were to leave, she put Nick's chausses, mail shirt and helmet in a coffer in her chamber, along with a pair of her own leather boots and gloves. When Guy came to bed, the quality of her silence told him that she would have none of him. However, he chose to ignore the warning and reached for her. She pulled away from him quickly and turned over to face the other way. It was the first night she had denied him since they were wed. A small frown creased his brow. Perhaps I should take her along, he thought. Then he considered breaking down her defenses, which he knew without doubt he could do in short order, but then he thought, She is just waiting for me to capitulate. I will not be ruled by the wench.

When he arose before dawn, she was sleeping so peacefully and innocently beside him that he did not wish to disturb her. Besides, he feared her tears and what they might do to him. His lips brushed her forehead in farewell and he was gone, carrying his sword from the room quietly. She waited two full minutes and then opened the coffer and dressed in Nick's attire. She skipped breakfast and made her way by stealth to the stables where Nicholas had promised to meet her.

"Now, tell him you will bring up the rear with the baggage cart, don't forget. Thank you for saddling your horse for me, I would never have managed in this damned chain mail," said Lillyth.

"It's too heavy for you, Lillyth, you will never hold yourself up in the saddle," he protested.

"I will manage for a few miles. Here they come," she hissed. "I will hide in the back stall."

Totally ignoring the sleepy-eyed stableboys, she crouched down in the stall and held her breath. Guy's voice came to her loudly. "Nick, where is your mail and helmet? You are not traveling without them!"

"Half-asleep, I guess," Nick apologized. "I'll get them. You go on ahead, I'll stay with the baggage cart for a while, then later on I'll trade places with one of you."

The party set out and Lillyth came from hiding. "Quick, give me your cloak, I'll stay behind the cart where I cannot be seen very well. It's still dark out anyway. Wish me luck."

Her face was alight with the excitement of the escapade and Nick shook his head. He only hoped Guy did not wipe that smile from her face too soon.

By the time they had traveled for an hour and it came a little lighter, Guy noticed his men looking at him askance, and he immediately wondered what was going on. Were his men planning to stay in London and go home with William at the end of the month? He dismissed that thought. If they were about to desert him, at least one of them would have been man enough to tell him before this. He glanced back toward the baggage cart and was surprised to see the rider in the rear duck out of his line of vision. He immediately knew it wasn't Nick because of the size, and he knew instinctively that it was Lillyth.

For a moment he was angry enough to strike her, then as he pondered what he would do, he cooled down a little. After all, she knew how angry he would be, but she had dared his wrath just to be with him. He softened a little. He knew if he went to her and ordered her home she would defy him in front of his men. He could make her obey, but it would not be a very pleasant scene. She had won her point, but if she wanted to have her own way, she would have to be willing to take the consequences! What he knew would happen sooner or later occurred. A wheel of the baggage cart became caught in a deep rut, and strain as they might the oxen team could not pull it out. Guy rode toward the cart and shouted, "Be a good lad, Nick, and take care of this, will you? I suppose you will have to unload everything, pull the oxen ahead out of the rut and then load everything back on the wagon again. We needed a rest anyway. When you have done, come and join us in a drink," and he rode off and motioned the other men to follow. They dismounted under some trees and Guy poured ale all around.

"You cannot let her struggle with that lot," Hugh protested.

"When she comes to beg my pardon and ask for assistance I will give it to her, and not before!" he stated.

He settled back, prepared to enjoy himself.

Lillyth was almost fainting from the weight of the helmet and chain mail, and the chore she now contemplated was gargantuan. She struggled with a few items, but she could not do the job. She took off the helmet and wiped her brow. She knew the moment had come when she must face Guy. Then, like a revelation, she thought, What if he knows I am here? Surely they would not leave Nicholas to cope by himself while they sit drinking under the trees? What if he is just waiting for me to beg his forgiveness? She tugged down a bale of wool, lay down in the roadway and rolled it on top of her. Then she gave a little scream, closed her eyes, and waited. Before she could take two breaths, Guy was kneeling beside her.

"Dear God," he prayed, "do not let her be hurt."

She peeped between her lashes and saw his face so white that she took pity on him. "Oh, love, do not worry, I am not hurt."

They must have presented such a ridiculous picture sitting on the roadway that Guy started to laugh. She struggled up a little and said, "Get this damned smelly wool off me, it's probably lousy."

"You little bitch," he laughed, "I'll have to get me a long rod to use on you."

"You have a long rod you use on me," she said wickedly.

"Lillyth, sometimes you shock me," Guy said.

"Help me off with this chain mail; I don't know how you endure it."

"We only have one tent with us, my dear, you will have no privacy tonight."

"Neither will you," she said mischievously.

"I do not mind an audience," he threatened.

"Oh, you would not!" Then she saw he was teasing her.

When they arrived in London, Guy found them a comfortable inn and took two bedchambers. Their room was spacious with a lovely fireplace and a window overlooking the busy inn yard. Guy left Lillyth alone while he and his men took the cloth to William's court. He was determined to sell the wool today so that no guard would be needed all night. He asked his men if they would like to deliver the other order of cloth to Robert at Berkhamstead, which would leave him free to show Lillyth about London for a few days. The men readily agreed, and he put Hugh Montrose in charge because he knew the way, having been with Guy on his previous journey.

Chapter 21

As Hugh had ridden away from Godstone he had found it a wrench to leave Adela behind. The farther away he got, the more she was with him in thought. He worried that she might be molested in his absence, though he had warned her over and over not to take foolish chances by walking alone, not even in the daylight. He had almost decided to ask Adela to be his wife. He had been a confirmed bachelor all his life, mainly because he had never seen a union that brought happiness, but as he observed Guy and Lillyth, he realized he was letting the years slip away and it was time to grab his happiness with both hands, before it was too late.

Back at Godstone, Adela sang to herself as she went about her day. Her thoughts dwelled again and again on Hugh Montrose, and she realized that she looked forward to her man's return rather than dreading it as she had in the past. She laughed to herself as she thought of the day she had unstitched the mattress to remove the knotted ligature. She felt most benevolent toward Morag and decided to take her some damson jam preserves as a treat. She wanted to ask

Morag about that ancient custom young women observed when they wanted a proposal of marriage. If she remembered correctly, the rite involved baking a cake with flour and soot, eating one half and putting the other half under your pillow. Or was it baking a cake with black and white beans in it? If you got a white bean, the answer would be yes. Well, Morag would be able to tell her.

Morag was not at her own hut, but was with one of the peasant women who was in labor. Accouchements always had a morbid fascination for a woman, so Adela went along to Elfrida's hut. The hut was crowded with women. Elfrida's daughter lay on a rush mat on the floor, swollen with child. She had apparently been in labor for two days, and they had sent for Morag as a last resort. Morag felt caught between the devil and the deep blue sea. She gauged that the girl was too far gone and would die anyway, so she was loathe to touch her. She did not want to be blamed, and human nature being what it was, she knew she would be blamed if she tried and failed. She observed the women's attitudes closely. The younger women, who would probably find themselves in like case, begged for help for the girl. The older women, past childbearing age, were more callous, saying it was nature's way to suffer in childbirth.

Finally Morag was challenged to act or lose her position in the village pecking order. Without touching the young woman in any way, she directed the other women to fill an empty eggshell with hops and malt, heat it in the fire, and make the mother-to-be swallow it.

Adela watched in horror as they fed it to the woman writhing in labor, and it induced the wretched creature to vomit and then to scream. The talk inside the hut was ghoulish. One woman declared the child was too big to come and would crush the girl's insides and she would bleed to death. Another agreed, saying, "It's the heads! All the children born in that family have big heads. It will tear her to pieces to deliver it."

Adela left the stench of the hut and ran up to the hall as fast as she could.

"Lady Alison, you must come quickly! Elfrida's daughter has been in labor for days, and they are resorting to spells in their ignorance. It is like a nightmare in that hut. I hate to go back there, but we must try to help the poor soul."

When Alison saw the girl lying in a pool of sweat, her waxy pallor indicating that death was standing patiently, waiting until the last possible moment, she took over instantly.

"Clear this hut!" she ordered. "You too, Elfrida—outside."

She looked at Morag. "You know better than this, woman, for shame! Go up to the hall with Adela. She will give you clean sheets. And go to my stillroom and fetch me some pennyroyal. You will recognize it by its pale purple color."

When Alison was entirely alone with the young woman, she examined her and found that the child was coming buttocks first. Gently and slowly, she inched the little body back up the birth canal as far as it would go, turning it into the proper position for delivery. The girl gave a few pathetic screams, but she had screamed for so many hours she was almost beyond it. When the two women returned, Alison issued orders left and right. They lifted the girl onto the clean sheets and mixed the pennyroyal with warm water. It had a hot, aromatic taste which immediately stayed her disposition to vomit. The herb would help expel the child whether dead or alive. It was like a miracle. Suddenly two feet were presented, then the buttocks slipped out and finally the shoulders and head were freed with a little help from Alison. She heaved a sigh of relief, as did Adela and Morag standing to one side.

The young mother had mercifully swooned and would likely recover if there was no hemorrhaging. Alison sat back on her heels. "Women have a thousand things in their lives they just cannot face, but somehow we do. We cope!" The other women silently agreed with her.

"Send in Elfrida, she will be able to manage now."

Adela walked slowly back up to the hall. She asked herself if she really wanted another marriage and all it entailed. The answer came back a resounding yes! This was what life was all about.

When Guy had concluded all the London business and the men were on their way to Berkhamstead, Guy and Lillyth found themselves alone for the first time since they had met. In the privacy of the snug chamber their love blossomed freely. He could not bear for her to be far away from him, and his hands and lips sought her ceaselessly.

"There is so much in London I want to show you," he had said, but one kiss led to another and another, and they did not leave their chamber for three days. They lived for love; it stayed with them night and day and they cared for nothing else. They would sit for hours, she leaning back against him, he stroking her hair and caressing her. They laughed and often spoke the same words at the same time. They were immersed in each other so much they became as one. Their nights held a magical quality and each dreaded the time when their idyll would come to an end. They bathed together, enjoying to the full the warm sensuous feeling of the water upon their nakedness. They shared the same wine cup and tasted the sweet nectar on each other's lips. They lay in bed long hours after the sun was up each day and for one whole day did not bother to dress, and so enjoyed each other to the fullest possible measure.

One evening after her bath, she sat naked on the edge of the bed, her hair a golden-red cloak. He gazed at her, enthralled. "You are glorious. What is that you are doing?" he asked curiously.

"Rubbing my body with mint leaves so that I will smell good for you."

"And taste good," he added.

"I never thought of that," she giggled.

"I think of little else," he said, his voice ragged with desire. He lifted her hair behind her shoulders so he could see her naked breasts. She had to bite her lip to stop the moan of desire from reaching his ears. "Don't suppress," he whispered, "I love it when you cry out in the throes of passion. Lord God, you smell and taste so delicious. I like some of your English customs."

"What do French women smell of?" she murmured.

"Garlic," he lied.

"Guy! That is an untruth. I have heard what they say about the French."

"That we are the world's best lovers? That we have forgotten more bed tricks than other men ever learn?" he whispered suggestively.

"Such as?" she murmured with breathless anticipation.

He pushed her back onto the bed and turned her over onto her stomach, straddling her. His fingertips began their featherlike touching at her shoulder blades. He stroked her back so lightly, so teasingly, she shuddered with anticipation. His fingertips stroked the backs of her legs and came up to her buttocks. He traced the soft little creases beneath the cheeks of her bottom, then turned her over to begin the featherlike caresses over her breasts. "This is called *patte-d'araignée*, designed to drive you crazy, but right now I am the one who is mad with desire." He began to kiss her, but he did it differently than he had ever done it before. He gave her French kisses, the long, melting ones, where the tongue caresses the mouth of the beloved. She became so aroused she experienced five or six distinct pulsations between her thighs, without him even entering her.

"Ooh," she said, surprised at her body's response to his kisses.

"*Maraichinage*," he explained.

"Why do these things sound so wicked and sensual when you say them in French?"

"Ah, *chérie*, there is more."

"No, no. Please Guy, it is too much, I cannot take any more."

He laughed in his throat. "I have only just begun," he promised.

They sang and laughed and whispered love poems, their voices roughened with desire, until their souls as well as their bodies were joined. On the fourth day they walked miles around London, sampling the food from the street vendors, sailing upon the great river and laughing at all the funny people they encountered. Guy bought her trinkets and ribbons and anything that caught her fancy. Lillyth gave Guy a medallion inscribed, "To my beloved, my most beloved husband." An urgency came upon them to return to their haven, and as Lillyth stood looking pensively through the window, wishing they could go on like this forever, Guy came up behind her and clasped his hands beneath her breasts. She could feel the heat of his body through the thin material of her underdress. The mere touch of his hands aroused her. He undressed her, and pressed kisses upon every part of her body. She lay full upon him and teased him with her breasts and thighs, and when he would have rolled over to bring her beneath him, she shook her head and straddled and mounted him for the most glorious ride of her life.

On the fifth day, Guy's men returned, and they all enjoyed themselves on their last day in London. Guy had been invited back to William's court, so on the last evening he dressed in his best, told Lillyth not to wait up for him, and took himself off. The court was crowded and he recognized many friends and acquaintances. The main topic being discussed was William's return to Normandy. Robert de Mortain was to remain in residence at Berkhamstead, and William's other brother, Bishop Odo, was to remain in London and act as head of state until William's return, probably before Christmastime.

Guy pledged his fealty to Odo and promised to fight whenever he was needed against uprisings of the Saxons or attack from foreign sources. He found it hard to extract himself from the company. Eleven o'clock stretched to midnight, and it was well past one when Guy left for the inn with too much French wine under his belt. He lost his way twice, and before his faltering footsteps found their way back to the inn it was three in the morning. Lillyth had been beside herself with worry, and when she saw the condition he was in she was naturally angry.

"Where have you been?" she shouted.

"At court," he answered shortly.

"You have been carousing, and William does not allow that at his court! You have been off with a whore somewhere. You absolutely reek of wine. If you think you are going to share my bed, you may think again, sir!" she asserted.

"Where will I go?" he asked plaintively.

"You can go next door with your men," she said, and forcefully pushed him from the room and locked the door behind him. After a while she thought forlornly, He has probably gone back to her. I should never have told him to leave. She ran to the door, unlocked it and peeped outside into the dim hallway. There he stood, swaying slightly, in exactly the same spot she had left him. Relief swept over her. "Oh, for heaven's sake, come in here," she scolded. She guided him to the bed, laid him down and removed his boots and cloak. She got into bed and was determined to show him how angry she was, but before she could think of a remark that would cut deeply enough, her ears were assaulted by a loud snore. She opened her mouth in exasperation when her sense of the ridiculous got the better of her and she started to laugh. She rolled back and forth, hugging her knees, until the tears rolled down her cheeks.

When they arrived back at Godstone, the building had gone ahead in leaps and bounds.

Spring was in the air, and the work to be done now that the season was approaching necessitated that Guy be away from the hall from dawn to dusk. While Guy had been away in London, the man they had extracted from the St. Denys fief had been recovering from open lash wounds which covered his back. His wife and her family were very grateful to Guy for all he had done for them and vowed that he would never run away, so Guy felt secure in the extra lands he hoped to plant. He decided to put in a crop of hops for the brewing of ale. An idea had come to him to export barrels of ale to France in exchange for wine. He liked the atmosphere of the brewhouse with its roaring log fire built under the huge copper kettle. The wooden fermenters gave off their aromatic vapors, and these mingled with the sharp smell from the kettle, and the mellow aroma that came from the cooling pans. He believed a good brew of beer began with good clear water, which they had in abundance in Godstone. Handmade casks were already in production by the coopers.

Guy also had a plan to teach all the peasants proficiency with the bow and arrow. He overcame his knights' reluctance at the idea. They firmly believed in a code of chivalry that did not permit the lowborn to bear arms of any nature. He had argued that the peasants would be able to hunt and provide food for themselves, and, further, they would be prepared to help if defense was needed. One by one the knights came around to his mode of thinking. André was able to carry a full workload and walked with a barely perceptible limp. He, along with Aedward, took the running of Oxstead from Guy's shoulders, and Guy was most pleased with the way his brother was maturing and taking on added responsibility.

Now that Emma could hide her pregnancy no longer, Lillyth decided to take a hand in the matter. She sent a note to Esmé asking that he attend her. He answered the summons immediately, hoping he could be of special service to the lady of the hall and gain her husband's special thanks.

"Ah, Esmé, Edyth and I will be riding over to Oxstead this morning. We will need an escort we can rely upon. Would you do me the honor, sir?"

"The honor is mine, my lady, it will be a privilege to serve you." He bowed low.

"Thank you. I am sure we will be ready to leave by the time you have had the horses saddled."

"I will saddle them myself, to ensure it is done properly, madame."

When he had gone, Lillyth called, "Edyth, where are you? I have come to brighten your day! We will ride over to visit André at Oxstead, and to kill two birds with one stone, I will see if I cannot plant a few seeds in the fertile mind of our most charming Esmé."

Edyth was thrilled. André had almost declared himself on two occasions before Guy had sent him up to Oxstead. She had missed him desperately and hoped he had been affected the same way. She would be devastated if he discovered one of the women of Oxstead more to his taste.

During the ride Lillyth chatted with Edyth and politely included Esmé in the conversation. Lillyth's talk was all of her husband and his plans. She turned to Esmé. "My husband will be most pleased when André and Edyth are married. Oxstead is a large undertaking and Guy feels strongly that married men are much more responsible."

Edyth opened her mouth in surprise, so Lillyth quickly closed one eye in a conspiratorial wink before she could say anything. She said to Edyth, "A hall is to be built at Sevenoaks for when Nicholas takes over there. Guy realizes his brother is very young, that is why he will choose a married man to be Nicholas's second-in-command." She turned and smiled at Esmé. "A wife is almost a necessity; do you not think so, sir?"

"Ah yes, no doubt our commander's ideas on wedded life have undergone considerable changes since he was lucky enough to win such a lovely bride."

"Guy believes a man who hasn't courage to marry lacks courage in most other things," she said sweetly. She changed the subject swiftly. "Edyth, remind me to check on the linen supply at Oxstead. If there are not enough sheets, we must set the women to weaving some. Guy is teaching the peasants so many new skills, I think it would be a splendid idea to teach the peasant women fine weaving and stitchery. You never know when you will uncover an artistic talent like Lady Emma's."

Esmé fell silent and a crease of concentration appeared between his eyes. The corners of Lillyth's lips lifted as she saw that the seeds she was trying to plant had fallen upon fertile ground.

Guy fell into bed exhausted. However, he was never too tired to reach out loving arms for Lillyth. Tonight as he brushed her breasts, she winced.

"What is it, love?"

"My breasts are sore. Funny, I don't remember bumping into anything."

"Mm, you were sick this morning, *n'est-ce pas?* Sweetheart, I think perhaps you are enceinte."

She sat up quickly. "Oh, Guy, do you think so?"

They smiled into each other's eyes, almost too happy for words. He pulled her down beside him and slipped his hand over her belly.

"Are you afraid, *ma petite?*"

"Only a little. It is a gift you have given me, which I will give back to you. I know you want a son more than anything in the world."

"First, I want you, then I want a son," he corrected. *"Je t'aime, je t'adore,"* he whispered.

She lay against his heart, filled with the wonder of it all.

By the end of March, Godstone had produced more goods which could be traded, and Guy thought it a good idea to travel to the coast in William's train as William returned to Normandy, so that he could send the goods back to France. He had cloth, bales of wool, kegs of English ale, furs and animal pelts. He extracted a promise from Lillyth that she would not follow him as she had before. He also urged her to divulge her condition to her mother. She had wanted to keep the child a secret between them for a little while longer but agreed to share the knowledge with Lady Alison to make Guy feel less apprehensive about leaving her.

By the beginning of April, spring was definitely in the air. The woods were filled with violets and the birds were busy building their nests and selecting their mates. When Guy returned from the coast, he found their chamber filled with daffodils and the windows open to the pale sunshine.

* * *

Rolf told him that St. Denys had paid a visit in his absence. With his own eyes he had seen the man who had formerly belonged to him working quite willingly at the plowing without any urgings from an overseer with a whip.

"He did not look happy. I don't trust him. He will never let you plant those fields if he can prevent you," Rolf warned.

"We will see," said Guy noncommittally.

"The peasants' lessons in archery have been going well. Quite a few show a remarkable skill; it comes almost naturally to them."

Guy nodded his approval. "I would like to have a look," he said, so the two men went off in the direction of the butts.

The herds had all been put out to pasture and their winter quarters cleaned out thoroughly. The manure stood in piles ready to be spread on the fields. But the month of April was marred by what appeared to be an accident. Gerrard, one of Guy's knights, was found dead in the woods with an arrow in his back. After he was buried, Guy called his men together for a conference. Some argued that it was deliberate murder on the part of the Saxons and that they should never have been allowed bows in the first place. Others conceded that it could well have been a genuine accident, but in their opinion all archery for the peasants should be suspended until the culprit was discovered. Guy questioned every man in Godstone, but could get no explanation, no satisfactory answer to what had happened. He was reluctant to lay blame where he felt it did not rightfully belong. He went about silently preoccupied for days, coming up with an idea and later rejecting it. The peasants had been fearful since the body had been discovered. The heavy hand of justice, or more

likely injustice, was bound to fall, and they waited
with great apprehension.

It came to him in a flash and the more he
thought about it, the more convinced Guy was
that he had hit upon the truth. He sought out Rolf
and questioned him closely.

"When St. Denys was over here nosing about
did he learn of our peasants bearing arms?"

"Well, not that I know of, but he was here a
while before I was aware of it," Rolf answered.

"Is it conceivable?" Guy pressed.

"Now that I think about it, I do not see how he
could have been unaware of it. The men were
practicing and they walk about with their bows
quite openly. They do not try to conceal them.
What do you suspect?"

"I don't suspect, I know! St. Denys killed Gerrard as sure as I am standing here. He has been
looking for an opportunity to turn me against my
Saxons. He wants to foment trouble here at Godstone. The question is, what am I going to do
about it?" he pondered.

"I warned you he would not give up those
fields so easily but, by God, when a Norman
stoops so low that he will kill another Norman, he
doesn't deserve to live."

Guy informed the peasants without delay that
he had discovered the murderer and that they
were all totally exonerated. He assured them that
they would still be allowed to bear arms, and they
heaved a collective sigh and agreed among themselves that Montgomery was the kind of lord they
were lucky to have. Rumor was rife in Godstone,
and it was not long before everyone knew the culprit was St. Denys. Two nights later, Guy's problem of what to do about his neighbor was solved
for him. St. Denys was found drowned in the river
that ran between their properties. There was no

mark upon his body. Guy planted the fields and cast his eye on the rest of St. Denys's land. Before the summer was over he intended that the knights, as well as the land, would be his. He was a true Norman conqueror.

Chapter 22

May Day dawned. It was a beautiful warm morning, and Lillyth begged Guy to leave his work for one day so they could spend it together. She packed a picnic basket and they went across the meadows, through the woods and upstream before they picked a secluded spot, under magnificent leafy trees, beside the water. They dismounted and left their horses to wander freely and crop the sweet grass wherever they found it. In their private glade, they lay with fingers intertwined upon the grass.

"Guy, look at the bumble bee on that snapdragon. Now watch closely. She will go all the way inside and the flower will snap closed upon her, then when she has gathered the pollen, she will try to back out. It is the funniest thing you have ever seen. Here she comes, staggering backward." She put out her finger to touch the bee.

"Don't, it will sting you." He pulled her hand back.

She laughed. "Of course it won't sting me. It would die if it stung anyone, they only do that as a last resort if they are frightened or being hurt."

"How do you know all these things, sweet-heart?"

"I've always loved nature. I sit and watch by the hour in summertime." She rolled onto her stomach. "Look at the bluebells under the trees, they stretch out like a carpet, and just smell them—ah, heavenly."

"Would you like me to pick you some?" he asked playfully.

"Ah no, they wilt so quickly without water, and they look so much more beautiful growing."

He lifted the lid of the basket. "Here, you can put some water in this container and it will keep them fresh. Go and gather a few."

He watched her with loving eyes as she moved about gently beneath the trees, being very careful that she did not trample anything underfoot. She came back laughing. "My hands are all sticky with the sap from the stems. I'll just wash them in the water."

She beckoned Guy to join her, "Look at the beautiful butterflies dancing over the water." She held up her hand. "Come to me, butterfly!"

"*Papillons* will not come like a dog when you call, you silly child," Guy chuckled.

"I can attract one easily, watch!" Lillyth dipped her arms into the water and held them out toward the butterflies. Almost immediately one lit on her arm and she smiled into Guy's eyes.

"It's magic," he said incredulously.

"No. It is thirsty, watch closely. It will put out a tiny tube from its mouth and drink the moisture from my arm."

"How come I don't know any of these things?"

"Well, you know many other things that I am totally ignorant of, so we are even."

"Do you like us to be even?" he smiled.

"Oh, I like you even when you are odd," she

joked. "If you observe nature closely, it can teach you valuable lessons," she said. "For instance, see those two sparrows above in the hawthorn tree?" She pointed.

"I know enough about nature to see that he is going to mate her," he grinned.

"That is where you are wrong, my lord." She flashed him a triumphant glance. "She will have none of him, see how she scolds and pecks him? She won't allow him to mate with her until he has built a nest, ready to receive her eggs. For her, it is the same security that marriage is for me." She touched his face lovingly.

"What else can you show me?" he asked.

"Well, let me see if I can find one." She turned over the leaves on a bush until she found what she was looking for. It was a furry caterpillar. She plucked the leaf on which it sat and brought it over to Guy. "Now, if you are very quiet and listen very carefully, you will be able to hear it munching this leaf."

"Lillyth, lies all lies, you will have me believe anything!" He tossed the leaf aside and took her hand, "Come, let's have a swim, there is none to see us."

"The water is much too cold for me, darling. You swim, I'll watch," she urged. She did indeed watch fascinatedly as he divested himself of his garments. His skin was olive brown as if he were constantly tanned. To Lillyth's eyes his body was beautiful. He had a few old battle scars, but this only added to the sense of powerful strength his nakedness showed. He ran to the water and dove in. All his movements were clean and graceful as he cut through the water with hardly any splashing. He reminded her of an otter she had seen once, gliding sleekly through the water.

"You were right," he called, "it is pretty cold."

He waded out of the river and shook the excess water from his body. Then he came and stood over her, displaying his manhood to the full. She wanted to feel his strong arms about her, and she could feel in her imagination what it was to wrap her legs about his lean brown body. She took the linen cloth from the basket and reached out tentative hands to dry him, but as her fingers came into contact with his body, passion exploded in him and he was beside her on the grass, removing her clothes, until she lay as naked as he. He covered her with kisses, starting with her toes. He lingered hungrily over her legs, across her belly, and up to her breasts, which were very large and firm with her early pregnancy. She did not lie passive but caressed his back and moved her hands down to his taut buttocks. When she put the tip of her tongue to his nipples, they stood erect like her own. Her hand cupped him gently between his legs, tantalizing him beyond endurance before she allowed him entrance. Very quickly he was driving hard, his voice ragged with passion until she throbbed and pulsated beneath him. She could feel the hard earth beneath her back, rather than the soft bed she was used to, and perhaps this was the reason he seemed to have penetrated deeper inside her. The intensity became almost unbearable, and as their explosion burst simultaneously, she gave a shuddering cry and went limp.

Afterward, as she lay with her head in his lap and he fed her savories from the basket, her mischievous eyes twinkled up into his. "The Saxon youths have a rhyme they sing about May Day. Would you like to hear it?"

He nodded.

She reached up and whispered in his ear, "Hooray, hooray, the first of May; Outdoor fucking starts today!"

He looked at her sternly. "I believe you enjoy shocking me." The corners of his mouth quivered and he could not suppress the smile that came unbidden to his lips.

"This has been one of the happiest days of my life, love," she said softly. He took her hand and pressed it to his lips.

Their happiness was soon to be shattered.

The horses slowly ambled toward their stable in the late afternoon. The sun was going down and the shadows were lengthening. Guy and Lillyth were humming a French chanson when they spotted a small group also approaching on horseback. When they were in the yard, they recognized their visitors as Madame St. Denys with one of her men-at-arms. With them, however, was a stranger. St. Denys's widow pointed to Guy, and the stranger dismounted and spoke in French.

"My lord, Guy de Montgomery?"

"I am he," nodded Guy.

"Thank the saints. I have been trying to find you for over four months. I bring messages from your lady wife in Normandy, my lord. She plans to come to England and bring your children. Forgive my delay, my lord, but my crossing was postponed again and again because of storms and then I traveled up to Berkhamstead, thinking you would be with Mortain. Then on to London, and finally here."

"Yes, yes," said Guy irritably, putting out his hand for the sealed packet. "You must take refreshment now, we can talk later."

He looked swiftly toward Lillyth, who sat upon her horse as still and white as death. She was staring at the St. Denys woman, who in turn was smiling with sly satisfaction.

Lillyth's brain was beating out the words, It

cannot be, it cannot be, over and over. She groped for the reins to dismount, and Guy swiftly moved to her side, but she recoiled from him instantly and he could not bear the pain and accusation in her eyes.

He ushered his guests into the hall and sought out Alison with his eyes. "She knows everything! Help me," he whispered.

"I won't bear his bastard," vowed Lillyth as she quickly ran into the stillroom. She was momentarily insane with shock. She reached into a jar, counted out seven bayberries and immediately swallowed three. The horror of what she was doing overcame her and she flung the other four across the dirt floor and ran from the stillroom, crying. It took seven bayberries to abort a fetus. Less than seven would not work, but more could be dangerous enough to kill.

Alison found Lillyth in her own chamber. Lillyth raved and cried and called down curses upon Guy and would not be consoled. She sobbed and rocked herself and tore at her hair in grief.

"I cannot bear it, I cannot bear it. I wish I were dead! He has other legitimate children, while I am to bear his bastard. I will not do it—I will kill myself first," she sobbed. "He has betrayed me. There is nothing in this whole world for me. The world is empty. There is nothing! Nothing worth having, nothing worth trusting. This is hell! Hell is here on earth, not someplace we go to pay for our sins. It is here, now! Oh God, oh God, oh God." She was racked with weeping.

Her mother made a quick decision. "I will bring you a posset to soothe your nerves and calm you. I will be right back."

She hurried down to the stillroom, took seven bayberries from the jar and crushed them into a little honey. She mixed it with some raspberry syrup and swiftly returned to Lillyth.

"Drink this," she commanded, and Lillyth dutifully swallowed the concoction between sniffs and gasps.

Guy asked Rolf to attend to the needs of the visitors and slowly unsealed his letter. It was dated December 31, 1066.

> To my husband:
> I have had no word from you since you sailed for England three months ago; however, news reaches us daily of William's great victory and the untold wealth of the Saxons. My New Year's resolution is to share this wealth. If I guess correctly, you have not been behind in gathering much of this new land for yourself and your precious brothers, while I and your children are left behind to fend for ourselves. I am making preparations to depart Normandy. As soon as I hear from you, I shall sail immediately.
>
> Margarite de Montgomery

He crumpled the letter with his fist and smashed it into the table, then rose almost reluctantly. He must face Lillyth. He went up the stairs and sought her in her mother's chamber. As he went through the door Lillyth bent over in agony and clutched her abdomen. Blood pooled on the floor as she fell. He rushed over to pick her up and took her to the bed.

"She is losing the child," said Alison to Guy.

"No, no, I only swallowed three of the berries, I swear, I threw the others away."

Guy looked stricken, and Lady Alison went pale and muttered, "Oh my God! Tell me carefully, Lillyth, how many bayberries did you take?"

"Only three, only three," she said weakly.

"Are you absolutely sure? You couldn't be mistaken?"

"No, I took exactly three," she said weakly.

"She is hemorrhaging badly. I must try to stop it. Stay with her while I go to the stillroom."

He nodded. He went up to Lillyth and asked, "Why did you do this thing?"

She looked at him accusingly in her misery and silently swooned away. Her blood covered the bed and Guy was frightened.

"Oh God, don't let her die. If anyone has to die, take me," he prayed fervently.

The minutes until Alison returned seemed endless and he felt powerless to do anything for her. She bled for three days and hardly gained consciousness during that time. Guy and Alison took turns nursing her and sitting out their vigil. Time and time again they changed and washed her and put fresh linen upon the bed. Finally the bleeding stopped and Lillyth regained consciousness, but almost immediately fell into a deep, exhausted sleep.

On the fourth day she was sitting up in bed when Guy entered the chamber. She averted her face, but not before Guy noted that all the soft roundness had left her. Her cheekbones stood out as if they might pierce the fragile skin. He moved toward her, but she impaled him with her eyes and with quiet intensity said, "I hate you! You have killed whatever love I had for you."

He looked at her for a full minute and then said with equal intensity, "And you killed my son, just as surely as you killed your husband!"

Lillyth lay with her face to the wall all that day, and when night came she could not sleep. She felt completely empty. She mourned the loss of her child deeply. It was the same child that had brought her so much happiness such a few short weeks ago. She could not bear the loss; she feared she would lose her sanity. At first she could not abide thinking of Guy, and every time her mind conjured up his image, she pushed it away from her, out of her consciousness. Gradually, however, her thoughts turned to him more frequently and she probed the ifs and whys of their situation as one would probe a sore tooth with a tongue. She wanted to get away, anywhere would do. Lillyth felt she could not stand to be in close proximity to Guy day in, day out.

I hate him, I hate all men, she told herself over and over. By the time she took her first tentative steps down to the hall the next morning, Guy had departed. None knew where, only that he had packed his saddlebags and left, perhaps for Oxstead, perhaps farther.

Lillyth made a rapid recovery, physically. Within a couple of days she felt just as well as she had ever felt in her life, but emotionally she was dead. Day by day she erected a hard shell around her feelings and vowed over and over that none would ever hurt her again. From now on she would use men as they had used her.

By now she had learned the truth from her mother about the bayberries, and deep inside she resented the fact that her mother had made the decision to abort the child. A coolness grew up between them, especially since Lillyth realized her mother had known that Guy was married when he went through the mock ceremony at the church. Lillyth felt betrayed by everyone and consequently kept herself aloof.

After three weeks Guy returned. He was ill-tempered, stern-faced and short with everyone he came into contact with, and Rolf and his brothers resigned themselves that he had returned to the

way he used to be before Lillyth. The two avoided
each other to a great degree, but when this was
impossible they passed as strangers. She was out-
wardly calm, but inside she was a seething mass
of resentment. Whenever she saw Guy she felt ill,
and the moment she was alone she trembled from
head to foot from these encounters. So great was
the tension between them that it was almost a tan-
gible thing with a taste and smell of its own. Everyone was acutely aware of them, not merely
because of curiosity, but because the intensity of
the emotions involved affected all who came into
their presence.

Esmé had proposed marriage to Emma and she
was thrilled. Because of her obvious condition,
they had gone quietly to the church, then announced it afterward. Emma knew a moment of
panic when she learned how Montgomery had de-
ceived Lillyth but pushed it from her mind, telling
herself furiously that Esmé belonged to her, even if
there were a dozen wives waiting somewhere for
him.

Adela and Hugh had decided to marry, but she,
along with Edyth, who was now formally betrothed to André, felt she must hide her happiness
from Lillyth. The only way to do this was to avoid
contact or conversation with her. This, of course,
was not difficult as Lillyth had become withdrawn
and solitary.

Lillyth knew that the situation could not go on
as it was. It became unbearable for her. When she
learned that Father Sebastian was returning to
Berkhamstead, a plan began to take shape in her
thoughts. She knew she could stand it no longer at
Godstone and that she would have to go some-

where else. How to survive? She would need the protection of a Norman in this time of the downtrodden Saxon. Robert de Mortain's name cried out to her. Who stood higher in the land? Only the king himself! She had his ring, his invitation, what more did she need?

A part of her drew back when she admitted all that going to Robert would imply. She would become whore to a Norman. She laughed aloud at herself! She had already been whore to a Norman for over half a year. Why have scruples at this late hour?

Lillyth trusted none these days, but realized she must take the monk into her confidence. She decided to hold off until the day before he departed. She showed him Robert's ring and told him that she wished to travel with him, but that Guy de Montgomery must not learn of her proposed journey. When Father Sebastian had traveled to Godstone he had come on his own horse with a string of two packhorses. Lillyth put her things with his, ready to put on the packhorses at dawn. She took only a minimum of things with her. She needed her warm cloak, a serviceable riding dress, and only one outfit of velvet tunic and underdress. Excess baggage would be a burden and besides, each gown held a special meaning for her. Memories of Guy clung to every fold of the material. She intended to cut herself from the past ruthlessly.

She sat now in the small bedchamber she occupied alone. She planned to rise long before dawn for the journey that lay ahead. Her hair presented a slight problem until she decided to plait it in long, tight braids and wind them around and around her head. On impulse she decided to do it now and sleep very carefully without disturbing it. It took well over an hour before the last pin was in place. She laid out her riding dress and warm cloak, then undressed and, shivering uncontrollably, got into bed. She knew it was past midnight and planned to rise in less than four hours, but sleep would not come to her. Her feet were icy cold, and no matter how vigorously she moved them about the empty bed, warmth would not come to them. Suddenly she stiffened. Someone was trying to get into her room. Thank God she had remembered to place the bar across the little door.

With minimum noise and maximum effort, Guy broke the door open by dislodging the bar where it was embedded into the wall. He came into the room and managed to close the door behind him.

"Lil—I cannot stand being apart from you. To see you every day and not speak or touch is torture for me."

"Please leave me," she said quietly.

"I will not," he said harshly.

She saw by his face that he would not listen to her while she begged him to leave. There would be no discourse; his waiting was plainly over. He was in the bed now and the roughness of his hands told her that he was beyond pleading with. Struggling and screaming would avail her nothing, but she had another weapon she could use against him. Indifference! She would be completely passive, cold and unmoved. She would keep him from possessing her inner essence. What a fool she had been! If she stayed under the same roof as he, this was bound to happen sooner or later. Never again, she vowed.

"Legalities mean naught to me! You are mine. You will always be mine." His brain reeled with the nearness of her, but her stillness told him she wanted none of him. His fingers sought out the soft, silky place beneath her breasts and she found it very hard to remain passive and un-moved.

He tried persuasion. "Lillyth, you do not un-derstand. When a man is in close proximity to a beautiful woman without any outlet for his physical needs, it becomes too painful for him to bear."

She turned her head away from him on the pil-low and stared at the wall, thinking. He will make use of any argument or persuasion to gain power over me and have his way, but I shall stand outside of myself and be apart from his lovemaking.

"You are trying to punish me by being cold, but I will thaw you, my darling, resist me how you will." He forced himself into her and shuddered with ecstasy when he felt her tightness. She bit her lips to prevent herself from crying out. He began to move slowly and deliberately, every thrust de-signed to shatter her defenses and bring forth her response. She kept her mind and soul apart, but her body would betray her if she did not keep an iron control on herself. She clenched her teeth to-gether to prevent the low moans from escaping, and he cried out a sharp command, "Meet me, Lillyth!"

Her body was responding to him, but she would die before she would let him know it. He was an experienced lover and knew the value of verbal stimulation, so now he whispered all his lover's longings into her ears. His voice caressed her with honeyed compliments and his hands ac-companied his words.

Never by a word or a gesture did she show the effect he had upon her, but she had let down her love juices twice before Guy allowed himself the pleasure of fulfillment. He looked down at her

seemingly frozen form and his green eyes narrowed.

"I was right. All women are bitches!" he spat as
he removed himself from her presence.

Chapter 23

She wasted no time on tears, but started immediately to redo her hair, which Guy's lovemaking had destroyed. Her fingers trembled as she replaited the braids and pinned them up tightly. Without trying to sleep again, she dressed, wrapped her warm cloak tightly about her and sought out Father Sebastian. He slept apart from the others in a hut of his own, and Lillyth entered and shook him awake.

"I beg of you to leave now, my friend."

He looked at her quietly. "Tell me what your trouble is, child."

"Oh, Father, everything is such a mess. How can I tell you, I am too ashamed."

He patted her hand and said simply, "Child, nothing can shock me, but take your time. Your tale will no doubt unfold on the journey. I am traveling to London to see Bishop Odo before I go on to Berkhamstead. Will that inconvenience you, child?"

"No, no. I care not where I go, so long as we go from here quickly. Father, do you think we could travel west first and then make our way to London? I do not want to run away only to be brought back tomorrow or the next day."

"I am only familiar with the main road to London, but we can go in a roundabout way, I am sure, if it will ease your mind." He smiled at her kindly. "I don't suppose you have brought any food for yourself on this journey? No, I thought not. Well, since you are in a fret to get started, pack these wheaten cakes into your saddlebag. You will find your little horse is tethered with my own horses behind the hut." He chuckled. "You never gave a thought to how you would get your horse from the stables in the middle of the night without setting up a hue and cry, did you?"

She went pale. "All I could think of was leaving. I'm sorry that you have to do the thinking for both of us. I will try to be more considerate in the future."

"Come, I think we will be safe on the main road until daylight."

She patted Zephyr's muzzle and murmured to her softly, then she mounted and pulled her cloak tightly about her to keep out the damp chill. They set out at a very quick pace, Lillyth wishing to put distance between herself and the man who had betrayed her, and Sebastian wishing to set her fears at rest. They rode in silence for about two hours, and the first streaks of dawn stole red fingers across the black sky when Lillyth called, "Do you think any Norman soldiers will stop us?"

"Do not worry, none will dare to detain us. I carry a pass to travel from the king. It forbids any to offer me hindrance."

"I hope you are right, but from what I have experienced, Normans are very bold. They seem to do exactly as they please."

"Most Normans are very religious, child. My presence should be enough to protect you."

"If they are religious, how could they come burning and killing us Saxons so wantonly?"

"A Norman does not consider being a soldier and being religious as opposing each other. They go hand in glove, really. They always pray for victory before a battle, and give thanks afterward. The Norman is a superior being where military matters are concerned."

"Do you bear arms, Father?"

"I do not carry a sword, but I am in the battle nonetheless. I help the wounded and the dying. Bishop Odo does not carry a sword, but he has a heavily spiked ball that does a great deal more damage, I should think."

They rode in silence for a few hundred yards, then he said, "The horses need a rest and we will break our fast. I hear a stream up ahead. Let us rest there, child."

He built a small fire and set some water to boil, then fed the horses. Lillyth doled out a few wheaten cakes and she nibbled pensively. Her mind was miles away; Guy would be getting up now, perhaps he had already discovered that she had left. They would soon be searching for her, she thought apprehensively.

In fact, Guy had no idea that she had departed. He had risen early and was bringing men from Oxstead to help with the building. He was determined to avoid Lillyth at all costs. She could come to him; he would not go to her again. Alison soon discovered that she had left, but having a good idea where she had gone she decided to keep her own counsel.

Sebastian looked speculatively at Lillyth. "I thought you were happy with Montgomery."

She looked startled and blurted, "I was, but then I discovered he had a wife and children in Normandy." Her words were bitter.

He went on carefully, "Many men take lemans, it is quite a common practice. Of course, William frowns upon it because he is happily married, but most men are not so fortunate and they take their pleasure where they find it."

"But he married me! He had the priest wed us and we had a big celebration and invited everyone in Godstone."

"I see," he said thoughtfully. "You believed you were his wife, then discovered he already had one?"

She nodded miserably.

"You must not feel guilt or remorse over what has happened. It was none of your doing, and now, of course, I see why you had to leave. You would have been forced to continue on in the position of mistress, and after thinking yourself a wife, it would have been intolerable."

Lillyth could not bring herself to speak of the child and changed the subject quickly. "When we resume our journey, I think we should quit this road as soon as may be."

He nodded. "I think we should go east rather than west. It would be the illogical thing to do."

She smiled at him for the first time. They rode side by side for the rest of the day and Lillyth had ample time to study her companion. He was no older than Guy but very thin, as if he had lived a life of abstinence. His eyes were dark and piercing and he had a large hooked nose. Although he was not a large man, Lillyth suspected he had a wiry strength which would serve him well in a fight. They stopped only once to water the horses and did not stop again until the sun was low in the

sky. He told her to make a fire and went off to
scavenge for their supper.

Lillyth's back ached from spending all day in
the saddle, and she took a walk to find water and
relieve her muscles. By the time she returned with
the water, Father Sebastian was cooking eggs over
the fire. She noticed the fowl, not yet plucked, and
he said, "I will cook it tonight, then we will have
meat for tomorrow."

She laughed. "You stole them, didn't you?"

He spread his hands in a Gallic gesture. "Let us
say I found them before they were lost."

After they had eaten their eggs, Sebastian cut
and fashioned a spit to hold the bird over the fire,
and Lillyth gathered some herbs with which to
stuff the bird. She lay a long time that night before
sleep overcame her, because, tired as she was, she
could not get used to the hard ground with only
her cloak for comfort.

The next day they met other travelers going toward London, and Father Sebastian traded with
them for some food. Lillyth felt less apprehensive
now that they were not alone, and she wondered
why they had not been overtaken yet with riders
from Godstone.

Perhaps he is glad to be rid of me, she thought
coldly. Well, I am certainly glad to be rid of him!
she swore fervently.

Her back ached just the way it did before she
got her monthly courses and she did some mental arithmetic to see if this could be her trouble. After her bleeding over the miscarriage
ceased, she had spent a few days in bed, almost
a week. Then Guy had been gone almost three
weeks, plus another week had passed before he
forced his way to her bed. How odd that it was
five weeks since she had bled. She worried about

how she would be able to avoid embarrassment and maintain her modesty in such close proximity to this holy man when she started. The next morning she looked discreetly for signs of blood and, finding none, immediately set to worry about being pregnant once more.

One part of her recoiled from such a predicament, and the other part of her felt a longing for another baby. I must be mad, she admonished herself. How can I go to one man with another man's child inside me? she thought wildly. Other thoughts crowded into her mind. Perhaps she would not bleed this month because she had lost so much when she hemorrhaged. She began to panic. She felt weak, alone, frightened of the future. Frightened of the present, if it came to that. She felt truly sorry for herself and laid all her woes at Montgomery's doorstep. She sank to the ground, and laying her head upon her knees, she wept.

"What is your trouble child?" Sebastian asked kindly.

"I feel I cannot go on," she said weakly.

"Ah, you are so young and beautiful. The world lies at your feet. The future opens before you like a feast. Enjoy it! Take it in both hands and make it yours. Let the past go. Do not be defeated before you start," he urged.

She lifted her head and looked at him. A calm descended upon her and she thought, I will make a new start. I will be strong. I am a woman and I will face whatever life has in store for me.

A squirrel ran up a tree nearby and another chased it. She began to laugh. "The sun is shining, summer lies before me and I will enjoy it to the full." She felt one last pang of regret that Guy had not come to take her back to Godstone and then tried to dismiss him from her thoughts. "Come, my friend, London awaits us."

They rode into the city and Sebastian said, "You present a bit of a problem, child. I can hardly take you with me to Bishop Odo's court, so we will have to find you a place to stay until we resume our journey to Berkhamstead."

"I will go to the inn I stayed at before. They will know me, and it is a lovely place."

"What about money?" he asked doubtfully.

"Ah, you have not seen the new Lillyth in action! It is not a problem, merely a challenge," she laughed.

Lillyth squared her shoulders and entered the inn with the monk following. The innkeeper and his wife recognized her. "Madame Montgomery, welcome back. Is your husband not with you, madame?" she was asked.

"He has business outside the city. He will join me in a few days, but insisted I come ahead where I would be lodged more comfortably. I hope you will be able to find a room for me."

"Would the gentleman also require a room?" he asked looking pointedly at Father Sebastian.

"Oh no, he has business at court with Bishop Odo. You know," she added, "he is only acting as my escort. He will be taking the horses with him except for my mare. I would like her to have a good rubdown, and then feed her well. Also I would like a bath brought up to my room as soon as possible," she said with more authority than she felt. Sebastian carried her saddlebags up to her room, and they said a swift good-bye.

"Do not walk abroad, child. London is no fit place for a woman alone, especially a beautiful woman."

"I shall rest until you return for me, I promise.

Thank you for all your kindness to me, I will never forget it."

When he had gone she looked about her. She was thankful it was not the same room she had shared with Guy, but it was similar and evoked poignant memories. She pushed these thoughts purposefully from her mind as she undressed and bathed. She felt so warm and relaxed that she crawled into bed immediately and slept until morning, without even a dream. She awoke to the smell of bacon and sausage frying and was immediately overcome with nausea. This confirmed her fears that she was with child. Determined not to panic and return to the low spirits of the day before, she cleaned her hands and face and set about brushing the dust of the road from her garments. She took out the gold bracelets Guy had given her. She would take them to the goldsmith's shop where she had bought the medallion for Guy when they were last in London and try to sell them. She wondered briefly how much they would bring and decided not to take less than ten or twelve deniers. Lillyth decided that it would not hurt if she looked as pretty as possible, so she combed out her hair, framed her face with curls and carefully put on her cloak and pulled up the hood. She walked quickly along the street, paying no attention to the people who tried to detain her to sell their wares. She hoped she remembered the way as she turned down another street and stood bewildered for a moment. Ah yes, it was this way; on the opposite side. She hesitated only slightly before entering, and gathering all her courage, she went through the door and threw back her hood. She came face to face with the most elegant man she had ever seen. He was buying jewelery and had two manservants with him. Extremely tall and slim, he had silvery-blond hair and silver eyes to match. He was dressed in black from head to foot, relieved only by silver embroidery about his collar. He bowed to her and gestured toward the man behind the counter. "Ladies first." A flush rose to her cheeks as she offered the gold bracelets up for inspection.

"I would like to sell these. Do you think you might be interested?" she asked the goldsmith. She felt the gentleman's eyes upon her, and her breast rose and fell in agitation. The goldsmith slowly appraised the bracelets and said, "Five deniers?"

Her face fell. "I thought—I thought perhaps ten?" she inquire hesitantly.

The goldsmith shook his head and shrugged apologetically.

The tall man beside her said, "May I see them? Beautiful things are a weakness with me." His eyes never left her face.

She held out the bracelets to him and urged, "They would make any woman who wore them more attractive."

"I have someone in mind," he smiled. "I will give you ten deniers for them, *chérie*."

"Thank you, monsieur," she said softly. She hated this whole business of haggling, but the bracelets were the only things she had worth selling, and she knew she must get some money soon. He counted the money into her hand, and without looking into his silver eyes she went swiftly from the shop.

Once back at the inn, she decided not to venture forth again until Sebastian came to fetch her. It was four days before he came.

"Child, I have been worried to death because I could not come sooner. Have you been all right?"

"Yes, but I am glad you came. I was beginning to worry about you. I sold some jewelry and I have ten deniers. Now the problem is, do I use it to settle my bill here, or do I keep it for future needs?" she mused. She made her decision almost immediately. "If you will see to my horse, I will deal with the landlord. Come!"

She put on her most regal air, though her knees shook slightly as she spoke to the landlord. "My husband will be delayed for a few days. When he arrives, please give him the message that I have decided to go on ahead of him, and oh yes, I almost forgot, please tally up my bill and add it to Montgomery's."

The innkeeper was about to protest when he thought better of it. If he demanded payment now, perhaps the Montgomerys would take their custom elsewhere; there was no shortage of inns in London. She gave him a dazzling smile and swept into the yard feeling only a little guilt at the deception she had perpetrated.

The roads seemed busy with travelers, and since Lillyth had never traveled this way before, she took a great interest in the scenes about her. Father Sebastian knew it was a longer journey they were undertaking this time and had packed a good food supply to take with them. The third day there were fewer travelers upon the road, but they met an occasional patrol from Berkhamstead. Sebastian told Lillyth they had nothing to fear from these Norman soldiers, and she relaxed and enjoyed the beautiful countryside. The Chiltern Hills were dotted with sheep, and they stopped for fresh milk from grazing dairy herds. The weather held out fair for the entire journey as they followed the River Colne until it branched off to the River Gade, and Sebastian told her that they would follow this river until they came to Berkhamstead. Behind them on the road, the thud of hooves became louder, and a small group of horsemen overtook them. Lillyth was surprised to see the handsome fair-haired man she had met at the goldsmith's in London at the head of the horsemen. When they passed by, the man swept off his hat and bowed low in the saddle to Lillyth. She nodded her head and Sebastian asked, "Do you know him, child?"

"I saw him in London. Who is he?" she asked.

"His name is Ancelin de Courcey," he said shortly.

"He is very handsome," said Lillyth.

Sebastian snorted. "Handsome on the outside perhaps."

She raised her eyebrows at his tone of voice, but he did not pursue the subject further, so Lillyth let it drop. As they drew closer to their destination, Lillyth became nervous and apprehensive. Sebastian noticed the change in her and suggested they stop and eat so they would not arrive hungry, but afterward Lillyth became nauseated and her stomach muscles felt tied in knots. She retched until she became weak, and Sebastian urged that they hurry and get to Berkhamstead without further delay. He could clearly see she needed to be abed. When they arrived, they left their horses in the stables and Sebastian led her into the huge castle. By a backstairs route he took her to an upper level and led her to a secluded alcove where he bade her wait.

"I will try to find Robert de Mortain and have a private word with him."

"Here, take this ring. It will save a lot of explanations. What if you cannot find him?" she asked apprehensively.

"Then I shall return and we can decide what to do next. Lillyth, you look dreadful. Will you be all right if I leave you alone here?"

She nodded mutely.

The wait was endless. Pages and servants passed her by but paid little attention. There was nowhere to sit and her legs felt like water. I must not faint, she told herself sternly. She contemplated sitting on the floor, but knew this would attract undue attention. She began to count slowly, hoping this would make the minutes go faster, and when she reached a thousand, her mind could go no farther. Then she noticed Sebastian returning with another man.

"Lillyth, my dear," said Robert de Mortain, "you traveled all this way alone and I can see the journey has made you ill. Come, my dear, I will find you comfortable rooms."

"Oh thank you, Robert, it is so kind of you to receive me thus," she laughed with relief.

He looked at her face, so beautiful but so pale, and his heart went out to her. She was so young and innocent, what had that devil Montgomery done to her to make her flee her home? Robert led the way up another flight of steps and along a hallway. He opened two or three doors before choosing a chamber and ushered Lillyth and Father Sebastian inside. It was a comfortable bedchamber, but despite the sunshine outside, the room was cold. A smaller chamber with a trundle bed opened off it.

"I will have some food sent up and a servant to light a fire," Robert said.

At the mention of food Lillyth turned paler and murmured, "Thank you, my lord, but I could not eat a thing tonight, and Sebastian can light a fire for me."

"I will send women to look after you." He looked perplexed for a moment. "Those damned chattering girls my wife surrounds herself with are next to useless. I think I had better send my physician to you."

"Oh no, no, no," she pleaded, sinking down upon the bed. "I am not ill, my lord, just fatigued."

"I have it!" Robert exclaimed, pleased with himself. "My old nurse. She will mother you, perhaps even smother you," he laughed, taking her hands. "Father Sebastian will bring her here to you and I will come by later to see how you are feeling." He lifted her hand to his lips and the two men departed.

Lillyth was swept with a relief that was weakening in its intensity. Robert had looked so concerned and had acted in a paternal manner toward her. Perhaps he could be kind for kindness's sake and would require no payment from her.

Sebastian came back with a plain-faced, comfortable fat woman. She took one look at the pathetic figure huddled on the bed and threw her hands in the air. She turned upon Father Sebastian. "Shoo, shoo, you go now. We need no men here."

Lillyth thanked him before he was shoved from the room.

"I will undress you, just lie back. I know you have not eaten, but sleep is the most important. We French have a saying, 'To sleep is to dine!'" She hustled Lillyth into the bed. "Tomorrow I bathe you and wash your beautiful hair, but tonight sleep, sleep, sleep," she emphasized.

"My Lord Robert will be returning shortly," Lillyth began.

"Ha! He won't get past the door, that one! I shall tell him you are asleep. He will do as I say—he always has."

"You are very kind to me. What is your name?" asked Lillyth as she pulled up the cool sheets.

"My name is Bette. A plain name for a plain

woman, but your name is very beautiful, Lillyth. It quite matches you."

The elderly woman chatted on comfortably until Lillyth began to doze. She did not hear Robert come, nor Bette send him away. She heard nothing at all until midmorning. She rolled over in the big bed and opened her eyes. She was quite alone, but not for long. Bette came bustling in straight from the kitchens with cool milk and hot buttered scones with honey. She insisted Lillyth have it in bed. Afterward she helped her bathe and washed and dried her beautiful, long hair.

"You will do nothing but rest today, and if Robert comes I shall not allow him to tire you."

Lillyth laughed. "You do not sound very much in awe of him, Bette."

"I should think not! He was in my nursery, aye and his son too." She nodded. "Lillyth, dear, you haven't a thing to wear, but never mind, I shall speak to Robert."

"Oh no, you mustn't," she protested.

"Nonsense! He is a very generous man. Why, you should see the wardrobe his wife has and all those chattering creatures she keeps about her. Every one of them is extravagant to a fault. And she does nothing but nag him, poor man. I know what he likes. He needs someplace where he can come and relax for an hour. We will give him that place, you will see." She chatted on about their plans, and Lillyth smiled to herself.

A knock on the door sent Lillyth scurrying back under the bedcovers, but when Bette answered the door it was only a messenger with a small parcel. Bette brought it to Lillyth, who unwrapped it carefully. There lay the two golden bracelets. "I was the one he had in mind," she said, surprised.

"A little gift from Robert?" Bette asked.

"No, I believe they are from a gentleman called Ancelin."

"De Courcey! He is always about Robert. Be careful of that one, my girl. Looks are very deceptive. He has a wicked wit and makes Robert laugh, but the women hang about him something shameful."

Chapter 24

Lillyth finally had to insist on getting dressed, and that evening when Robert came to see how she was, she followed Bette to the door and opened it wide to permit him entrance.

"I am feeling perfectly rested, my lord, which is more than I can say for you. Please come in and make yourself comfortable."

"Thank you, Lillyth. I'm delighted to find you well again," he smiled.

Bette bustled over to get him wine, but Lillyth forestalled her and with an almost imperceptible nod toward the other room, dismissed the old servant. When they were alone Lillyth brought him the wine, took a cushion and placed it on the floor beside his chair and sat at his feet gazing up at him.

"I'd forgotten how fair you were," he said, picking up a tress of her hair and rubbing it playfully between his fingers.

"This is such a vast place. Although I haven't seen too much of it, it must keep you very busy." She encouraged him to talk about himself, and soon he was very relaxed and talking as if they had been friends for years.

He liked to talk, a thing he seldom got a chance

to do with his own wife, and Lillyth soon learned
that all he wanted, like most men, was a good lis-
tener. Soon he was talking about the vast preparations he had made prior to the invasion. He told
her that he had provided one hundred and twenty
ships. Her mind flew back to a time when Guy
had told her that it had taken all his resources to
furnish one ship. She drew her mind back to the
present quickly and she tried to imagine the
wealth it had taken to provide one hundred and
twenty ships with men, horses and provisions.

Robert had taken her hand and was stroking it
tenderly. "Lillyth, I have a small hunting lodge not
too many miles from here. Would you perhaps
consider going there with me for a few days? We
could take just a couple of servants with us—
someone to cook for us and of course a maid for
you. I feel in need of a rest—a little peace and
quiet. Do you think you could find it in your heart
to show me a little kindness?" he asked wistfully.

She thought cynically, Here is the payoff. You
never get something for nothing. She pushed her
apprehension away and said, "I should like that
above all things, my lord, but I certainly don't
need a maid, and I could do the cooking for just
the two of us. That way we can be alone. I would
feel so much more comfortable with no prying
eyes upon us."

"You can cook?" he asked, amazed.

"Well, of course I cannot rival your Norman
chefs with all the intricate dishes they prepare for
you, but simple things like omelets and stews are
fun to make."

He looked at her unbelievingly. "Would you really do that for me, Lillyth?"

"It would be my pleasure," she smiled.

He jumped up, enthused. "I'll make all the arrangements. It will take a few days, but you will

be busy the next couple of days anyway," he said cryptically. He bent and brushed his lips across hers. "I don't know when I have spent such a pleasant evening. Thank you, my dear."

She looked up at him and saw that the careworn look he had when he came in had vanished, and he looked years younger.

The next morning brought a bevy of people to her rooms. Seamstresses and men bearing furs and jewelry told her that she must make her choices. She cast an accusing glance at Bette, who only grinned and nodded her head in approval. Lillyth was woman enough to enjoy the attention and the beautiful materials and preen in front of the mirror the next day when the gowns were presented.

Lillyth did not go down to the great hall for her meals because Bette brought them to her rooms, explaining that there was always such a crush in the dining hall and everything was usually cold by the time it was served. But Lillyth was thankful to take her meals alone. She did not wish to come into contact with Robert's wife or any of her ladies.

Robert came for an hour each evening. He talked, laughed and relaxed in general, but did not press his attentions upon her in any intimate way. He always left her before the hour became unduly late, and then finally he told her to be ready on the morrow, as they would be leaving for the hunting lodge after breakfast.

Lillyth was surprised and a little unnerved to find that Robert's "gentlemen" were riding out with them. She was greatly agitated when Ancelin de Courcey himself carried the things down for her. He appraised her from head to foot with his cool silver eyes and said before they reached Robert's side, "If you do your work well during the next few days, I shall have a proposition to put before you when you return."

When they reached the castle ward, Robert held a pretty white mare with red leather saddle and harness for her. She exclaimed with a real delight, and Robert was obviously pleased with her reception of his gift. His gentlemen were acting as escort and also carrying food that had been prepared for them, a vast quantity of French wines, a pair of berselet hounds which hunted by sight, a pair of brachet hounds which hunted by scent, falcons, linen, candles and other luxuries.

Lillyth felt very self-conscious that the whole party of men took it for granted that she was Robert's latest mistress, but there was nothing she could do except hold her head high and act the part of a gentlewoman, which came naturally enough to her. After they arrived, it was quite some time before his men prepared a meal, made up two fresh bedchambers, laid the fires without lighting them and took care of the needs of the horses and dogs. Lillyth had her things brought into one of the chambers, and she decided to stay in there until the last of the gentlemen departed.

When they were finally alone Robert opened the chamber door. "You are so shy, Lillyth, but I must admit it is an endearing quality, and in truth I thought they would never leave," he laughed.

"This must be very rare for you, to get away from everyone and everything," she said.

"Not quite everything. I have a huge pile of dispatches from London to read, but they can wait. We've three whole days to ourselves. What shall we do first?"

Relieved to find he did not expect to play games in the big bed all afternoon, she replied, "Well, whatever we do, let us do it outside in the sunshine. It's such a lovely day, let's not waste it."

"Would you care to go hawking?" he asked her politely.

"I would really rather just go for a walk. Perhaps we could take a couple of the dogs with us?"

"It is quite dangerous to be in these woods on foot, Lillyth," he warned.

"I have no fear with you beside me, my lord," she answered truthfully.

Robert unleashed the hounds and they went crashing off through the underbrush. Robert and Lillyth walked hand in hand beneath the towering trees, while his other hand stayed on the hilt of his dagger in case danger threatened.

Brown leaves from the previous autumn swirled about their feet and made a delicious crisp sound as they crunched them underfoot. Lillyth stooped to pick up a few acorns, and Robert watched her appreciatively.

"You are a delight to the eyes in that pale turquoise."

"It is not very suitable for country wear. It would be more appropriate at a ball, but it is nice and cool. I have not thanked you properly for all the lovely things you have given me."

He shook his head. "Please no. Whatever you wish for, you may have."

If I could only say that to him, and mean it, thought Lillyth sadly, but I cannot give him my heart.

She fingered the acorns. "Aren't they curious, these little hard fruits?" She spied a gray squirrel, remained motionless and held her hand out to it. It came timidly at first, then more boldly. It took an acorn in its mouth and greedily took another in its claws before it scampered off to bury them.

Robert laughed. "Do you think it will come to me?"

"Of course," she said, giving him some acorns,

"but do not hold them between your fingers or you will feel its teeth as sharp as needles! Hold them on the palm of your hand."

The squirrel came back to Lillyth, but when she had nothing for him he ran up her dress and across her shoulders, sniffing her ears and pulling her hair. Reluctantly, it went to Robert and picked the acorns from his hand. "Cheeky devil!" he laughed.

That evening they dined royally on roasted pheasant with a delicious white wine. Pies of all descriptions and cheeses had been brought for their pleasure, and dozens of delicate tarts and pastries rounded off the meal. Lillyth was relieved that Robert was a good talker, and when a silence fell she only had to ask a question with wide-eyed curiosity, such as, "Do you believe the world to be round or flat?" to send him off on a lengthy explanation of his views and opinions.

Night was upon them and could be denied no longer. At last he said, "I will give you a little privacy while you retire, my dear. When I return I hope you won't be unkind and send me away."

She smiled tremulously, and he departed. Lillyth chose an expensive perfume from one of the many Robert had provided for her. She left one candelabrum burning, slipped into a white lacy bedgown and propped herself against the pillows. Her heart hammered as he came into the chamber dressed in a richly embroidered bedgown. His eyes avoided the tempting picture she presented, and he seemed nervous. He carefully blew out the candles and in the pitch darkness removed his robe and came into bed. Very tenderly he reached for her and kissed her. He became excited at the velvet smoothness of her skin, but he remained extremely gentle. He was intoxicated with her nearness, and his words became slurred as if he were drunk with the feel and smell of her. She was nervous and not in a mood to make love but offered no protest when he pressed her back tenderly and loomed above her. She was so dry and tight when he entered her that he thought with delight that perhaps she was still virgin after all. Before she had even begun to become aroused he had reached his climax and it was over. He immediately began apologizing. He apologized for his weight and moved away from her. He begged her forgiveness for hurting her, and she put out a reassuring hand and caressed his shoulder.

"Men have such base desires, my dearest. Thank you for submitting to them. You are the sweetest thing that has happened to me in many years."

He was so gentle, too gentle and mannerly, damn him, thought Lillyth. He slept, but Lillyth lay unsatisfied, lonely and bleak. In the middle of the night she rose softly and stood by the window. She had had a longing, a desire, to make him into a being that fit her deepest requirements, but it was impossible. Guy stood beside her in her thoughts and she could not bannish his specter. Love with him had been an exalting, blind madness, and the loss of that love had been like a brush with death.

A voice from the bed disturbed her thoughts. "Are you already regretting it, my dearest?"

She turned to him quickly with a denial on her lips.

"It was very precious to me, Lillyth. Would you like me to leave you now so that I won't disturb your sleep?" he offered.

"Oh, Robert, you are too kind and thoughtful." She went back to bed. "I don't want you to leave me, it would be too lonely for both of us. Just hold me, please."

The next day he was so happy and lighthearted, almost like a boy. It was infectious, and soon she was laughing with him. He was unfailingly thoughtful and kind. He looked rough and ungentle, a huge military man, but his manners, toward Lillyth at least, belied his appearance. He was almost shy with her, formal without being stiff.

She was taking a bath before the fire when he came in and he blushed crimson, begged forgiveness for intruding upon her privacy, and withdrew immediately. Unbidden pictures of Guy sprang up. He had always taken such pleasure in watching her bathe, and when she had emerged glistening wet he had never been able to resist sweeping her into his arms, while the water droplets still clung to her skin, to make violent love to her. Or when he was bathing, he would tease her by picking her up and pretending to drop her into the water with him. She sighed and forced her thoughts back to the present.

That night Robert came to her again under almost identical circumstances. Total darkness, too gentle caresses, and a quick release before she was ready. The only thing she could be thankful for was his unfailing tenderness toward her.

When their three days were up, Robert's gentlemen returned to escort them back to Berkhamstead. On the ride back, Ancelin de Courcey maneuvered his horse beside Lillyth's. He doffed his hat to her and bowed. "I congratulate you on your success. I can see that it went well; I only need to look at him to see that. I will be calling on you in a few days." He urged his horse to a canter and Lillyth dropped back to ride beside Robert.

Upon her return to Berkhamstead, Lillyth found that a much more sumptuous apartment had been prepared for her in one of the new wings. It was on the second floor, and the windows opened onto a lovely garden. She was delighted with the new arrangements, and Bette was there waiting for her, and beaming her approval.

Robert said a tender farewell, not caring that Bette was with them. "I will not be able to spend as much time with you as I would like, but we must guard your reputation and avoid a scandal, dearest. Ancelin, my dear friend, will act as a go-between. He is very discreet and you may put complete trust in him."

She doubted that very much, and she exchanged a knowing glance with Bette.

Chapter 25

Incredibly, it was almost a week before Guy discovered that Lillyth had gone. He assumed that she was being stubborn and avoiding him by keeping to her chamber. When he learned that she had gone and Alison had kept him in ignorance, he was incensed.

"Where could she possibly have gone?" he stormed. Alison did not dare to tell him, and after raving and shouting two solid hours, he ordered that his horse be saddled and announced he was going to London to find her. Rolf tried to calm him and offered to go with him.

"You have your work cut out here, bringing your wayward wife to heel," Guy thundered.

Upon arrival in London he went to the inn where he had stayed with Lillyth and was surprised to find that they expected him. He was so relieved to discover that Lillyth had been staying there that he actually felt weak. He invited the landlady in for a drink, and questioned her carefully.

"My wife is no longer here, madame?"

"No, my lord. She said to give you a message

that she had gone on without you and, er, she said to charge everything to your accounting, my lord."

"Did she, damn her," he shouted. "And where is it exactly she has gone?" He tried to moderate his tone.

"Why, my lord, don't you know?" she asked, surprised.

"I must confess, madame, that I do not. We had, shall we say, domestic difficulties, and she left without telling me where she was going."

"I see. Well, I do believe she and the monk she was traveling with were going to Berkhamstead."

"Monk?" His mind reeled. Of course, she left with Sebastian! He left at about the same time. Berkhamstead—Robert—it went through him like a knife thrust. "Of course. Where else would she go?" He sank onto the bed, his head in his hands.

"Are you ill, my lord?" the landlady asked, greatly concerned.

"Nay, I am just weary. Thank you, madame, I will see you tomorrow." He flung himself fully clothed onto the bed. She had betrayed him! Should he go after her? No, never! A black anger took hold of him and threatened to consume him. He tossed and turned the night away, and by morning there was no other course left open to him but to return to Godstone.

When he arrived home, he called Rolf and his brothers together. "I am going to post a proclamation among my men. I will give a hundred silver deniers for Mortain's head."

"You are mad!" Rolf shouted.

André looked grim. "William would destroy every man, woman and child in Godstone, then burn it to the ground. You know what William's vengeance is like!"

"The man has to die. There is too much pain in me, and he did it."

"Nay, brother, you did it yourself, and you know it!" Nicholas pointed out bluntly. The others blanched at his incautious words, but Guy just stared ahead, his eyes unseeing, his mind miles away. Murder was in his heart. He would find them together and kill both!

That night sleep would not come, so he drank himself into unconsciousness. The next day his temper was so vile every man stayed his distance and tread warily. The pattern was set and it wasn't long before his brothers feared for his sanity as one week sped into another.

"I think he needs a woman," André said to Rolf, when he was over from Oxstead.

Rolf laughed grimly. "He has lain with every woman over fourteen in Godstone this past month. There is only one woman can cure what's wrong with him."

"Perhaps if we showed him he was needed around here more, he would snap out of it," Nick suggested. "I could tell him the Saxons need watching or they lie down on the job and snore for an hour."

"You know they work hard for him, and so does he. It will be an early harvest this year. He'll buckle down soon. When there is work to be done, don't worry, he will do it."

Morag was not surprised when Guy swallowed his pride and paid her a visit. The women of the huts had quickly spread all the gossip that trickled down from the hall. Morag knew his every move. She knew when and with whom Lillyth had departed. She also knew which women had lain with the master and that not one had pleased him nor caught his fancy.

She looked at his face through hooded eyes. He was almost haggard. There was so much repressed

anger within him, waiting like a crouched predator to pounce, that she was afraid of him. "What
do you wish, my lord?" she asked, low.

"Answers!" he said savagely.

"You do not believe in my powers. You are
clutching at straws," she said quietly, wishing he
would not involve her, but knowing how futile
such a wish was.

"Careful, woman!" he warned.

"Give me your questions," she said.

"Why?" he flared. "Why did she do this thing?"

She looked at him for a long time, thinking how
foolish men were. He knew full well why. He just
would not admit he was at fault. "You pick what
you plant," she said simply.

"I will have you killed!" he ground out between
his teeth.

"Would that assuage your pain?"

He tried to hold his temper and said stiffly, with
much injured pride, "Will she ever return?"

"Put your own house in order. You have unfin-
ished business in France, my lord."

He grudgingly held out a small shiny coin.
Greediguts swooped down and stole it from his
hand. In that moment Guy wondered wildly what
he was doing in this witch's lair.

"I would rather have food than money, my
lord."

He looked at her incredulously for her daring.
"If you are hungry, eat that damned magpie!" he
thundered.

Guy was sickened by his own excesses and his
conscience was pricking him about his daughters.
He had not left them to fend for themselves as his
wife's letter accused. He had left his house and
land at her full disposal with many servants inside
the house and peasants to work the land. She had

an ample living, but nevertheless he had abandoned the role of father, and he made up his mind to rectify the matter. As soon as the harvest was taken care of, he would travel to France and bring his children back to Godstone. His wife would be free to keep the chateau and remain in France or sell everything and go to London to William's court if she so desired, but he would not have her at Godstone.

Lillyth was lonely these days, even though Robert's gentlemen paid discreet court to her, and she was busy keeping them at arm's length. She had always been used to a household filled with other women, but circumstances made it impossible for her to mingle with the other ladies at Berkhamstead. She did not need Bette to explain that she must keep entirely separate from Robert's wife and her household of ladies. Lillyth knew they could not have been ignorant of her existence, but it was a thing that was hushed and hidden and not acknowledged by any lady of breeding.

Ancelin de Courcey was a frequent visitor, one she wished she saw less of. Whenever he found her alone, he tried to persuade her to join forces with him to influence Robert to seek more power in the kingdom.

"Why should Odo live like a king in London, while Mortain is left in a backwater like Berkhamstead? He is the king's brother, and while William is out of the country he should be regent. We should all be in the capital, not in this godforsaken hole."

"My Lord Courcey, you exaggerate the influence I have over Robert," Lillyth protested.

"Not so, Lillyth. Mortain is besotted with you and your pretended innocence. He hates whores.

He said to me after one such encounter, 'She actually made the advances!' " He laughed. "You are that rare combination of child-woman. I can see the woman. I know for instance that you have known a raging passion with some man. Your mouth gives you away, your breasts are too full and your walk is seductive and alluring. Robert sees only the child in you, and it holds him in thrall. I am trying to get you on my side by persuasion, but I could use other methods against you, Lillyth. You underestimate my influence with Robert. For instance I can go to him and say, 'Your lady requires your presence,' or I can say, 'The lady says to tell that bastard she sleeps with to get here on the double.' "

Lillyth colored at his coarse words.

"It would be a very easy thing to let Robert think you are sharing your favors with me, and that, my dear, would destroy you," he threatened.

Lillyth smiled at him to cover the fear she felt. He was very dangerous and she would have to rid herself of him!

"I will try to do as you wish. When Robert comes this evening, I will discuss going to London."

"Be subtle! Now I fear I promised Robert's brat William to go riding with him. The boy is forever hanging about me. Would to God I had the same kind of influence over his father."

Lillyth sat and coolly calculated what she would say to Robert. She debated whether she should tell him of the child first, then decided, better not. Some men would not be pleased to think they were fathering a bastard, and Robert might be one of them. She rehearsed the things she would say to him over and over again. She must rid herself of de Courcey and it must be done swiftly.

Robert came alone, and after Bette had greeted

him fondly and brought him a dish of the almond
paste figurines he loved to eat, she left Lillyth
alone with him. Lillyth brought some soft slippers
she had embroidered for him, and he relaxed in
front of the fire, sipping his wine thoughtfully.

"I see Ancelin is much in your company these
days, sweet lady," he began.

She tensed. My God, what was coming?

"He is a most attractive man, do you not think
so, my dearest?"

"I never noticed," she said lightly.

"My God, Lillyth, if you prefer him to me, only
say so but I will not share you with him," he said
desperately.

She went on her knees before him. "Sweet my
lord, who has been spilling evil thoughts into your
ears? I have something I must speak to you about
even if it shocks you and gives you a distaste of
me."

"Speak," he said coolly.

She lowered her eyes. "You know that I was
married to a Saxon?"

He nodded.

"Well, he was a man who preferred men in his
bed to women."

His eyes widened. "So that is why you were a
virgin!"

She let the remark pass. "I believe Ancelin de
Courcey to be such a man. I have noticed many
things, and, my lord, this is the part that really dis-
tresses me. He is in your son's company overmuch!"

He sprang up. "Splendor of God!" He clenched
his fists. "It took the eyes of an innocent like you
to spot such evil filth!"

She trembled with trepidation.

"I shall send him back to Normandy, but of
course he won't stay there. William is returning

with Matilda and his family. They will be quartered in London of course. Let him try to corrupt William's sons, if he dares."

"My lord, if he knows this information comes from me, I fear for my life!"

"Not to worry, my dearest. I will get rid of him on a pretext. He will think I am sending him on an important diplomatic mission. I know how ambitious he is. He will jump at the chance to quit this place. If you will excuse me, I will see to it immediately."

Lillyth never saw Ancelin de Courcey again.

Her pregnancy was becoming visible, so Lillyth knew she must tell Robert. A few days later when he came in the evening, she waited until he was relaxed and laughing, and then she broached the subject.

"Robert, I have some news that may displease you."

"Nonsense, what could you do that would displease me?" he smiled.

"I am enceinte," she said softly, and the tears threatened to spill over, down her cheeks.

"Sweetheart, don't cry. This is marvelous news to a man my age. Any man would be pleased, not angry. Are you sure?"

"Oh yes, very sure." She smiled through her tears.

"I won't lie to you, Lillyth. As a man I am very happy, but it does present difficulties. You must know how William feels about these things. He is most narrow-minded, and someone is certain to run to him with the news as soon as it becomes known." He frowned deeply. "William is to return before the end of the year, but I cannot bear the thought of being separated from you. We will consider adoption for the child to a wealthy family."

Lillyth looked distressed at his words.

"The other alternative is to find you a husband, a complacent one, you understand?" He smiled kindly.

"I do not wish to marry, my lord," she begged sweetly.

"Good. I could not bear the thought myself," he laughed. He put his arms about her and hugged her to him. "Do you feel well enough to . . . to . . ." he hesitated.

She smiled kindly. How easy it would be to refuse him, but she could not bring herself to hurt this man who had only shown her unselfishness.

Once King William had deposited his wife and family in London, he sent word to Berkhamstead that he would be coming to see how the building had progressed. His letters were cool. He also made a point of letting Robert know that de Courcey had given him every detail of life at Berkhamstead. Robert braced himself for the censure he knew would come, but he was unprepared for the depth of William's ire. He was summoned to William's presence as if he was a mere esquire.

"It is common knowledge that you have taken a Saxon leman," he said with distaste. "Rid yourself of her!"

"You can command me in all things save this one," replied Robert, flushed.

"Bones of Christ, I raised you high, I can bring you low!" William threatened.

"William, William, we are brothers. Let us not fight," Robert reasoned. "If you could just see her, you would understand my enchantment. Lord God, William, after seventeen years of marriage does your eye not seek out a beautiful young woman sometimes? If you can deny it, I will know you are inhuman."

William looked at Robert in silence. His anger evaporated, but his face was still set and hard.

"Your mother was married to our father, Robert. Mine was not! You can have no conception of the misery that is visited upon a bastard. I learned to survive. No doubt it played an important role in shaping my destiny, so determined did I become to gain men's respect for my strength. However, let me convey to you how my mother fared. She was branded whore from one end of France to the other. She will be remembered as that tanner's daughter with the stink of hides still clinging to her. I watched her shed enough tears to drown me! I learned to swim, but I vowed never to father a bastard. You think to honor this woman by making her your mistress, but you only dishonor her. Send her away before the mob descends upon her like a pack of slavering wolves to tear her dignity to shreds."

It was finally decided that Lillyth would go to Mont St. Michel, where the Benedictine monks had built a spectacular Romanesque church and monastery. It was situated on a small island off the north coast of France, just out from the Normandy border. Father Sebastian had helped build the abbey. Working with native granite, they had replaced the simple chapel that had stood there for two centuries. Father Sebastian agreed to go with her; she was also to take Bette. Robert tried to press other servants on her, but she refused.

Now that the decision had been made and the time of departure drew near, Lillyth found that she was vastly relieved.

The child filled her thoughts and she could not bear giving all her time and attention to others. Robert had been courtly, kind, even fatherly toward her, but any man who could think of giving his child away did not have a hope of holding onto Lillyth. I know the child is not his, but he does not know that, she told herself.

She just wanted a safe haven, where she could be private for the last few months of her confinement. Lillyth did not want her condition known. She did not want to give unnecessary pain to another woman; she had had too much herself for that. Her condition was quite obvious to her, and only by wearing very loose clothes could she conceal it from others. She stayed in her suite most of the time or wandered through the lovely gardens, her thoughts filled with the new life within her. She knew in her heart that she would never return. Where she would go or what she would do remained a blank that she did not wish to concentrate on for the present, and she was most thankful that she would have a couple of months of blissful peace in which to make her plans.

She consulted Father Sebastian about what she should take with her. He gave her a graphic description of how cold the winter would be on Mont St. Michel, and accordingly she packed only her velvet dresses and the warmest cloaks. That evening Robert came early and brought the white-robed Benedictine with him.

"Lillyth, you have traveled with Father Sebastian before so you know you can put your complete trust in him. I have a fleet of ships strung out along the coast, but I think you would be best to travel along the coast road until you come to Havant. I have some ships at anchor there. Remind me to give you letters to present to the captain, Father. The best course is into the Channel Islands, past the tip of St. Helier and into the Golfe de St. Malo. I will also give you dispatches for Mortain, Father, it is only a few miles inland from Mont St. Michel. I would greatly appreciate it if you would find out how things go in Mortain for me as soon as you have seen that Lillyth is comfortably established."

Robert walked with Sebastian to the door and said in a low voice, "See me tomorrow and I will give you enough money to make your journey easy. Look after her for me." Father Sebastian nodded and took his leave.

Robert stretched out before the fire and took Lillyth's hand. "I won't be here either after tomorrow. There is trouble in the north. Some men who have been outlawed and put to the horn are rising up, gathering sympathizers every day, and they have to be put down. I have ignored them long enough."

"Saxons?" asked Lillyth.

"I am afraid so, dearest. I know how concerned you must feel when something like this happens."

"Nay, my lord, my only concern is for your safety," she protested, and added silently, Dear God, don't let Guy have to go.

Gently he took her into his arms and looked deep into her eyes. As if he could read her mind he asked, "Lillyth, were you in love with Montgomery?" His voice sounded ragged.

Her eyes widened in surprise. "I . . . I thought I was."

"I have never asked you what happened at Godstone. I did not want to pry."

"I deeply appreciate that you asked no questions of me, Robert. Must you do so now?" she pleaded.

He bent forward and softly took her mouth. He murmured against her, his words beginning to slur. "Did you love him more than me?"

She floundered for an answer that would satisfy him. "Robert, there is a vast difference between you. I don't only love you, I *like* you."

"And him?" he asked.

"I hate him!" she said so vehemently that Robert was left in no doubt how deep were her feelings for Montgomery.

He sighed, but he was too aroused to draw back now. "Lillyth, you're going to have to let me, sweetheart."

Chapter 26

Only relief, vast relief, did Lillyth feel at leaving.
After endless delays about luggage by Bette, who
wouldn't stop fussing, the party of three was es-
corted to the coast by a group of Robert's soldiers who traveled back and forth regularly.
They had a more direct route to the coast which
went straight south from Berkhamstead. They
did not go near London, nor Godstone. Lillyth
was taking her white mare for her own use, as
well as Zephyr. They had extra horses with them
because it was a long, hard ride. It took them
fourteen days of riding to reach the coast with
long rest stops because of Lillyth's condition. It
was not a beautiful time to travel, but the roads
were dry from cold frosts and, amazingly, the
weather held fine. They stayed at an inn for four
days until the ship was readied. Lillyth remained
close to quarters because a seaport was a rough
place to be in these days, although she would
dearly have loved to walk along the beach in the
sea air. Finally, on the fifth day, she was settled in
a small cabin with Bette, and they weighed anchor.

* * *

Guy had worked his people double time until the harvest was reaped, then announced his intentions of going back to Normandy. But by the time the myriad of preparations for winter were all attended to, it was late November before he was free to leave. His brothers offered to go with him, but he refused them curtly and said he was traveling alone. At the same time that Lillyth was embarking from Havant, Guy also found a ship that would take him to France, but his destination was St. Valery, the place from which the great Norman army had set sail the year before.

One day out in the Channel they met up with an early gale, and his ship was blown off course to the west. At one point, just after the gigantic storm had settled down, the two ships came within sight of each other. Then, when the Channel took on a calmer attitude, his ship swept back eastward on course, and Lillyth was taken inexorably on toward her lonely destination.

She was violently and inelegantly sick from the moment her feet touched the deck. She had been ill a few times in her life, but nothing, she thought miserably, was as bad as seasickness. During the storm she was torn between fears of dying and then fears of not dying. She prayed silently, then aloud, then screamed blasphemously, fists raised and clenched, until all her strength had been spent. Then she lay shivering in her bunk and wished with all her heart that Guy was with her to lean on. She found herself praying for death, then frantically tried to cancel her prayers, because she would never see the face of her love again, and also because she wanted more than anything in this world to hold his child in her arms.

When the danger was past and her fear had abated, she was back to hating him once more. The ship came into harbor and the little party disembarked. Father Sebastian said, "When the tide is up, Mont St. Michel cannot be reached before morning. We will spend the night at Barre le Heron. We will need a guide to take us across the great sandbanks. Only a few know where the quicksand lies."

Lillyth was silently appalled at the sight of the island with the great tides rolling around it. The next morning did nothing to dispel her apprehension as she viewed the flat infinity of sand. Small rocks jutted everywhere, encrusted with mussels and other shells, and tiny crabs crawled in profusion.

They led their horses across the causeway and into the castle gateway. Above them the path rose steeply to where the buildings covered the highest point on the island. The castle was a simple affair, but the monastery was imposing. Their horses were stabled in the castle courtyard and inside there was only the dining hall, the gatehouse walls and a single tower in which Lillyth was given rooms. Later she would see the monastery and the first-floor alms hall where the poor received charity from the white-robed Benedictine monks. The second floor held a graceful guests' dining hall and a magnificently lit scriptorium where the monks prepared books for their extensive library. The monks dined on the top floor in the refectory and beside this were arched cloisters for those who sought quiet meditation.

As one day blended into another Lillyth regained her health and strength. She spent many lonely hours in the lookout at the top of the gatehouse. The sea was sometimes gray and turbulent, and the wild cry of gulls brought a sharpness to her lonely idyll. Other times it was flat and oily and looked even more menacing than when it was rough. There was no fresh water on the mount, and every day horses took out empty casks and brought them back filled while the tide was low. To the south lay Arderon and to the north, Genets. Invariably her thoughts were brought back from their wandering by the homey noises of the hall, with its clatter of dishes and barking of dogs. There was nothing to do here but think.

It was soon brought home to Lillyth that she still loved Guy with all her heart and soul. She was hopelessly homesick and would have given ten years of her life for one glimpse of that fierce, proud face with the glittering green eyes. What did it matter that he had a wife? Fifty wives could not diminish the love she felt for him and him alone. What a fool she had been to throw it all away!

Why? she asked herself over and over, and could only think that it must have been her pride. Now she felt humbled and lonely but not alone, for didn't she have his gift there, beneath her heart?

The last remaining leaves had turned to magnificent red and brilliant yellow when Guy rode up to his home in late November. The dogs went wild as he came into the yard. He curbed their exuberance with a few stern commands and greeted his elderly retainer with a huge grin. The old man's eyes were sad, and tears stood in them as he surveyed his lord.

"What is it, Gaston?" he inquired intuitively.

The old man shook his head and said, "Come inside, my lord, and I will tell you." He poured wine for Guy, and two little girls came shyly forward to inspect the stranger.

"Margarita? Angelique?" he inquired. "Don't tell me you have forgotten your father?" He held out his hand and the smaller one came forward slowly, her little dark face serious and solemn.

"Where is your mother?" He turned to Gaston. "Don't tell me she has deserted them?" he asked angrily.

"In a manner of speaking, my lord. I do not know how to tell you, my lord, but she is dead. She is buried in the little plot on the hill."

Guy sat stunned, his arm about his daughter. The housekeeper came bustling in to look for the children and stopped in her tracks.

"How did she die, when?" Guy asked, still not able to fully take it all in.

The man and woman exchanged glances and the woman said quickly, "It was a lung fever, my lord, she caught a severe chill. I nursed her for days but I could not save her." She did not give him details of the wild New Year's party, the drunken revelry, and that Margarite had lain outside in the snow all night before she had been found.

"How long ago?" Guy asked distantly.

"She became ill at New Year's, she died January tenth. It has been almost a year now."

For a moment he sat still, then blinked rapidly and seemed to hold his breath. "Did you say January tenth?"

They both nodded in agreement. He began to tremble. He had married Lillyth on January twentieth, that made her his wife in reality. A warmth started in his chest and the waves spread up his neck and cheeks and went to his head. He stood up and swayed, he was so lightheaded. His man stepped quickly forward to assist him, but Guy threw back his head and laughed wildly. The children retreated and the man and woman exchanged glances again, this time fearing that the shock of the news had unhinged him.

He sobered quickly and said, "Tomorrow I would like to speak with everyone about my plans. I would like to thank you, madame, for looking after my daughters. I fear I have shamefully neglected them."

He bowed and went upstairs to a bedchamber and did not come down again until noon the following day. He inspected the fields and the outbuildings, took inventory of the livestock and harvest. Everything seemed small after Godstone. When he returned to the hall, the household was gathered. "I want to thank you all for carrying on in my absence. I intend to sell up here. You may stay if that is what you desire, or you may come to England with me. I will find a mademoiselle to take charge of the children and ready them for the journey to England. I must return there at once on personal business, but I shall return very soon, so you will have time to pack your things and prepare your families for the journey. If you have any questions, I will try my best to answer them."

With one set purpose in mind he rode back to the coast and took ship for England. The seas were rough, but he curbed his impatience as best he could at the number of days the voyage took, and when he finally landed, he headed straight for Berkhamstead without stopping at Godstone. It was December and the bitter winds cut into him as he rode north.

His spurs clanged on the stone floors as he

went forward to his dreaded audience with Robert de Mortain. There was a deathly silence as the two men looked at each other. Each man tried to gauge the other's strength, and Robert was the first to lower his eyes.

"I have come for my wife," said Guy flatly.

"Your wife?" Robert asked with surprise.

"You heard me aright," said Guy coldly.

"She is not here," said Robert softly.

Guy crashed his gauntlets onto a table. "I demand to know where she is." There was so much violence, barely controlled, ready to erupt, that Robert sought quickly for words to defuse him.

"Demand? How can you demand anything? When Lillyth came here she was ill and I took her under my protection." Robert realized with a blinding surety that she must have been with child when she arrived, that was the reason she had been so ill.

Guy stood there, white-lipped, fists clenched, his eyes two burning coals in his head.

Robert continued, "To protect her from vicious scandal I sent her to France. She has gone into seclusion. I will not tell you where. The decision is hers; if she wishes to see you, she will come to you; if not, she is welcome to return here."

Guy turned on his heel and quitted the hall, his mind seething with impotent anger. "What a damned mess I have made of everything," he cursed. He thought of Godstone and was consumed with longing. He would go home, perhaps he would be lucky and she would be there waiting for him.

As man and horse covered the miles, the feeling that he would soon be with his beloved again grew stronger with each hoofbeat. When he arrived he was mentally and physically exhausted, and when he experienced the full disappointment of not finding her there he was emotionally bereft.

He came down with an ague. It was the first time he had been sick for many years. The fever mounted dangerously and Alison nursed him unstintingly. When she heard his ravings for Lillyth, she knew in her heart she had done them both a grave injustice to let her daughter run away from him. Christmas had come and gone before he fully recovered.

The first day he was out of bed he visited Morag. This time he did not demand anything.

"Morag, I have put my house in order. Lillyth is my legal wife. Can you not tell me where she is?"

"She is in France," she answered.

"So Robert told me, if I can believe him."

"He spoke the truth."

"Tell me where in France, and I will give you food for a year," he promised.

She shook her head. "All I see is a huge stone fortress, surrounded by water."

A picture of Robert's castle in Mortain with its surrounding moat sprang into Guy's mind. That's where he would begin his search. "Will I get her back?" he asked hesitantly.

"Yes, but you will have to learn to share her love," she told him.

"Never!" he thundered, so savagely she stepped back in alarm.

Then she smiled knowingly. She would not ease his suffering by telling him it was his son he would have to share her with.

* * *

William was in London with his family, and
Guy and his knights were required at court. He
was in a turmoil of impatience to get back to
Normandy, but it was many weeks before he was
free to do as he wished. At the first possible moment he took ship once more for France. He returned home immediately and set about finding
a buyer for his property. Although more than
two months had gone by since he gave instructions to pack up, nothing was in readiness, and
he realized that without his firm direction and
watchful eye, it would never get done, so the
weeks stretched into each other without Guy
finding a suitable buyer.

Since he felt anchored to the place anyway, he
decided he might as well put his time to some
useful purpose. He made a resolve to get to
know his children. When he looked at their
pinched, sad faces his heart contracted, as he
compared them to the Saxon children he had
seen back at Godstone. Even though the Saxon
children were peasants, they were rosy-faced
and happy. Most of them, in fact, were cheeky
and full of mischief, and that was the way he
wanted his girls to be. He took them riding
with him, made a point of eating his meals at
table with them, and every night when he
went to bid them good night, he managed to
tell them some bold adventure. He made sure the
stories had some ridiculous parts, because he
loved to see their tight little faces break into
smiles.

As he touched his finger to a sleeping cheek, a
longing for Lillyth swept over him that he could
not control. He went for a walk in the icy night to
chill the blood that was tormenting him from head
to foot. Desire licked at his body like flames,

scorching his nerve ends until he wanted to scream. He would wait only a few days more, then he would be on his way to Mortain to find her.

Chapter 27

Lillyth screamed once. The pain was so sudden and intense she could not help herself. Bette came rushing in. "Whatever is it, Lillyth?"

"My labor has started," she said slowly.

Bette wrung her hands. "*Mon dieu, mon dieu*, it is too early! Premature babies do not survive," she blurted before she caught herself.

Lillyth looked across at the old woman who had been everything to her for the last few months—mother, nurse, companion, servant, friend. "Bette, do not fear, the baby is not premature. I was with child when I came to Berkhamstead. Robert is not the father."

The old woman looked outraged. "What are you telling me? Who then?"

"He was a Norman knight. He conquered Godstone, where I lived, and became the new lord there. I fell in love with him against my will, and God help me Bette, I still love him."

"Did he throw you out when he got you with child?"

"Splendor of God, no, woman! He wants a son more than he wants anything in this world." Another contraction came, but this time she had been waiting for it.

When it passed Bette said, "It will be many hours yet, Lillyth. I do not think you will deliver before tomorrow."

Lillyth nodded, "The labor of love—help me to be brave, Bette," she pleaded.

To occupy Lillyth's mind, Bette asked, "Well, what went wrong if he loved you and wanted the child?"

"I did not say he loved me, Bette. I said I loved him. He married me in the church, but then I found out there was already a Madame de Montgomery!"

"You don't mean Guy de Montgomery, do you, child?" asked Bette.

"Ah-ah-ah, oh, it is passing, thank God. Yes, I am speaking of Guy, do you know him?" she asked, her face lighting up.

"He has been a friend of Robert's for many years. He is a lovely young man. Poor, but he always carried his responsibilities like a man, even when he was only a boy. I understand his marriage was not a happy one. Strange, is it not, that friends so often end up wanting the same thing? I have seen it often with brothers, too. They are always attracted to the same woman," she mused.

Lillyth laughed. "I've thought about that too, but I do not think it is because of similar tastes. I honestly believe it is man's nature to covet the thing his brother or his friend has, and they will not rest until they get it." Her midsection went rigid once again and she gasped for air until it passed.

"Lillyth, my conscience will trouble me sorely when we try to pass this child off as Robert's."

"My dear, we are not going back to Berkhamstead. I am going home to Godstone. Even if he does not want me, I know Guy will want his child, and I also want the child brought up at Godstone and to know its father. My child will be a bastard, but after all the king is a bastard and he overcame the handicap. When this is over and I am strong enough to travel, you must decide whether you wish to remain here in France or go back to England. You may come to Godstone with me, or return to Berkhamstead; the choice is yours."

"I will think on it," Bette promised. "Why don't you lie down for a while now, try to save your strength for when hard labor starts."

"I feel suffocated. Let's walk out upon the gatehouse walls. I know the wind is strong enough to knock me over out there, but if we cling together we can get some fresh air, then I promise I will lie down for a while."

Lillyth lay in agony. Her pains were coming hard and fast now. She had been in labor for fourteen hours and she was very weak. The baby was the wrong way around and Bette was worried to distraction. "Lillyth, if only I had some help. The child must be turned," she cried frantically.

"Go quickly to the abbey and get Father Sebastian. He will help us, Bette," gasped Lillyth.

"I dare not leave you, child," cried Bette.

"Please, you must! I will hang on here. It will only take a few minutes, please?"

Bette rushed from the bedchamber and as if this was the cue the baby had been waiting for, it started to come immediately. Lillyth gave one convulsive scream, and miraculously the child was born. The cord was wound around the baby's neck. Frantically Lillyth lifted the child onto her abdomen and gently unwound it. The baby was breathing normally for a few moments, then its breath became very shallow, and Lillyth fancied it had a bluish tinge to its skin. She did not know what to do, but quickly she took the cord between her fingers and gently began to massage and pump it. The child's breathing returned to normal and once again it became a healthy pink color.

Bette hurried in with Father Sebastian and went into action immediately. Lillyth's relief was so great she fell into a swoon. When she regained consciousness, the child was safely swaddled and tucked in beside her.

"It's a boy!" Bette said excitedly.

"Yes I know, isn't he beautiful?"

She put the baby to her breast and was overcome with a great enveloping maternal love, the like of which she had never experienced before. Then she slept the clock around.

"My little Norman," she crooned lovingly. "That is what I shall call him, Normand de Montgomery! The most beautiful name in the world."

Within a few days Lillyth was able to get up and care for the baby. She was so happy that she soon regained her strength and counted the days until she was sufficiently recovered to make the journey home. Bette decided that she would return to Godstone with Lillyth for the present, and Father Sebastian felt it his duty to escort the women to England.

Finally, in desperation, Guy sold his property for much less than it was worth. At last he was free to go to Mortain and find Lillyth. When he found no trace of her, he was disappointed and dejected. He was also faced with the dilemma of

twenty odd people waiting for him to transport
them to England. He was willing to search from
one end of Normandy to the other if necessary, but
his obligations were such that he could not take
off without making alternate arrangements for everyone. It was now March, and he finally managed
to persuade the new owner to delay moving in
until April to give him the extra time he needed.
Robert had many castles and strongholds throughout Normandy, and Guy set out immediately on
his search.

When at last they departed Mont St. Michel,
Lillyth did not even glance backward. She had
never been so ready to leave anywhere in her
whole life. She felt triumphant, as if she were riding out with full honors of war, trumpets sound-
ing and banners raised.

There had been some terrible storms at sea in
the early part of March, but mercifully when
they set sail in April they had a calm, uneventful
crossing and Lillyth almost knelt and kissed the
soil of England when once again she set her foot
upon it. It was with slight trepidation that she returned to Godstone. She was determined to
swallow her pride and accept whatever place
was offered her.

Her homecoming was so joyful that she was
overwhelmed with tears. When she discovered
that Guy had gone to France to find her, her heart
soared. Alison forbade any to tell her that she was
Guy's legal wife, rightly knowing he would wish
to tell her himself. André and Nicholas made such
a fuss over the new little Montgomery that she
had to rescue him continually from their attentions. The child looked exactly like the three Montgomery brothers, and there could be no denial of
his parentage.

Life had gone forward at Godstone in her absence. Emma and Esmé had their child. Edyth and André, now married, were expecting a baby of their own, and Rose was betrothed to Nicholas.

Lillyth was pleased when she learned that Aedward had finally married Edwina despite her peasant ancestry, and Adela and Hugh were by now an old married couple.

Guy was weary of his futile search, and April was fast drawing to a close. He asked the same questions over and over again, but to no avail. When he saw a couple of white-robed Benedictine monks helping the poor one morning, it came to him suddenly that Lillyth was at Mont St. Michel. That was what Morag's words had meant! It was so close to Mortain he could have kicked himself for overlooking it. Without a moment's delay he set out for the coast. He waited for no guide to direct him across the sands to the lonely island but urged his horse across before the tide was fully out. On the vast stretch of sandbacks he experienced a moment of panic when the water seemed to be getting deeper. Could he have miscalculated in his desperate haste, and was the tide actually coming in? It was with heartfelt relief that he saw the mist clear ahead so that he could see the sand stretched out in front of him. A monk met him at the gateway and tried to answer his demands for his wife.

"There were two ladies here, staying in the castle, but they departed for England just last week. Father Sebastian was with them. That is all I can tell you, my son."

He rode to the mainland furiously before the tide could sweep in again and headed back for his daughters and the people who had been waiting so patiently. He was elated at the thought that

Lillyth was returning to England, but fear that she would return to Robert gripped his heart. He swore he would find her and make her return to Godstone whether she would or no.

Chapter 28

It was a fine May morning when the cavalcade arrived at Godstone. Lillyth had heard the horses and wagons approaching, and she ran out joyfully to meet them. He was home at last! She stopped dead in her tracks at the sight of him. Now he was leading two little girls and an attractive young woman. Her heart was in her mouth as she dreaded the moment of coming face to face with his wife. He dismissed the young woman with a curt, "Thank you, mademoiselle," and Lillyth's heart leapt with joy.

He planted his feet firmly on the ground before her and said, "Splendor of God, Lillyth, you have led me a fine chase!"

She was bereft of speech as she sank down before him in a demure curtsey. He raised her up and a current like lightning went through her at his touch. "May I present my daughters, Margarita and Angelique?"

The two solemn little girls came forward, but before they could dip the knee she swept them to her in a motherly embrace and kissed them both. "Welcome to Godstone, my darlings, welcome home!" she cried.

In the hall, Guy was surrounded by his brothers and Rolf, all laughing and talking at once.

André began, "Guy, wait until you see . . ." but Lillyth quickly put her finger to her lips in a warning gesture and he finished lamely, "Wait until you see how the building has progressed."

"I'll come at once," he said goodnaturedly, "but first all our people must be found quarters, they are tired after their long journey."

Lillyth spoke up quickly, "I will look after the children, go with your brothers and see to all your people, I know they are anxious to talk to you. We will have a homecoming feast prepared, my lord. Welcome home." His eyes followed her hungrily as she took a hand of each child and led them upstairs to the bedchambers. She directed Guy's luggage to be placed in their old bedchamber, fed her son and put him to sleep in her mother's chamber. The children's nurse, along with Bette, helped her bathe the little girls and she gave them a small meal to tide them over to dinnertime.

She put on an underdress and tunic of pale green that had been Guy's favorite. The hall was merry tonight. Guy sat beside Lillyth and his eyes never left her. There was a tension between them that grew stronger as the hour advanced. Neither of them had much appetite for food, and although many of their favorite dishes had been prepared, they both toyed with the meat. Finally Guy spoke, "Robert . . ."

Lillyth opened her eyes wide and looked directly into his. "Treated me as a father would treat his daughter," she said firmly.

The pain left his eyes and Lillyth knew the lie had been worth all the courage it had taken to utter it.

His eyes danced. "I have something to tell you, *chérie*."

"I have something to show you, my lord." She laughed prettily in anticipation.

He longed for the moment when he would tell her she was his wife. He wanted to see the happiness come into her face as he uttered the words.

She longed for the moment when she could put their son in his arms.

He waited for some indication from her that she would be willing to share his bed, greatly fearing further rejection. Her hand brushed his and immediately he was aroused. She sat with her eyes demurely lowered, a light flush upon her cheeks, but he knew instinctively that she was aware of his physical condition and was enjoying his discomfort.

Finally she took pity on him and said, "Come, the hour grows late. I will escort you to your chamber and you can tell me what you have been bursting to tell me all day."

"You are a shocking tease, madame."

When the door was closed, he took her fiercely into his arms. His mouth bruised hers as his kisses grew to fever pitch and his hands sought to remove her garments.

"Tell me," she murmured, staying his hands as best she could.

Guy had starved for her so long, he was beyond words at this moment. He was driven to reclaim her body and soul, to put his brand upon her and mark her as his, both in her eyes and in the eyes of the world.

Soon, she too was beyond words, beyond even coherent thought. Suddenly her need was as great as his. While they had sat together, touching yet not touching, she had become swollen and slippery with need.

When he had her naked, she groaned in protest that it took longer to denude his powerful body. Until she again felt his strong hands upon her, she had forgotten that sometimes he made love savagely, like a storm, until she almost shrieked with pleasure. His lust threatened to consume them and as he fell upon her and possessed her totally, she gave herself up to the whirlwind, yielding all, wishing she could lie beneath him forever while he took her again and again and again. Once he had brought them to their first cataclysmic release, they would have the rest of the night to make slow, sweet, tender love.

It was a long time before she drifted back to consciousness; finally, they had banked the raging fires of their desire long enough to share their secrets with each other. As he let a handful of her glorious hair drift through his fingers to spill across his chest, he said, "Sweetheart, my wife died before we were married. Our wedding ceremony was a valid one; you are my wife in very truth."

"Oh, my love," she sobbed, tears like stars filling her eyes. "Wait there just one moment, I have something to show you."

Reluctantly he let her go, but when she returned with his son, he went on his knees before her and kissed the hem of her gown. He took his child in his arms and thought his heart would burst from pure happiness. The baby cried lustily, and Lillyth sat on the bed and gave him her breast.

Guy watched in fascination. "Another Norman come to conquer your heart and tear down your defenses."

She smiled mistily as she put the baby back to

sleep and returned quickly to the arms of her husband.

He kissed her deeply and breathed, "Ah, Lil, I love you more than life!"

I have conquered him at last, she thought, but as his hands possessed her body wildly, she thought, But thank God I will never tame him.

America Loves Lindsey!

The Timeless Romances
of #1 Bestselling Author
Johanna Lindsey

THE MAGIC OF YOU   75629-3/$5.99 US/$6.99 Can
Amy Malory is as wild and reckless as the most incorrigible of her male cousins. And now she has set her amorous sights on a straight-laced American ship captain.

ANGEL   75628-5/$5.99 US/$6.99 Can

PRISONER OF MY DESIRE   75627-7/$5.99 US/$6.99 Can

ONCE A PRINCESS   75625-0/$5.99 US/$6.99 Can

WARRIOR'S WOMAN   75301-4/$5.99 US/$6.99 Can

MAN OF MY DREAMS   75626-9/$5.99 US/$6.99 Can

Coming Soon

KEEPER OF THE HEART   77493-3/$5.99 US/$6.99 Can